Ode to Aurora

Ash Wildridge

ISBN: 979-8-9950530-2-6 (paperback)

Book Cover by GetCovers

Editing by Paige Schroeder

First edition 2026

To my family, both biological and bonded, for bearing with all of my rambling ideas throughout the years. Now you can finally see what they have molded into.

To my lovely wife, Christina, for I could not have achieved my dreams without your support. May our love for each other follow us into all of our next lives.

To all of my fans, friends, and readers, for I could not have gotten started without you. I hope you all enjoy what is to come in these following pages.

Content Warnings

Before reading this novel, please note that it contains subject matter that may be deemed as sensitive to some readers. These subjects include:
Religious imagery and themes
Graphic depictions of violence
Alcohol consumption
Sexual themes
Mentions of LGBTQ+ phobia.

With this said, please read at your own discretion.

Table of Contents

One
Awakened

She feels nothing but a searing pain across her whole body. She strains to lift her right arm in front of her face, only to be met with the sight of burning, melting flesh and exposed bone. Her weak, shallow breaths only serve to make her chest ache and provide no relief to the pain. Her thick hair, clumping together due to the blood leaking from somewhere on her head, falls in front of her face and obstructs her vision. As her vision flickers and fades, a cruel smirk and glowing grey eyes with star-shaped pupils come to the forefront of her memories. The echoes of loud, mechanical thuds fill her ears, and her body trembles in the aftermath of being dropped through the sky until she'd landed in the ink-colored, grassy turf below her with a sickening "CRACK."

As soon as the recollection of the impact against the ground enters her mind, the angel shoots up in bed, gasping for air. Relief floods her system as her lungs fill with oxygen, her chest rising and falling with each breath. She presses a hand to her heart and finds it beating beneath her palm, the tempo strong and rapid. Looking around, she finds herself sitting in a hospital bed with the shrill beeping of vital monitors echoing rhythmically to one side. She touches her face and finds that her head is not bleeding, and her arm is not disintegrating before her eyes. The small wings on either side of her head droop to her shoulders as she calms.

The room she finds herself in reeks of sterility, the scents of rubbing alcohol and bleach permeating every available surface.

The walls are painted plain white, and the uncomfortably stiff hospital bed she's laying on is tucked into an alcove with pale wooden cabinets on either side. The floor-to-ceiling windows across from her glow brightly with the mid-morning sun, despite the blinds being tilted just enough to keep it from shining in her eyes. She's covered in a thin, papery medical gown, and the uncomfortable fabric scratches against her skin.

"What...?" she whispers, still mentally shaken and physically trembling in the aftermath of her nightmare. As she remains seated in the hospital bed, her neck begins to ache. She rubs it, only to feel the smooth and toughened skin of a scar. She swallows around a thick knot that forms in her throat, trembling more as she tries to remember what had happened to give her a wound in such a vital area.

"Oh! Miss Taylor!" an unfamiliar voice chirps from the doorway to her recovery room. She carefully turns her head and sees an angel, donning nurse scrubs and with her wings flared out in surprise. The white and pale blue feathers indicate her angelic origin of a sympathy angel, which are known for being skilled in medical care and healing magic. After a moment, the nurse continues to speak. "You're finally awake!"

"How long was I... Out?" Angelique asks, voice crackly from lack of use and shaky with sudden nerves.

"100 years, dear." The angel enters her room and writes down the numbers displayed on the vitals monitor, the wings behind her ears fluttering slightly as she works. "Your recovery time was quite fast, given what you've gone through. Since you're awake, though, I *do* need to complete an examination of your physical state as well as evaluate your memory. Can you handle it right now?"

"Um... Sure?" Angelique hesitantly agrees. *I was in a coma for 100 years? What could have happened?*

The nurse looks her over, testing her motor skills and reflexes as she speaks. "Do you remember your name?"

"My name is Angelique Taylor."

"Do you know where you are?"

"I'm guessing Heaven Central Hospital."

"Do you know what year it is?"

"No, I don't."

"Do you remember what happened to you?"

She shakes her head, wincing at the additional ache in her neck. "No. I don't."

The nurse grabs her clipboard to note all her findings. "It makes sense that you don't recall what happened to you. I'm surprised you remember as much as you do, given the aftereffects of being decapitated."

The blood drains from her face as a pit of dread forms in her stomach. "I was decapitated?"

"Yes. It was a clean cut, so the doctors were able to use a combination of scientific tools and specialized healing magic to reattach your head. You were barely conscious until the anesthesiologist cast a spell to put you under, and your body has been in recovery since the procedure."

"So it's been 100 years..." She hugs herself tightly. "Such a long time... I hope Aurora has been okay..."

The nurse tilts her head curiously. "Who's Aurora?"

"She's my work partner. We've been guardian angels together since we graduated from the training course." She looks around, the cold, sterile emptiness of the room fully sinking in. There's no sign that anyone aside from her had ever stepped foot in the room. "... Wait, where is she?"

The nurse frowns, a tense air of guilt filling the space between the two angels. "No one by the name 'Aurora' has ever come to visit you, dear. Perhaps she moved on?"

"What? No, no, Aurora would never do that!" Tears sting and prick at her eyes. "She's my partner! She'd never leave me! She promised!"

"I'm... I'm not sure what to tell you, Miss Taylor, other than I'm sorry. Your friend has never once stepped inside this room; dare I say, even the hospital."

Angelique allows her tears to trail messily down her face and sniffles pathetically. "I have to go find her. There has to be a reason she hasn't visited." She throws aside the blanket covering her legs and moves to get up, the wings on her back flaring out behind her as she grows more and more distressed. A few white and jade-green feathers and a handful of soft down flutter to the floor, making a slight mess of the room.

"W-Wait, Miss Taylor!" The nurse darts forward and helps Angelique steady herself on her feet. "You have to be examined by the doctors before you're able to leave!"

"I don't care! I need *answers!"* She weakly pushes at the nurse, trying to break out of the other angel's firm hold despite the searing strain of her muscles. She cries more, whimpers escaping her as she slowly falls to her knees. Her head-wings curl around her face in an attempt to hide the fresh onslaught of tears brewing in her eyes. "I need to know *why*... Did I really mean *nothing* to her?"

The nurse kneels in front of her, holding onto her wrists. "That's something for you to figure out at a later time. For now, your focus should be ensuring that you are both healthy and physically stable enough to leave this hospital. Once you get discharged, you can charge headfirst into getting all the answers you want. Deal?"

Angelique wipes her eyes, still sniffling. "Okay. I... I can do that."

"Good. Now, let's get you back into bed, and I'll fetch the doctors once you're settled." The nurse helps Angelique stand and steady herself once more, before settling her back onto the cot she'd apparently been unconscious on for 100 years. "I'm off to fetch the doctor for you."

"Thank you..." She watches as the angel leaves the room, her wings fluttering ever so slightly. As soon as the nurse is out of sight, she flops back against the cot and groans. "What happened to you, 'Rora...?"

About ten minutes later, a tall angel in long, plum-purple robes and a snow-white doctor's coat enters the room, spreading sanitizer on his hands. The golden cuffs, collar, and belt decorating the man's robes glimmer in the fluorescent lights above them, indicating that he has some sort of status amongst the angelic populace. The heart-shaped pupils of his piercing silver eyes shrink a bit as he critically evaluates the room. His two sets of white-and-blue wings tuck themselves closely to his sides, and his two-tiered halo bobs underneath the doorway's maximum clearance as it hovers above his head. His deep navy hair is pulled back into a ponytail that loops between the lowest tier of his halo and halfheartedly drapes over one of his shoulders.

"Miss Taylor, I presume?" he queries, his deep baritone voice nearly echoing in the near-quiet of the room as he brushes his deep navy ponytail off his right shoulder.

"Yes, that's me," Angelique answers, trying to sit with a straight back.

"It's good to see you're finally awake, young lady. My name is Dr. Raphael; you may know me as the Archangel of Health."

"Now that you mention it, you do look familiar..."

He chuckles. "I'll assume that's a good thing. For now, though, I'm here to see if you're ready for discharge."

"I hope I am... I really need to get out of here so I can figure out where my partner is."

Dr. Raphael smiles sympathetically, the expression almost forced and weak. "You guardians and your work ethic, I swear... In any case, let me review Serafina's notes and check your strength. Being in a coma for 100 years will definitely leave you a bit shaky on your feet."

After looking at the clipboard full of nurses' notes and helping her stand stably on her own, Dr. Raphael discharges Angelique from the hospital.

"I've given you some supplements and a handful of exercises to help you regain the strength in your arms, legs, and wings. If you ever need anything else, let me know. Alright, Miss Taylor?"

"Yes, sir." She takes a quick moment to summon a shimmering wave of pink and gold magic, which transforms the papery medical gown into her typical white-and-pink uniform dress, complete with a thick ribbon choker wrapped around her neck to hide her nasty scar. She makes her way to the hospital pharmacy, where she grabs her strengthening supplements. From there, she leaves the hospital, lightly fluttering her wings to try and exercise them as she walks.

Angelique steps outside the blank white walls of the hospital and is forced to shade her eyes from the blinding sun that glows overhead. It takes a few moments for her vision to adjust to being outside on such a sunny day, at which point she realizes... She has no idea where she is. Sure, she'd previously been to one of the various clinics spread around the sprawling metropolis of Heaven's central city, but that was over 100 years ago. She'd never even broken a bone until this near-death experience on what was apparently her most recent mission, so her ability to traverse her way home from the hospital is, rather unsurprisingly, nonexistent.

She heaves a heavy sigh and tucks her discharge paperwork close to her chest. As her anxiety rises, lightning bolts of pain course down her forearms and into her palms as she stares at the marble sidewalk, trying desperately to fight back tears as her mind runs wild.

I don't know where I am.

I don't know where I'm going.

I don't know what I should be doing.

I don't even know what happened to me.

Why am I even here?

There's no way I should be alive right now—

She cuts off her panicked train of thought as her lungs burn for air. Taking a deep inhale, her body relaxes. She looks around, trying to focus her mind on anything else. She eventually finds her other senses coming back to her, at which point she perks up at the sound of a vehicle approaching. Looking to her left, she sees a large blue bus slowing to a stop before continuing on its way.

There must be a bus stop across the street! She hurries across the golden, brick-patterned street until she reaches the other marble sidewalk. The bus driver looks her over with an annoyed expression, apparently sensing her apprehension to board.

"Destination?" he grumbles.

Angelique freezes. "Uh... Guardian Angel Headquarters?"

"Not this route." He pulls a lever, slamming the doors closed in front of her face. The engine rumbles as the bus begins to move, leaving Angelique standing dumbly on the sidewalk.

She puffs out her cheeks in a bit of a pout as she plops herself down on the sun-bleached bench behind her. *How rude! And he wasn't any help, either...* She digs around in her pocket for her phone, ignoring the shakiness of her hands as she opens the internet browser. The small, sparkling heart charms dangling from the lower-right corner of the case jingle slightly as she types rapidly on the slick screen.

"Bus routes..." she murmurs to herself as she finds the webpage for the Heavenly Transport Service. After scouring the page for the correct information, she finds that she's in the northern sector of the capital city, Cloud Nine. She's in the district of Baystar, and the next bus she'll need to take arrives in about an hour.

She groans, only to quiet as she hears her stomach growling. "... Actually, I'll have plenty of time to stop at a café and eat some lunch."

Angelique finds herself wandering around in search of nearby cafés, nearly jumping with joy when she finds a small establishment squeezed between two much larger buildings. She heads inside and, after interacting with a bored-looking cashier and a server who practically tossed her bagged lunch on the pick-up counter, walks out with a turkey sandwich in one hand and an iced caramel latte in the other.

She once again sits on the bench and waits for the bus, which arrives as she scarfs down the last remnants of her meal and tosses the packaging in a nearby trash can. She hops on, paying the fare on her way, and takes a window seat as the bus starts off on its journey. She finds herself watching the iridescent skyscrapers and towering apartment buildings pass by. She even spots a few fashion outlets with displays someone like her could only dream of wearing one day. The bus makes its way across a large steel bridge with a road sign on the side of the road. In large, bold, white letters, it reads: **[Welcome to Pearl Hill]**.

The name of this town seems familiar...

Just then, she spots the grandiose campus that she would always remember, no matter what could have occurred to her beforehand. The buildings themselves are made of swirled marble, with berry-colored veins coursing through each structure. Angels soar to and from the campus in steady motion, creating an equal exchange of those returning to and leaving from the large building.

The bus comes to a stop and the driver glances into the rear-view mirror, beckoning the lone passenger to exit with a simple nod. Angelique hops off, her anxiety once again spiking as the bus pulls away. Fighting back the urge to turn tail and run, she makes her way down the path, which leads to a large set of gilded front doors. The intricate golden handle, decorated with carvings of wings and eyes, stares at her until she gives a strong yank. As the door creaks open, she's greeted by the 100-foot-high ceilings of the primary assignment hall, with thousands of mailbox compartments along each wall and the giant pillar in the center of the room. Dozens of other guardian angels flutter around collecting their assignments, while the angels in secretarial roles bob and weave their way through the flurries of feathers in order to fill the empty mailboxes.

She makes her way to the front desk, where an angel with white and pink feathers—a patience angel, she reminds herself—sits writing out a scroll with a typewriter. The other angel's attention turns to Angelique as she approaches. "Can I help you?" she asks, her voice light and gentle.

"Uh... I hope so. My name is Angelique Taylor, I just got released from the hospital, um—"

"Angelique Taylor?" the angel echoes in awe.

"Yes?"

"Oh, that's amazing! You know, we were so worried about you when we first heard what happened, but then we heard you were in a coma and—" She pauses to catch herself. "Er— I'm so sorry, that was rude of me. I've heard so much about your case, I always wondered if or when you would be able to return to duty..."

Angelique smiles weakly, caught off-guard by the other angel's admiration and enthusiasm. "Well, thank you so much for your concern. Is Master Barachiel here?"

"Master Barachiel should be in his office. Come with me, and we'll go see if he's available." She stands and beckons for Angelique to follow her. Obediently, the life angel does as told. Her gaze travels as she walks, darting between the angels gathering scrolls of assignments until her steps halt outside a large office door. A golden placard with text spelling the archangel's name in large, bold letters is fastened into the wood beside the small glass window, which reveals the figure of the Archangel sitting alone inside his office.

The man is tall and muscular underneath his berry-colored robes. His golden cuffs, belt and collar are decorated with symbols of eyes like Dr. Raphael's. Long, silver-blonde hair is tied into a long braid and rests over his right shoulder, where the loose strands at the end curl into a small ringlet. His bangs fall into his silver, square-pupiled eyes ever so slightly. His golden two-tiered halo floats above his head, and his white-and-pale-green head-wings flutter slightly as he reads over a small stack of paperwork.

The secretary that led Angelique to the office knocks on the door as she opens it, her smile becoming a bit forced around the edges. "Master Barachiel—"

"Mythra, how many times do I have to tell you, it's not very *patient* to barge into a room *as you knock*," the Archangel snarls, not even bothering to look up from the files on his desk.

The feathered wings on either side of the secretary's face press close to her cheeks as they redden in embarrassment. She hugs one arm across her frame as she continues to speak. "But Master Barachiel—"

"*What* could be so important this time? Another typo on a scroll?" he sneers mockingly.

"No!" she yelps, only to cover her mouth with her head-wings the moment after. "I— Um— What I mean to say is... One of our guardians just got discharged from Heaven Central Hospital."

The Archangel's pointed ears twitch at the last sentence. "Is that so?" he asks, finally raising his head. He brushes a stray silver-blonde ringlet from his face and looks to the door, where Angelique is somewhat hidden behind the secretary's wings. "Which one?"

"Her name is Angelique Taylor, sir." She steps aside and pulls her wings close to her body as the aforementioned guardian angel fully enters the room and curtsies.

"Master Barachiel, it's good to be back," she greets, trying to hide the shakiness in her voice that she hadn't encountered while speaking to the secretary.

"Ah, Angelique!" Barachiel cheers, standing up, "It's lovely to finally have you back amongst our ranks! Dr. Raphael just sent me a letter, so I'm assuming it's your return to work notice." He roughly claps a hand to Angelique's back, grinning widely.

Angelique manages to fight back a flinch at the rough contact; instead, her heart pounds in her chest with a surge of anxiety. "Oh, um... Of course! I assume I'll be working in reception until my wings are stronger?"

"Nonsense!" he laughs, bright and nearly deafening, "You're going to get right back out into the field!"

"What?" Angelique and the secretary both gawk in unified confusion.

"You can't honestly expect me to have one of my best guardians on desk duty, can you?" Barachiel muses, "Sure, your old partner might be gone, but—"

"That's the other thing I wanted to ask about, sir. I heard my partner Aurora never came to visit me in the hospital..." She frowns worriedly. "What happened to her?"

"Pretty much what it says on the tin," he responds with an offputting nonchalance, "After you were decapitated, she disappeared. If you want, you could always talk to Lord Gabriel or Lord Uriel for a more definite answer. Since Lord Gabriel is the Overseer of Prophecy, his gift of visions might be able to help you the most."

"Thank you, Master Barachiel. I'll go find him and—"

"Your first priority should be getting back into the field, Miss Taylor," Barachiel states, his voice almost turning into a low, authoritative growl. His silver eyes, which are as piercing as Dr. Raphael's, bore into her as he clenches his teeth.

The blood freezes in Angelique's veins at the low tone and sharp gaze of her boss. "Ah... Right, of course... Um— What should my first assignment be?"

The Archangel's demeanor almost immediately flips, his narrowed eyes brightening and a wide smile forming on his face in place of his previous scowl. "That's my girl! Now—" Without turning his head, he smacks his hand on a much taller stack of papers, which wasn't visible from the doorway, and snatches the top sheet off the pile with a shimmer of magenta and gold magic. "Here is your assignment. I'm sure you'll do an excellent job, since you're back."

With an unsteady confidence, Angelique takes the paper and briefly looks it over. Across the top in bold, blocky, golden letters is the title **[Holy Protection Order]**, and underneath it reads, **[The family of King and Spyr Lockley]**.

The secretary peers over Angelique's shoulder, and the color drains from her face. "Uh, sir—"

"Now... We're all set here, and you two need to get out of my office," he declares, making a shooing motion with his hand. "Angelique, I eagerly await your report once your assignment is complete." With that, a magical gust of wind and berry-colored sparks sends the two angels tumbling out of the office. The door slams shut and locks with a loud click.

The secretary sighs as she gathers herself from the floor and turns her attention to a frazzled Angelique. "Well, you heard Master Barachiel... I suppose you'd better get going."

The guardian angel holds the Holy Protection Order tightly to her chest. "Right..." she murmurs with a heavy heart, "I can always speak to Lord Gabriel about Aurora at a later time..."

Two
Right at Home

When she arrives at the Guardian Angel Headquarters' central courtyard, Angelique makes her way to the feature known as "the Looking Glass." The small marble decoration looks more reminiscent of a birdbath than a millennia-old relic, but despite the elegantly-carved pillar the basin stands on, it's the mirror-like water that proves the landmark to be magical in nature. Angelique leans forward to look into the silvery water, brushing her hair behind her ear so as not to contaminate the pool.

"Show me King and Spyr Lockley," she commands, her voice quiet and clear. The reflection in the water melts and shifts to show a group of several tall apartment buildings. The complex surrounds a large parking lot, with each of the buildings separated from each other by well-maintained lawns. The vision in the Looking Glass zooms in, presenting the house near the entrance to the apartment complex. There, a young couple stands outside; the taller of the pair is carrying three grocery bags, while the shorter holds only one. The latter also appears to be cradling a bundle in their arms. The vision remains fixated on the couple until they duck inside the much smaller building, at which point the vision fades.

Angelique hums. "I should be able to find them easily enough..." She maneuvers her way out of the courtyard and strides confidently to the edge of the clouds, which sits about 50 yards from the campus. She peers over and looks out upon the human realm of Earth. The humans look like tiny ants bustling between towns, cities, and landscapes as they go about their daily lives.

She takes a deep breath, tucks her head-wings close to her cheeks, spreads the wings on her back... And jumps.

The wind whips through her long, dark brown hair as she tries to maintain her balance despite plummeting through the air. Her wings shake from the force, as expected of anyone exerting a limb they hadn't used in 100 years, but manage to catch onto an updraft of wind. The sudden catch causes her body to lurch a bit, but she steadies herself and continues to glide through the air, occasionally flapping her wings when she reaches more steady winds.

It doesn't take long for Angelique's descent to the human realm to finish as she soars over a bustling city with skyscrapers, shops, and apartment buildings, all of which are oddly similar to the central metropolis of Heaven. The houses scattered throughout the city are coated in colorful vinyl sidings not too unlike the location of her newest wards. The more common house colors, which consist of rustic reds, pale beiges, and snowy whites, make the search for the midnight blue buildings from the Looking Glass's vision much easier. She soars above the city until she finds a cluster of buildings whose deep color sticks out like a sore thumb covered in the same shade of the midnight blue.

She manages to land in a quiet, hidden alleyway without hurting herself or attracting too much attention with her rough and shaky landing. As she regains her balance, she notices various posters plastered along the alley walls. She almost takes a moment to examine them, but decides against it and moves to exit the alley she'd flown into once she catches a pungent whiff of the nearby restaurant's dumpster. She sniffs herself quickly and after deducing that her landing spot had *not* made her reek of old food, confidently approaches the front office of the apartment complex.

Angelique's nervous system tingles with a sense of unease as she approaches the cluster of buildings. She frowns, unsure of what danger her new wards could possibly pose to her, but continues onward. Her wedge-heeled sandals thwack against the pavement with each step until she finds the building, which turns out to be a cozy-looking house with a silver plaque plastered onto the wooden front door. The sign reads, **[DHA Apartment Complex Main Office]**. She plasters on a brave smile, raises a fist, and knocks firmly on the door.

"Come in," a kind voice calls from inside.

She turns the knob, steps into the house, and finds herself standing in a small cream-colored foyer with a reception desk against the far wall. There's an archway leading to a living room behind the desk, and through an archway to the left sits a tidy dining room. Her attention snaps back to the desk in front of her, where a thin person with platinum-blonde hair and blue, almost purple, eyes sits. They're cradling a sleeping infant, who is wrapped in a baby-pink blanket, close to their chest. A loose-fitting lavender sweater drapes slightly off of one of their shoulders, and the black leggings they wear underneath their thigh-length tunic rest snugly against their legs. Leaning on the counter is a moderately tall man with wavy, dark auburn hair. He's wearing a maroon long-sleeved protective coat, which one would normally find in a chemistry lab. Slightly-baggy black pants are tucked into white shoes made of thick, protective plastic. Both of them perk up curiously upon seeing Angelique, and the person sitting behind the desk appears to narrow their eyes in a display of distrust.

"Can we help you, miss?" the standing man asks, straightening his stance at the newcomer's presence. His gaze darts to her angelic features, which she'd forgotten to hide upon landing in the human realm.

Angelique swallows around the thick bundle of nerves that had suddenly formed in her throat. "I'm looking for the Lockley family," she states, voice wavering slightly.

“What is this about?” the person sitting at the desk queries with a quirk of their brow.

She pulls out the rolled-up Holy Protection Order and unfurls it, revealing the names of the Lockleys in golden ink. “I’ve been assigned to them as a guardian angel. I’m hoping you two can assist me in locating my wards.”

The man in the lab coat frowns and takes hold of the parchment. His emerald eyes squint as he reads it over, a curious tilt of his brow the only expression on his face aside from his lopsided frown. “I see... This is a genuine Holy Protection Order.”

“For us?” the person at the desk asks.

The angel’s eyes brighten as she looks between the two adults. “Oh! *You’re* the Lockleys!”

“We are. My name is Kingston, but everyone calls me King,” the standing man states, holding out a hand to Angelique for her to shake. “The beautiful person sitting at the desk here is my spouse, Spyr. The little one is our daughter, Irida.”

Angelique shakes King’s hand firmly and nods politely to Spyr. “Well, it’s a pleasure to meet you all. My name is Angelique Taylor, and I’ve been assigned to be your guardian angel.”

“You said that already,” Spyr notes with a cautious stare and a somewhat indignant hum. “In any case, since it seems you’ll be here for a while, would you like us to set you up with an apartment? We have a few available, and I can print a lease pretty quickly.”

“Oh, really? If it’s no trouble, I would greatly appreciate it! I have no idea where else I would go, and I’d prefer to stay close to you all in case something should happen...”

Spyr nods silently and gently places Irida into the lavender-colored baby carrier sitting on the floor next to their chair, then types away at the computer. The printer at the end of the counter whirs to life as it produces an oddly short lease agreement. They grab the small stack of papers and hand it to their husband.

King takes the lease documents and turns back to Angelique. "I'll take you through a viewing; right this way!" He leads her down the winding sidewalk to an apartment building on the far side of the large parking lot. They end up on the top floor, in the warmly-lit hall of a large apartment suite. King produces a silver master key with a flick of his wrist, and unlocks the door with ease.

The apartment is spacious, with medium-tone hardwood floors throughout. To the left side stands a small kitchen, complete with granite countertops and wooden cabinets painted a midnight blue, almost matching the building's exterior. The handles on the cabinets shine a brilliant golden color in the bright overhead lights. The right side of the ice-blue entryway contains a boot tray, coat rack, and small dining table with four country-style wooden chairs.

In the ruby-red living room, a simple black couch sits near an elegant coffee table and across from a small flat-screen television perched on the wall. Soft grey curtains stand on either side of the floor-to-ceiling windows, which look over the entirety of the complex.

"Oh, wow..." Angelique whispers, the wings near her ears flapping excitedly, "It's beautiful!"

King sits at the dining table and pulls out a pen. He speaks as he fills out the landlord's section of the lease form. "You can thank Spyr for the layout and colors." Once he's filled out his portion of the forms, he points his pen at Angelique and gives her a firm stare. "Now, onto the complex's rules. Number one, there are to be no pets without us knowing."

"Pets? Oh, uh, I don't have any pets," Angelique stammers as she also takes a seat.

"Alright, let's check that off then." He places an "X" on one of the boxes. "Number two, you don't plan to host any giant parties and disturb your neighbors, right?"

"Absolutely not."

"Good. And lastly..." His gaze moves from the document to her face with a steely expression. "If you were to find out that there is a demon living on these grounds, what would you do?"

Angelique sits in stunned silence, only able to blink at the sudden change of attitude and tone of the conversation. "Well, uh..." She looks at her hands as she fidgets. "... If they weren't bothering anyone, I'd leave them alone. If they were causing trouble, I'd let you and Spyr know. If they tried to attack me, I would defend myself with the least amount of force necessary."

A few beats of silence fill the apartment.

"Welcome to your new living arrangements, Miss Taylor," King declares as he signs a section of the lease. He turns the paper around and hands her the pen. "If you would please sign in the section labeled 'tenant,' your accommodations can start right away."

The angel's head whips up and she looks at the human in shock. "Um... Are you sure?"

"Of course I'm sure. You answered the last question exactly as we expect from our tenants."

"O-Oh! I was afraid you were going to be disappointed in my answer."

"Why would I be disappointed?" King asks with a quirk of his eyebrow.

"Because I'm more of a pacifist than most guardian angels..."

"Well, if that's true, we won't have any problems. Spyr and I are pacifists, too."

"Oh thank goodness," Angelique sighs in relief. She takes the pen, signs the lease, and hands both the papers and the pen back to King. "Here you are. Um... What will I owe for rent? Or a security deposit?"

"Since you're doing us a service, why don't we leave it at an even barter? You keep dangerous demons away from us and our tenants, and you get to live in this cozy apartment?"

"I can do that. Thank you so much!"

"Ah, think nothing of it. Spyr and I are always trying to help people find their way." With the new lease agreement tucked close to his chest, he stands and makes his exit. A single bronze key is left on the table in his stead, which Angelique takes.

She makes a beeline to the fridge and looks inside, finding it empty as expected. She gathers her few belongings and summons her wallet... Only for it to dawn on her that, once again, she has no idea where she is or where the nearest grocery store is located.

After a quick search on her phone and with a destination now in mind, she hides her wings and halo with a simple glamor spell and heads out of the apartment. She manages to purchase enough familiar ingredients and cooking utensils to confidently make herself a fresh, home-cooked meal, and makes her way back to her new home.

"Ugh, I need to invest in sneakers," Angelique groans as she struggles to carry her bags of groceries back into her apartment. She drops the bags to the floor and nearly collapses once the door is shut. She takes a moment to catch her breath, then drags her bags over to her fridge and other nearby cabinets. It takes her about forty-five minutes to organize everything neatly and make room for the cooking utensils she'd bought. She's nearly sweating by the time she's done, at which point she takes a bag filled with personal care items to the bathroom, which is located down the hallway to the right of the front door.

The room itself is painted a calming shade of sage green, with the toilet hidden behind the sink. A large mirror shows Angelique exactly how tired she looks from her long day. Turning around, she sees the shower is hidden by frosted glass doors, guarding any occupants inside from being fully exposed. She steps inside the shower for a moment to place her hair care products, body wash, and facial cleanser onto the built-in tile shelves. *I can't wait to relax under a hot shower once I'm done for the day...*

Her relaxing thoughts are temporarily halted by the loud growling of her stomach. She returns to the kitchen and stares at the electric oven with a flat stovetop. Deciding on spaghetti bolognese, she fills a pot with water and places it on the stovetop. *This can't be much different from the oven back in my old dorm...* She flicks the dial for the right-rear burner. It takes a little while for all of the food to be prepared, but once it's bubbling with readiness, she grabs herself a portion and sits to eat.

After she eats her dinner, packs away the leftovers, and washes the dishes, she makes a beeline to the bathroom. She relaxes under the warm spray of water, sighing in contentment as the sweat and stress are washed from her form. Once she's sufficiently dried off with a freshly-purchased towel and has brushed her much cleaner hair, she plods down the opposite hallway to the apartment's singular bedroom.

The pale lavender room is comfortably large, with a closet nestled into the right wall. A few feet in front of the door a queen-sized bed covered in deep purple bedding stands proudly on an elegant bed frame. Overhead, a ceiling fan with flower-shaped blades holds a singular bright bulb, which somehow illuminates the whole room by itself. With a yawn, she crawls onto the bed and pulls the cord to turn off the ceiling light. She buries herself underneath the covers and rests her head against the plush pillows.

It's been a very long day, she tells herself, *I'll get back to work in a more serious manner once I get some more rest...*

You mean you don't want to end up in another coma?

Angelique shoots to a sitting position in her bed at the second, much more cynical inner voice. She frowns, staring at her hands as they tremble once again. Tears fill her eyes as she touches her bare neck and feels the tough skin of the scar once again. A choked whimper escapes her, and before she knows it, she's breaking down into sobs as she lays back against the bed. After about thirty minutes, at which point she's cried herself out, she whispers to no one in particular.

"I want to go back to how things were... Why did everything have to change?"

Three

Midnight Mission

Slowly but surely, over the next three weeks, Angelique adjusts to her new environment. It takes her a bit of fiddling with the television to figure out how to use it, but the simple remote is easy enough for her to learn. She maintains the upkeep of her new apartment by washing her dirty dishes daily and taking the garbage out regularly. After each long day, she enjoys a hot shower and scrubs the stress from her body before collapsing into her new, comfortable bed.

Despite the weeks that it takes for her to grow accustomed to her apartment and her new routine, her anxiety never fully settles. She frowns when she rubs roughly at her stinging hands and arms, wishing for her anxiety to finally ease. When she notices it hasn't gone away by the end of the month, she groans. *It's got to be the anxiety from being back at work,* she reasons, unsure if she fully believes her logic. *I haven't found any demonic traces the entire time I've been here!*

With a new self-confidence from her small mental pep-talk, she heads to the main office for the DHA Apartment Complex. Unfortunately, Spyr and King still act suspicious of her based on the way they both will hold their infant close to their chests every time Angelique draws near. Spyr especially does not seem to appreciate the angelic guardian's presence, judging by the frequent suspicious glances or irritated glares they send her way. Every time she catches herself on the receiving end of such disdain, she can't help the self-consciousness that forms a pit in her stomach and a lump in her throat.

One evening, as her wards' distrust of her eats away at her more than usual, she flings the covers off of her and leaps from her bed. She pulls a warm, long-sleeved, turtleneck sweater over her baby blue nightgown, slips on her sandals, and grabs her keys as she heads out of her apartment, only stopping to make sure the door shuts quietly behind her. She takes the elevator to the first floor, hugging herself as she makes her way out onto the moonlit paths of the apartment complex. Her night walk is uneventful until she hears a quiet chittering coming from a small bush next to King and Spyr's house. She sneaks closer to the house, using the noise-muffling quality of her wings to aid her investigation.

Upon further approach, she sees a small crimson-skinned creature hiding in the bush. It stands at around three feet tall on the tips of its hooved feet. It can barely reach the first floor window sill, where it peers inside with its large-yet-beady eyes. Obsidian-dark horns curl from its upper forehead, much like a bighorn sheep, and a long tail with an arrow-shaped tip sweeps against the ground as its voice quietly crackles in its thin throat.

"An imp!" Angelique gasps, her voice catching loudly in her throat.

Surprised by the sudden noise, the imp whips around, baring sharp claws as it hisses at Angelique. From what she could recall from her orientation days, imps were considered pets of a certain subspecies of demon... Those that brought death and destruction to the human world. Angelique's blood runs cold as panic courses through her veins.

There must be a death demon nearby... But I haven't felt any traces!

Breaking herself out of her thoughts, the angel summons a bow and quiver and nocks an arrow, but as she aims at the imp, it turns and dashes away, hissing more. She takes to the sky and chases after it, hovering low to the ground so she can keep the crimson creature in her sights. As her target bolts between alleyways, she's forced to tilt and fly at awkward angles between buildings until she finally catches up to it.

She hovers in the sky, locking onto the imp as it tries to dart through a large green park. Right as she releases her arrow, however, her target falls over itself, causing her to miss and her arrow to lodge into the ground. She pulls her wings close to herself and plummets down, opening them back up just in time for her to land with a thud against the grass. With a swing of her arm and a glimmering wave of pink and gold magic, her bow morphs into a silver short sword. She stands tall and charges toward the imp...

Until she feels a tug on the front of her long nightgown.

In her rush to attack, she'd nearly forgotten how poor her coordination in long clothes had always been, even *before* she'd been in a 100-year coma. She's sent tumbling to the ground, and her sword strikes into the earth right next to the scrambling imp.

The small creature grabs hold of the sword's hilt and manages to tug it out of the ground. As it wields the weapon against its owner, the creature uses a small amount of magic to transform the sword's size to a much smaller, imp-sized dagger. Angelique watches in horror as the imp grins maliciously and moves to strike her with the blade.

Just then, she hears a loud '*SHING*,' and the imp's body drops to the ground, bisected across the middle. Thick, ink-black demon's blood drains into the nearby grass from the creature's lifeless body. A silver-bladed glaive prods at the upper torso, as if checking to make sure the imp is truly dead.

The long handle of the glaive is held by a somewhat muscular woman who stands only a couple inches taller than Angelique. The woman's shoulder-length brown hair is mostly pushed back behind one pointed ear, and a set of long black horns protrude in a zig-zag upwards from her head. A purple jewel-style tank top covers her midsection, tucked into a pair of high-waisted shorts with two pairs of silver buttons at the front. Dark grey over-the-knee socks and black knee-high leather boots cover most of the woman's legs. A long tail with six thin spines near the tip and a pair of large, leathery bat wings with spikes on the top ridge protrude from her lower and upper back respectively. Upon closer inspection, the woman's face is rather beautiful in its roundness, and her vibrant blue-purple eyes hold skull-shaped pupils within them.

"Heh," the woman laughs, "What are you, a rookie? You don't charge into battle in long dresses, little angel."

"Who... Who are you?" Angelique asks as she pushes herself back to her feet and hugs her sweater closer to her body. Her head-wings press tightly against the pink ribbon choker around her neck as suspicion courses through her. She grabs for the dagger that the imp had transformed and hugs it close to herself as well, preparing to fight in case the other woman would pose a threat to her own safety.

"You chased this thing through the whole city?" the woman asks, ignoring the question. Based on the way she lowers her glaive and wills it to disappear in a flurry of black and purple magic, she doesn't see Angelique as a threat.

"I did," the angel confirms, also dissipating her blade in a flurry of pink and gold sparks.

"That's impressive, for somebody who can't keep herself on her own two feet."

"Flying is completely different from running. You have wings, so I'm sure you know that." After a moment, Angelique's eyes brighten with a realization. "Wait a minute... You're a death demon."

"Ah, yes. Such an astute observation, Angel."

"You just killed an imp!"

"Uh-huh. Any other *thrilling* commentary to add?" the demon snarks as she picks up the lower half of the imp by an ankle and summons a large trash bag to shove it into.

"Heaven tells us imps are pets for... Your kind."

The woman bursts into loud laughter, her tail wagging wildly as she cackles. "'*My kind*' hunts these things for sport. They're glorified target practice!" She grabs the imp's upper half by the horns and unceremoniously throws it into the trash bag as well, then deftly ties two firm knots at the mouth of the bag.

"... So they're not pets?"

"Not even close. Hence why they're perfect for us death demons to hunt." She shoulders the bag and places a hand on her hip. "Now, if you don't mind, I'm off to report this to my wards." She turns and begins to walk away.

"You have a ward? Er- More than one?" Angelique queries with a quirked eyebrow. "What are their names?"

The demon stops and turns to face Angelique again, glaring at her with glowing, narrowed eyes and making Angelique's stomach shrivel into lumpy knots. "Why do you want to know, huh?"

"Well... Because that imp was watching *my* wards."

After a moment of tense, somewhat awkward quietness between the two otherworldly beings, the demoness turns back around and lashes her tail. "Why am I even considering answering you? You're not my boss," she mutters. She turns on the balls of her feet, tail flicking in irritation, and struts off in the same direction as the apartment complex.

Angelique watches her go for a moment, until her frozen thoughts catch up to her. She scurries after the demon, making sure to keep a safe distance from the other woman's intimidating, almost threatening, aura. She pursues the demon back to the DHA Apartment Complex and watches as she makes a beeline to the main office. After a firm knock, the door opens and allows the demon and her imp-filled garbage bag inside. Angelique uses another small burst of magic to coat herself in an invisibility spell as she darts inside the house just before the door fully shuts.

"I got another one for you guys," the demon declares, strutting into the living room and holding the trash bag as if it were a first-place trophy. "So you should be able to rest a little bit safer tonight."

"Thank you," Spyr murmurs wearily. They plop down in the rocking armchair with a soft groan. "I knew I had eyes on me, but..." They trail off with a defeated sigh. "I didn't want to worry any of our tenants. I should've known it was one of my ex-clients." As they talk, the platinum-blonde is washed over by a wave of periwinkle-colored magic, which reveals their true form as their glamor dissipates. Their blue eyes turn a vibrant purple color with heart-shaped pupils in the center; a pair of black, slightly curved horns protrude from their head; a long spade-tipped tail wraps around their waist; and a set of bat-like wings curl into the shape of a heart around their thin body.

As Angelique watches the transformation from the shadows, her jaw drops in shock. *Spyr is a demon?! So that's why they haven't trusted me all this time...*

King kisses his spouse's forehead between their horns. "It's alright, honey. The imp is dead now, so we're closer to being safe."

"Right..." They lean in close and nuzzle their nose against their husband's, then turn their attention back to the female demon. "Thank you again for protecting us, Stellar."

The other demon—Stellar, apparently—smiles at the sight before her. "It makes sense why you don't want these types around; especially with little Irida growing so quickly. She's almost four months old, right?"

"She is." Spyr tears up. "She already grew out of her newborn scrunch..."

"Aww! That means she's growing well. And with you two as her parents, I'm certain she's a happy baby, too." Stellar's tail wags again, showing exactly how joyful she is for the small family. "Now, what do you say I get rid of the *garbage* for good?" She waves her left hand in a circle as it glows with magic, forming a glowing portal in the nearby wall. The insides of the portal shimmer, as if it's filled with a thick mixture of pastel glitter and shining stars. Stellar grabs the trash bag containing the imp's corpse, and chucks it unceremoniously into the portal.

As the door between realms closes, Stellar wipes her hands against each other. "By the way, during my hunt tonight, I encountered an angel that was also after the same imp," she muses, "Has she been hanging around you two?"

The angel in question, still hiding, feels a lump form in her throat at the mention of her presence.

"Oh... Angelique..." Spyr murmurs, curling into a bit of a tighter ball in their chair.

"Angelique is here acting as our guardian angel," King clarifies. "We were somehow issued a Holy Protection Order, so she's been here on an assignment to protect us. The paperwork must have gotten mixed up, since we've nearly had angels try to attack us previously..."

"It's a good thing you've got me around, then," Stellar chuckles, "If the paperwork gets changed while she's here, your safe haven would become fish in a barrel..."

A heaviness forms in her chest as her heart sinks. *They really think I'd turn around and attack them...?*

"Speaking of... Angel," Stellar calls, looking over her shoulder in the direction of Angelique's hiding spot, "You can come out now. I know you're there." She holds out her right hand, which summons her silver-bladed glaive once again.

The angelic guardian swallows a thick, anxious knot in her throat and dissipates her invisibility spell. She steps out into the warm light of the foyer, holding up both of her hands in a show of peace. She hears Spyr's breath hitch, and watches as King stands protectively in front of his spouse as her presence is revealed.

"Please believe me when I say I'm not here to hurt anyone," she pleads, her voice shaking slightly as she speaks.

"You're only saying that because the Holy Protection Order hasn't changed," Stellar declares with a snarl, pointing the blade of her glaive down to stomach-level and preparing to attack.

"I've never been on a demon extermination mission," she counters, "You saw my attempted performance tonight. I would *not* be the one here if these grounds were under threat of angelic action."

Stellar's eyes narrow, but she pulls her glaive back to a neutral position beside her. "You make a good case, angel. You're definitely not a fighter."

"Exactly." She looks over Stellar's shoulder to Spyr and King. "It's like I told you when I first moved in, I'm a pacifist. If it gives you any kind of faith in me, I got out of the hospital the same day I came to protect you two." She takes a deep, shaky breath and continues to plead her innocence. "My partner is missing, and in all honesty... I want to find her and make sure she's okay." She summons the Holy Protection order and closes a trembling hand around the rolled parchment. "I'm sure there's got to be something we can do to prevent Heaven from changing this order."

Stellar snorts at the final statement. "Once Heaven finds out demons are living here, they'll change the order in a heartbeat. They won't be willing to leave a safe haven for demons unharmed." She holds out her arms, motioning to the area around them. "The only reason this place is even *here* is because of King and Spyr. They've been dealing with demon hunters for over a year since its creation, living in fear that one day Heaven will find out about them and send an angelic squadron to eliminate this place for good."

Angelique stands proud as she slowly lowers her hands to her sides. "I'm not about to tell Heaven what's going on. If this is how they make people feel... I don't want to be like them." She grips tightly at the skirt of her dress. "Whether you're humans or demons, you're under my protection, and I won't let anything happen to you."

"How are we supposed to trust you?" Spyr hisses.

"I'll work to prove it to you that I *can* be trusted."

The female demon watches her with analyzing eyes for a moment, until her deep frown morphs into an amused smirk. "Fine then." She moves her glaive to her left hand and holds out her right. "My name's Stellar Evernight."

Angelique takes the offered hand and shakes it firmly. "Angelique Taylor."

As they break the contact, Stellar hums. "Well, considering the late hour, I suppose it's about time you get back to your apartment and try to sleep. You've had a long night, Missy."

Angelique glances at the clock on the wall, which shows the time as being half-past midnight. "I suppose you're right." She turns around, baring her back in a show of trust to the demons and human. "I'll see you all in the morning. Thank you for giving me a chance."

She leaves the main office and slowly meanders back to her apartment, trying desperately to process everything she'd just learned. She opens her apartment door on autopilot and makes her way back to her bedroom. She flops onto her mattress and manages to quell her stress long enough to allow her to succumb to sleep.

Four
Heaven and Earth

The following week, after just over a month of the Lockleys being under her guardianship, a letter is delivered to Angelique. One glance at the pristine white-and-gold envelope announces the sender: none other than Heaven's Holy Council. She carefully tears open the envelope and takes out the letter, which is folded into neat thirds and decorated with a gilded border. After quickly reading it over, her blood runs cold. Written on the page in glimmering golden ink is an announcement that she is being brought before the Holy Council to verify the safety of her wards. She writes out a quick reply confirming her attendance, and another letter is received soon after to provide her a court date for three days later.

On the day she's assigned to appear in court, Stellar, King, and even Spyr are waving her off.

"Good luck, Angel," Stellar says with a small chuckle and a wave, "Something tells me you're going to need it."

"Don't remind me. I get stage fright with my friends, let alone in front of my bosses..."

"I'm kidding. I'm sure you'll be fine." Stellar flashes her a small smile. "You'd better get going; you don't want to be late."

Angelique takes off into the sky, soaring to Heaven with ease thanks to her significantly stronger wings. She makes her way to the courthouse, which is perched on a hill overlooking the city. The giant building stands brilliantly tall among the cityscape, and its marble columns are streaked and speckled with gold. She makes her way up the matching marble steps, her hands trembling from a sudden onset of anxiety as her footsteps echo below her. Taking one last glance behind her she gasps at the beautiful view. The skyscrapers and other tall buildings nearly glow under the warm rays of sunlight, the metal giving off a nearly blinding, iridescent sheen.

Angelique turns back around, staring at the large golden doors that lead inside the courthouse. She opens one gilded door, revealing eerily-empty halls, with only a single angel at the front desk. She takes slow, careful steps inside to try and minimize any echoes bouncing off the gold-and-marble walls. The charity angel sitting at the front desk raises her tired, almost irritated gaze as she tucks her white-and-orange wings close to herself. Her voice comes out nasally as she asks, "Do you have an appointment?"

"My name is Angelique Taylor. I'm scheduled to meet with the Holy Council at eleven o'clock to—"

"Look, I'm sure you're a *very* sweet girl, but I really don't care," she grumbles, "If you'd like to leave collections for the Holy Council while I check you in, the plate is right over there." She points a thin finger to her left, bringing a small clay plate to Angelique's attention. It has a few large monetary notes already placed inside, which surprises the angel.

"Oh, um... I-I didn't bring my wallet..."

One of the secretary's eyebrows raises, but she doesn't comment as she clicks three times on her computer screen. "Alright, head to Courtroom A. It's the last room on your left," she explains, motioning down one section of the grandiose hall.

Angelique heads in the direction she's pointed and makes her way to the aforementioned room. She pushes open another large gilded door and finds herself in a courtroom with green walls that sparkle like fluorite stones, thanks to the sunroof 30 feet above. She finds herself on what appears to be a stage, with a pair of microphones perched at the far end. As she makes her way to the center of the courtroom, she notices two large, empty jury boxes on the left and right sides of the room, as well as one smaller jury box perched about halfway up the far wall. It takes her a moment to see, but the elevated jury box holds a panel of nine Holy Councilmen. Each of the old, wrinkled men have three sets of angelic wings sprouting from their back. The balding men sit somewhat curled in on themselves, looming over the courtroom like hungry vultures awaiting their next meal.

Below the panel of Holy Councilmen stand six of the seven Archangels in their brightly-colored robes. Each set of robes is covered in golden hems, and the collars, cuffs, and belts all bear eye-shaped markings. Lord Barachiel, acting out his title as the Overseer of Guardians, moves forward and speaks with grandeur.

"We are gathered here today to bear witness to the trial of Miss Angelique Taylor," he declares to the mostly-empty room. The blood rushes from her face as her boss states his words so clearly, as if she were truly on trial for doing something wrong.

Well, I suppose premeditated perjury is a crime... She folds her wings close to her body and neck, and places her shaking hands behind her back, all in an attempt to better straighten out her posture and make herself appear more confident.

"Now, what did this young lady do?" one of the Holy Councilmen wonders aloud in a hoarse and crackling voice.

"Nothing bad as of yet," Lord Selaphiel states firmly. The Overseer of Prayer moves forward, holding his teal robes close to his body. His two sets of white-and-butter-yellow wings flare out as he moves in front of Barachiel and leans in close enough to look directly into her eyes, despite the forced eye contact feeling as though he is peering into her soul instead. "However, if we do find anything to be amiss in your testimony, Miss Taylor, we will be forced to take disciplinary action."

Angelique tries to keep her voice steady. "Nothing will be amiss, Master Selaphiel. I can assure you."

"For your sake, I hope that is true." He turns on his heels and marches back to his position below the panel of Holy Councilmen.

An Archangel in plum robes, who Angelique recognizes as Dr. Raphael, steps forward. "Since I was the first to meet Miss Taylor, I will speak my testimony first. Miss Taylor was in a coma for 100 years after she was decapitated during a solo mission. Her former partner, Miss Aurora Grey, has been missing in action since the incident, and is suspected to be the one who beheaded Miss Taylor. Since Miss Grey has yet to return to Heaven, she is now presumed dead."

Angelique's eyes fill with tears. *I know Aurora would never do that to me... They have to be wrong! But she's still considered missing after 100 years... Is it even possible for me to find her anymore?*

One of the other members of the Holy Council speaks. "Miss Taylor, based on what you recall of your time under Dr. Raphael's care, would you say that his claim is accurate?"

"Yes, sir. While I can't accurately recall exactly what happened when I got decapitated, let alone who the culprit is, I know from my time in Heaven Central Hospital that I was in a 100-year coma."

At the mention of her uncertainty in regards to who beheaded her, the councilmen and Archangels quietly murmur amongst themselves.

"Miss Taylor, you were returned to full duty under the watch of Lord Barachiel, is that correct?" another councilman asks.

"Yes, I returned to full duty the same day I awoke from my coma."

"And you have since been assigned to protect a small family."

"I have."

There is more murmuring amongst the high-ranking angels. "Tell us about this family," the Archangel with red robes and white-and-orange wings demands.

Archangel Michael!

Angelique stares at the man and swallows around a lump in her throat. "They own a gathering of apartment complexes in the human realm. I have even been given one for as long as I am their protector."

"And what information have you gathered on this family? Why are there imps and demons coming after them?"

I need to be careful here... One wrong word and it's all over for the DHA.

"I have yet to gather the full story as to why they are being targeted. However, seeing as they are my wards, I will do everything in my power to protect them from any visible threats." She places a hand to her chest, just shy of the ribbon choker covering her decapitation scar. "Even if it means sacrificing my life in the process."

One of the Holy Councilmen, donning a brilliant golden robe, stands and places both of his bone-thin, wrinkled and liver-spotted hands atop the jury box. "And what would you do if you were to find out that one of your wards was, in fact, a demon themself?" the seraphim queries. Murmurs fill the courtroom at the mention of demons.

Do they know about Spyr?!

Cautiously, she steadies her voice as she prepares a lie on her lips.

"I would exterminate them for the safety of my human ward, as well as the other humans on Earth."

The room is silent for a moment, until the Archangel Gabriel, dressed in ocean-blue robes, speaks. "I believe Miss Taylor to be telling the truth," he states.

At the Overseer of Prophecy's words, a wave of calm washes over the room's occupants, and Angelique has to use all of her willpower not to fall to her knees in relief. *From what I've heard, Archangel Gabriel can tell when someone is lying... Let's hope it's only a rumor.*

"In that case, Miss Taylor," Archangel Jegudiel, the Overseer of Reward, states, "You are free to leave." He makes a shooing motion as he turns to the other Archangels, his emerald-colored robes flowing as he moves.

As Angelique is about to turn on her heels, something odd occurs to her. "Before I depart, may I ask why there are only six of the Archangels in attendance today?"

At the mention, Barachiel sends Angelique a silencing glare. "It is not your place to question the Archangels, Miss Taylor. I would suggest you leave... Unless you want to stand trial for blasphemy."

She bites her lip hard, kicking herself mentally for daring to speak out of turn. "My greatest apologies, My Lords. I will take my leave now." She turns and scurries off, fighting back tears as her blood runs cold, a bone-deep ache permeating her veins. *I can't believe I questioned the Archangels! I should be killed for daring to ask such a thing!*

Angelique darts out of the courthouse and spreads her wings, adrenaline coursing through her veins as panic floods her mind. *I need to get away, I need to get away, I need to get away—!* She takes a running leap off the courthouse steps, praying that her strengthening exercises have helped her enough to allow her a fast and safe flight away from the embarrassing scene, which replays over and over in her head. Luckily, a strong breeze helps to lift her away from the ground, and with a few strong flaps of her wings, she's soaring over the central city of Cloud Nine. She covers her ears with her hands and her head-wings, fighting back the tears forming and stinging in her eyes.

You're so stupid! I can't believe you questioned your bosses! You should have known better, you stupid, stupid girl!

As her mind races, her body operates on autopilot until she finds herself flying above the heavenly city. She doesn't pay attention as to which district she's soaring above until she reaches the cloud's edge; even then, she only comes back to her senses as she's diving through the air. She mindlessly coasts through the air until she's able to locate her apartment building, at which point she aims directly for the roof. She manages to once again catch herself before face-planting into the building, but she falls to her knees nonetheless. Tears continue to make her eyes burn as she looks out toward the beginnings of a sunset, at which point she notices a familiar form is sitting on the roof as well, their legs dangling over the edge. Stellar lightly kicks her feet, her glaive laid across her lap, and doesn't even look over at Angelique as she speaks.

"How did it go?"

Angelique sighs and hugs herself, too drained of energy to even attempt to get up and approach the demon. "I messed everything up," she confesses, curling in on herself. She allows tears to flow as she sniffles and elaborates. "I testified that everything was fine, and I think they bought it, but then I turned around and asked why only six of the Archangels were present and now I..." Thick globules of tears cloud her vision, and as she tries fruitlessly to dry them away with her hands, wrists, and head-wings, she breaks down into more sobs.

Please stop crying, she pleads to her body, *Not in front of Stellar... Please... She already finds me pathetic and weak, I can't just—*

A slightly calloused hand rests on her shoulder and a soft handkerchief wipes at her eyes. Blinking away more tears, Angelique comes face-to-face with Stellar, who has silently moved to her side. She's half-leaning, half-kneeling in front of her as she helps the angel to dry her tears. The demon's expression provides no insight into her thoughts aside from what appears to be a worried pout.

"Wait, what are you—?"

"You're gonna make a mess of yourself if you keep crying, silly angel," she coos, her voice just loud enough for Angelique to make out her words.

"I—" She sniffles— "I can dry my own tears, thank you!"

"I'm sure you can, but having someone take care of you has to be a little bit nicer than bottling everything up." Stellar plops down onto Angelique's lap, her inner thighs pressed against the angel's legs in a slight straddle. She leans forward a bit more to better help wipe the angel's tears away.

"Wh— I don't bottle everything up!" Angelique huffs, bucking her knees in an attempt to get Stellar off of her lap. Her action only succeeds in shoving the demon forward, further into her. They crash into each other, avoiding a collision of their heads, and lay on the roof of the apartment building for a moment. Their chests press against one another, and Angelique can feel a slight vibration coming from the demon— a crackly, nearly silent purr.

"Hold on, you purr?"

"Pardon?" Stellar asks, quirking an eyebrow and scrunching up her nose as if she were offended. "What the Hell are you talking about?"

"You're purring! You're not making any noise, but—" Without thinking, Angelique wraps her arms around Stellar's midsection and pulls the demon closer against her own body.

The vibrations of Stellar's purrs grow louder at the touch, and a crackly rumble forms in the demon's throat. Her tail wags lazily from side to side, much like a cat's tail when it receives scratches under its chin. Despite this, Stellar's face reddens considerably at the closeness.

At the demon's blushing face, Angelique's breath hitches. She removes her hands from Stellar's sides and places them on either side of her own head. "I'm so sorry. Please forgive me."

The demon huffs, puffing out her cheeks cutely. "I'm not going to attack you just because you hugged me or heard me purr, y'know."

"But—"

Angelique's plea is cut off by Stellar tilting her head to rest comfortably on her chest, as if her breasts were pillows. A pair of arms snakes to her sides and rests there. Stellar's legs are still straddling the angel's thighs, and the demon's purrs increase in volume more as she settles against Angelique's body.

"Uh... Are you comfortable?"

"Mm-hm." She glances to Angelique and meets her eyes. "Why? Am I squishing you?"

"Nope! Nope, not at all..." She lightly wraps her arms around Stellar's midsection, settling in as the demon's purrs soothe her anxious heart. Slowly, her eyelids grow heavy and she fights to keep them open.

"If you need to rest, Angel, by all means, *rest.*"

"But I don't want to leave you..."

She could swear a smile covers the demon's face. Her eyelids drift closed and she can barely make out a whisper of, "You're not leaving me. Not for long, this time."

The next thing she knows, she's waking up and finds herself back in her own apartment, placed delicately in her bed. She tries not to be disappointed as she gets ready for the day.

Five

Hunting the Hunters

Angelique and Stellar continue their unlikely partnership as they work to protect the Lockleys from any unwanted demons who make their presence known. After dealing with a particularly fussy Irida one afternoon, Spyr and King head upstairs to cuddle and nap. Stellar sits on the roof of their house, glaive across her lap once again as she stands guard.

"You haven't exactly been able to explore the city since you got here, have you?" she asks as Angelique moves to sit beside her.

The angel pauses and frowns a bit. "Not really, no... I've been too worried about the Lockleys to do any type of reconnaissance."

"Maybe you should do that. If you know the area well, you'll be able to keep them safe more confidently." She nudges Angelique with her elbow. "Besides, they don't need two of us to stand guard while they take a quick rest."

Angelique hugs her knees to her chest. "I suppose you're right..." *I can't exactly tell her I want to stay with her so I can hear her purr again...* "I guess I'll go, then." She slides off the roof and lands on the grass below her. As she moves to leave the grounds of the apartment complex, she hides her angelic features and makes her way down the sidewalks into the bustling city.

She finds herself surrounded by towering buildings that contain both offices and shopping centers, and curses internally as her anxiety kicks in again. *I have no idea where I am or where I'm going, and I'm all alone...* With her nerves aflame, she tries to remain walking in one direction, so she can turn around and walk back once she's done enough recon for the day. As she wanders through the energy-filled city, she can't help the feeling of being watched.

It takes her a little while to fully recognize why she's so on-edge: the city is full of both human *and* demon energies, the latter of which feels oddly weak. As she passes a telephone pole, she notices a shimmering, magic-coated poster hidden from human eyes. Curious, she decides to take a look.

[A safe haven for demons of all kinds!] reads the poster, with symbols for each of the nine varieties of demons grouped together in a circle. Angelique hums. *From what I've seen throughout my time here, the DHA truly is a safe haven...*

Throughout the city, she finds more posters for the DHA. One advertisement for the DHA Apartment Complex proudly proclaims, **[Low-income housing available. Officially endorsed by King Mammon.]**

Huh? Mammon? The King of Greed is trying to help demons find their way? She frowns. *Then Heaven does have things twisted...*

She continues on her way, looking around nervously. She could swear there was someone following her, and it only unsettles her worse.

She stumbles upon one final poster with two familiar faces: King and a visibly pregnant Spyr cuddled together, with them nuzzling each other adoringly. The latter is beaming, which Angelique has never seen. *They really don't trust angels if they won't even smile around me...* Her heart sinks, but she reads over the text on the poster. **[Find your sanctuary with the Demon-Human Alliance! Founded by an inter-realm couple, the goal of the DHA is to ensure the safety of demons on Earth.]**

"We should look into updating these posters now that Irida's in the world," a familiar voice says behind her. She turns to see King standing only a couple feet away.

"King? What—? You were back at home, weren't you?"

"I was, but Spyr woke up and was craving a sweet treat. I told them I'd grab them something, they went back to sleep, and then I saw you reading one of our old advertisement posters. I didn't mean to make you jump, though."

"Oh, it's fine! I wasn't expecting you to be here. You said you were off to grab them something sweet?"

"Yes; would you care to come with me?"

"Oh, um... Sure!" She trails after the human, the air between them awkwardly quiet. "Can... Can I ask you a question?"

"Of course. What's on your mind, Miss Angelique?"

"Why doesn't Spyr trust me?"

The man takes a moment to contemplate his answer. "They don't trust most people. For a while, it felt like they didn't even trust *me*, but luckily I was wrong." He smiles fondly as his thoughts drift to his spouse. "Their father died to demon hunters when Spyr was very young, and when their mother moved on and got together with her second husband, he turned out to be a cruel brute of a man. The two of them were abused over the smallest things, so Spyr learned to put their walls up around anyone. Obviously, when we first met, that meant me, too. They don't allow other demons or humans too close to their heart, let alone angels, so... Please don't take it personally, Miss Angelique. They've been through a lot and are intensely protective of our baby."

"I see... Is Irida the first for you both?"

"She is. I've done my best to keep Spyr resting, since they dealt with an oddly long bout of morning sickness throughout their pregnancy, but they feel guilty if they aren't productive for a few hours, never mind a few months. Hence why I'm off to get them a bowl of the ice cream we helped to create."

Angelique's ears perk up. "Wait, you make ice cream?"

"Oh, yes!" The man's demeanor brightens further as he beams. "Spyr helped me to create special demon energy mixers that can either be consumed like a human energy drink or used to flavor human foods. We've found they're easy to make into ice cream, so we hired someone to deliver our special soft serve throughout the city."

"Different demons need different types of energy?" she asks curiously, "Heaven only tells us that demons prey on humans..."

"Based on what I know of Heaven, they say lots of things they're not entirely sure of," King chuckles. "But yes, different demons need different energy sources. For example, Spyr is a hybrid of a greed and a lust demon. If they were to eat, say, an ice cream made for gluttony demons, it would make them sick. Never mind their lack of a spice tolerance for the pride ice cream..."

"That... Makes sense, actually. How do demons consume natural energies once they find them?"

"Well, most demons find people who exude too much of the energy they need. If they overeat, though, the human they feed from becomes ill." As they turn a corner, they find an ice cream truck with a small line of people waiting to order. "Aha, here we are."

King and Angelique both enter the line and wait patiently to order, but the sensation of being tracked like prey doesn't settle for Angelique.

It had to be King, right...? Who else would it be? Unless they're after King as well, but—

Her thoughts are cut off as they finally arrive at the window. Angelique quickly realizes the server is a demon with smooth, curled ram's horns.

"Ah, Mr. Lockley! How are you doing today?"

"I'm doing well." He motions to Angelique. "This is a friend of mine. She's in town for a bit, so I decided I'd treat her to one of our specialties."

The demon casts Angelique a somewhat suspicious glance before returning his attention to King. "Whatever you say, Boss. Are you getting anything for Spyr?"

"You know I am."

"Do they want the special citrus or the strawberry?"

"Can I get one of each for them? Knowing my luck I'd pick the one they aren't craving."

"On it, Boss!" The ice cream truck driver whips around and gathers two styrofoam bowls, fills them each with soft-serve ice cream, and places lids firmly on top. The one on the left is a nearly neon shade of green, and the one on the right is a fluorescent magenta color. "Here you go. Anything for yourself?"

"I'll take the regular apple cinnamon."

"As you wish." A dish of pale beige ice cream is placed between the other two dishes. "And for you, little lady? Which would you like?"

"She'll take the vanilla and I'd like a special chocolate," another familiar voice speaks from directly behind Angelique. The angel jumps and whips around, blushing brightly when she sees Stellar standing behind her.

"Wh— Weren't you back with—"

"I was, but Spyr was *super* disoriented after they woke a second time, and wasn't sure where King ran off to. They wanted me to come find you both and bring you back home, since they were looking for him. I figured I should grab a snack for myself while I'm out and about! You don't mind, right?"

"I don't see why not, Miss Stellar!" the ice cream truck driver laughs. "And Boss, don't even try it! You know I'll never make you pay for your own treats."

King rolls his eyes, putting his wallet away in his pocket once again. "Alright, if you insist."

"Of course I do!" He sets the last two bowls of ice cream—a pure-white vanilla and an ink-black chocolate—on the counter. "I will, however, bag these all up for everybody." He swiftly places lids on the last two dishes, pulls out a paper bag with handles, and loads all of the treats into it. He places five spoons in the bag and hands it over. "There you are, everyone! Have a good day!"

Stellar gathers the bag and carries it along as King leads the way back to the apartment complex. The three of them chat about small things as they walk, until a memory clicks in Angelique's mind.

"Oh, before I forget... Stellar mentioned that demon hunters are after you and Spyr because you two founded the DHA. Is that still true? I haven't seen anyone hanging around since I arrived..."

King sighs. "Sadly, yes, it's still an issue. The last time we had to fight off the demon hunters, several of their members got injured, so we haven't seen them since before Spyr had the baby."

Stellar snickers at the memory. "Spyr kicks ass when their family is threatened, so they scared those hunters pretty good." As her giggles fade, a concerned frown forms on her face. "It *is* a bit worrying, though, what with how silent they've been... Have the threat letters stopped?"

"Those have also been on pause, which is odd. It's not as if the demon hunters would take a vacation just because their targets have an infant to care for..." They turn onto a much less crowded street; an odd occurrence in a bustling city.

Just then, a loud *THUD* is heard behind them as someone in thick-soled boots jumps from a nearby fire escape. The woman is dressed head-to-toe in black, from her turtleneck sweater and cropped leather jacket to her thick army-style pants. Her curly red hair and pale skin bear a stark contrast to the rest of her garb. She pulls a knife from the holster on her left leg and turns her nose up at the three of them. The patches on the upper portion of her sleeves bear the resemblance of a cartoonish, silver demon head encircled by a crimson circle with a slash in the center. "You can thank *me* for that," she declares with a haughty huff.

"Rachel..." King snarls.

She rolls her eyes. "You can't possibly still detest me after all this time—"

"You have *personally* attacked my family. How am I *not* supposed to detest you?!" He holds his hands out to his sides, and in a wave of periwinkle magic, a pair of handheld sickles chained together at the handles forms in his palms. Angelique freezes, surprised at the human's ability to magically summon a pair of kusarigama.

Rachel, however, narrows her eyes and scowls. "Is it seriously going to be like this? You forget how well I *know* you, King. If anyone's going to beat you in a fight, it's going to be *me.*"

"You couldn't beat me back when we worked together. What makes you think I'll let you win now?" King throws one bladed end of his kusarigama, holding the weighted chain in his left hand in order to reel it back. Rachel parries the attack from the curved blade, knocking it back through the air and allowing King to narrowly catch it by the handle. The pair continues to trade blows, narrowly avoiding becoming injured in the flurry of bladed attacks.

"If they keep this up, somebody's going to get hurt," Stellar growls, "And I will *not* let it be King's blood that gets drawn." She turns to Angelique and half-passes, half-tosses the bag of ice cream into her arms. "I'm going to put a stop to this."

"What?!" Angelique shrieks, "What are you going to—"

"Human weapons can't hurt me. I'll be fine." She summons her glaive and dashes forward, throwing herself in front of King. She curls her wings into a large round shield, which manages to deflect the throwing knife Rachel had pulled from an inner pocket of her jacket.

The demon hunter hisses as her weapon skitters across the sidewalk, the blade crumpled as if it were made of cheap aluminum foil. She casts a glare to the demon and pulls out another knife—this time made of silver. "Whoever you think you are, you have a lot of nerve getting in the middle of our fight—"

"Oh, I'm not getting in the middle. I'm putting an *end* to this," Stellar growls, her voice much more cold and calculating than previously. Her wings flap, raising her into the air and exuding a powerful aura in the process. She raises her glaive as the blade glows with a mixture of purple and black magic, and a large, protective dome forms around the four of them. "King and Spyr are under *my* protection, and I will not allow the likes of *you* to interfere with their lives and happiness."

"Hah! You say that as if I care what some demon—"

"'Some demon?'" Stellar scoffs, feigning offense. She chuckles darkly, *cruelly*, as her sclera eclipse and turn from their usual white to an inky black. She holds up one open hand, causing glowing purple chains to rise from the ground and swirl around Rachel like a group of snakes. She slams her fist closed, and the chains close in, wrapping tightly around the demon hunter and clicking shut around her neck and waist. Rachel nearly falls over as she's caught off-guard by the attack, but the demon hunter manages to keep herself on her feet.

Until it dawns on the hunter: she's being held by two fingers underneath her chin.

"You truly don't have any idea who I am, do you?" Stellar coos coldly as she remains hovering in the air.

"No... No, ma'am," Rachel stammers, her voice caught in her throat as an icy chill courses down her spine.

"You should thank your lucky stars that you're not on my *list* yet. As Executioner, I could rip your soul from your body and drag you into the deepest depths of Hell where you belong. But, seeing as it is not *quite* your time, I'm going to do you a *one-time* courtesy and spare your miserable, hateful life today. However, if I find out that you threaten my wards; send them hateful letters; or even *look in their direction,* I will take action and remove your name from the census. Am. I. Clear?"

Rachel nods, eyes wide and her lower lip trembling.

"Good." Stellar snaps her fingers, causing the chains around Rachel to disappear. She shoves the redhead out of the way as the magical dome dissipates as well, uncaring as the hunter stumbles into the alleyway she'd ambushed them from. "You two, we should get going. No clue if there are others of *her kind* hanging around."

King and Angelique pale at the commanding tone and pass by Rachel without a word. The walk back to the apartment complex is eerily silent for the first few minutes, after which Angelique drums up the courage to speak.

"So... Who was she?"

Stellar glances over her shoulder with a playful hum. "Do *you* want to fill her in, King, or would you prefer I recount your tale?"

King snorts. "I suppose I will. You exaggerate mortal lives too much, Stellar."

"Hey, now!" They laugh for a moment, after which King speaks again.

"So, as I'm sure you heard, Rachel and I used to work together. In fact, we were dating back in college."

"You had an intense taste in women," Angelique murmurs. Her face burns at her words, and she stammers out a quick, "I'm *so* sorry, that slipped out—"

King laughs. "You're not exactly wrong, but she wasn't always this crazy. When she learned about the study of demonology from one of her classmates, *that's* when everything went downhill. She would gather crystals with 'powers to ward off evil'; she'd collect weapons like those throwing knives and learn how to properly use and care for them; she even went out late at night searching for demons to chase off, once. Her search came up fruitless, luckily, so no one got injured.

"But, her shenanigans didn't stop there. One day she decided to drop out of school and become a demon hunter in some... Cult, for lack of a better term, and begged me to do the same. I was almost finished earning my master's degree in synthetic chemistry, so I told her I would join her once I graduated."

"Did you actually join her?" Angelique questions, "From the way you talk about her, she sounds..."

"Insane? I'm sure, and I saw it, but I had my own motives for going into the demon hunting field. See, I was a synthetic chemist back when I had a nine-to-five day job, and it's done me well. But from what I *did* read in the demonology books she loaned me, it seemed like demons could only eat certain types of energy. I decided to dive headfirst into my own field research and started interviewing my targets about the reasons they were on Earth. I learned that most of them were looking for a place to start fresh, away from whatever trauma they'd experienced previously." He shrugs. "So I was a poor-performing demon hunter."

"And I'm guessing you two split because of differing views?" Angelique guesses.

"For the most part. She's been bitter ever since, though, and has decided to take it out on my family." King looks at his left hand, where a simple silver wedding band sits on his ring finger. "I met Spyr not long after they were originally accosted by Rachel, you know."

"Did you break up with her, and then... Hit it off with them?"

"Exactly."

"So *that's* why she has such a grudge against Spyr!"

"Mm-hm. I ended things with her the night she found them, and about a month later they found me working in my old house's garage. I'd turned it into a makeshift laboratory so I could try making synthetic demon energies, and they decided to stick around and help me out. We fell in love, founded the Demon-Human Alliance, and were given the permissions and land to build the apartment buildings we own. Other than that, the rest is history; I have a beautiful and intelligent spouse and we have an adorable daughter. What more could I ask for?"

Her eyes sting with the beginnings of sentimental tears. "Aww! You two are so cute!"

"I get a bit emotional hearing their story, too," Stellar adds.

"Speaking of, thank you very much for protecting me back there. I probably could have handled her, but I'm a bit out of practice..." King rubs the back of his neck in embarrassment.

"It's no skin off my back. Now, let's get you and the sweets back to Spyr. I'm sure they'll be happy to hear what we did to Rachel~!"

"Oh, you could say that again," he laughs.

They arrive back at the DHA apartment and head inside the main office, where they find Spyr curled up in their armchair in the living room. They appear to be half-asleep as they cradle Irida close to their chest. "Mm... King?"

"Hey, baby. I'm back, and I got you a treat like you wanted." He motions for Angelique to bring the bag of ice cream over. He pulls out the vibrant green and bright magenta ice creams, which makes the demon chuckle.

"You're so good to me."

"Of course I am; I love you."

Angelique backs away from the couple to watch the scene from the doorway, once again teary-eyed. An arm wraps itself around her waist and tugs her closer to the fourth figure in the room. Her face heats up as she rests her cheek against Stellar's shoulder, but relaxes once again when a rough purr escapes the other woman.

"What do you say we dig in, too?" the demon suggests, "It would be unfortunate for us to come all this way and have melted ice cream."

"Oh, right. That's a good idea." She pulls out their treats and two of the remaining spoons. They both dig into the ice creams and relax into each other's presence.

Six

A Shift in Perspective

Two weeks have passed since the encounter with Rachel, and Angelique has gained a new appreciation for the DHA's cause. Combined with Stellar's consistent presence, the two protectors keep a watchful eye over the Lockley family. The demoness even helps to gather supplies for King's energy mixers, which he makes easily thanks to his knowledge of synthetic chemistry, the recipes he's compiled, and the laboratory in the basement of their home.

"Thank you again for your help, Stellar," King sighs tiredly. "I don't know how to repay you."

"Just make sure demons live a long and healthy life here," she chuckles, passing him a bag full of ingredients.

"We're doing our best." He sorts the various ingredients among the shelves as the mixtures in three Erlenmeyer flasks bubble and boil. As the mixtures condense, they practically glow with bright and colorful demon energies.

Angelique watches from the corner of the basement laboratory in awe. "Making synthetic demon energies is rather simple, huh..."

"Oh, it is now that I have proper recipes. Before I figured out the flavors and makeups of each energy source, it was a lot of trial and error. Luckily, Spyr's especially knowledgeable thanks to their background and experience."

"Can all of these demonic energy flavors be consumed by humans, too?" Angelique asks.

"Yes, they can. We humans don't get sick from consuming demon energies, but they create a small abundance of them in our bodies. Sometimes I like to stock up on greed or lust mixers to make life easier for Spyr, now that we have Irida."

"And I appreciate that very much," the aforementioned demon declares as they make their way down the basement stairs. "By the way, lunch is ready. Come take a break with me."

"We'll be right up, my dear." King quickly and efficiently cleans his workspace. Once he reduces the heat to ensure the bubbling mixtures won't make a mess, he leads the way back up the stairs and into the main living area of the house.

Just before the four of them sit at the table, Stellar's cell phone begins to ring. She pulls it out of her back pocket and steps away to answer with a surprised chirp of, "Oh!" She presses the device to her ear, smiling brightly as she greets the caller with a cheerful, "Hey, Dad. What's up?"

Stellar's dad is calling her? Huh... I wonder what her family is like... Angelique muses to herself as she tries to listen in on the demon's conversation.

"Come home? Why?" Stellar continues, a frown now evident in her voice. "I'm still with the Lockleys, though. Is it urgent?" There's a tense pause. "... In Hell? How?" A sigh. "Alright, I'll be home in a bit, but you'll have to send Briar, Nast, and Viper so they can take over for me."

At the mention of Stellar being replaced by three other demons, Angelique's heart sinks. *If she's going home to Hell... Does this mean I'll never get to see her again? I don't want to deal with any other demons... They're probably going to be so hostile and—*

Her panic is cut short by a nudge against her shoulder. Looking over, she's surprised to see Spyr giving her a gentle, concerned expression. "Is everything okay?" they whisper, nodding their head in Stellar's direction.

"Oh, um... Yeah, I'm sure everything's fine, Stellar can handle—"

"I mean, are *you* okay?"

Despite the inquiry being innocent in nature, Angelique swallows around a lump in her throat. Before she can answer, Stellar comes back into the dining room. "So, it turns out there are some pretty odd traces back home and I'm the one they want leading the investigation," she declares.

"... Huh? What kind of odd traces?" King asks, confused.

The answer comes out unexpectedly calm and blunt from the demoness as she answers: "There are traces of an angel."

"... An angel? In Hell?" Spyr repeats, stunned and confused.

"That's what the report says... Look, you guys are as confused as I am, but my brother's concerned and told my dad, who decided I'd be the best option for the investigation. As the Executioner, it's my job to keep my people safe from any threats... Imp and angel alike." She waves the unspoken concerns off with a casual shrug.

"Wait, wait, wait," Angelique interrupts, waving her hands rapidly in confusion, "You said 'your people' like you're some type of royalty. If you're a guardian like me, surely that's not the case, right?"

"Who said I was just a guardian?" Stellar laughs.

As she speaks, a large, swirling portal forms behind her. Out step three death demons, each dressed in black metal armor and carrying a different type of weapon. The first demon holds a greatsword at her side; the second one has a bow and quiver strapped to their back; and the third warrior has a sheathed shortsword on a belt wrapped around his waist. They turn their attention to Stellar.

"Lady Executioner! What is our task?" They all salute Stellar as if she were an army general.

"You three will be taking over my current duties on Earth," Stellar declares, waving a hand to King and Spyr as she presents them much like one would when displaying a priceless art piece. "The family you'll all be protecting is the Lockleys, and their organization is the Demon-Human Alliance. You will need to protect them from imps, demon hunters, and angels. Are you three prepared for the task?"

"Yes, sir!" they declare loudly.

"Good. Get into your positions. You are dismissed." With her command, the three death demons drop their salutes and head off to scout the house and perimeter.

King scratches the back of his head, a bit flustered. "You brought your three highest elites to protect us? I didn't realize we were so special, Your Highness."

Stellar snorts and rolls her eyes. "For the love of *everything,* please drop the formalities. Briar, Nast, and Viper will call me if anything suspicious happens while I'm gone." She glances at Angelique and smiles innocently despite the angel's expression being frozen in awe. "Not that I don't trust you, Angel, but their cell phones will connect to mine while I'm in Hell."

"You're *royalty?!* And a *general?!"* Angelique gasps, *"Why* did you let me think you were a normal guardian?!"

"Because I knew you'd react like *this,* silly girl." She cradles Angelique's cheek in one hand. "I hope you can forgive me for wanting to be treated as any other demon for a little while."

Angelique's face flares pink with heat. "I can forgive you... I just... Don't want to offend you."

"Believe me, you won't offend me by treating me like a friend." She lets go of Angelique's face. "In any case, I suppose I should be going. I don't want to keep my father waiting." She heads to the front door, only stopping when she hears quiet footsteps behind her.

"Um... Before you go... Is this... Goodbye?" Angelique asks, trying to hide the tremor in her voice.

"Hm? What do you mean?" she asks, turning away from the door to properly face her companion.

"Am I never going to see you again?"

"Why wouldn't you? I'm sure we'll meet on missions every now and then." She leans in close and gives a teasing smirk. "What's the matter? Are you going to miss me?"

Angelique huffs, unable to fight back a bright blush. "So what if I am?"

Stellar quirks an eyebrow in surprise. "Oh?" Her tail wags like a curious and playful dog. "If that's the case, why don't you come with me?"

"... Huh?"

"I'm sure the elites will be able to keep the Lockleys safe, if you want to come visit Hell with me."

"Oh! Um... As much as I'd love to, I... I really shouldn't leave the Lockleys," the angel explains, "Since they're my assignment."

"My elites will keep them safe," Stellar repeats.

"I wouldn't want to impose on you—"

"You wouldn't be imposing at all! You'd be my guest."

"My bosses—"

"Won't know about this unless you tell them."

Before she can counter the demon's argument, she's interrupted by her own thoughts. *You could look for clues about Aurora while you're down there,* a voice whispers in the back of her mind.

"... Actually... Sure, why not? Let me say goodbye to the Lockleys and then I'll join you."

Stellar grins. "Go ahead. But don't you worry, we'll keep an ear out to make sure things are running smoothly."

Angelique scurries back into the dining room, where King and Spyr wait with knowing expressions on their faces. "You're going to Hell with Stellar, right?" the demon asks. When they're met with a nod, they smile brightly.

"Alright. I suppose we'll see you later," King says.

"Thank you. We'll be back as soon as everything gets sorted out."

"Enjoy yourself and don't get into too much trouble."

The angel rolls her eyes playfully and heads back to Stellar's side. The demoness smiles at her and takes her hand. "Ready to go?"

"As ready as I'll ever be."

"Good girl." She waves her hand and forms a glittering portal. "Now, hold on tight."

"Huh? Hold onto what?"

"Me." She grabs onto Angelique's other wrist and leaps backward into the portal, tugging her along into the rift. Angelique yelps and squeezes her eyes shut, even covering her face with her head-wings. She prepares to fall, but feels the wings on her back instinctively begin to flap. She finds herself thankful the exercises had given her enough strength since her release from the hospital, especially since she'd hardly been flying while on Earth.

She opens her eyes and gasps at the scenic view before her, which is enhanced by the height she and Stellar are hovering at, about fifty feet in the air. Off in the distance, a fire-colored sun is hanging low in the sky, casting everything in a warm glow. Similarly to the capital city of Heaven, a large city spreads out beneath them, with houses and apartment buildings covering the base of a nearby hill. The familiar sight of ink-black grass spreads across the remaining distance as far as the eye can see.

"Oh, whoa..."

"Welcome to Hell, Angel," Stellar declares proudly beside her, "This is the city of Petraglow, the capital of the Death Sector."

"It's so pretty..."

Stellar raises an eyebrow in surprise. "Yeah? I'm sure it's nothing compared to the pure sunlight and soft clouds of Heaven."

"It's completely different, which is what makes it so beautiful." She looks over to Stellar in awe. "You just... Live here. You get to see this every day."

"I do."

"I'm almost jealous."

Stellar snorts and laughs. "Don't be. You have to be deemed a bad person to be able to live here."

Angelique pauses as a realization sets in. "Heaven's rules don't make any sense, do they..."

"They make sense to the rule makers, at least," the demon grumbles, "They can twist their laws and proclamations into whatever they want on a case-by-case basis. If they find out they don't like someone in Heaven... Poof, they're gone in the blink of an eye because everything twists in the council's favor."

"... How do you know this?"

"My dad has told me a lot of stories over the years."

"It sounds like it... Speaking of your dad, am I going to get to meet him?"

"You bet! His house is right this way!" She tugs Angelique forward, and they fly down to the walkway. Stellar's heels click elegantly as she makes her way up the path to the large hill the city is built around. On top of the hill sits a large manor-like palace with a black brick exterior. It stands proud and isolated, with the outer perimeter of the property surrounded by tall, black speckled marble columns with wrought-iron fencing between them. Silver arrow-shaped spikes decorate the top of the fencing, providing a vaguely threatening sight to the passerby. A grand gate blocks the path from directly entering the estate.

The angel follows Stellar, only to freeze in her tracks when she sees three extremely large dogs lazing in a pile just inside the gate, and two more average-sized dogs resting nearby. The extra-large dogs sense their presence and immediately perk up, growling threateningly. As they stand up, it's revealed that they are not three giant dogs, but one giant dog with *three heads*. Stellar's full height only reaches to the underbelly of the oversized, three-headed Doberman pinscher-rottweiler. The demon places her hands on her hips as it leans down to sniff her through the bars of the iron gate, uncaring of the saliva dripping from the other two heads.

"Uh... That's Cerberus..." Angelique manages to say as she watches in shock.

"Yeah, I know. They look super threatening at first, but I promise they're a gentle giant." She produces a key and unlocks the gate, beaming as it slowly swings inward and frees the giant hound. "Isn't that right, bubbies~?"

Cerberus barks and drops to the ground in a "play" position, its long tail wagging happily as it recognizes Stellar. A chorus of barks comes from the three heads, the volume surprisingly quiet compared to its towering size.

Stellar laughs and begins to pet the two heads on the sides, making kissing noises as she nuzzles the middle head's snout. "That's right~! Stellar's home~!" she cheers, her voice bubbly and excited as she greets the Hellhound. She laughs more as they lick her, drooling all over her arms and hair. "Oh, God, now I need another shower! You messy, messy dogs!"

The two smaller dogs approach Stellar as she coos and cheers and laughs. One is a large, long-haired mix between a Newfoundland and a flat-coated retriever, and the smallest dog appears to be a purebred black labrador, which yips cutely in an attempt to gather Stellar's attention. The demoness manages to break away from Cerberus' slobbery onslaught and pet the other two dogs.

"Hi, Rue~! Hi, Helena~! Did you all miss me?" she coos, giggling as the smaller dogs press against her legs and rumble happily. She looks back over her shoulder at Angelique. "Come on up, they won't bite you. You smell like me."

"... I do?"

"I brought you here, didn't I?" she chuckles.

"I suppose you're right..." She takes a few hesitant steps forward, freezing once again when the three dogs lean forward to sniff her. She holds her hands close to her chest as fear courses through her whole system. The dogs all let out deep, harsh growls, saliva dripping from their jaws as their fierce gazes bore into the angel before them.

She flinches back, using the wings on either side of her head to cover her face as she lets out a terrified yelp. She hears Stellar move, and when she peeks through her feathers she finds herself guarded by the demon. Stellar's holding one arm out protectively in front of her, and giving the dogs a fierce glare.

"That's enough, you three," she snarls out, "She's not dangerous."

The dogs back off, their eyes still locked onto Angelique.

"She's safe," she repeats, "Back down."

At the command, the three Hellhounds back away and head to another section of the property's lawn.

"Um..." Angelique begins.

"I am *so* sorry," Stellar interrupts, "I'm sure they'll grow to like you, the more time you spend here." She takes one of Angelique's trembling hands and shuts the gate with her tail. "I told you, you're safe with me."

"Right... Right." She squeezes Stellar's hand lightly. "Let's go meet your dad."

"Are you sure you're ready?"

She nods as the dogs walk up the path. "I think so. Maybe just... Let me know what I should look out for?"

Stellar hums as she formulates her words. "My dad can be a bit... Eccentric, let's say. He dotes on my brother and I a lot." She rolls her eyes playfully, a smile on her face. "He'll be ecstatic when he sees I brought a friend home. I doubt he'll care that you're an angel, either. He trusts my intuition, just like everyone else."

Angelique relaxes at the reassurance. "That makes me feel a lot better. Thank you."

"Good. Now, let's head inside." She leads her up the concrete walkway and onto the front patio. Before Stellar can even knock on the door, it opens.

The man on the other side towers over them, standing approximately seven and a half feet tall. A long black cloak with dramatic tears along the hems drapes from his shoulders, covering the elegant grey-and-silver pinstripe suit he wears. A pair of spiked wings and a long spiked tail protrude from his back, the appendages matching those of his daughter. His face is hidden by a goat skull mask, its horns curled around in a circle and ending just above his ears. His own horns zig-zag upwards like Stellar's, but the tips of his have begun to lose their inky hue and have faded to an ashy, pale grey color. A set of piercing red eyes widen under the mask, and a deep chuckle resonates from deep in his chest.

"Stellar! It's so good to see you're home already!" he declares. He removes the mask, hanging it on a hook inside the door. A middle-aged face smiles down at the girls, slight wrinkles crinkling with the kind expression. He places his hand on Stellar's shoulder, pulling her into a side-hug despite their intense two-foot height difference.

"Hey, Dad," Stellar greets, returning the hug.

Angelique stares at the two death demons, caught off-guard by the man's intimidating height yet gentle demeanor. "Whoa..." she whispers.

The man in the suit turns his attention to Angelique, still smiling. His expression morphs to one of light-hearted curiosity as he speaks. "Oh, hello there. Who might you be?"

Stellar steps back to the angel's side and pulls her close by the waist. "This is Angelique Taylor, the angel that's been working with me to protect the Lockleys."

The much larger demon's gaze shifts to his daughter as he raises an eyebrow, a silent question passing between them. He must be satisfied with her nonverbal answer, though, because he claps his hands together. "Ah! Right, yes, Angelique! It's a pleasure to finally meet you!" He holds out a hand for her to shake. "My name is Elias Evernight. I'm known as the King of Death Demons."

She takes his hand and shakes firmly, swallowing a lump in her throat. "It's... It's a pleasure to meet you as well, Your Majesty."

"There's no need to be scared, dear girl," he states calmly. "Why don't you two come inside? The staff are almost finished preparing lunch."

"Good thing we didn't eat with the Lockleys," Stellar giggles. She takes Angelique's hand again and leads the way through the palace and into the opulent dining hall, where vibrant red walls surround a long table made of elegantly-carved cherry wood. The seats surrounding the table are made with the same carved wood, obviously a part of a set, and have cushions made of soft, thick, basket-weave material attached to both the base and the back of each of the chairs. As everyone takes a seat, six staff members in servant outfits and aprons march out from the kitchen, carrying large dishes of food and placing them onto the table.

"It smells awesome, Dad," Stellar praises, nearly drooling at the scent of the finely-cooked food.

"I requested the kitchen to prepare your favorites as soon as I got off the phone with you. I had a feeling you'd be home for lunch."

The servants begin portioning out the different dishes, which include a crisp salad, creamy pasta dish, and a main course of braised pork. The combination of rich scents makes Angelique's mouth water as she thinks back to the home-cooking she and Aurora would share back in their joint dorm at the Guardian Angel Headquarters.

"It must have been a long time since you've been home, Stellar," she comments in awe as she brings herself back to the present.

The demon shrugs and digs into the meal. "Time is relative in this house. Adrian's gone much more often than I am, but we always come back." She takes a large bite of the braised pork. "Speaking of my brother, where is he, Dad?"

"He was invited out by Ryzen."

"Ah, I should've guessed." She looks over at Angelique. "He'll be back later, and I'll introduce you to Ryzen once we pay a visit to the Blasphemy Sector."

They all eat, the angel groaning appreciatively as the food nearly melts on her tongue. "This is so good~!"

"I'm glad you also find it delectable," Elias thanks.

"It's very good, Your Majesty."

The King of Death chuckles again. "As I'm sure Stellar has stated, there's no need for formalities between us."

"Ah... Speaking of that..." Angelique turns to Stellar with a befuddled expression. "What is your rank, anyway?"

"Me? Oh, I'm the Princess of Death. Though, *technically—*" She shoots a playful glare at Elias— "I should be an archduchess since I'm adopted. But a *certain somebody* insisted that both his kids be equal in rank so they're treated the same."

"Ah, yes, forgive me for such *grave sins,*" the man laughs.

Angelique smiles at the playful atmosphere between the two royals.

"Before we get too caught up in the joys of reunion," Stellar begins, "What exactly *did* Adrian find with traces of an angel?"

"Ah, right..." Elias sighs. "While it is distressing, it can't be too dangerous if he's been out with his friends, so why don't we have him brief us on the specifics once he's back?"

"That sounds like a good idea. It sounds like he was vague with the details, anyway."

"He was."

The conversation remains lighthearted until the meal is finished, at which point Stellar stands and tugs at the angel's sleeve. "C'mon, I'll show you around the manor!"

"Oh, alright!" Angelique stands and follows Stellar to the doorway. As they're about to leave the dining hall, though, their path becomes blocked by an unfamiliar young man. His ink-black hair curls loosely around his face and horns, which are the same zig-zag style as the other demons in the room. A short, dark, torn-looking cloak covers from his shoulders to his elbows, obfuscating most of his cropped hoodie and checkerboard-patterned undershirt. Baggy black jeans with decorative tears on the thighs and knees are held up by a navy blue belt wrapped around his hips. Two smaller belts and four thin silver chains dangle from the belt loops, wrapping around to the loops in the back in a stylish manner. Black sneakers protect his feet as he walks through the halls of his family home. Despite being taller than Stellar and standing around six feet tall, his height is still dwarfed by Elias. If the two men were to stand side-by-side with one another, the newcomer would only reach the older demon's shoulders.

"Ah, Adrian! You're home earlier than expected!" Elias calls from his seat at the dining table.

Stellar's tail wags, a bright smile forming on her face. "Hey, Adrian! How was hanging out with Ryzen?"

"It was fine, but he and Tyrian miss you. You'll have to stop over at some point and catch up," the young man comments. His gaze drifts to Angelique, silently looking her over as a frown forms on his face. "Who are you?"

Stellar places a warm palm against Angelique's shoulder. "This is Angelique, the angel helping me protect the Lockleys. Angelique, this is my brother Adrian."

"A pleasure to meet you," the angel greets with a shy wave.

“Hm. Likewise,” the young man responds stiffly. He raises his head and looks past them. “Dad, I’m going to fill them in and head back out.”

“That’s fine. I’m assuming you’ll be on your way once you’re caught up, Stellar; Angelique?”

“Most likely,” the demoness replies, “So we’ll see you later, Dad.”

“Alright. Be safe and have fun!”

Adrian turns his attention back to his sister and her companion. “Let’s go sit and talk this over,” he suggests, turning around on the balls of his feet. He quickly makes his way down the hall and into one of the nearby rooms.

Angelique moves to scurry after him, but is held back by a firm grasp on her wrist. She turns and meets Stellar’s gaze, a heated blush coating her face.

“What is it?” she asks.

“Take your time. We may be dealing with another angel, but since it doesn’t seem they’ve harmed anyone yet, there’s no real need to rush.”

Angelique pauses to process the words, before a confused frown forms on her face. “Wait, so you’re saying we’d only be rushing around trying to sort this out if someone had been injured or killed already?”

Stellar raises an eyebrow. “Yeah, why?”

“Shouldn’t we be trying to prevent anyone from being hurt?”

The demoness chuckles and lets go of Angelique’s wrist. “You guardians and your ‘save the world’ mentality, I swear…” She places her hands to her hips. “It’s not realistic to expect everyone to survive when a disaster strikes. It just gets people’s hopes up, only for them to come crashing down with the hard truth of reality.”

Angelique looks at her hands, picking her fingernails as shame creeps into her chest. “Is it really so wrong to hope for the best?”

Stellar shrugs. "My philosophy is, 'If you set your expectations low, it's hard to be disappointed.' Dad says it's an optimistic view on pessimism, but..."

"That's a sad way to look at life," the angel comments worriedly.

The demon shrugs again. "I mean, hey, so long as I make it through the day, who cares?"

Angelique grabs Stellar's hand again. "I'll show you that life is worth living, for more than one day at a time. I swear."

Stellar gives an amused smirk. "Alright, challenge accepted." She squeezes Angelique's hand firmly. "Now, let's go meet with Adrian."

They head down the hall and into a comfortable-looking living room. The tall ceiling is warmly lit by the elegant black iron chandelier, which is coated in glimmering white crystals. A fireplace sits unlit beneath the large flatscreen TV hanging from the stone mantle. The walls are almost fully covered by ten-foot-high wooden bookshelves, each of which holds hundreds of books. Surrounding the cozy fireplace sit three large golden-framed couches decorated with soft diamond patterned black cushions. A large glass coffee table with drink coasters is nestled atop a woven red-and-gold carpet between the large seating areas. Sitting perched on one of the couches is Adrian, a manila file folder in his fingerless-glove-covered hands.

"It's about time you two got here," he huffs with a playful expression in his navy blue eyes, "I thought I was going to turn to dust."

Stellar rolls her eyes and takes a seat across from him. "Yeah, yeah, you say that as if you weren't out with Ryzen and Tyrian until I came home."

"It was only Ryzen," he corrects, "Tyrian had to stay home with his husband and their little one. Did you know those two are expecting another baby?"

"What? No!" Stellar gasps. "Oh, those brats... I'm going to smack them for not telling me!"

"Who...?" Angelique wonders as she takes a seat next to Stellar on the couch.

"The King of Blasphemy and his partner are going to be second-time parents," Adrian clarifies.

"Aw, that's so sweet!" the angel coos.

Stellar clears her throat. "Sorry, Adrian, we got distracted again. I was told by Dad that there you've gone all around Hell and found angelic traces?"

Adrian nods, a sudden seriousness to his expression. "Yes, I have. I believe it started in the Blasphemy Sector, but it's hard to tell because the traces were well-disguised. Whoever the angel is, they must have a demon alongside them leading them around the place." He hands his sister the manila folder. "I tried to discuss this with Ryzen, but he wasn't sure what I was talking about. According to him, he's just been going between the palace and Earth, so our best bet would be to consult the other palaces."

Stellar frowns. "Why couldn't we speak with Tyrian?"

"He's busier than Queen Bee because of his husband and their toddler. He needs time to rest, so Ryzen is going to let me know when the palace is available for a meeting."

"But someone could get hurt if an angel's here!" Angelique counters.

Adrian shoots her a stern, silencing glance. "It's not our place to dictate the lives of those in the other palaces. If Tyrian needs time to be a good husband and parent, he will *get it.*"

The angel swallows thickly and curls her hand in her skirt. *Me and my big mouth... I'm already overstepping my bounds—*

A hand rubs lightly against Angelique's forearm. "I see where both of you are coming from," Stellar declares softly, "So I will respect Tyrian's request. We'll investigate elsewhere until we hear that the Palace of Blasphemy is taking visitors."

"If I may suggest, perhaps you should start with the Palace of Pride," Adrian muses.

"That sounds like a good idea," Stellar agrees, standing up. She turns to Angelique and holds out a hand. "Come on, Angel, we're heading to the Pride Sector!"

Angelique's face flushes as she takes Stellar's hand and stands from the couch. As she turns to leave the living room, a sudden shiver inches its way up her back. With a quick glance over her shoulder, her blood turns to ice as she sees Adrian silently watching her with a suspicious glare. She swallows the lump forming in her throat and tries to focus on the warmth of Stellar's hand.

Seven
Creative Liberties

As Stellar pulls her along, Angelique does her best to keep up with the demon's oddly fast pace. "You seem excited to go to the Pride Sector," she jokes breathlessly once they're outside the palace walls and headed for the iron gate.

"Not particularly."

"Then why are we going so fast?"

Stellar slows to a stop, then turns to face Angelique. "You felt the glare my brother was giving you. I'm keeping you safe." Her voice is matter-of-fact as she squeezes the angel's hand snugly. "He doesn't like that you're here with me."

"... Is it because I'm an angel?"

"I... I don't know for sure. You'd have to talk to him, but I strongly advise against it right now." She loosens her grip on Angelique's hand slightly. "I don't want him to blame you for something you had nothing to do with."

"Oh... Okay." She squeezes Stellar's hand and plasters on a small, brave smile. "Let's keep going."

The death demon swings open the wrought iron gate, unbothered as the hinges creak. She wanders ahead of Angelique, her tail swaying lazily from side to side as she walks. "By the way, Angel?"

"Hm? Yes?"

"You might want to hide those wings on your back. We're going to be doing a lot of walking, and it's easy to sprain your wings if you bump into somebody."

"Oh! Right, that makes sense." She tucks her wings close to her body and activates a small surge of magic, which makes her large, feathered appendages disappear. "Should... Should I hide my head-wings and halo, too?"

"Do you want to get a bunch of dirty looks?"

"No..." She frowns and uses the same spell to hide her other angelic features from her appearance. "Why do the people here hate angels so much?"

"Well... Even those who are content with the lives they've built here feel jilted by Heaven. Not everyone here is as awful as Heaven makes them out to be." Stellar's tail wraps loosely around her ankle as she speaks, careful not to slice open her leg with its spines.

"I believe you," Angelique replies, "The demons I've met so far don't seem like bad people."

The demon princess gives a lopsided grin. "I'm glad to hear that. We're still taking the subway, though."

"... Huh? Subway?"

"You know, like the ones they have on Earth. You didn't think I was going to make your life easy and teleport you everywhere, did you?"

The angel's face burns in embarrassment despite the playful tone. "Oh, no, of course not! I could never ask you to do something like—"

"Relax, Angel, I'm picking on you," Stellar coos as she places a hand to Angelique's shoulder, "I want you to see what it's like for *everyone* here, not just the royals and nobles."

The angel perks up at the explanation. "Oh! That'll be nice!" She beams and bounces on the balls of her feet. "I'll get to see how everything works!"

"You will. Now c'mon, we've got a train to catch." She grabs Angelique's hand and once again begins to pull her along with a significant spring to her steps. The angel scurries alongside Stellar and can't help but giggle as they race down the hill that leads from the Palace of Death. The Hellish sun shines warmly on the land as Angelique and Stellar make their way into the city below.

The concrete path below them grows larger and diverges to turn into the sidewalk of a scenic city street, much like one found in the metropolis of Heaven or the busy cities of Earth. Hundreds of buildings, both large and small, sit nestled against one another. The city is incredibly walkable, despite its immense size and the dozens of vehicles coming and going. Houses and businesses fill the gaps between skyscrapers and apartment buildings.

"I never expected the Death Sector to be so densely populated..." Angelique notes in awe.

Stellar snickers beside her. "If it makes any difference, it's not *only* death demons living here."

"Really? But if demons are free to move between sectors, why do the sectors even exist?"

"The sectors were made for the royals to split up their territories and designate where sinners go to start, based on their sins. No one is confined to certain sectors or trapped in little societal bubbles." Her tail wags slightly as she speaks. "Granted, there are some stereotypes between the different subspecies of demons, but we all know not to judge a book by its cover. Every demon is their own person."

"So demons treat each other like humans do? Or... At least should?"

Stellar nods in affirmation. "You're right. And besides, it's pretty easy to get along with each other when the worst people get punished the way they should."

"What do you mean?" Angelique asks, tilting her head and raising an eyebrow in confusion.

"You've seen an imp before; remember the night we met?"

"Of course I do, how could I forget?" As the words escape her mouth, her face grows even warmer. *That sounded way more romantic than I meant for it to...*

Stellar continues her explanation, not apparently noticing the angel's inner turmoil. "Imps are the souls of the people my family deems dangerous to the general populace of Hell. Murderers, rapists, pedophiles... People like that. Since they're labeled as threats, we death demons hunt them to keep everyone else in Hell safe."

"Why don't you execute them as soon as they turn into imps?"

"To be honest, it's more fun to play a game of cat and mouse with those demented creatures. Plus, it helps the new reapers learn the ropes."

Angelique hums to herself. "Interesting..."

"Oh? How so?"

"Well, in Heaven we're told that imps are dangerous because their presence means a death demon is nearby, ready to steal our ward's life. But it sounds like death demons are trying to protect all kinds of people from imps, including demons. So it sounds like an angel saw a hunt in progress, and didn't figure out that imps are considered pests..."

"I'd be willing to bet you're right." Stellar turns her attention away from Angelique and beckons toward a large subway station. "Here we are, Petraglow's subway hub. Since we're going between sectors, we'll need... This platform, over here." The demon princess once again takes Angelique's hand and leads the way. They enter the subway station, make their way to a platform labeled by a large number "2," and take a seat on a nearby bench as they wait for the train to arrive.

"Don't we need to pay for a ticket?"

"No? Why would we?" Stellar replies, confusion clear in her voice and on her face.

"Well, if we don't have a ticket, we could get turned away..."

"The subways in Hell are paid for and maintained by the royals," she clarifies.

"... What?"

"Yeah, the royals pay to keep the subway system running, so the common folk don't have to spend money to get to where they need to go. You have to pay for public transportation in Heaven?"

"Well, yes... It's usually pretty cheap, since Heaven is a large city, but we *do* have to pay to ride the bus."

"That's annoying. How many angels do that instead of walking or flying?"

"Enough to justify the buses as an option," Angelique mutters.

"What does the Holy Council do with all the money they get from collections?"

"I..." She pauses. "... You know what, I don't actually know. Keep the city running, I guess? Fund the Guardian Angel Headquarters so angels can train to be guardians?"

"Hm. Sounds like they need to be more transparent with how they spend the people's collection money," Stellar comments with an unimpressed expression, "Because if people don't know what the Holy Council does with their money, how do they know they're donating to the right cause?"

"I... I don't know. I suppose they don't."

Stellar glances to the large TV screen that displays the estimated arrival times of the subway train. "The next subway to Pride will be here any minute," she declares as she stands, "Let's go."

Angelique stands and remains close to Stellar as they approach the boarding line. Sure enough, within a couple minutes, the subway train arrives and slows to a stop on the tracks. The doors open wide to allow the small handful of passengers to disembark, before Stellar and Angelique are permitted to board. They find a pair of comfortable seats as the doors close and the train begins to move.

Angelique twiddles her thumbs and bounces her right leg as the subway ride proceeds. Aside from the working machinery beneath the train car, the only other audible noise is the soft music playing from the speakers.

"Are you anxious about this trip, Angel?" Stellar asks gently, placing a hand on Angelique's bouncing knee.

"I mean... A little bit, why?"

"I can't tell if you're bored from the subway ride or trying to burn nervous energy," she giggles.

A sudden heat forms in her face. "I have nothing to worry about. You said I'm your guest, and you'd never let anything bad happen to me."

"That's right. What a good girl, remembering what I told you," she coos.

A lump forms in Angelique's throat as she averts her gaze, choosing instead to watch the scenery pass through the windows. *Why am I getting so flustered? I never even felt like this around Aurora...* She pauses as more worries about her missing friend come to the forefront of her mind. *How am I ever going to find her down here? Everything is so different, and I've got to stick close to Stellar so I don't get lost...*

Before she knows it, the subway train has started to slow. The LED screens above the windows read, **[Now approaching Stratsford, Pride.]**

No time to worry about that right now, I guess... I have to focus so Stellar doesn't figure out why I actually agreed to come to Hell.

Once the two girls disembark from the subway car and make their way out of the station, Angelique freezes and looks around the capital of Pride in awe. While Stratsford is a bustling city like Petraglow or the entirety of Heaven, the various buildings throughout the city are covered in layers of graffiti art. Large office buildings are covered in intricate, spray-painted murals, and the smaller houses are decorated in what appear to be mostly practice pieces.

"Wow...!" she gasps, "It's beautiful here!"

Stellar nudges her. "What, you've never seen a few murals before?"

"Nothing like this! The ones back home are hundreds of years old and made with precious gems and gold..."

"I take it spray-paint is frowned upon in Heaven?" the demon jokes.

"You have no idea." She takes Stellar's hand as the demon leads the way forward, still admiring the various artworks at every turn through the city. After making their way around the city for a bit, the two of them stop outside a large gallery. There are various posters hung beside the doors and on the light posts surrounding the building, all advertising an exhibition. Angelique stares at the advertisements, then over to the doors of the gallery.

"Do you want to check it out?" Stellar offers.

"I... I do, but do we have time for this?"

"We'll *make* time for it, Angel." The demon princess beams and squeezes her hand, leading the way inside. By the time the two of them leave the exhibition, the sun is hanging low in the sky, casting the city in a warm red-orange glow, and Angelique's stomach growls. Her face reddens as it lets out a loud noise, which draws Stellar's attention. "If you're hungry, I know the *best* place to eat."

"Oh, I..." She sighs. "I'm sorry. I know we were going to the Palace of Pride, but then I got distracted and now I'm holding us up."

"Nonsense. You're my work companion and guest, so let me treat you to dinner." Stellar takes hold of Angelique's wrist and leads her through the city once again. The angel remains unsure of their destination until they come upon a small diner with a modest appearance. The sign next to the front door reads, **[The Gemstone Diner]**.

"A diner...? I thought this was going to be a super-fancy restaurant."

"Nope! I like down-home comforts, as I'm sure you noticed back at my father's manor."

"You have a point... You may be a princess, but you don't turn your nose up at people living simply. It's nice."

"Is that so?" The demon pulls open the door to the diner and motions for Angelique to enter ahead of her. As the door closes behind them, they're greeted by a girl standing dutifully behind the hostess stand.

The girl doesn't appear to be more than fifteen years old. Her coily black-and-blue hair is tied into small, intricate braids and tied back into a low ponytail. Thin, segmented horns protrude out of her head and a long tail with a beehive-shaped end pokes out from under the knee-length skirt of her blue waitress dress. An apron is wrapped snugly around her waist and tied into a large bow at the back. A pair of purple eyes with flower-shaped pupils dart to them and brighten as she speaks in an upbeat yet professional tone. "Hello there; table for—? Wait. Auntie Stellar?"

Stellar waves and smiles. "Hey, Lana."

Angelique looks between the two of them and, despite her confusion, waves as well. "Hello."

The girl—Lana, apparently—beams at them. "It's been so long since you came in! I should tell Mama and Fari that you're here!"

The death demon giggles. "Alright, but can we take a seat first?"

"Of course, Auntie!" Lana grabs two menus. "Right this way."

Angelique and Stellar are led to a booth that's relatively close to the kitchen entrance. Once they're seated, Lana curtsies and retreats to the hostess stand, leaving them to scan over the menu and make their decisions.

The angel looks over the options with a hum. Despite the restaurant being considered a classic diner, there are options one wouldn't typically expect; such as a salad sandwich on homemade French bread, or a BLT sandwich with grilled goat cheese and various protein options.

"Need help deciding?" Stellar queries playfully, "I know there are a lot of good options."

Angelique nods as a warmth forms in her cheeks. "Yes, please. Everything sounds so good..."

Stellar points to a few menu items. "I'm a sucker for the chicken and biscuits, the homestyle burger, or the classic Caesar salad."

"Chicken and biscuits sounds good..." She swallows thickly to keep from drooling.

Stellar grins. "I'll take the homestyle burger."

Just as they decide, a girl who's shorter and stockier than Lana, but has the same horns, eyes, and tail, scurries over. Her tightly-coiled black-and-red hair is styled to emulate lopsided bangs. She wears a similar dress and apron to Lana, except hers is a bright cherry red. She beams brightly and nearly bounces on her toes as she cheers, "Auntie Stellar! It really is you!"

"Hello, Fari," Stellar greets, holding out her arms in an invitation for a hug. The girl giggles brightly and nearly leaps into the embrace.

"It's been so long since I saw you, Auntie!"

"Well, it sounds like I'll have to come back more often to make up for my absence."

"Yes, you will!" She pulls back from the hug and pulls an order pad and pen out of a pocket. "So, what can I get you two?"

"We'll take two glasses of water, an order of chicken and biscuits, and a homestyle burger without onions."

"Alright, I've got you covered!" She goes to place the order with the kitchen staff, leaving the two of them alone once again.

"She's a sweet girl," Angelique comments.

"You've got that right. Lana may be more quiet and reserved, but she has just as big of a heart," Stellar chuckles.

"I'm guessing they're sisters?"

"You would guess right. They're twins."

Fari comes back over with their drinks, and they both thank her as she leaves once again. After taking a few sips, engaging in some more small talk, and a few comfortable silences, the angel asks a question that had been nagging at her since they stepped into the diner. "Why do they call you Auntie? I didn't think you have any siblings other than Adrian, and they look nothing like him."

Stellar laughs quietly. "I helped their mother when she was having them. She was a nervous wreck because she went into labor while she was on the clock at her last job. She used to be a hairdresser, and stayed long enough to finish her client's hair. Anyway, she was stressed because she was all alone ever since her husband died, so I took her hand and helped her through the process. So... Now I'm the girls' godmother."

"Ohhh... That's so sweet!"

"You could say that again," a sultry Southern woman's voice interjects. The girls' attention is drawn to a tall woman with her tightly-coiled hair braided with black and purple extensions and wrapped into a large braided bun on the back of her head. She's wearing a white chef's jacket stained by a handful of sauces and spices, a pair of long dark trousers, and purple-and-pastel-orange sneakers. Her demonic features match those of the young hostess and waitress in the diner. She holds two dishes in her hands; one plate donning Stellar's burger, and the more curved dish is filled with steaming, thick chicken stew and two biscuits on top.

"Hey, Henriette!" Stellar greets with a wave. "You didn't have to bring the food out yourself!"

"Nonsense! It's been a while since I got to see and talk to you, so I want to indulge myself a little." She smiles kindly, her eyes nearly shining as she sets the food on their table. "Speaking of; I've never seen you around before," she comments, her gaze fixating on Angelique.

The angel swallows thickly under the woman's scrutiny. "Uh... My name is—"

"This is Angelique," Stellar introduces, "She and I are working on a case together."

"A case, huh..." Henriette glances between them. "Alright, since she's your friend who's working with you, I suppose I'll leave you be." She leans in close to Angelique and stage whispers, "Make sure she keeps on top of her condition for me, okay?"

Huh?

"Huh?" Angelique asks, confusion clear as day on her face as her own attention snaps from Henriette's teasing to Stellar. "What is she talking about?"

"Oh, sweetie, you haven't told her?" Henriette chides Stellar disapprovingly. She takes hold of one of Stellar's wrists and holds up her hand, showing Angelique that the skin on the death demon's hand, from her fingertips down to the first knuckle, have begun to turn an ink-black color. "This is the same condition that brought her to the hospital the night I had my girls all those years ago."

Stellar pulls her wrist from Henriette's grasp. "It's nothing to worry about. It's not bad right now, and I've dealt with far worse instances."

"So you say, but you'd better keep a close eye on that, little one. You know exactly how bad it gets, and how quickly." Henriette then heads back into the kitchen.

Stellar turns her attention to her food, pointedly ignoring Angelique's concerned gaze. She takes a large, somewhat messy bite of her burger as her tail lashes slightly against the booth seat.

"I'm sorry if I'm overstepping, but... What *is* that? It looks almost like frostbite..."

Stellar huffs. "It's called corruption. It's a long story, but I'd rather not talk about it over food..."

"Oh... I understand." Despite her claim, a frown still forms on Angelique's face, until she takes a small bite of her chicken and biscuits. Despite the plain appearance, the rich flavors of the soup dance on her tongue. The biscuits are buttery, the vegetables are firm but not undercooked, and the chicken has obviously been well-seasoned prior to being shredded and added to the pot. "Oh, whoa... This is delicious...!"

Stellar's tail calms as the topic of conversation changes once more. "Henriette grew up in the Gluttony Sector, and she's always had a passion for cooking. She built this restaurant from the ground up after I convinced her to make her success a tribute to her late husband, Charlie."

"Oh... That's such a cute story, though. The food is delicious and her husband's memory lives on in this little diner, now."

"It would be better if he was here to help her, but he was executed by his community for being in a relationship with Henriette since he was human."

Angelique freezes mid-bite. "... The girls are half-demons?" She's met with a nod. "He loved her, though, right?"

"More than anything. He chose to be executed rather than denounce his love for her."

"So they were like King and Spyr..." She frowns, eyebrows scrunching together in befuddlement. "I don't see the issue."

Stellar quirks an eyebrow, but hums. "So long as the relationship between human and demon is built on genuine love and adoration, there's no issues... Right?"

"Exactly. If everyone is happy, there's no need for anyone else to throw a fit about a couple's loving relationship."

"Hm." Stellar takes another bite of her burger. At the lack of response, Angelique turns back to eating again.

Once their meals are finished, Fari approaches once again. "You two can leave whenever, Auntie Stellar," the teen explains, "Mama said your food was on the house."

Stellar rolls her eyes dramatically. "Of course she did. How about I leave all three of you a hefty tip, instead?"

"You know tipping isn't required," Lana huffs playfully as she walks by.

The demon princess sighs dramatically, still grinning. "Alright, if you all insist." She stands and looks over to Angelique expectantly. "You coming? There are a few more things I want to show you before we find a hotel for the night."

"Oh! Um— Yes, I'm coming!" She scrambles after Stellar and thanks the teens as they leave the diner. Once they're a few yards away, the demoness speaks once again.

"I still slipped the girls forty dollars," she confesses, "They deserve it."

Angelique stifles a laugh at the admission. "I agree."

"Now, we really do need to look into grabbing a hotel for the night. Come on; we don't have forever!" Stellar grabs firmly onto Angelique's wrist and tugs her along the street.

"Wha— Hey! Slow down!"

Eight
Party Time!

"Congratulations to this year's graduates! May you all serve Heaven with courage and righteousness!"

The hundreds of angels in the auditorium stand with a round of applause, and the former students toss their graduation caps into the air. There's the sound of a cannon firing off, and a flurry of downy feathers and colorful confetti drifts to the floor. Angelique searches through the crowd of excited new guardians, only for her gaze to land on a girl she almost recognizes. After a few moments of scrutiny, it finally occurs to her who the familiar form is.

That's Aurora! she finds herself gasping. She turns and races toward her partner, but as soon as she approaches, the other angel turns away from her and begins to leave. Angelique reaches out to grab her old friend's hand...

And bolts awake, nearly throwing the blankets off the bed. As her surroundings slowly register to her sleep-addled brain, she lets out a groan and flops back against the mattress. The first rays of Hellish sunlight peer through the curtains, brightening the unfamiliar, fancy-looking room.

She looks over to her left and sees a familiar form huddled under the blankets of the other bed. For a moment, it almost looks like Aurora, until the demon's horns and shorter hair make it clear: her partner is not the one by her side. Stellar rubs her eyes as she wakes. "Mm... Mornin', Angel," she murmurs, "How'd you sleep?"

“Huh? Oh, um... I slept fine, I suppose,” she half-lies, gripping tightly at the covers.

“I’m not so sure. You wouldn’t have had a nightmare if you slept well, right?”

“Uh... Well... I—”

Stellar snorts. “Relax, Angel, I’m joking.” She gets up and uses a wave of magic to change her star-and-moon-patterned pajamas into her usual daily attire. “Once you’re ready for the day, we’ll go downstairs and see if there’s an event at the Palace of Pride.”

It doesn’t take long for Angelique to prepare herself for the day ahead of her. Once she’s changed her clothes and brushed her hair, she looks over at Stellar. “I’m ready.”

They stop at the front desk. “Do you happen to have an advertisement from the Palace of Pride regarding when the next exhibition ball is going to take place?” Stellar asks.

The receptionist, a demon with the curled horns of a pride demon and the teardrop-shaped pupils and finned tail of an envy demon, perks up at the query. “Actually, yes!” They grab a flyer and hand it to the Princess of Death.

Stellar looks it over, her tail wagging when she finds the needed information. “It seems we came to Pride at the right time, Angel; the next big exhibition ball is tonight!”

“Wait, really?” Angelique reads over Stellar’s shoulder. “Oh, and it starts at 5:30!”

“You’re right,” Stellar declares with a bright, planning grin, “So we have plenty of time to pick out dresses for the occasion.”

“... Huh?”

“I’m not going to have us walk into an event held at the Palace of Pride without dressing for the occasion! Don’t you want to dress up a bit?” she teases with a smirk.

“Uh... I suppose not...” The angel’s face burns. “But I’m not sure if I’ll find something I like...”

"Well, luckily for you, I know a dress shop whose owner is both a designer and a seamstress. He can use magic to make sure any dress you enjoy fits perfectly." Stellar beams as she leads the way out of the hotel. "I'll treat you to breakfast first, and then we'll find something pretty to wear!"

They head to a café, where Stellar buys them both breakfast sandwiches and pastries. Once they've eaten their fill, they spend the day shopping at a boutique and each pick out a dress and some makeup to wear to the exhibition ball. Angelique's rose-pink dress gives her a princess-style silhouette without it being too bulky to move in, and has a ribbon tied around her waist into a large bow behind her. The fluffy skirt drapes in layers to look like an upside-down rose. The straps of the dress fasten behind her neck, making her ribbon choker appear as though it's part of the dress instead of an accessory. Stellar's dress of choice is indigo in color with silver moon and star patterns on the corseted bodice. Where the corset ends at her waist, the tulle skirt flares out a bit until it ends at the floor, where it bundles up to appear as though Stellar is walking on thick white clouds. Long bell sleeves drape over her shoulders and cinch at her wrists, bringing the attention away from her corruption-coated fingers. When Angelique notices that her companion's skin has now started to turn ink-black up to the second knuckle of her fingers, she frowns and can't help but fuss.

"Your hands are turning darker..." she murmurs.

"I know, but it's really not bad! Don't you trust me?"

She tries to push her nagging concerns to the back of her mind. "I do."

"Then I promise, I'll be okay. I know my body, and I know my limits. It won't be long before we meet with Lucifer and Lilith, get the information we need, and get out of here."

"Alright." She takes Stellar's hand and squeezes it. The demoness squeezes back, soothing the angel's frayed nerves. Their hands remain intertwined as they make their way to the Palace of

Pride. After their walk through the city, they find themselves at another large manor-like palace similar to the Palace of Death, aside from the brick exterior being painted a deep, rich red. A crowd of people in formal attire waits outside the closed wrought-iron gates, which peek out of tall rose bushes with crimson blooms. The energy among the crowd is filled with excitement and anticipation for the moment the gates open and allow them onto the grounds.

As they approach the Palace of Pride, whispers from all angles reach Angelique's ears.

"Is that Princess Stellar?"

"Who's with her?"

"Could she be her muse?"

"Maybe she's coming back to present some new artwork!"

"Wow, there are a lot of people..." Angelique murmurs, a tension forming in her chest at the realization. A gentle squeeze around her hand brings her a small amount of comfort, and she looks over at her companion. Stellar offers a soothing smile.

"If you get overwhelmed, say the word and we'll leave, okay?"

"Are you sure? I know we wanted to speak with the Rulers of Pride about the traces..."

"I'm positive. These parties gather folks from all throughout the Pride Sector, so they can easily get crowded. If we have to leave before we can discuss the case, we can come back sometime tomorrow. I'm sure I could even get a private audience with them."

"Alright... If you insist, I'll keep better tabs on whether or not I'm overwhelmed."

The death demon winks. "What a good girl!"

A heat forms on Angelique's face just as a handful of servants exit the building and make their way to the large gates and the awaiting crowd. Two large, muscular demons with thick horns on either side of their heads come out and open the heavy metal gates, and the remaining servants beckon to the awaiting masses. Slowly, the gathering of demons flows through the open gates, their dress shoes and high heels thumping and clicking down the grand concrete entryway. Almost on instinct, Angelique clings snugly to Stellar's arm, and the two of them walk alongside the rest of the party-goers with their arms linked like a couple.

They're brought into a grand entryway with 60-foot-high ceilings and golden chandeliers shining brightly overhead. The crowd enters a very large ballroom with warm white walls. The dance floor in the center of the room allows for plenty of movement space without crashing into any chatting bystanders off to the sides. Two sets of stairs stretch from the floors on either side of the room, their golden banisters glimmering in the brightness of the room. For a moment, Angelique quirks an eyebrow at the existence of the stairs.

Who would allow their guests into the rest of the palace?

Her worries are quelled, however, once the full crowd has been shuffled into the ballroom. The hallway lights on the upper floor go out in a flash, leaving the halls almost as black as the night sky. Standing atop the balcony overlooking the ballroom is a pair of demons: a woman wearing a shimmering red dress, and a man in a black suit. The man clears his throat and speaks loudly, his deep and refined voice echoing through the large room.

"Welcome everyone, and thank you all for coming to tonight's exhibition ball!" he declares excitedly, throwing his arms out in front of him in a grand gesture. Suddenly, the plain white walls shimmer as dozens of art pieces are revealed to have been hung up. Those in attendance all gasp in awe as the various works are revealed, before bursting into loud cheers and applause.

"I am your gracious host, Lucifer Morningstar, and I do hope you'll all have a lovely time while you're here tonight." He bows elegantly, and the lights shining above him dim as his speech finishes. With that, classical music begins to play throughout the room, and the guests mill about. Some stick to the sides to chat; others admire the new artwork on the walls; and then there are those who choose to grab a partner and head to the dance floor.

Angelique's attention snaps to her companion as Stellar moves forward, toward one of the art-covered walls. "Where are you going?" she asks, trying not to allow her brief panic to coat her voice.

"I figured you'd be thirsty, so I was planning to get us something to drink at one of the refreshment stands. Do you want to come with me?"

Before she knows it, the angel is nodding frantically at Stellar's offer. The demon princess gives an understanding smile and takes hold of Angelique's shaking hand. "Alright, the refreshments should be this way." She leads the way through the busy ball room, murmuring quiet "excuse me's" to signify their need to pass through.

They make it to the refreshments table, which has large displays of cut fruit, towers of crackers and cheese, and three large bowls filled with iced drinks. One of the drink bowls contains water, and the other two hold fruit punch. Stellar grabs two of the small glass tumblers that sit nearby, fills them about halfway with the fruity drink, and offers one glass to Angelique.

"Hopefully you like fruit punch," she chuckles, taking a sip from her own glass.

"Uh... Yes, I do," Angelique agrees as she grasps the cup in her hand. She takes a small sip of the liquid, thankful for the perfect amount of sticky sweetness. When she looks back up, she sees Stellar standing at the end of the refreshment table, looking at the artwork on the walls with a wistful expression in her eyes.

"Do you miss it?" Angelique guesses.

"Hm? Miss what?"

"Being creative. You... You seem like you had big dreams for yourself when it came to whatever your passion was, but had to give it up for some reason."

Stellar takes another sip of her drink. "You could say that, I suppose. I used to draw a lot; most of my projects stopped at the sketching or concept stages, though." She leans back against the wall as a sigh escapes her lips. "Whenever I tried to work on a *real* project, like writing a book or comic or drawing a more detailed piece, something would always go wrong. Be it the aches I get from my... Condition, or never being able to pass the planning stage without hating my work." She sips her punch again. "It can be hard to look at others living your dreams of success."

"I understand that," Angelique murmurs, "After all... This may be the Pride Sector, but there's always a bit of envy where personal success is involved."

Stellar hums into her glass. "I always used to tell my dad I should've been an envy demon."

"I'm not so sure, Princess. After all, you're extremely skilled in your line of work," a woman's voice interjects. Both girls look over as the voice's owner approaches, and Angelique's face flushes when she recognizes the woman by her shimmering red dress.

The woman who had stood beside Lucifer Morningstar as he gave his grand, welcoming speech stands before them, taller than both Angelique and Stellar; the demoness's height is only added to by her sleek black high heels. The dress she wears has a thigh-high slit over her right leg, and the fabric changes from a rich, crimson red at the sweetheart neckline to a dark, cherry merlot color at the bottom, where it drags lightly against the floor. The woman's large, curled horns end amidst long, thick black bangs, which are mostly pushed behind her ears. The rest of her wild, wavy hair shines with a violet undertone as it drapes down to her hips. A few thick strands even drape over her left shoulder, slightly obfuscating a small tattoo on her collarbone.

"Thanks for the vote of confidence, Your Majesty," Stellar snorts. She turns her attention to Angelique and holds out an introductory hand to the woman in red. "Angelique, this is Queen

Lilith Morningstar of the Pride Sector. Queen Lilith, this is Angelique; she's my companion for a case I'm working on."

Lilith smiles sweetly and gives a small wave to Angelique. "Hello, dear. It's lovely to see that little Stellar finally brought a friend to one of our events." She casts a playful purple-and-gold glance to the other royal demon.

"It's an honor to be here, Your Majesty," Angelique responds, clutching her glass a little bit tighter as her anxiety rises in her chest. *What will happen if she finds out I'm an angel? Will Stellar get in trouble?*

Lilith pushes a stray strand of hair behind Angelique's ear. "You don't have to be afraid, dear. I can tell your intentions aren't the malicious sort."

Angelique's head shoots up, ears perked at attention. "You can tell I'm...?"

"Of course. It may have been a long time since I was in contact with an angel, but I know their traces. Speaking of, you two are working on that case, right?"

Stellar nods in the affirmative. "Yes, we're here to investigate, but a party like this isn't the best place to discuss such things... Too many sets of ears. We don't want anyone to eavesdrop and spread panic."

"Such a responsible reaper," Lilith coos in an almost motherly manner. Just then, the tattoo on her collarbone begins to glow with a soft white light. She brushes her hair back over her shoulder and presses her hand to the glowing skin, which makes it glow a bit brighter. "Apologies, girls; my husband is looking for me."

"After the centuries you two have spent together, I can only imagine how much he despises straying from your side for too long," Stellar jokes.

"I'm sure you can guess, but you'd probably be wrong—"

"There you are, my love!" a familiar voice cheers. A pair of suit-clad arms wraps around Lilith's waist and pulls her close in a hug. The man of the hour, Lucifer Morningstar, stands behind his wife with adoring red-and-indigo eyes meeting hers. His short, thick, dark curls sit neatly on the top of his head, and there's a tapered fade that thins out toward his ears and the back of his head. "I've been looking for you for nearly ten minutes! I was so worried something happened!"

"Darling, you know I can handle myself," Lilith counters playfully. She presses a soothing kiss to her husband's cheek, which makes a broad, adoring grin form on his face.

"Yes, I know, but—"

"Besides, Your Majesty, if anything were to happen to Lilith, I'm right here." Stellar moves forward from her place against the wall of art. "My companion and I would make sure she returns safely to your side."

The King of Pride's attention snaps to the Princess of Death, and his eyes nearly sparkle as her presence registers to him. "Oh, Princess Stellar! I had no idea you were in attendance tonight."

"We happened to be in the area for a case," she clarifies, "So we decided to stop in and say hello before we had to conduct more official business with the two of you." She takes hold of Angelique's wrist, tugs her close to her side, and wraps her arm around the angel's waist. "This is my companion, Angelique."

"An angel, hm?" Lucifer muses quietly.

Angelique's face burns at the scrutiny, but she manages to curtsey in greeting. "It's an honor to meet you, Your Majesty," she says, her voice trembling slightly with her nervousness. Her hands tremble ever-so-slightly around the half-filled glass of fruit punch.

"Well, so long as you're Stellar's guest, I suppose there's nothing to worry about. We Royals trust her intuition with our lives." Lucifer's gaze relaxes as he speaks, even though he stands a bit straighter. He wraps an arm around his wife, almost mirroring Stellar's grasp on Angelique.

Stellar bows to the Rulers of Pride, much to Angelique's surprise. "As always, your trust in me is greatly appreciated." As she stands at her full height, the Princess of Death asks, "So, when should we hold a meeting to discuss the case Angelique and I are working on?"

"How about closer to the time before you two decide to leave? That way, we can pull you into a quieter area to decompress, discuss the issue at hand, and then you can leave through a different entrance?" Lilith offers, "I know events of this size can be a bit overwhelming for some."

"That works," the two younger women respond in unison.

"Perfect. Come find us when you're getting ready to leave." The Rulers of Pride return to the party around them. As Lucifer waves good-bye, Angelique notices a tattoo peeking out from under his wine-red shirt sleeve.

"Do they have matching tattoos?" the angel whispers to Stellar.

"They do. Did you see how Lilith's tattoo glowed when she touched it?"

"Yeah... How did it do that?"

"Their tattoos are imbued with magic."

"... Huh?"

"When they got their tattoos scribed into their bodies, they infused the ink with a small amount of their souls."

Angelique blinks, staring at her companion like a deer in headlights. "What? They used their souls to—"

"Create a communication link with the ink. If they can't find each other, they touch their tattoos and use a tiny bit of magic to activate the ink. It glows and allows them to find their way to each other, kind of like a game of magical Marco Polo."

"Oh! That's... Actually quite sweet."

"Isn't it?" Stellar beams and finishes off the rest of the punch in her glass, then sets the cup on the tray of a passing servant. "What do you say we do some dancing?"

"Oh, no, I don't know how to—"

"No time like the present to learn!" The death demon grabs onto Angelique's wrist and pulls her toward the dance floor, uncaring of the angel's startled yelp.

"Wait! I... I need to finish my drink!"

"Then you'd better start chugging, Angel."

"Uh—" She sighs and presses the glass to her lips, sipping the fruity drink quickly until there's nothing left in her glass. She places the empty cup on the tray of another passing servant, and grips Stellar's hand tightly. "Alright, I'm ready."

Stellar laughs and tugs her the rest of the way onto the dance floor. Once they step onto the well-waxed floor, Stellar twirls around, pulls Angelique close, and rests her free hand on the angel's waist. She smiles coyly and looks into her companion's eyes as she asks, "Ready, Angel?"

Angelique swallows a thick lump of nerves in her throat before answering. "Yes."

The two of them begin to dance, Stellar leading the way through their shared movements. Somehow, Angelique manages not to step on either her or Stellar's dress, or the latter's toes. The skirts of their dresses swirl and flare out elegantly as they sway their bodies among the other party-goers.

As the dance continues, Angelique finds herself smiling and laughing. A warm, comforting feeling settles in her chest, and she murmurs out a quiet, "It's so nice to have you as a partner."

This isn't your partner, the voice in the back of her mind snarls, *Are you giving up on Aurora so easily after everything the two of you have been through together?*

"Er— Dance partner!" she corrects, her body trying to freeze at the voice's angry growl. "You, uh... You really seem to know what you're doing."

The cynical voice in the back of her mind quiets in satisfaction with the clarification, but Stellar hums, clearly disbelieving. Luckily, she doesn't press the issue. "Would you believe me if I said I have very little ballroom dancing experience?"

"No."

"Well, it's the truth," she confesses.

"Then you are *full* of surprises."

"You have no idea, Angel."

The ball continues, with Stellar and Angelique taking breaks between dances to admire more of the hanging artwork or gather refreshments. After a while, Stellar half-sighs, half-groans and leans heavily against a nearby wall.

"Are you alright?"

"Yeah, but my feet and back hurt. I'm not used to wearing heels like these."

"Then maybe we should get ready to leave. Let's see if we can find the Morningstars."

"Are you sure? I can deal with this longer if you want to stay."

"No, I'm okay. I may be having fun, but I'd prefer it if you listen to your body and take care of yourself," Angelique insists.

"Heh, you really took Henriette's words to heart, huh?"

"While I did take her request to keep an eye on you seriously, that's not the only reason."

"Oh? And what, pray tell, is the other reason?"

I care about you and your wellbeing, a softer, less angry mental voice declares. "Something for me to know, and you to never find out."

"My, my, playing hard to read, huh? Alright, I suppose I'll honor your request. Let's go find Lucifer and Lilith."

The two of them leave their rest spot and head back out into the ballroom. The room is a bit less crowded since about a third of the attendees had taken their leave for the night, so it was a bit easier than previously to locate the Royals of Pride. The two of them are locked in a romantic slow dance, swaying gently to the rhythmic melody playing from the speakers.

"Pardon the interruption, Your Majesties, but we were planning to leave soon. Could you spare a few moments to speak in private?" Stellar asks, taking on a more formal way of speaking.

Lucifer's ears perk up at Stellar's voice and he turns to look at her. "Of course we can spare a few moments for you, Your Highness." He tugs Lilith off the dance floor and beckons for Angelique and Stellar to follow them.

They make their way through the ballroom until they find a staff entrance leading to the large, elaborate kitchen, where some of the chefs are still cooking fresh plates of hors d'oeuvres. Servants dart in with dirty dishes and leave with plates piled high with the delicious-looking food. They continue through a less populous section of the kitchen and find themselves in a dimly-lit hallway.

"The home office is this way," Lucifer states, leading the way with Lilith closely behind him and the two younger women at the tail end of the procession. They enter an office similar in atmosphere to the living room at the Palace of Death. There is a large desk off to the right-hand side, across from a small red-and-gold sofa and a golden coffee table with a glass top.

Lucifer and Lilith each take a seat in one of the chairs behind the desk, leaving Angelique and Stellar to sit on the sofa. The two-cushioned couch provides enough space for the two of them to sit, their thighs nearly touching due to the closeness. Angelique fights back a blush as she tries to focus on the conversation ahead.

"So, girls," the King of Pride begins, "I hear you're investigating the angelic traces throughout Hell."

"We are," Stellar confirms, "Due to King Tyrian of Blasphemy taking leave to care for his young child and his spouse, we were advised by my brother to start the investigation here. I'm not sure what information you have to give, but we would appreciate any leads you can provide."

"Well, to speak plainly, we didn't notice there was an angel in our sector until they'd already left," Lilith admits, a flash of shame crossing her face, "The angel you're searching for must either be extremely skilled in disguises, or have a demon at their side helping them to traverse through Hell."

"Just like my brother theorized..." Stellar muses, clenching her fists tightly into the skirt of her dress. "Do you have any other information, like where the traces were coming from or heading toward?"

"We couldn't tell exactly where the traces were coming from, but they appeared to be heading for Ship's Haven."

"Where is that?" Angelique asks.

Stellar, however, already seems to be calculating the route based on the name of the town. "If those traces are correct, then they went from Pride to Envy..." She frowns, confusion clear as day on her face. "What could they possibly be doing?"

"If that *is* the route they've taken, they may have gone to Blasphemy and signed an Oath of Peace. Or, their demonic companion could have brought them into their home sector," Lucifer suggests.

"In the worst-case scenario, it could be the angel is on a recon mission and holding some poor demon hostage..." Angelique murmurs, hugging herself with an arm as a flare of anxiety makes her stomach turn.

Stellar's eyes widen at the suggestion, and her tail lashes. "You don't think..."

"I'm not sure," the angel clarifies, "But it's a possibility."

"I'm sure once there are more clues, the answers will become clear," Lilith soothes.

"For now, if you want to catch them, I'd pursue their path into the Envy Sector," Lucifer adds.

Stellar stands, clearly tense. "Thank you, Your Majesties. I'll make sure the threat is dealt with as soon as possible." She holds out a hand to Angelique. "C'mon, Angel. We have a train to catch."

"Uh— Okay." She takes Stellar's hand, a bit surprised at the change in her companion's demeanor. She has just enough time to quickly wave good-bye to the Rulers of Pride before she's tugged out the door and through the dim hallway, in the opposite direction of the ballroom. "Stellar?"

She doesn't get a response, aside from the lashing of the princess's spiked tail. They reach a large door made of glass panels at the end of the hall when Angelique tries to speak again.

"Stellar?"

Stellar pushes the door open and continues onto the concrete side patio. They head through the gardens and find themselves at the front entrance, at which point Angelique's distress rings true in her voice.

"Stellar, please slow down! You're hurting me!"

At the plea, the demoness almost immediately halts, loosens her grip on the angel's wrist, and turns around, worry in her eyes. "Sorry, sorry... Are you alright?"

Angelique sighs in relief. "I'm alright, but you were pulling a little hard..."

"Alright... If you insist..." She pulls her hand away and holds her hands close to her chest. "Just... Don't hesitate if I hurt you again. Sometimes I don't know my own strength..."

Angelique shows the demon her unmarked wrist. "See? I'm alright." She places her other hand on Stellar's shoulder. "It's like you said before; we don't necessarily have to worry too much unless something's already happened, right?"

"Right. Um— Sorry, I... I got caught up in my head. I don't *want* anyone to get hurt, but... I know that can be hard to prevent."

Angelique offers a tired smile in return. "How about we head back to the hotel? We can change our clothes, maybe get some rest, and then head for the Envy Sector whenever you want. Okay?"

Stellar's shoulders slump and her posture becomes much more relaxed, likely due to her pain and exhaustion. "Please... That sounds lovely right now."

The two of them head back to their hotel, Stellar discarding her high heels on the way. Once they're back in their room, they change into their pajamas and crawl into bed. Stellar lets out groans and whimpers as she settles in, and Angelique falls asleep to her worries about her companion.

Nine
Sunset Shores

When the sun is high in the sky the next morning, Angelique and Stellar check out of the hotel and head for the subway station once again. Luckily, they wait less than ten minutes before the train pulls into the station and waits for passengers to board. The two of them take their seats as the large vehicle begins its journey to Ship's Haven, the capital of the Envy Sector.

"Is there anything I should know before we get there?" Angelique asks after an extended stretch of silence. "I know we'll be having an audience with the Queen of Envy, but... What is the sector like?"

Stellar leans back against her seat, crossing one leg over the other as she considers her words. "Leviathan's sector is filled with different types of self-improvement classes. You can think of it as an area full of shops with comfy clothes, simple makeup, and hobby workshops."

"... That sounds awfully similar to Pride."

"It is, in certain ways. The Envy Sector's main difference is the beachy, resort-like atmosphere thanks to its proximity to the coast."

"So it's full of beaches?"

"Beaches and hot springs, yeah. But demons that aren't from Envy are only permitted to swim or relax in certain bodies of water, though."

Angelique raises an eyebrow, her nose scrunching at the implication. "Why?"

"Most of the waters along the coast have a high concentration of souls."

"... Huh? Souls?"

"Mm-hm. The ocean surrounding Hell is filled with the souls of those who have lived long lives down here."

"I didn't know demons had a proper lifespan. Last I knew, angels don't have lifespans unless they're killed..."

"It's like that for us, too," Stellar clarifies.

"Then... How is there a sea of souls...?"

"Well, technically it's how we manage the population. We don't offer this to newcomers, especially if they're distraught about being in Hell... But those who have lived for a long time can take an audience with my father, and give up their life force to return their souls to the sea. The process is painless and voluntary.

"Leviathan has powers over the waters in Hell, so every so often she'll clear special swimming areas for non-envy demons. If one of those demons were to touch the soul-filled waters, it would negatively affect their health; like how a human would get sick if they were to swim in polluted waters on Earth, or take too much medicine."

"Oh! Envy demons have a resistance to those effects?"

"Yes. It's not recommended for them to swim *exclusively* in the Sea of Souls, but they have a much higher constitution for it than other demons. Leviathan is effectively immune to the effects of the sea, since it's her domain." Stellar outstretches a hand, which has inky skin down to the base of her fingers, in front of her. "I'm not sure what the sea's effect would be on angels, but I can't imagine it would be much different. If the concentration were lower, however..."

"Would it have a less potent effect?" Angelique guesses.

"Bingo! In fact, it would have the *opposite* effect. Water with a low concentration of souls acts as a highly-effective healing agent. My father has a laboratory in his palace that's got a few different pods full of a healing soul-water mixture. He can put someone in the pod and after a few hours, their normally fatal wounds will be fully healed with only a few faint scars left." She smiles weakly. "I'll have to show you sometime. I can vouch for the effectiveness; it's the reason I have so much battle experience and so few scars to prove it."

"I'm sure the healing pods aren't the only reason," Angelique huffs, "From what I've seen of you in a fight, you're very strong and efficient with your attacks."

Stellar chuckles, her smile becoming more genuine. "You think so?"

"I don't *think* so, I *know* so."

"Aw, aren't you a flatterer!" she giggles, ruffling Angelique's hair a bit, like a pet owner would their excitable dog.

"Hey!" the angel huffs, "I mean it, really!"

"You haven't seen me *actually* fight," Stellar clarifies, her tone turning stern and serious, "So let's hope it stays that way."

"What do you mean? Your fight with Rachel—"

She snorts. "It was child's play, trust me."

Angelique frowns, suddenly much more worried about her companion. "If you say so..."

After another hour, the subway pulls into the station and lets the passengers off. As they step out of the train car, Angelique and Stellar find themselves sighing contentedly at the warm rays of sunlight shining on them. The light, breezy air is soft, humid, and warm against their faces.

"You weren't kidding about Envy being a popular retreat destination," Angelique gasps. "It's so nice here!"

Stellar places her hands on her hips, a proud grin on her face and her tail wagging lazily behind her. "See? I told you this whole city is *super* close to the beaches~!"

"I knew you were serious, but it's so relaxing here, I can't see how anyone would want to leave!"

The death demon wraps one of her arms around Angelique's waist, tugging her away from the subway station. "I'll check us into a hotel, and then we can start examining the beaches. If I recall correctly, there might even be a Water Purification Festival planned in the next few days, so we could attend it while we're here."

"Is that when Leviathan removes the souls from the dedicated swimming spots?" the angel guesses.

"Mm-hm. She does it once every three months. And if my gut instinct is correct..." She looks around and points in the direction of the nearest beach, which is framed by a large archway made of hardened sea salt pillars. Shells and glimmering sea glass are pressed into the now-dried salt, and seaweed drapes like curtains from the top of the arch. Other, smaller salt-and-shell pillars frame the edge of the beach, with sun-bleached planks of ipe wood closing the distance between them to make more natural fencing. Beyond the barrier is a large expanse of sand, colored similarly to the dark volcanic ash that flows into the sky during an eruption. The foreshore glows slightly with tiny, luminescent remnants of soul that cling to the wet sand.

"Whoa! Does the beach always look like this?" Angelique asks in awe.

"Yes," a voice says from behind them, making the angel nearly jump out of her skin. They turn around to see a demon with slightly curled horns protruding upwards from the edge of their hairline and a long, fin-tipped tail. "Sorry, I didn't mean to startle you."

"Oh— It's fine!" Angelique squeaks, hot shame heating her face.

"I take it you've never been to Envy before?"

"Ah... No, this is my first visit."

"Then you came at the perfect time. I'm an event organizer for the Water Purification Festival. It's being held tomorrow, so depending on how long you'll be in town, you'll have the chance to witness Queen Leviathan's powers at work."

Angelique's eyes brighten eagerly at the mention. "Wait, really?" She turns to Stellar and beams. "Our timing is impeccable!"

Stellar chuckles. "It definitely seems so. Now, shall we go find a hotel?" They bid good-bye to the event organizer and she leads the way along the boardwalk toward a large stretch of hotels and other shops. The angel takes in the sight of the glowing sea as Stellar heads into a nearby hotel to check for any available rooms. As she leans against the railing, her thoughts drift to her companion.

Stellar doubts her abilities, despite being known as the Executioner among the ranks of death demons? She frowns. *She's so skilled, I'm almost jealous...*

Her memories drift to her earliest missions with Aurora; how their story began when they graduated from the Guardian Angel Training Program at the same time as each other. The two of them were almost always by each other's sides, and their skills were evenly matched. Whenever they'd decided to spar in their downtime, they had an equal amount of wins and losses.

Ever since she awoke from her coma, however, self-doubt had begun to creep into the back of Angelique's mind. She was 100 years out of practice, her closest ally was missing, and she was now traipsing through Hell with one of the Royals—someone that she would've been convinced was her *enemy* 100 years ago—acting as her guide and guard.

"What's got you looking so contemplative?" Stellar asks, breaking Angelique out of her thoughts. The Princess of Death is leaning back against the boardwalk's railing and had obviously been trying to speak to Angelique as her mind swirled with uncertainty. The concern in her vibrant blue-purple eyes makes the angel's stomach churn.

Here you are, being a burden to her again...

"Oh, it's... Nothing. Just admiring the view of the water, y'know?"

Stellar hums, once again clearly disbelieving, but turns to face the sea nonetheless. "It's pretty, isn't it?"

"Yeah... Really pretty." Angelique's gaze unknowingly wanders to her companion as she speaks, admiring her profile. Stellar has strong, muscular arms and hands toughened by years of battle experience, though they're a bit less calloused than one might expect. Her physique is not as thin as Angelique's own, but she's certainly not unhealthy; she looks like a firmly-stuffed teddy bear, perfect for squeezing tightly after a long, stressful day.

The angel is pulled from her accidental admiration of the Princess of Death when Stellar looks over at her and quirks an eyebrow expectantly. "What's up? Are you hungry?"

"Oh, um... Yeah, I could eat."

"I know a really good seafood restaurant nearby, if you want to try it."

"Sure! I'll try anything once."

After they've eaten their fill and paid the bill, they head to their hotel room. It's simply decorated, with ocean waves painted onto the lower halves of each wall. Two queen-sized beds once again take up the majority of the space.

"The people of the Envy Sector enjoy the beaches and ocean a lot, don't they?" Angelique muses as she looks around the room.

"Yeah, the inhabitants of each sector tend to be proud of their natural environments and individual cultures," Stellar answers as she kicks off her shoes and plops down onto one of the beds.

"I know we're mostly going to be visiting the capital cities so we can talk to the Royals, but..." Angelique shifts her weight before taking a seat on the opposite bed. "Will we be able to spend some time sight-seeing? I doubt I'll ever be able to come back to Hell and visit, so—"

"Of course," Stellar answers almost instantly, her tail flicking upwards in eagerness at the query. "We'll visit as many places as we can before we finish our mission."

The angel beams, and if she had a tail of her own, it would be wagging violently. "Thank you. It... It means a lot that you've been so accommodating of my presence here."

"I wouldn't have offered to bring you to Hell if I didn't want to," Stellar clarifies sternly. As Angelique opens her mouth to argue, the demon continues, "And if you're about to say something about me not needing to accommodate you as much as I have, I promise it's no skin off my back to make sure you're comfortable while you're here."

The angel shuts her mouth almost instantly, surprised by the demon's words and demeanor. "I'm surprised you've been treating me like an old friend when we're hardly more than coworkers..."

The comment visibly upsets the demon. She nearly pounces on top of Angelique from her position on the other bed, pinning the angel to the mattress she's sitting on as her tail lashes. Angelique lets out a half-squeak, half-yelp at the sudden contact; the noise seems to soothe the rage dancing in the demon's eyes. Instead, Stellar leans in close and nuzzles their cheeks together, much like a cat rubbing against their owner's legs. It takes a few moments for Angelique to register the purrs coming from the demon princess as she presses against her.

"Uh... I take it you didn't like me saying that?"

The purr in Stellar's throat is still unceasing as she speaks. "You remind me of someone I knew a long time ago. I was really close with them, so hearing you say that, it... Scared me."

The dark-haired woman frowns worriedly and gently grasps what she can of Stellar's form— namely, her elbows. "Why did it scare you?"

The brunette rests her head against Angelique's shoulder. "Because I lost them before I got to tell them how I felt."

A sudden surge of emotion makes Angelique's eyes sting with unshed tears. "Oh... I'm so sorry, Stellar."

The demoness takes a deep, calming breath that silences her purr before replying. "It's alright. I'm... I thought I would be over it by now." She pulls back, off of Angelique and out of her grasp, and wipes roughly at her eyes as tears spill. "I miss them so much, y'know? Whenever I think about them, it hurts."

The angel struggles to fight back her own onslaught of tears. "I know. I'm... I have someone like that, too. I don't know where she is, but I want to find her, even though I have no idea where to look."

Stellar laughs, a broken sound tearing itself from her throat. The spines on her tail flare out as it raises, making her muscular form look all the more intimidating. She speaks, her voice now weak, pained, and cynical all at once. "Is *that* why you agreed to come with me in the first place? You're only here to find your friend?"

Angelique feels the blood drain from her face at the growl-like tone of her companion's voice, and she shoots up with a cry of, "No! Well— Yes, but it's not the only reason!"

Stellar's simmering rage appears to quell, and she watches the angel with narrowed, uncertain eyes. "... Go on," she demands, crossing her arms over her chest as the spiked end of her tail lashes a bit in irritation.

"I... I really do want to help you figure out what's going on, and I've enjoyed my time with you immensely. I want to keep learning about Hell and its people, because it's so different compared to Heaven and what they've claimed. I... I like it here. I like spending time with you."

The death demon hums, her tail lowering to wrap around her legs as she processes Angelique's words. "... I see." She sits back on the bed she'd claimed as hers. "I'm sorry for my outburst," she whispers, "I was afraid you were using me for your own gain."

"I would never do that to you," Angelique declares, reaching her right hand out to the demon, palm-up in a show of peace. "You're my friend, just like she was."

Stellar smiles weakly, exhaustion overtaking her form as she places her left hand in Angelique's. She separates their hands after a moment, then lays down and tugs the comforter over her body. Slowly, as she begins to fall asleep, she murmurs a soft, "Thank you. You're my friend, too."

Angelique takes a moment to catch her breath as she wraps herself in the covers of the other bed, a hand placed over her racing heart. As she watches the demoness sleep, she slowly settles and finds herself able to drift off after about another hour.

Ten
The Sea of Souls

The next morning, Angelique and Stellar get ready for the day, the latter acting as if the tensions from the previous night had never happened. Stellar takes them out to another small restaurant on the boardwalk for a brunch of eggs and bagels with cream cheese and lox. They eat at a table outside as the sunrise morphs from vibrant oranges and golds to a pale blue sky.

"What time is the Water Purification Festival?" Angelique asks as they walk along the ash-colored beach in the early afternoon. Waves lap at the sand, slowly washing away the footprints they leave behind.

"The festivities start around six o'clock tonight, but Leviathan will make her appearance after the sun has set, around eight-thirty."

"So we've got a while before we can take an audience with her..."

Stellar hums. "If waiting is making you anxious, we could try to meet with her sooner. It's only one o'clock, so we'd have plenty of time to discuss the case."

"... Are you sure it's not too much? I don't want to intrude if she needs to prepare..."

"If you're with me, I'm sure everything will be fine. C'mon, let's go see what she knows; the last one on the sand's a rotten egg!" The demon turns on her heels and dashes through the sand toward the sun-bleached, pale grey brick path that connects the central city of Ship's Haven to the boardwalk.

Angelique yelps and turns to run as well, her sandals filling with black sand as she tries to keep up with her companion. Once she stops on the brick path, she leans over and clutches her knees. The unexpected chase leaves her limbs burning and chest heaving as she tries to catch her breath.

Stellar, however, is laughing, also a bit winded as she places a hand to her chest. Angelique watches her laugh for a moment, only for worry to clench at her heart as she notices the demon's hands. The ink-black corruption has crawled down her fingers even more than when they'd first arrived in the city and begun to color the palms of her hands.

"Stellar..."

"Yeah?" She laughs, "I know it was a dirty trick, but I figured you'd have some fun if we raced!"

"Your corruption is getting worse." She strides forward and grabs Stellar's hands, turning them over to present the darkening skin. "Is this... Because of what happened last night?"

The Princess of Death sighs at the question, and tries to tug her hands out of Angelique's careful hold. "Probably," she admits. "But you don't have to worry about it."

"It's too late for me not to worry about you. You're my friend, remember? And I don't want this to get worse."

Stellar groans, throwing her head back in exasperation. "I don't want you to tiptoe around me."

Angelique's eyes narrow and her grip on Stellar's hands tightens. "I refuse to tiptoe around those I care about, so you don't have to worry. I just... I don't want you to get hurt."

"I'll let you know if it gets too bad, okay?"

"Okay. You have a deal." The two of them settle against each other and intertwine their fingers as they walk beside one another. Their path goes through the center of the city, which is filled with resorts advertising hot springs, swimming pools, and water-based sports and activities. As they approach the Palace of Envy, Angelique is once again left staring in awe.

Large, clear glass tubes twist into half-circles around the outer perimeter of the manor's grounds, acting as a fence. The water inside the tubes is dyed a rich, royal blue, and flows through rapidly like ocean currents. The gate at the center of the fence is made of glass with decorative scale designs and a large dragon's head motif in the center.

"A fence made of glass? What happens if it cracks or breaks?"

"It won't. Leviathan placed a spell over all the glass in the manor to prevent it from breaking; the fence around her manor is as functional as an iron fence, but it's less off-putting." Stellar places a hand to the snout of the glass dragon and pulls, opening the gate enough for them to enter.

"Queen Leviathan won't be mad if we just... Walk in?"

"I highly doubt it, but if she is, I'm sure she'll understand once we explain the situation with the angelic traces." Stellar tugs Angelique through the gate and pulls it closed with her tail.

The manor grounds are nearly as beautiful as the beach. They find themselves walking along a large stone bridge with an expansive pond beneath them. Various stone fountain structures protrude out of the dark water, spitting elegant streams from the various outlets until they flow into the tiered basins. Bubbles in the water indicate the presence of marine life, most of which are large, brightly colored koi fish with bone-shaped markings along their backs and sides.

"Oh, wow! Look at how big these fish are!"

"If you consider those big, you should see Leviathan's sea monster form during the festival!" Stellar laughs.

"... She can actually turn into a sea monster?"

"Yeah. Did you not know that?"

"Well, Heaven says a lot of things that apparently aren't true. I wouldn't be surprised if they lied about her abilities, too..."

Stellar snorts, then bursts into bright giggles. "Be careful, Angel, or you'll end up in the Blasphemy Sector."

Angelique pouts. "Why? It's not like you'd tell anyone that can report me to the Holy Council."

They approach the large front doors, and Stellar knocks strongly against the sturdy wood. After waiting a few moments, the door opens and a familiar face peeks out.

"You're the event organizer!" Angelique blurts.

The demon from the previous day blinks in surprise, their ears twitching as recognition flashes across their face. "Oh! Yes, that was me!" They stand tall and pull the door the rest of the way open. "I didn't recognize you yesterday, Princess Stellar."

"Don't feel bad, Minuette; I didn't recognize you, either," she laughs. She stands on her tip-toes to peek around their shoulder, looking for any sign of the Queen on Envy inside the palace. "Is there any chance we could have a quick audience with Queen Leviathan before the Water Purification Festival?"

The servant looks over in the same direction as Stellar and hesitates, contemplating. "There should be enough time between now and the ceremony for you to speak with her. Come along." They turn and lead the way through the grand hall. As they near the foyer, the sound of rushing water can be heard. Once they enter the room, it becomes apparent *why* the sound could be heard with such booming clarity.

There are several waterfalls cascading from various points in the walls, before collecting into a two-inch-deep indentation in the floor. In the center of the shallow, artificial moat sits a singular throne decorated with scale patterning and colorful seashells. Behind the throne is the widest waterfall, which pours from a platform about ten feet in the air.

Dancing atop the platform is a tall woman with a long, indigo braid. Her ocean-and-aqua-colored, knee-length dress flows around her as she twirls and dances, and thin strips of aqua-colored mesh flare out dramatically like a spinning jellyfish. Her long, serpentine, fin-tipped tail flows elegantly behind her as well.

As their quiet steps echo through the foyer, the fins on the sides of her head twitch, and her fluid movements cease. The demoness turns her attention to the newcomers trailing behind her servant. "Princess of Death?" her quiet voice inquires, echoing in an eerily ethereal way as her voice echoes through the chamber of waterfalls.

"Hello, Queen Leviathan!" Stellar calls, waving to the other Royal.

The servant clears their throat as they address Leviathan. "Princess Stellar and her companion requested an audience with you before the festivities tonight, Your Majesty."

"I see. Minuette, you are dismissed until our guests leave."

"As you wish, Your Majesty." The servant turns and meekly scampers off to a staff-only section of the palace.

Leviathan wills two large waves of aqua and blue magic to flow from her hands, the sparks drifting elegantly into the water. As soon as they touch the liquid, the magic causes rivulets to rise from beneath her feet and swirl around the Queen of Envy until her form is fully concealed. The sphere of water slips down the rushing waterfall, landing with a plop and falling away in a dramatic show of poise and elegance. Leviathan walks forward, her thick-soled sandals leaving ripples in the water with each step.

"It's lovely to see you again, Stellar. If I may ask, what brings you here?"

"We were hoping to discuss the angelic traces that have been found around Hell, if you have the time or intel."

"I can make time. I do have a question, though... Who are you?" Leviathan turns her pale, aqua-green eyes to Angelique. Her teardrop-shaped pupils scan the angel as the queen stands rigidly at her full height. The angel only reaches the demon queen's shoulders, which makes her gulp at the analytical gaze.

"This is my companion, Angelique," Stellar answers easily, pulling her close by the shoulder until their sides are touching. "We're working together to discern the source of the angelic traces in Hell."

"I see. You have never given me reason to doubt your intuition before, Stellar, so I will trust your judgment," the Queen of Envy states.

"I appreciate it, Your Majesty," Angelique murmurs as her voice trembles.

Leviathan turns her gaze back to Stellar, who has yet to let go of the angel. "In any case, I'm assuming you came here from Pride? According to what I've heard, that's where the traces in my sector originated from."

"Yes. Lucifer and Lilith didn't even know the traces were present until the source left the sector, so we were hoping—"

"Ah, so it's not my own senses growing dull."

Angelique freezes. "Wait, you also didn't sense the traces until they were out of the sector either?"

"No," she says matter-of-factly.

"Then their demonic companion must still be helping to hide them..." Stellar muses, lightly tapping her fingers against the ball of Angelique's shoulder as she thinks aloud. "There haven't been any sort of distress signals in the same location as the angelic traces, right?"

"No. The angelic traces were faint, and there were no signs of distress in the area."

Stellar groans in mild aggravation. In response, Angelique speaks. "That means they're already gone, right? Do you have any idea where the traces were heading?"

"The route they took leads toward the Wrath Sector. I'm not sure if the angel was truly aiming to confront King Satan or simply pass through his domain, but I would head there and see if he has any more information." She crosses her lightly-scaled arms as her tail sways lazily. "I heard Prince Sarien is also home on his summer break from college, so that's even more reason for you to pay the Wrath Sector a visit."

Stellar's tail begins to wag at the mention. "Wait, he's home from college already?"

"Hold on, who's Sarien?" Angelique pipes up, confused.

"Sarien is the Prince of Wrath, the only son of King Satan and his late wife, Queen Lameia," Leviathan answers simply. "He's been off studying at a college in the human realm and finally got the chance to visit home. The young Royals have been friends for a while, so I'm sure Stellar would like to visit him while he's here."

"You're right, I would," the demon princess agrees. "We'll head for Wrath tomorrow, since we want to stick around long enough to see the Water Purification Festival in full swing."

Angelique bounces on her toes. "Yes! I'd love to see your performance at the festival!"

"Then I expect to see you there." Leviathan turns around and waves a quick good-bye, her steps leaving ripples in the shallow water beneath her.

The demon and angel duo take the hint and leave the Palace of Envy. As the glass gate closes firmly behind them, Stellar freezes in her steps. The spines on her tail extend as the limb lashes violently behind her. Her wings reappear as well, flaring out and nearly smacking poor Angelique in the head.

"Whoa! Stellar, what's wrong?"

"Didn't Leviathan say the traces were heading in the direction of Wrath?"

Angelique quirks an eyebrow in a combination of concern and confusion. "She did."

"Then why do I sense more traces in the area?"

"What?!" Despite her rising fear, the angel closes her eyes and tries to concentrate her senses on her surroundings. As she focuses her attention, she feels a wave of angelic energy flow in from the center of the city. "There's no way the traces could be this strong if the source was truly in Wrath."

"We need to move. *Now.*" The demon summons her silver glaive and spreads her wings, taking off with one strong and swift movement. As Angelique reveals her wings and tries to take off after her companion, she finds herself falling behind.

I can't believe this...! she scolds herself as she flies shakily through the Hellish sky. *I was doing my wing exercises until we came to Hell, and now that I'm a few days behind on them... Ugh! How could I be so weak?! I have to catch up!*

The angel chases Stellar's trail to an alleyway between a few of the shops on the boardwalk. She lands harshly a few feet away, clutching one hand to her chest. "Did... Did you find anything?" she pants out.

"No," Stellar snarls, "The trail ends here."

"In an alley..." Angelique leans against a nearby building. "Could this be somewhere the source rested after being in disguise for so long?"

The death demon discards her glaive with a pulse of her magic and hides her wings once again. "I don't know. Maybe I'm getting trigger-happy because my corruption is acting up..."

"Is there anything we can do to help mitigate the symptoms?"

"I doubt anything aside from a soak in the healing tanks back home will help... But maybe once we're in the Sloth Sector, we could check with King Belphegor to see if they've found any other solutions since I last visited."

"We'll do that," Angelique declares as she hides her wings once again. "We'll head to Wrath tomorrow and make our way to Sloth unless something in the other sectors needs our attention."

Stellar approaches the angel, holding out a hand that has now turned ink-black up to her wrist. "C'mon. Let's take one last stroll around Ship's Haven before the festival tonight."

Angelique's heart pangs with worry at the demon's worsening condition, but takes hold of the offered hand nonetheless. They leave the alleyway, lightly swinging their intertwined hands despite the exhaustion present in both of their bodies after the dead-end chase. Before they know it, the sun has begun to set, so they make their way over to the beach where the Water Purification Festival is to be held.

The ash-colored sands are teeming with festival-goers and excited onlookers. Tall bamboo torches are spread along the beach, providing warmth and light as the sun begins to disappear over the horizon. Charcoal barbecue grills are scattered about as skewers of meat, fish, and vegetables are cooked over the flame-licked grates. Music resonates from small groups that play various percussion instruments, most of which are drums with tropical flower designs carved in the wood. A few of the musicians even hold castanets made of clam shells or play a tune by blowing into large conch shells.

"Wow... It's so beautiful here," the angel whispers in awe.

"They say visitors that come during the Water Purification Festival rarely want to leave." Stellar chuckles as she tugs Angelique toward one of the grills with seasoned fish. After they're each given two seafood skewers, they continue their trek along the beach and devour the offerings. They stand off to one side and watch as the sunset colors the deep, dark waters of the Sea of Souls in vibrant, warm hues. Once the sun has fully disappeared over the horizon, the water glows a bright aqua color thanks to the heavy concentration of souls.

The music near the entrance to the beach halts as the time comes for the Queen of Envy to make her appearance and cleanse the waters. Stellar and Angelique make their way over in time for the torches to change color from warm reds and oranges to vibrant, oceanic blues. The music starts again, this time in a more elegant and practiced manner than the previous upbeat, festive tunes as a familiar figure strides under the archway. Leviathan stands tall as she walks forward with an unhurried pace. The tulle strips of her underskirt make it appear as though she is gliding along the sands as she makes her way to the wave-damp foreshore. Before she enters the water, though, she turns to face the crowd that has eagerly gathered around her path on the beach and the music halts once more.

"I want to thank everyone for attending this season's Water Purification Festival. I trust you all have been enjoying the event thus far, and ask that you wait patiently until I return to the shore before entering the water. Without further ado..." She twirls back around on the balls of her feet to face the glowing waters before her.

The music returns to the more energetic beat from before Leviathan's arrival; this time, however, the percussionists hit the batter heads a bit stronger than they had for the first melody, creating a powerful beat. The Queen of Envy steps forward until the Sea of Souls laps at her toes, at which point ripples of her blue and aqua magic flow from her feet. With her next step, she remains perfectly on top of the waves and begins her dance.

She leans down as if to brush her fingertips against the rippling water beneath her, only to stand once again and extend her hands gracefully to the moonlit sky. She lowers her hands back to waist-level, then sways her arms from side to side and takes several more powerful steps forward. The glowing particles in the water beneath her dart away, creating a glowing watertop runway as she walks forward with confidence.

Once she finds herself a sufficient distance from the shore's edge, she rises onto the balls of her feet and twirls around to create a giant, bioluminescent stage with each small leap atop the water.

With a brief pause in her movements, small cyclones of water rise from the water and swirl into the air around her. After five glowing cyclones have surrounded Leviathan, she wraps her arms around her torso, making the water swirl around her until she's surrounded by a large orb of water. Angelique finds the sight to be reminiscent of the Queen of Envy's descent from the waterfall platform in her palace.

Instead of descending to the water, though, the ball of water ascends into the air thanks to the power of the cyclones. The size of the orb expands greatly as the water rises into the air and glows almost blindingly, before bursting and creating a large shockwave of energy that spreads over the beaches of Ship's Haven and into the city. In an instant, the glowing soul remnants in the water are pushed away, creating a barrier several thousand feet from the shore.

In the aftermath of the shockwave, Leviathan remains floating in the air thanks to the powerful flaps of her fin-like wings. Under the light of the brightly-lit moon, her body shifts and transforms into a 150-foot-long, serpentine sea monster. Four large, claw-tipped flippers extend from the monster's abdomen, much like those one would find on a seal. Two spiny dorsal fins extend down the length of Leviathan's back, from the large fins on either side of her thin, elongated, dragon-like face to the tip of her tail. The creature leans backward after its transformation is complete and dives into the water below, creating a hefty splash upon impact. The waves made by her splash lower from tsunami-level heights to just above average as they reach the shore.

Angelique stares in shock at the display of elegance and power as the other festival-goers cheer and applaud. The spines of Leviathan's back can be seen rising from the water as she once again approaches the ash-colored shore. Before her snout hits the sand, she transforms back into her humanoid form and struts out of the waves and onto the beach. The applause rises in volume as the musicians bring their melodies to a powerful end.

"Pretty impressive, huh?" Stellar nudges Angelique with her elbow. "You've never seen anything like this, right?"

"No... Never..." The angel's gaze shifts to her demonic companion as she takes her hand, ignoring the slight trembling of her fingers. "Thank you for letting us stick around long enough to watch this."

"Eh, don't worry about it. This trip around Hell is as much of a vacation for me as it is a cultural tour for you. Besides, I always found Levi's displays of power to be awe-inspiring."

"You never told me that," the Queen of Envy huffs as she approaches the two of them.

Stellar's cheeks flare red at the other royal's sudden presence. "Well, maybe I didn't want to stroke your ego."

"You and I both know I don't have enough confidence to be an egoist, Stellar."

"That's true, but my point stands. Your performances are amazing."

"Thank you." Leviathan smiles at the two of them. "Feel free to stay and mingle for as long as you want, but I know you two will most likely want to catch the first train to Kilmarnock. Make sure you get plenty of rest before you leave."

"We'll make sure of it, Levi. Thanks again for everything."

As the Queen of Envy turns and wanders down the beach, Angelique frowns as something comes to the forefront of her mind. "Shouldn't we have told her about the traces we found in the alleyway earlier...?"

"I don't want to make her worry on a festival night. I'll send her a text in the morning."

"Alright... If you say so." The angel can't help the concern and looming dread that crawl their way up her spine. However, she pushes the worries to the back of her mind as she and Stellar continue to enjoy the festival.

Eleven
The Wild, Wild Wrath

In the morning, as planned, Angelique and Stellar head to the subway station and board a train heading to Kilmarnock, the capital city of the Wrath Sector. Angelique watches the scenery pass outside the window as the train starts its journey away from the tropical resort of Ship's Haven and darts between small mountains. The warm beaches slowly give away to drier, sun-charred plains, which catches Angelique by surprise.

"It's like a desert out here..." she murmurs.

"Wrath is full of desert-like areas and grassy plains," Stellar explains. "The dry heat is especially good for the ore-rich reserves found here."

The train passes a large mine that has turned the grassy landscape even more dry and desert-like. Large clumps of shining rocks and spires of various minerals can be seen in the deep hole as a group of wrath demons wielding pickaxes and hammers swing at the ore-rich reserves.

"Oh, whoa..." She turns back to her companion with wide eyes. "What exactly do the wrath demons do with the ores they find in the mines?"

"A lot of them can be traded and used for different things. Namely, any gems can be made into jewelry, alongside a lot of the gold and silver veins... They *do* find pieces of magic-infused obsidian and coal every so often, which can be turned into energy sources for us... And of course, iron ores can be used for a variety of things— especially for soul-infused jewelry pieces."

Angelique quirks an eyebrow at yet another mention of usage for one's soul. "Didn't you say souls can be used as a healing agent and make up a lot of the sea? Plus there are Lucifer and Lilith's tattoos... They can also be infused into jewelry?"

"Well, yeah, but it's a really lengthy process, so it's really only used for special occasions... Like a couple getting engaged or to pass a family heirloom from a grandparent to a grandchild."

Angelique purses her lips as she thinks. "... Is that how King is able to use magic despite being, well... A human on Earth?"

Stellar grins. "You nailed it, Angel. King's wedding ring is made out of a special silver that Spyr commissioned while they were visiting once. They came to my dad and asked to have a small portion of their soul removed and infused into the raw materials for the ring. My father led them to a master craftsman, who made their ring."

"Oh, wow! Is that a common practice for couples who are getting married?"

"Yeah, it's pretty commonplace."

"Wow... I would have had no idea... I wish we angels had something so romantic. Giving a piece of yourself to your lover is so..."

"Passionate? Binding? Dangerous?" Stellar offers.

"... Huh? Dangerous?"

"Well, yeah. Imagine giving a piece of yourself to your lover, only for them to refuse to marry you and end the relationship instead. It would be the world's worst heartbreak."

Angelique doesn't register the fierce scowl on her face. "Are you saying this because you're a pessimist, or because of personal experience?"

The sudden change in Angelique's demeanor makes Stellar burst into bright laughter, to the point she hugs her stomach.

"Man, what was that reaction for? You sound *offended* for me, Angel!"

"Well, if someone did that to you, they obviously didn't know what they were missing," she blurts, crossing her arms over her chest.

The laughter dies in Stellar's throat as she turns to the angel with an expression of genuine awe and surprise instead of her previous amusement. "Wait, did you seriously think someone rejected a marriage proposal from me?"

The angel finds her face burning as her scowl fades. "... That didn't happen?"

"No! Why would you think—?"

"Well— I— You just... You sounded so hurt by the idea of being rejected..."

Stellar's confused gaze softens. "I see... Well, I can confidently say I've never had a marriage proposal get rejected. I've never been proposed to, either."

"Oh..." Angelique ducks her head, thankful for the curtain of her long, dark hair that falls in front of her face and hides her red-hot embarrassment. "I guess I was just... Worried, for you."

"While I appreciate the sentiment, Angel, I'm going to let you in on a little secret." The shuffling of fabric can be heard as Stellar scoots closer and leans in close, so her whispered words are breathed against Angelique's ear.

"I've only ever been in love once, and haven't dated anyone since," the princess confesses.

The angel's head shoots up. "Wait, really?"

"Yeah. It wouldn't be fair to try and 'move on' from my first love if my heart wasn't truly in it, right?"

"Right." Angelique smiles softly. "See? You're not as cynical as you make yourself out to be. You still care about other people."

Stellar's cheeks darken a few shades, and she looks away with a huff. "Don't let that get around, you hear me?"

"My lips are sealed, and your secret's safe with me."

"Good."

The two of them laugh and continue to relax in their seats until the train pulls into the Kilmarnock Subway Station. As they move to disembark from the train, Stellar's tail flicks curiously. Noticing the movement, Angelique turns to her companion with an equally curious hum.

"What is it?"

"We might have to be careful stepping out. Stick close to me." She places a hand on Angelique's shoulder as she leads the way off the train and out into the station's platform. Everything appears to be relatively normal, much like the other places they've encountered on their journey... Until they step out of the subway station.

A large blast of orange and gold magic soars toward the two of them; in response, Stellar shoves Angelique down by the shoulder. The angel is barely able to put her hands out to catch her fall before she finds herself face-down in the pavement with Stellar kneeling at her side. The demon spreads her wings and raises her tail in a defensive posture, and Angelique can barely raise her head from the ground in time to see a figure dash forward and move to tackle Stellar.

The death demon is unfazed, however, and uses a small burst of her black and purple magic to shove back against the figure, sending them flying fifteen feet away. She stands and summons her glaive with another magical surge, then dashes forward, sweeping forward with her weapon only to be parried by a faintly-glowing lance. Each of the combatants jump back and ready their weapons before once again lunging forward. The glaive and lance beat against each other in succession, the sharp sounds of metallic collisions filling the air.

Angelique scrambles to stand, but remains frozen on her feet as Stellar thrusts her glaive upward into the air, knocking her opponent's lance loose from their grasp as they fall backward and land flat on their back. The weapon lands with a clang behind the death demon, who points the blade of her glaive at the assailant's chest.

"Your time away at college has made you rusty, Sarien," the princess declares, her voice frosty.

The demon on the ground below her laughs softly, running a hand through his curly, dark brown hair. "Yeah, I figured as much... Can you truly blame me for wanting to relive our little squabbles?"

"I suppose not." She dissipates her glaive with a flick of her wrist, and instead extends her hand out to the young man on the ground. He takes her hand and she easily pulls him to his feet. "I have a guest, though; you're lucky nothing happened to her, or I *wouldn't* have held back."

The demon's eyes brighten at the comment. "You brought a friend? Can I meet her?"

"I don't see why not. Come with me; you can grab your lance while you're at it."

"Yes, ma'am!"

Stellar turns and struts her way back to Angelique's side, the other demon trailing behind her. Now that the two of them aren't locked in combat, the angel is able to take a better look at him. He's a young man who stands about three inches taller than Stellar, with short, thick horns sprouting from either side of his head. His horns curl slightly upward, almost like those of a young longhorn cow. His long hair is pulled back into a low ponytail, and the warm sunlight makes it appear as though he has pale golden highlights. His eyes are the colors of the sunset, and his star-shaped pupils meet her own gaze as a bright, excited smile forms on his face. He's wearing a white graphic T-shirt featuring a pair of comedy and tragedy theater masks, and a blue, white, and sea-green infinity-style scarf is wrapped around his neck. His high-waisted pants have one black leg and one with a pastel rainbow checkerboard pattern. His slip-on sneakers are the same colors and designs as his pant legs.

"Sarien, this is Angelique," Stellar introduces, placing a comforting hand to the angel's back. "Angelique, this is Prince Sarien of the Wrath Sector."

"Hello! It's nice to meet you!" Sarien greets, holding out a hand to shake.

A bit caught off-guard by his enthusiasm, Angelique hesitantly shakes his hand. "It's nice to meet you, too. We heard from Queen Leviathan that you're back from college?"

"I am! We're on a break right now, but I go to a college in the human realm for creative writing and musical theater." His tail wags behind him as he speaks. Despite the movement, Angelique notices that his tail has small barbs sprouting near the sharp, spiked tip.

"I still have no idea how your father, a man who takes no shit on a good day, managed to spawn a pacifist like you," Stellar jokes, lightly punching Sarien in the shoulder.

"I'm sure he ponders that question as much as I do," the Prince of Wrath half-laughs, half-sighs. "I'm still glad he doesn't mind... I couldn't wish for a better dad."

"How many times have we had to tell you, 'he loves you, so he'll support your goals no matter what'?" the death demon huffs, crossing her arms over her chest.

"Too many," he groans, throwing his head back dramatically. The two demons laugh and turn their attention back to Angelique.

"I deeply apologize for my rudeness," Sarien says meekly, "It's been a while since Stellar and I last saw each other, but that's no excuse to neglect the presence of a guest."

"Oh, I don't mind," she assures him, "It's nice to see I'm not the only one Stellar can hold a banter with."

"Oh? She banters with you, too?" Sarien raises a curious brow. "Do tell!"

"Well, we—"

"We don't have time for that!" Stellar interrupts, her face turning a deep shade of pink in embarrassment. "Sarien, would you mind leading our way to the Palace of Wrath? You can make the trek into a tour, too."

The Prince of Wrath quirks his eyebrow in surprise and confusion. "Sure, we can head to the palace. Did you need to talk to my dad about something?"

"Yes, actually! And you should stick around when we talk to him, so you can be filled in, too."

"Alright. This way!" He turns, leading the way into the town. Stellar grows more relaxed in the company of her friend. Angelique hums to herself as her thoughts drift to Stellar's original flustered reaction, and she absentmindedly takes the demoness's hand in her own, giving her a slight squeeze in a brief attempt at comfort.

They're led through the city, which is filled with blacksmiths and jewelers. The window displays hold dozens of precious gems, metal art pieces, and weapons of varying quality. Sarien gives a quick history lesson on the city's origins as they traverse through the streets.

"Most of our citizens are either jewelers, smiths, miners, or metalworkers," Sarien explains. "We have dozens of mines throughout the sector, each with different resources. After a while, we leave the ground to rest and recuperate so it can reform and provide us with even more natural resources."

"The resources here aren't finite like they are on earth?" Angelique questions with a tilt of her head.

"Nope!" The Prince of Wrath's tail wags. "Since Hell is a magic-filled place, it's able to replenish even the rarest natural resources with enough time. It's like how on Earth, there's a proper rotation of crops to allow the soil to replenish certain nutrients while taking others."

"Does the soil also need to rotate to contain the proper nutrients for crops down here?"

"If I recall correctly, it does; you'd have to ask Queen Bee to be sure, though. Maybe King Mammon would know, too..."

"Huh? Why would the King of Greed know about the agriculture of the Gluttony Sector?"

"Because King Mammon and Queen Beelzebub are twins," Stellar clarifies.

"... They *are?!* I had no idea!"

"Most citizens of Heaven don't know they're twins, so I don't blame you," Sarien sighs. "They think all of the Kings and Queens have no family, which isn't exactly true. I mean, my father is Lucifer's cousin, and Queen Asmodeus has a cousin, too..."

"Don't forget Tyrian and Ryzen," Stellar cuts in.

"I could never forget them! And of course, there's also you and Adrian."

"I'm not sure if that counts, since I'm adopted."

"It does," Angelique blurts. "Elias brought you into his family and raised you and Adrian together. You two treat each other as if you're siblings, so you *are* siblings, no matter if it's a blood relation or not."

Stellar's tail sways lazily behind her. "My father didn't do much raising of me, but, I suppose you're right. Adrian and I get along like we've known each other all our lives, so it may as well count as being a blood family."

"See?" the angel teases.

"Yeah, yeah, I see." She squeezes Angelique's hand tightly and diverts her attention back to the demonic prince. "Let's go meet with your dad, Sarien."

"Right! We're almost there." Their guide leads them to a large manor—undoubtedly the Palace of Wrath—and pulls open the large, wrought iron gates despite his lean frame. "Dad should be out back training a new recruit or two, so we need to go this way."

"Why does Satan need recruits?" Angelique asks, trying to hide the slight tremor in her voice, "He's not going to... Attack anyone, right?"

"Not at all! My father is *far* past that time of his life; he calls his students 'recruits' so they don't feel demeaned. Even though they're never going to be stronger than the King of Wrath, they're still deserving of respect and are treated as such."

"Oh, so I shouldn't be worried?"

"Not unless you pose a threat," Sarien says, his tone both light-hearted and entirely serious. The kind smile he flashes after the thinly-veiled warning makes a shiver course down Angelique's spine, and she has to fight every urge telling her to hide behind Stellar for protection. She must have grown a bit more rigid than previously, however, because the Princess of Death squeezes her hand reassuringly. She doesn't even register that her companion has leaned over to whisper to her until a warm breath puffs against her ear.

"I'll keep you safe, remember, Angel? You're here with me, and I won't let anyone or anything hurt you."

Angelique swallows thickly, trying to fight back the heat rising into her cheeks.

"Good girl." Stellar pulls back and continues to tug her along; meanwhile, Angelique has to hold back an embarrassing noise at the loss of warmth and close contact.

They make their way around the outside of the palace and through one of the small gardens to reach the backyard—if one can call a vast training ground a 'backyard.' The area contains a large, circular, dirt combat arena in the center. Off to either side are a firing range with targets for archery and a shed with a large wooden sign that reads **[Melee Weapons]**. In the center of the combat arena are two demons locked in a duel. The shorter figure is brandishing a sword and makes continuous attempts to strike at their opponent.

The opponent in question is obviously the King of Wrath despite their casual attire, which consists of a tight-fitting orange tank top, a pair of baggy sweatpants, and red sneakers caked with dirt. The word "WRATH" is printed down his left pant leg, much like the name of a sports team on a piece of branded leisure wear. His thick, curly, deep brown hair is pulled back into a long ponytail. He's not even brandishing a weapon against his opponent, instead opting to smack the sword away from himself with his hands, which are bare aside from black boxing wrap that covers from his knuckles to his wrists. Like Sarien, a pair of thick horns protrudes from the sides of his head and a tail with barbs and a spiked tip extends from his lower back.

"Is he fighting bare-fisted against a sword?!" Angelique gasps, shock clear on her face as she watches the larger demon easily beat back each strike of the blade.

"Yeah, he doesn't often use weapons against new recruits."

Stellar raises an eyebrow. "Isn't that one of the recent arrivals?"

"Yep! Dad has been helping him learn coping mechanisms for his anger. They've already tried boxing and martial arts, so it looks like they're testing if swordplay or fencing will fit best for him today." He waits at the edge of the combat ring, tail swaying lazily as he watches his father and the recruit. Stellar and Angelique remain at his side as well, watching the two demons locked in combat.

"You're pretty good with a sword," Satan chuckles as he bats the blade away from himself once again, a bright grin having formed on his face.

"You say that, but I'm hardly doing anything," the smaller demon huffs, panting and slashing at the king.

"You have a knack for this, kid. You don't have to be good at something right away in order to enjoy or continue it." The

King of Wrath catches the recruit's next downward strike in his left hand, stilling the blade almost instantly. "You're getting tired and sloppy, so take a few minutes to rest. Make sure to grab a drink and sit; your legs are shaking."

The younger demon stares at the king in surprise for a moment, stunned at the sudden inability to move the sword, before his head dips. A quiet murmur of, "Yes, sir," can be heard before he releases the hilt of the sword and trudges to the far edge of the combat arena, legs trembling with every step.

As the King of Wrath moves to place the sword back in its scabbard, which had been placed a few feet away, Sarien raises his hands to cup the sides of his mouth and loudly calls out, "Dad! We have guests!"

Satan's ears visibly twitch and his head whips around to them at the sound of his son's voice. "Hey, kiddo! How long have you been standing there?"

"Only a few minutes, I promise." The younger wrath demon steps into the combat arena and approaches his father, wrapping him in a firm hug. "How did he do?"

Satan returns the hug, rubbing his son's back. "He did quite well, considering this is his first time holding a sword. Did I hear we have guests?" He raises his head once again and looks over to the edge of the combat arena where Angelique and Stellar are still standing.

Stellar raises an arm high and makes a large arc in the air as she waves. "Hello, Your Majesty! How is the new recruit's training going?"

A deep chortle escapes the king. "Hello there, Princess Stellar! The training is going well." Still holding his clinging son close, he shuffles over to the girls. Once he's only a few feet away, his attention turns to Angelique. "You must be a friend of Stellar's."

"I am," Angelique says with a curtsy. "I do hope my presence isn't seen as a threat, Your Majesty."

"If *Stellar* is the one bringing you around Hell, I am sure you do not pose a threat. If she deemed anyone to be dangerous, they would either be dead or on an incredibly short leash. Isn't that right, Princess?"

Stellar rolls her eyes and places her hands on her hips in mock offense; however, she can't keep a smile from forming on her face as she holds back laughter. "Why does everyone make me out to be so dangerous, huh? It's not like I've ever threatened anybody who didn't deserve it."

"That is true," Satan agrees with a laugh. "In any case, what brings the two of you to Wrath? You don't visit us very often, Stellar, let alone with company at your side."

"Yeah, you said you had something important to discuss..." Sarien adds, worry filling his eyes, "Is something wrong?"

"We should probably talk about this inside," Angelique suggests, "We don't want anyone to overhear..."

"Alright, then right this way."

After Satan gathers his grey soft-shell vest from a nearby bench and dismisses the recruit for the day, the King and Prince of Wrath lead the way into their palace. Stellar and Angelique follow close behind the Royals of Wrath as they're led through the palace, which has rooms for indoor fencing and swordplay, boxing, and martial arts. Eventually, they find themselves in the throne room, which still has three thrones despite the lack of a Queen of Wrath.

Angelique's eyes soften at the empty throne, which still appears well-maintained despite the amount of time since Queen Lameia's passing. She bites her tongue to keep from mentioning it, and tries to keep her focus on the task at hand.

Stellar looks around, tail lashing a bit considering the rather open area they find themselves in. "Are you sure this is a good place to discuss this? If someone eavesdrops on this conversation—"

"I'm sure everything will be fine," Satan assures her, "After all, you're working on a solution for whatever this issue is, and you're plenty competent."

"I'll trust your judgment, then. This is about some odd traces that have been found throughout Hell."

Sarien tilts his head curiously. "What kind of traces?" he asks.

"Those of an angel," Angelique answers. "We're trying to locate the source, but it seems whoever it is may be bringing a demonic companion around with them. So far, the detected traces have been faint, and they were only discovered after the source left the previous sectors."

Satan's brows furrow in concern. "Which sectors have they already been to?"

"Pride and Envy so far. The traces leaving Envy were headed in this direction, so we wanted to see if you two had found anything."

"If not, we'll be heading north to either Sloth or Lust and continuing our investigation there," Stellar adds.

"As far as I'm aware, there haven't been any angelic traces..." Sarien murmurs. His tail lashes a bit as he turns to his father with furrowed brows. "Did you hear anything about something like this, Dad?"

Satan crosses his arms over his chest. "I did."

"What?!" Sarien and Stellar yelp at the same time.

"Please tell me that means you already chased them away from Hell..." Angelique pleads, pressing her palms together in pseudo-prayer.

"Sadly, I did not." The King of Wrath's tail lashes as the three other pairs of eyes stare at him. "I only discovered the traces after you and your fiancé went out to that party in Lust, Sarien. I didn't want to worry you, so I've been trying to do some of my own investigative work. Luckily enough, it seems like Princess Stellar is already further along on the case than I am."

“Which way were they going?” Stellar demands, her voice a near growl as her tail lashes violently.

“The traces were found to be heading toward Lust as well. I imagine they made their way to the capital city of Aria, since it’s a known party hub thanks to Queen Asmodeus and Duchess Selene.”

The color drains from Sarien’s face. “Why didn’t you tell me? If something had happened while I was there, I could have done something!”

“You and I both know you would have likely gotten hurt had you confronted the source of the angelic traces. I didn’t want you or your fiancé to get in harm’s way.”

Stellar summons her glaive and grips it tightly; her knuckles would have turned white had the skin of her hands not already become night-colored due to her aggravated corruption. “Give me *one* good reason not to attack you where you stand.”

“I outrank you, and you are on *my* turf,” Satan declares, the evenness of his voice unwavering as he speaks with a blade pointed at his chest.

Angelique bites her lip and places a gentle hand to Stellar’s back, hopeful that the warm touch is comforting enough to soothe her companion’s temper. “It’s alright, Stellar,” she tries, “Like you said, nobody’s gotten hurt, so you don’t need to worry—”

“*You* were the one worried about that when we first got here!” the Princess of Death snaps, her attention whipping around to the angel at her side as an irritated glare fills her eyes. “What changed?!”

Angelique lets out a panicked, squeaky apology and pulls her hand back, instinctively using her arms to cover her face and neck. She squeezes her eyes tightly shut as she pleads, “I’m sorry! I didn’t mean to—”

“Stellar, look at me,” Satan commands, hardly raising his voice. Once the death demon’s gaze is fixated on him once again, he nods. “Good, thank you. I understand you’re angry at the news about the traces, but you don't need to take your emotions out on anyone but me. Since you're so upset, why don't we spar? It could help," he offers.

The Princess of Death lowers her blade to the floor and hangs her head in embarrassment and shame. "... Yes, sir," she murmurs, her voice hardly audible.

"What was that? Loud and clear, recruit."

"Yes, sir! I accept your invitation!"

"There we go! Good kid." He places a hand to her shoulder. "Inside or out?"

"Inside."

The King of Wrath turns Stellar around and leads her back to the indoor combat arena, leaving Sarien and Angelique in the throne room. The ringing in the angel's ears slowly dissipates, at which point the Prince of Wrath raises his hands in a show of peace and speaks.

"It's okay. You're safe now. Nobody's going to hurt you."

Angelique snaps out of her head at the kind and reassuring words. "... What happened?"

Sarien's eyes soften. "Stellar yelled and you got scared. Dad's taken her to the indoor arena for a spar."

A thick lump forms in her throat at the mention of sparring. "She's not in trouble, is she?"

"Who, Stellar? Not in the slightest." The prince's tail wags slightly. "It's just something my dad set up. Whenever he finds someone having trouble regulating their emotions—especially someone as trigger-happy as Stellar—he offers to spar with them to help reduce stress."

Angelique swallows around the tension in her throat and looks at her trembling hands. "I didn't mean to... I've never been scared of her before, so why *now* did I...?"

"Because you've never seen her truly angry?" he suggests. "Stellar does what she can to bottle up her negative emotions, but after a while, it just... The bottle shakes and the cap comes loose."

"I... I know what you mean. I don't get angry, but... When I get overwhelmed, I burst into tears and can't stop them."

"Me, too." He smiles softly at her and holds out a hand. "How about we go watch my dad and Stellar's spar?"

"I... I'd like that." She takes his hand and squeezes lightly. As he leads her down the hall, Angelique slowly gathers her courage and asks, "Is Stellar like your dad was, back when you first lost your mom?"

"Hm? What do you mean?"

"She's... Standoffish, let's say."

"Standoffish, huh... She hasn't been mean to you, right?"

"What? No, no! She hasn't at all!" She bites her lip as she tries to search for the words that best explain her observations of her demonic companion. "It feels like she's afraid of trusting people, but wants so *desperately* to try... Like, one minute she's distant and calculating, but in the next, she's cuddling me and purring..."

A small laugh escapes the Prince of Wrath. "It sounds like she's trying to play it cool for a girl she's got a crush on," he snickers. "I've had too many guys try that trick on me, so I can usually spot people behaving like that from a mile away."

Angelique stares at Sarien as he speaks. "Wait, Stellar likes girls?"

"Uh... Yeah, she's into girls *exclusively*. I swear I saw her gag when we passed some shirtless guy at the beach one time..."

"I had no idea she's a lesbian."

Sarien quirks an eyebrow and stares at her in blatant disbelief. "With the way she dresses, it wasn't obvious? How long have the two of you been working together?"

"Uh... A couple months?"

"... Alright, so you're the typical oblivious girl who can't tell when another girl is hitting on her."

"Wha— Hey! I can't tell when *anyone* is flirting with me, thank you!"

"So you're bisexual?"

Another anxious lump forms in Angelique's throat, but she finds herself nodding in agreement to the question.

"Well, you'd better not let anyone in Heaven find out."

"... Huh?"

"The last time an angel was found to be even *questioning* if they were gay, they got thrown down here so fast they almost died on impact." He pauses. "... Or wait, did they die and get revived by King Elias...?"

"That's awful!" Angelique gasps.

Sarien sighs. "Yeah, it is, but it's not uncommon. Heaven doesn't want any of its citizens to be anything but cisgender and straight, so Hell is full of LGBTQ+ citizens. I mean... My fiancé knows he's going to end up down here, so..."

"I'm sorry you all have to go through that. It's not fair to anyone..." She squeezes his hand a bit more. "... Let's go check on your dad and Stellar."

"Alright, if you insist." They continue until they find the entrance to the indoor combat arena. Through the magically-reinforced glass windows, they can see Stellar leaping into the air as she brandishes her glaive, while Satan swings an incredibly large greatsword around to block her frequent attacks. Their blades meet repeatedly, and grunts of exertion can be heard from both combatants.

"Whoa... They're so skilled..." Angelique gasps, "I've only seen Stellar fight a few times, and most of those times were against opponents who didn't stand a chance."

"Am I one of those who didn't stand a chance?" Sarien teases with a light-hearted laugh.

"Uh— Well— I, um..."

"It's okay if you say 'yes'; I know I'm nowhere near as skilled as Stellar."

"You were able to hold your own against her for the most part. I can't say that about the imp or the demon hunter I watched her fight."

"... Really? I was?"

"Yes. Then again, when she fought the demon hunter, it looked like more of a scare tactic than anything... But my point stands!" Angelique nudges him. "You're not as weak as you seem to think."

"Well, thank you." They head inside right as Satan knocks Stellar back and sends her crashing into the floor, where she sprawls out on her back.

"Ugh..." the Princess of Death groans, propping herself up on her elbows. She looks over to her glaive, which had scuttled off toward the far wall with the harsh deflection. She rolls over onto her knees and slowly gets up, panting and sweaty.

"Did this help you, Princess?" Satan asks as he watches her slowly rise to her feet.

She opens her mouth to answer but lets out a harsh cough instead, covering her mouth with her arm as she struggles to catch her breath. She slowly trudges over to her glaive, her movements sluggish with exertion, and grabs it before making it disappear with a small pulse of magic.

Angelique frowns and approaches her demonic companion. "Stellar?" she calls, "Are you okay?"

"Yeah, I'm... I'm fine."

The angel's gaze drifts to the princess's shaking hands, where the corruption has begun to crawl up her arms; her wrists are now fully blackened, and the darkness is slowly covering her forearms. "Your condition is worsening. We need to go to the Sloth Sector and get you treated as soon as possible."

"No," she counters, "We need to go to Lust and track the source of those traces."

"You're exhausted, Stellar. If you keep this up, you'll be of no help with this investigation." She takes one of the darkened hands into her own, but is surprised to see Stellar flinch and pull away before their fingertips even touch. "Does... Does it hurt?"

"Not any worse than usual. I just... Don't want to hurt you."

A small, worried frown makes its way onto the angel's face. "I know you never would."

"You flinched."

"Huh?"

"When I yelled. You flinched and tried to hide from me..." Tears trail down the demon's cheeks. "I don't want you to be scared of me. I don't want to hurt you."

"I always jump at loud noises," Angelique explains, "It's got nothing to do with you."

"Still... I'm sorry."

"Stellar," Satan speaks from behind them, "You don't need to punish yourself. It was an accident, and I think we all know that."

Angelique nods in agreement. "See? Everyone knows you didn't mean to yell." She holds out her arms in a silent request. "So... Is everything okay between us?"

Stellar looks from Angelique's outstretched arms to her face as she cries more thick tears. "... Yeah," she murmurs, "Yeah, we're okay." She takes one step forward, only for her knees to give out underneath her and send her tumbling to the floor as she passes out from exertion.

The angel dives down with a yelp to catch her fall, and manages to with relative success. The demon's head is resting on her shoulder, with weak breaths ghosting across the skin of her neck. When she tries to move, though, Angelique finds herself stuck crouching with Stellar's dead weight leaning heavily against her. With a bright blush to her face, she looks over her shoulder and quietly asks, "Um... Can somebody help?"

Satan steps forward and scoops the both of them into his arms with ease. "You girls can stay in one of the guest rooms until she wakes." With Sarien close behind, the King of Wrath carries the women up a staircase and into the guest suite of the palace. The prince chooses a vacant room and opens the door, allowing his father to enter despite his filled arms. Satan gently places the two women onto the large, queen-sized bed.

"If you need help getting her situated, do not hesitate to let us know."

"I should be able to manage from here, but thank you, sir."

"Of course, Angelique." He pets her head and smiles. "You're good for her." He turns and leaves, opting not to comment on the bright blush forming on Angelique's cheeks.

That evening, Angelique settles into bed beside Stellar, who still had yet to awaken. The angel frowns at her companion's sleeping face, worries plaguing her heart, and decides to cuddle closer. As she closes her eyes, the voices in the back of her mind speak.

Is this what Aurora went through when you first fell into your coma?

How do you know Stellar will appreciate how close you are right now?

What would Aurora think if she could see you like this?

Angelique sighs, defeated, and opens her eyes once again. She rolls over onto her back and resigns herself to a restless night...

Until her ears register the sounds of a gentle purr coming from her sleeping companion.

She looks back over to Stellar, surprised at the soft vibrations. "Are you awake?"

"Ngh..."

"Stellar?"

"Mm..."

"Can you hear me?"

"Nn...?"

Angelique laughs quietly. "You're still not awake enough to talk, huh?" She turns back onto her side and curls close to the demon once again, their hands lightly intertwined between their bodies. "I hope you won't mind this, tonight."

Twelve
Fair Trade

Angelique is woken in the morning to something shifting on the opposite side of the bed. Slowly, her eyes flutter open, allowing her to sleepily watch as Stellar carefully lifts herself off the mattress. The demon seems unaware that the angel beside her had woken up at the small movement, until the latter decides to break the morning's quietness.

"You're finally awake," she mumbles, remnants of sleep still coating her voice.

Stellar jumps and immediately meets Angelique's tired gaze. "Oh, sorry. I didn't mean to wake you—"

"It's okay." Angelique sits and rubs her eyes. "I'm glad to see you're okay, too."

Stellar huffs, a pale pink hue coating her face. "You didn't need to worry—"

"I was decapitated and placed into a coma for 100 years. I get to be worried about my friends, and whether or not they'll find themselves in a similar situation."

"... Decapitated, huh? I've never heard of anyone surviving something like a beheading."

"Neither had I until I woke up from my coma... As a matter of fact, I have no idea *how* I survived. The Holy Council seems convinced that Aurora did it, but—"

"Who's Aurora?" Stellar asks. Her voice is quiet and level, as if she's trying to remain calm in her questioning. "Is she the friend you're trying to find?"

"Well... Yes. I need to know for myself whether or not she's safe, and if it turns out she is, I want to see if she knows what happened the night I was decapitated."

The Princess of Death clicks her tongue. "If she's alive down here, she'll have changed her name."

"That's fine. I'm sure I'll recognize her if we stumble across her."

"And if you *don't* recognize her? Or what if we don't find her, hm? What will you do then?"

"I suppose I'll have to keep coming back until I *do* find her. Besides, you and I are friends, so I don't want to abandon you after this mission is over. I want to stay in touch!"

The demon stares at her with wide eyes. "... You seriously still consider us friends? After yesterday, and—?"

"Well, yeah. You still called us friends after we had the misunderstanding back in the hotel room in Envy. And I know you keep saying we're companions, but isn't that another, more professional word for friends?"

Stellar chuckles, her tail wagging slightly as she speaks. "I suppose you're right, Angel."

Angelique beams brightly. "There it is!"

"Huh? What are you talking about?"

"You haven't smiled since yesterday afternoon. It's nice to see you're back to being yourself." She hugs her knees close to her chest. "King Satan mentioned something about you not needing to punish yourself before you passed out, so I was worried you'd retain that mindset after you woke up."

"Oh... Well, Satan and I had a good spar, and it wore me out enough to bring me out of my spiral." She places her hands on her hips in a self-confident manner. "You won't be getting rid of me that easily; I've survived much worse than a bit of negative self-talk."

"Good. I don't want to lose one of my closest friends any time soon." Angelique stands and gets ready for the day. "The last good friend I had, other than Aurora, went MIA for a while before it was determined that he was likely killed in battle."

"Was he a guardian like you?" Stellar asks curiously.

"Yeah, we met at work. He was in a clerical role for a long time, but after a while, he was put into the training program and graduated as a full-fledged guardian angel."

"Why wasn't he a guardian from the jump?"

"Well, he wasn't a life or diligence angel. He was a charity angel, and they're typically placed in administrative or customer service roles."

"It sounds like the system was against him, if you put it like that. Maybe they only permitted him to become a guardian angel to prove a point."

"What point would they be trying to prove?" Angelique asks, confused.

"Not to deviate from the norm."

She frowns. "... Would they seriously sacrifice someone just to keep everyone else in line?"

"I've heard of greater punishments for far lesser crimes."

Angelique thinks back to her conversation with Sarien the day prior.

"Well, you'd better not let anyone in Heaven find out. The last time an angel was found to be even questioning if they were gay, they got thrown down here so fast they almost died on impact."

"... Like falling in love with someone who happens to be the same gender?" she guesses.

The demoness quirks an eyebrow. "Yeah, something like that. What brought that to mind?"

“Well, Prince Sarien and I had a conversation yesterday while you and King Satan were sparring... He mentioned it would be best for my safety that Heaven never learns I’m—” She cuts herself off, a hot blush covering her face.

Stellar quirks a brow in surprise at the reaction. “You’re what?”

“... Bisexual...”

“Oh. Huh, I had no idea.” Stellar shrugs and wraps an arm around Angelique’s waist, tugging her close. “With that in mind... It sounds like I need to protect you from even *more* bad decisions while you’re here.”

“Huh?!” she squeaks, trying to ignore the way her body subconsciously leans into the protective hold. *Her hands are warm and her arms are strong...*

“I can’t have you getting distracted by someone’s sad attempts at flirting when we have work to do,” she jokes with a sly and playful grin. “So for now, while you’re with me...” She leans in close enough for her voice to lightly ghost over the angel’s ear. “You’re *mine.*”

A light, pleasant shiver courses its way up Angelique’s spine at the words, making her close her eyes. Before she can stop herself, she hears her own voice echoing a soft and breathy response to Stellar’s words.

“All yours...”

“Good girl,” Stellar coos against her ear. She moves her hand from Angelique’s waist to the middle of her back and applies light pressure. “Now, let’s head downstairs before Satan and Sarien wonder where we are.”

Angelique uses almost all of her willpower to prevent a quiet whine from escaping her throat. She steps forward on shaky legs, somehow managing to keep herself upright. She tries to focus on Stellar’s hand, which has been placed on her lower back, to ground herself.

They make it safely to the Palace of Wrath's opulent dining hall, where Satan and Sarien have been sitting in wait. The seats of the chairs are plush like those in the Palace of Death, but with a warm, sunset-orange upholstery. The table is covered in a long, pristine white cloth with colorful placemats under the plates and silverware. Upon entering the dining hall, Satan's ears twitch and he lifts his head.

"Ah, there you two are!" the king declares in relief, "I was about to send Sarien to check on you."

"Dad, don't tease them," the prince huffs. "We're glad to see you're okay, Stellar."

"I can imagine. Our spar yesterday broke me out of my spiral and made me sleep for... Fourteen hours?"

"Approximately," Satan agrees.

"You must have needed the sleep," Sarien adds. "Now, come eat. You two are going to be heading out soon, right?"

"Yeah, but we need to figure out where we're going," Stellar grumbles as she sits at the dining table. "We can either go chase the angelic traces in the Lust Sector, or make a pit-stop in Sloth to check on... This." She holds a hand up to show off her corruption.

The blood drains from her face as worry overtakes her. She lightly touches Stellar's arm, trying to once again ground herself instead of allowing her panic to spiral. "I say we go to Sloth. I don't want this to get any worse, if we can help it."

"But if we don't go to Lust, we could lose the target even more than we already have."

Satan and Sarien exchange glances with each other, then avert their attention back to their guests. "Why don't you two play rock-paper-scissors for it? If Stellar wins twice, you head to Lust; if Angelique wins twice, you make your way to Sloth?"

"Works for me," the demon princess declares, "What do you think, Angel?"

"Let's try it." She balls up her right hand into a fist and places it over her left hand's open palm.

"Alright. When we say 'shoot,' we reveal?" Stellar suggests, also readying her hands.

"Yes. And... Go!"

"Rock, paper, scissors, shoot!"

Stellar keeps her fist balled up as a 'rock,' whereas Angelique extends her index and middle fingers in a motion of 'scissors.'

"Stellar one, Angelique zero!" Sarien announces excitedly.

"Rock, paper, scissors, shoot!"

This time, Stellar extends a flat hand for 'paper,' and Angelique extends her fingers again in another motion of 'scissors.'

"Ooh, it's all tied up!" Satan comments, chuckling at the display.

"Rock, paper, scissors, shoot!"

For the final round, Stellar extends a flattened hand once more, whereas Angelique keeps her fist balled up.

"Dang it!" the angel exclaims, pouting as her demonic friend laughs brightly. "Alright, fine, we'll head to Lust, but no matter where the traces go, we'll head to the Sloth Sector next. Deal?"

"Deal." Stellar grabs Angelique's hand and shakes it firmly. "You know I'm a demon of my word, too."

"You are," she agrees with a laugh.

It's not long before a group of servants come out bearing a hearty breakfast across several trays. Most of the food appears to be pancakes and sausage, with a small tray of scrambled eggs as well. Once everyone has eaten, the girls stand and head toward the front doors of the Palace of Wrath.

"Wait! Before you go!" Sarien calls, "Let me make you a lunch for the road!"

"Alright," Stellar sighs dramatically, "Do what you like."

While they wait for Sarien to prepare them bagged lunches, Satan turns to them. "It's been lovely having you stay here, girls.

Sarien doesn't leave for the next semester of college for about three weeks, so come back and visit any time. I'm sure he'll greatly enjoy the company."

"We'll make sure to come back again if we have the time, Your Majesty," Angelique agrees with a bright smile. "And thank you again for your hospitality."

"It was nothing."

It's only a few minutes later that Sarien comes out bearing two thick paper bags, the tops folded over neatly. "Here you go!" he cheers, passing the parcels over to the guests. "Have a safe trip, now!"

The two women leave the palace and make their way back to the subway station, where they wait for the next train to head to Aria, the capital city of the Lust Sector. As they sit on a bench and wait, Angelique shudders and hugs herself.

"Something wrong, Angel?" Stellar asks with concern.

"No, no, I'm fine... It feels a bit like I'm being watched, but it's been on and off for a while. I'm sure it's nothing, really!"

Stellar frowns and looks around the subway platform, her back growing rigid with tension. Her pointed ears twitch as she scans the area for anything out of the ordinary, only for a defeated sigh to escape her a few moments later. "I don't sense anything, but... We'll keep an eye on it, okay?"

The angel nods, but finds her gaze drawn to the demon's tightly-clenched fists. "Alright... Besides, if anything were to happen, I'd have you right here with me. Right?"

"Exactly."

They break into the bagged lunches Sarien had prepared, finding a simple lunch of turkey and cheese sandwiches, small bags of chips, apples, and chocolate-chip granola bars. Once they finish their lunches and throw away their trash, it's not much longer before the train arrives at the station and allows the women to board. The train takes off down the tracks, making the trek from the warm and dry plains and deserts of Wrath to a lush forest environment as they near the Lust Sector.

"Oh, whoa... I never expected Lust to be filled with such lush green trees!" Angelique gasps.

"Yeah, most people who have never been to Lust are surprised at all the rich plant life it's got." Stellar leans back against the seat and watches out the window. "More often than not, people from Sloth and Lust trade plants and herbs with different effects."

Angelique swallows thickly. "Like aphrodisiacs and medicines?"

"Yes and no. Most of the aphrodisiacs found in Lust are heavily regulated to prevent anyone accidentally getting drugged. Azzie doesn't want anyone getting hurt, even though most of the people here for sexually assaulting someone are turned into imps and hunted by us death demons."

"But aphrodisiacs still exist?"

"Yeah, they do. If someone manages to get their hands on one, it's either for heightening their own pleasure sensations or for loosening their nerves. The drugs can only be given out by prescription, and the clubs and hangout areas are strictly monitored to prevent medication sharing."

"I take it the staff are super strict if they find out aphrodisiacs are being shared?"

"Oh, *yeah.* If a staff member finds out, they have no qualms about kicking them out and banning them for a lengthy period of time. There's a special magic network created specifically to keep track of stuff like that. If we run into Duchess Selene, I'm sure she'll be happy to explain how the system works. I don't know all the details, but from what I've heard, it's been effective so far."

"Duchess Selene, huh..."

"Yeah! Depending on where we end up, I'm sure we'll find her. She's Asmodeus' cousin, and helps her manage the clubs more often than not; they make a pretty good team."

"I look forward to meeting her."

"That's the spirit!"

After a while, the train pulls into the station and allows the passengers to disembark. Upon exiting the building, the girls find themselves in the middle of the bustling city of Aria, which is filled with bright and beautiful flowers scattered about. Most of the residences they're able to see have window boxes filled with bright, fresh blooms of begonias, fuchsias, zinnias and geraniums. Large raised gardens are spread along the streets, between the pavement for vehicles and the sidewalks for pedestrians. It gives the city a bit of a cleaner, more beautiful atmosphere than one would likely find on Earth.

"Wow… The city's so pretty! Look at all the flowers!"

Stellar watches as Angelique admires the blossoms along the street. "The Lust Sector has always been a pretty place; I think that's why Azzie staked her claim here."

"I bet Queen Asmodeus has a beautiful garden."

"She does." She takes Angelique's hand and leads the way further into the city. "C'mon, let's go find a nice hotel to stay at."

The girls easily find a hotel, and Stellar pays for a room. Angelique's stomach lets out a loud growl, so they stop to eat a fancy meal at the hotel's built-in restaurant. They make their way to their hotel room, and find a pale pink room brightly lit by a small chandelier. There's a large, king-sized bed pressed against one wall and full-length windows that overlook a large portion of the city. A television is mounted on the wall, above a dresser opposite the bed, and playing soft, relaxing music from its speakers. A plush chair and a planter stand fill the far corners of the room.

"I will *always* be amazed at how beautiful the hotel rooms in Hell are…" Angelique murmurs as she steps into the room. After a moment, the presence of the lone bed in the room fully hits her, and her face turns bright red. "Oh, um…"

"Relax, Angel," Stellar chuckles, "It's a big bed, so we don't have to cuddle or anything if you don't want to."

"That's not it!" she yelps.

"Oh? What's with the reaction?"

"It's just... I didn't think you'd *want* to share a bed with me. Last night was a fluke because you were unconscious, so..."

The Princess of Death flops down onto the bed. "I don't mind. You weren't uncomfortable with it, right?"

"Not at all."

"Then we can share a bed. If you want, I'm even willing to sleep on top of the covers—"

"That won't be necessary," Angelique blurts. "I... I liked cuddling you."

Stellar smirks. "Are you sure your little friend Aurora won't be upset?"

"I'm sure. Once we reconnect and I explain everything to her, she'll understand."

"How can you be so sure, Angel?"

"Because..." She hesitates. "She knows me."

"To me, it sounds like you two were more than friends."

Angelique's cheeks burn more. "No, she... I doubt she thought of me that way."

"But did *you* think of *her* that way?"

She looks away from her companion, glancing at the wall as she answers. "I don't know."

Stellar hums and takes off her boots. "Sounds like something you'll need to figure out before we find her. Feelings are complicated enough, let alone when possible unrequited love is involved."

"You could say that again," Angelique huffs. She kicks off her sandals and drops onto the bed beside her, mimicking Stellar. She scrabbles for purchase on the fluffy comforter, despite it being pinned underneath her body weight.

"You *do* know getting under the covers is way easier if you aren't laying on them, right?" Stellar teases as she stands, lifts the edge of the blankets, and climbs underneath them.

"Of course I do! I just... Don't want to get up."

A bright laugh escapes the demon. "Quite a problem, then."

"I know, right?" Angelique giggles, forgoing her efforts. "Can't you use a little bit of magic and lift the covers for me?"

"What? Aren't you able to do that?"

"But you're already cozy under the blankets!"

Stellar sighs dramatically, but laughs. "Alright, I suppose I can do you this favor." A small pulse of magic makes the blankets lift, spinning Angelique as though she were trapped in a tumbling dryer as they're ripped from underneath her. The angel squawks at the sudden movement, but quickly relaxes as she's covered by the soft and warm blankets.

The angel immediately settles in with a dopey grin on her face and half-lidded eyes. "Thank you, Stellar," she coos as she cuddles up to her companion.

The demon's smile turns gentle and reverent as Angelique settles beside her. She wraps an arm around the angel's waist and tugs her close, so she can rest her chin atop the other woman's head. "You're welcome, Angel. Now, close your eyes and get some sleep."

"M'kay."

The angel does as asked and finds she's able to quickly succumb to the sweet whispers of sleep. She finds herself floating in a black void, as she usually does on the nights she doesn't dream, until a faint but familiar voice calls out to her.

"—lique?"

"Angelique?"

"Angelique!"

After a few attempts of the voice calling her name, she fully recognizes the source.

"Aurora?" she calls back.

"Yes! It's me!" An image of her missing friend forms in front of her, complete with large white wings with a jade-green stripe. The other woman is dressed in a white romper with puffed-out legs and strappy sandals much like Angelique's own. The angel's long, dark brunette hair flares out around her, as if she's floating in water as opposed to air.

Angelique grows teary-eyed at her partner, until she notices her friend's eyes are fully shaded, obscuring them from her vision. *"It's been so long... Am I forgetting what you look like?"* Her hands tremble as she reaches out to the image of Aurora.

The vision, however, takes one of Angelique's trembling hands in both of her own and holds it close to her chest, just above her heart. Aurora whispers, *"You could never forget about me. Right, Angie?"*

"That's right... I could never forget you. Not any part of you." The angel presses close to the vision of her companion, allowing herself to cry. *"I promise, I'll come find you."*

"You don't have to look far," the vision coos, *"I am much closer than you think."*

"Then you must be close..." Angelique clings to the image of her missing partner.

"I've been with you all this time, Angie."

"In my heart?"

"In a way." The gentle smile on her face morphs to the expression of someone who knows more than they care to tell. *"For now, just rest. You deserve it."*

"Okay..." Angelique nuzzles close to her partner's visage. *"I promise, we will be reunited."*

Thirteen
Fresh Flowers

Angelique groans as she wakes in the morning, only to quiet at the feeling of being wrapped in warm arms. Her face burns as she finds herself nuzzled close to Stellar, even to the point that her head is tucked under the demon's chin. Stellar is still asleep, based on the quiet snoring escaping her and the gentle rise and fall of her chest. Embarrassed, the angel tries to wiggle her way out of her companion's arms, only for the grip around her waist to tighten and a leg to be lightly tossed over her own, fully pinning her between Stellar's octopus-like grasp and the soft mattress below them. Angelique lets out a hushed squeak at the closeness, but manages to relax and close her eyes again after only a few moments of the quiet, warm embrace.

Stellar grumbles after about fifteen minutes, letting out a tiny groan as she forces herself to open her eyes. She chuckles under her breath when she notices their predicament, and slowly maneuvers herself off of Angelique. Right as she's about to sneak out from under the covers, the angel emits a tiny, almost unconscious whine. The noise makes Stellar freeze, her tail perking up.

"Are you awake, Angel?" she whispers the question.

"Ngh... I was comfy..." Angelique huffs, pouting cutely.

Stellar runs a hand through Angelique's hair as she settles back onto the propped-up pillows. "I know, but we have to continue our investigation, right?"

"Ugh... Yeah..." Angelique slowly reopens her eyes, rubbing the sleep from them as she turns her attention to the demoness next to her. "You were gonna sneak away?"

A response lodges itself into Stellar's throat as a pink color coats her cheeks. "Well, I wanted to brush my teeth and stuff before you woke up."

"Why?"

"Can't a demon want to look pretty for their partner?" Stellar huffs, crossing her arms over her chest.

"I suppose you have a point. Morning breath isn't pleasant for anyone." Angelique sits up and brushes her hair from her face, uncaring when one sleeve of her nightgown has draped itself off her shoulder. "Mm... I'm sure my hair turned into a tangled mess, too..."

She's brought out of her sleepy, half-awake state by a pillow flying toward her and hitting her in the back of the head. Upon turning around, she sees that Stellar's face has reddened even more than its original dusting of heat.

"What?" she demands with a half-hearted scowl.

"Change your clothes and let's get going. If we're unlucky, we'll have to wait for the night life before we get any leads." Stellar tosses the blankets off of her lap and makes a beeline to the bathroom, where she shuts the door loudly.

"What's her problem this morning...?" Angelique mumbles to herself. She adjusts the sleeve of her nightgown and slowly crawls out of bed. After only a few minutes, she changes into her usual pink-and-white dress; once she's changed, she uses a wave of magic to summon a hairbrush and begins to run it through her hair, which is in fact a bit tangled, but less messy than she was expecting. "Huh," she murmurs, "I must not have been tossing and turning all night."

"Believe me, you were," Stellar says as she exits the bathroom, having cleaned herself up and changed into her day clothes. "I could barely sleep with you adjusting your position every five minutes, but once I put my arm around you, you settled right down."

A vibrant, heated blush covers Angelique's face. "If I was keeping you up, you could've knocked me off the bed! I'd be fine sleeping on the floor!"

"Is that how friends treat each other?" the demoness counters with a knowing smirk.

"... Well, no, but—"

"No buts. You insist we're friends, so I won't be treating you any worse."

Angelique huffs. "Fine. I prefer cuddles to cold floors, anyway."

"Good girl. Now, c'mon, let's see what we can find out about the traces." She grabs Angelique by the wrist and drags her out of the hotel room and into the streets of the Lust Sector.

She finds herself once again drawn to the beautiful foliage spread throughout the streets, be it flowering trees or hanging window boxes filled with colorful blooms. "It's even prettier here during the daytime..." Angelique whispers in awe, unsure of where to look. Several nearby buildings have murals painted on the walls, similar to those in the Pride Sector. "The flowers and art here are so impressive... They must be well taken care of."

"They are," Stellar agrees, a small smile on her face. "The people of Lust love to take care of the plants and artwork around here. Oddly enough, they take pride in their work—pun intended."

Angelique rolls her eyes and elbows her lightly in the side in response. "That was such a bad joke!"

"But you're smiling!" Stellar laughs.

She feels the urge to reveal her head-wings and cover her flushing face in slight embarrassment. They remind her of the times when Aurora would crack bad jokes and snicker at her various reactions—some laughter, some groans, some gentle shoves. "I guess I am, huh..."

Stellar's eyes soften at Angelique's expression, and a hum escapes her. "You're missing her, aren't you?"

The question snaps Angelique out of the trance she'd apparently been in. "Huh?"

"Something I did made you miss your partner, right?"

"Oh, um... A little. She used to crack these really bad jokes just to make me smile or react in some funny way."

"She sounds like fun."

"She was." She squeezes Stellar's hand and fights back the urge to cry. "Oh well. We'll focus on that later; right now, we've got a mission."

"Are you sure?"

"Yes. We don't need to stop because of me."

"Stopping and taking a break are two different things," Stellar counters. "You're obviously still grieving her, and grief is never easy for anyone."

Angelique looks away from Stellar, staring at her feet. "... Could we maybe stop for food somewhere? I don't know what time it is, but I think I'm hungry."

"Yeah, we can. Let me see where the nearest restaurant is... Are you craving anything in particular?"

Angelique shakes her head, a guilty look on her face. "No... I'm sorry if that makes it harder."

"Not at all! There are plenty of good places around here. In fact..." She looks around and perks up, her tail wagging. "There's a favorite spot of mine! Do you want to try it?"

"Sure! What type of food is it?"

"It's your typical bar and grill, so things like burgers, pizza, chicken wings..."

"So long as the chicken is boneless, I should be fine."

"Great!" They march forward, heading toward a building with a bright, red neon sign above the entrance that reads **[T's Fire-Up Grill]**. They head inside and are greeted with a warm, inviting atmosphere even with the late morning hour. Booths line the walls of the restaurant while various tables are placed neatly in the remainder of the space, far enough apart to provide sufficient walk space, while close enough together to feel cozy. Several seating areas are already filled with patrons, some of which are munching on their fresh and steaming meals.

The hostess, a greed demon with slightly curled horns and a scoop-tipped tail, greets them sweetly. She leads them to a corner booth, beaming as she sets the menus on the table. "Your waiter will be over soon. We hope you'll enjoy your time here!"

"Thank you," Angelique responds as she walks away. She looks over the menu, mouth watering at the thought of the barbeque chicken mac and cheese. "Wow, I must *really* be hungry..."

Stellar's ears twitch and she tilts her head curiously. "Hm? What makes you say that?"

"Usually I don't eat anything other than breakfast food first thing in the morning."

"Well, it *is* later than you usually wake up." She smiles coyly, her tail wagging a bit and thumping quietly against the booth.

The angel blushes. "I suppose you're right. I don't *have* to eat breakfast foods in the morning... But I guess I'm a little bit... Hesitant, when it comes to breaking my routines."

Stellar hums. "Changing assignments must be a pain in the ass for you."

"Yeah... It's like changing jobs for humans. You get used to doing something one way, then you have to change everything because you're working with someone new."

"Amen. It's definitely hard if you're not great with transitions or changes."

Just then, the waitress assigned to their table—a young demoness with short horns protruding from beneath her bangs—comes over, her tail wagging as she greets the patrons. "Hi there, folks! My name is Nyxia, and I'll be your server today. Can I start you off with something to drink?"

"Just water," both women say in unison, catching them both by a bit of surprise.

"Alright! Have you decided on your food yet, or do you need a bit more time?"

"We'll need a little longer, please," Stellar says.

"Okay, then I'll grab your drinks and give you a few more minutes." She packs her order pad away and bounces off, her tail swishing from side to side as she walks. As she leaves, Angelique notices the demoness's tail has long strands of hair at the tip, like a mixture of a cow's and horse's tail.

"Is she a sloth demon?" she whispers curiously.

Stellar nods. "Yeah, sloth demons are the only demons with hair on their tails. They also have the shortest horns and fur-insulated wings."

"Interesting..."

The two of them take a few minutes to finalize their decision about their orders, which they place when Nyxia returns to the table. They find themselves in a bit of a comfortable quiet, until another figure approaches.

"Stellar? Is that you?"

The demon's ears twitch as she perks up, surprised to hear her name called. "Huh?"

A woman with long, wavy, brunette hair and horns that curl backward from where they sprout on her head approaches, her white stiletto heels clicking against the floor with each step. She's wearing a shimmering white cardigan over a loose-fitting, iridescent cropped tank top. A purple leather skirt cinches around her waist and drops to her upper thigh, where it meets a single-banded leglet with a purple, heart-shaped gem. Her bright purple-pink eyes widen when she sees the other demoness, and her spade-tipped tail wags. "Oh, it *is* you!"

"Oh, hey, Selene!" Stellar greets, her own eyes brightening.

The woman's heart-tipped tail wags from underneath her skirt as she speaks. "It's been so long! What are you doing all the way over here in Lust?" She leans in for a hug, and Stellar turns her body to properly return the gesture. Despite the innocent motion, Angelique feels a simmering heat deep in her chest.

Why is this woman being so clingy to Stellar? I know she's probably her friend, but even Sarien wasn't attached to her like this...

"I'm here with a work friend for a case," Stellar answers casually as they break the hug. It's only then that Angelique notices the way Selene's shirt is styled, which reveals quite a bit of her cleavage. The angel's face burns in both embarrassment and more of the simmering sensation.

"Oh! I didn't see you there in the corner!" Selene squeaks, turning her attention to the angel. "I'm so sorry!" She extends a hand in a kind greeting. "My name is Selene. I'm an old friend of Stellar's!"

"She's also the person we were looking for," Stellar chuckles. "Meet Duchess Selene of the Lust Sector."

"Oh, it's... Nice to meet you," Angelique responds, her voice a bit hesitant thanks to the sensation in her stomach. "My name is Angelique."

They shake hands, and Selene gives a kind, pink-glossed smile. "Aww, you're such a sweetheart!" she cheers, her voice bright and even a bit sultry. "You remind me of my fiancé and our boyfriend!"

The comment makes Angelique freeze in surprise. "Is that so?"

"Yep!" Selene turns to look behind her, beckoning someone over. "Ryver, Haley, come here!"

Two more figures make their way over from the entrance of the restaurant. One has their long, dirty-blonde hair pulled back into a neat ponytail. They're wearing a latex bodysuit with hip-high cutouts that show off their long legs. On top of the bodysuit, they're also wearing form-fitting black pants with mesh-covered cutouts along the outer thighs. The pant legs flare out into a glittery fabric just past their knees. Over their arms, they wear a cropped pink jacket.

The other, more muscular figure is a young man with short brunette hair styled in a loose quiff. He's wearing a red, cropped halter top over his broad chest and fingerless fishnet gloves over his arms and hands. On his legs he wears a pair of tight leather pants, and red-and-black leather dress shoes protect his feet from the floor. The two newcomers also have spade-tipped tails and horns that curl back from their foreheads, just like Selene.

"Ohhhhh, one of you was a human, right?" Stellar asks.

"Both of us were, actually," the short-haired man corrects. "I'm the only one who, uh… Kicked the bucket."

Angelique stares between the three Lust Demons with shock. "Wait, you *died?*"

"Mm-hm. This is my afterlife." He waves with one hand and wraps the other around their long-haired companion's waist. "My name is Haley, and this here is Ryver. They've been here for a few years longer than I have, so they've slowly turned into a demon over time."

Ryver nudges Haley with their hip, letting out a tiny, pouty huff. The short-haired man laughs and hugs them close by the waist. "I never said you being down here is a bad thing, baby," Haley clarifies. "In fact, I'd say I'm lucky to have met you both."

"Oh, wait! I remember you!" Stellar blurts, "Your soul got separated from your body!"

"Yeah… It was a good lesson in not attempting strong magic when you have no idea what you're doing." Haley rubs the back of his neck shyly.

"What kind of magic were you trying to perform, if you don't mind my asking?" Angelique queries.

"I was trying to turn myself into someone my old celebrity crush could truly love… Something backfired, and it separated my soul from my body instead." He sighs. "At least I was put in the care of these two. I love them with all my heart." He nuzzles his nose against Ryver's, causing them to squeak before returning the gesture.

Selene grins at the sight, before perking up. "Wait, why don't we all sit together and catch up? Since you were already seeking me out, maybe I *can* help with your case."

"Oh, you don't need to," Angelique starts, only to be cut off by her companion.

"Sure, I don't see why not," Stellar says at the same time. After casting a quick, curious glance to Angelique, the angel swallows thickly around a ball of nerves in her throat.

"I mean... You don't have to feel forced to sit with us," she half-heartedly clarifies.

"Oh, it's no problem at all!" Selene cheers, taking a seat beside Stellar. The death demon scoots around the booth to sit closer to Angelique as Ryver and Haley also pile into the booth. Before long, Nyxia comes back over and takes the newcomers' drink orders.

"Before we get into catching up or discussing our case... You know which club Azzie's going to be at tonight, right?" Stellar asks her friend.

"Yes, I do!"

"Great; unless we can find her before tonight, we're going to need it."

"What's going on?" Ryver asks, fidgeting a bit in their seat.

"It's a long story. We've been chasing angelic traces all across Hell."

"Angelic traces?" Haley echoes, confused.

Stellar nods. "It seems there's an angel being led around Hell by a demonic companion. We're trying to catch them and get answers."

"Yeah, that would be a question for Azzie," Selene sighs, "I haven't heard, seen, or felt anything of the sort. I hope she would tell me if something like that was happening, but... She's always been awfully independent."

"My dad is always getting on my case about my hyper-independence, too."

"Luckily, that's what you've got me for," Angelique blurts.

Stellar leans against Angelique in playful affection. "You're right. Somebody's got to keep me on a bit of a leash."

The angel squeaks, face burning hot at the hidden implication. "Stellar!"

Her friend bursts into giggles, and the others follow suit soon after. Angelique notices Ryver's face is about as red as her own as they reach up to play with something around their neck. Upon closer inspection, they're wearing a baby-pink collar with a soft inner lining, and the item they're playing with is the bunny-shaped tag.

Also noticing Ryver's reddened face, Haley leans in close and whispers something into their ear, which sends a shiver down their spine.

"Is everything alright, Ryver?" Angelique asks curiously.

They nod, still blushing madly.

"Ooh, did Haley make a sexy promise~?" Selene guesses, grinning coyly. "Good bunny."

Angelique stares between the throuple, confused. Stellar leans in close and whispers into her ear, "It's a kink thing. They're trying to get Ryver all hot and bothered."

The heat in her face burns even hotter than before, to the point that Angelique could swear her skin was melting off her cheeks. She takes a much-needed sip of her water as their waitress returns with a full tray of food. She sets down each of the plates and heads off again.

The others move on from the previous conversation to eating their meals with ease, almost as if they'd done this a hundred times before. Angelique tries to do the same, even glancing at Stellar to gauge her partner's own conversational transition. She notices a slight color to her cheeks, which makes her smile to herself. *At least I'm not the only one still flustered...*

It doesn't take long for everyone to finish their meals. As the last few bites are shared, the topic changes to the girls' next move for the day.

"So, are you planning to stick around all day until we go find Azzie?" Selene asks.

"Pretty much," Angelique and Stellar both answer in unison, only for the demon to continue. "We were planning to get in contact with Queen Asmodeus sooner than later, but I'm sure a tour around Lust would be nice, as well."

Selene beams. "Alright, we'll lead you around Lust for a bit. How about we make a stop at the botanical gardens?"

Angelique perks up. "I love botanical gardens!"

The four demons' tails all wag. "Then it's off to the gardens with us. C'mon; I'll pay for lunch and we'll be on our way."

They all shuffle their way out of the corner booth and leave the restaurant. Selene leads the way, hips swaying with each step, followed closely by her lovers. Stellar and Angelique take up the rear.

"Is everything alright?" Stellar asks, "You were acting a bit odd back in the restaurant."

Angelique feels heat rush to her cheeks. "Yeah, I'm fine."

"Are you sure? Once Selene showed up—"

"I'm sure!" she yelps, "I'm alright! Everything's fine." She turns to her companion with an attempt at a genuine smile, only for it to come out a bit forced at the edges. "I'd tell you otherwise. I promise."

Stellar narrows her eyes, clearly disbelieving, but sighs. "Alright, then." She moves forward in a bit of a rush, carefully wrapping the tip of her tail around the angel's wrist and tugging, pulling Angelique behind her until they catch up with the lust demons. It doesn't take long for the five of them to arrive at a large wrought-iron archway, with matching metal flowers curling around it like a trellis. Wrought iron letters that read **[Hellion Botanical Gardens]** stand tall above the pathway.

"Here we are~!" Selene coos, tail wagging, "Now, there are a bunch of branching paths, so be careful not to get lost!"

Stellar rolls her eyes playfully and heaves a dramatic sigh. "We're not children, Selene."

"I know, but you can still get lost in this place like it's a maze as an adult."

"Yeah, I was the idiot who got lost the last time we came here," Haley confesses, "She's saying that to me in particular."

Ryver laughs. "She'll make sure to punish you if you don't pay attention and get lost again this time."

"I won't." He takes Ryver's hand as they both intertwine their tails, curling the appendages around one another. The latter kisses Haley's cheek in response as they both wander into the garden, leaving Selene, Stellar, and Angelique at the entrance. Selene follows her lovers, at which point Stellar takes Angelique's hand.

"Instead of being extra wheels, how about we go this way?" Stellar suggests, leading the way down a different path into the garden.

The girls find themselves surrounded by dozens of bright, beautiful blooming flowers. Some can be found on earth in abundance, but others are in shades Angelique had never seen before. Off in the distance stands a large weeping willow with oddly-colored leaves and flowers.

"Wow, what is that?" Angelique gasps in awe.

"Whatever it is must be new," Stellar muses, "Because I've never seen it before."

"I see..."

"We'll be able to see it in no time, I promise." She tugs Angelique along one of the paths, leading the way into a tree-dense area with bright foliage. Dozens of bright flowers dangle from the vines and trees; many of which the angel is able to identify as orchids. One type of flower, however, looks like a brightly-colored stage with beaded strands dangling from the large, wide petals. The stamens in the middle look like a trio of dancers posing for an unseen camera.

"What flower is this?" Angelique asks curiously.

"It's a passion flower. Its symbolism in the language of flowers means 'the death of a loved one.'"

Angelique stares at Stellar in shock. "But it's so pretty..."

"Flowers can be deceiving," she counters.

"Still... That's such a sad meaning!" The angel pouts. "It could mean something else, like... Teamwork, or togetherness."

Stellar hums. "Why are you so afraid of death? We both know there's an afterlife."

The angel pauses, unsure of the exact answer.

"Have you ever had a ward die?"

"No. Aurora and I always kept them safe until our assignment was over."

"Is it because *you* almost died?"

"... Maybe? I don't know."

Stellar's tail sways as she thinks. "You don't want to disappear and not have made a difference in the world?" she guesses.

Angelique freezes. "... Yeah, that sounds about right."

"If it makes you feel better, you're not the only one who thinks like that; a lot of people down here do, too. Folks tend to wait a very long time before they consult my father about giving up their souls."

"How long do demons live, exactly?"

"As long as they want, unless they're killed by an angel or demon hunter. I'd bet angels are in a similar boat. You're about a thousand years old, right?"

Angelique blushes brightly. "Do I look that old?"

"Not at all. You still look like you're 25 in human years." She grins. "I was guessing, since I'm 1,300 years old, myself."

"Oh. I never would have guessed we were the same age."

"Oh? We are, hm?" Stellar leans in close enough for Angelique to feel the demon's breath against her own reddened cheeks. "I bet that's why you're so comfortable around me. Birds of a feather flock together, after all."

"At least until the cat comes," calls a familiar, teasing voice. The girls look over as Selene approaches, holding a white blooming flower in her hand.

Angelique feels a sudden tension from her partner, but opts to ignore it when she notices the beautiful flower. "Oh, what a beautiful flower! What kind is it?"

A smirk curves along her cherry-red lips. "It's a—"

"A white narcissus," Stellar interrupts, moving to put her body between the other demoness and the angel. "Why do you have that?"

The former pouts at the reaction, a smirk in her eyes. "Is it not your favorite flower anymore?"

Angelique's brows press tightly together in a mixture of confusion and concern. "Stellar, what is she talking about?"

"Oh, did the Princess of Death not tell you? She used to *adore* white narcissus. Not only as a pretty flower, but as a drink, too!"

"It was *once*—"

"Ah, yes, because the pain of your memories made you want to drink poison. I can't help but wonder what else you may have tried instead..."

"Enough!" she yells, forcefully shoving Selene away. At the rough contact, the other demon's form fades into thick black ink, a grin still on her face as it dissipates. The narcissus flower is the only thing left behind on the concrete pathway.

Angelique lets out a startled yelp as she tries to back away. She feels a chill as her lower back presses against the wrought iron fence, and a fearful shudder courses up her spine. "Stellar… What just happened?" she pleads, voice barely above a whisper in her fear.

The demon hisses as she speaks. "That wasn't Selene."

"What? What was it?"

"A fragment of my corruption." She hugs herself tightly and continues. "When corruption gets bad enough, it spills out and makes falsehoods that look and sound like those you consider friends and family. They tell you horrible things and mock you for your struggles."

"That's awful!"

Stellar approaches the lone narcissus flower. "Luckily, there's always something 'off' about a fragment. They can never get everything perfectly right." She stomps harshly on the bloom, crushing it under the thick sole of her boot. "Selene hates wearing lipstick. She finds cherry red to be especially gaudy."

Angelique thinks back, her fear dissipating when she recalls Selene's pink lip gloss. "I wondered why she was being so mean to you out of nowhere. She seemed really nice when we first met her…"

"Trust me, she is." Stellar turns back to Angelique with an apologetic expression in her eyes. "Let's keep going. I want to see that new willow tree."

Angelique takes Stellar's hand as they continue through the gardens, worry tugging at her heart when she sees the demon's corruption has made its way even further up toward her elbows. She shakes herself out of the spiraling concern and tries to focus on the present moment with Stellar. The two of them find themselves admiring the foliage, and they choose to avoid the section that's labeled **[Poisons Around the World]**. Eventually they make their way to the large willow tree, which is surrounded by the concrete paths. The bark is a strange black color, almost as though it's made out of steel instead of wood. The blooms hanging from the branches shimmer in shades of blue and purple, like stars in a distant galaxy.

"Wow..." both women gasp in awe.

"This must be a new Hellish variant of a weeping willow..." Stellar muses, stepping off the path to admire the tree more closely. In the meantime, Angelique looks around for an information plaque. She finds one a few feet away, and she reads the information with eagerness.

[Emoticast Willow

This tree is a specially-grown addition to the botanical gardens that patrons can interact with. Grab a friend, place your palms to the trunk, and watch as your body heat changes how the willow tree looks!]

"Oh, Stellar, we should touch it!"

"Huh?"

"It changes colors based on the warmth of our palms!" She grabs Stellar's hand and marches up to the trunk of the tree, unaware of the heat radiating from her companion. "Ready? Let's touch it together."

"Uh... Alright, I guess so."

"On three. One, two... Three!"

They each place one of their hands to the coarse bark and look up, waiting for the leaves and flowers to change colors. After only a few moments, the blue and purple hues shift and become a single warm, bright, cherry blossom pink.

Enraptured by the color-changing blooms, Angelique lets out a gasp. "It's so pretty, Stellar!" she cheers, unable to look away from the spectacle above their heads.

"Yeah," the demoness echoes, her voice much softer, "It's beautiful."

The angel turns and beams at her companion, who gives a small smile in return. They remove their hands from the tree, watching as its blossoms and blooms remain the vibrant pink hue.

Distantly, as they stand there admiring the beauty of the color-changing tree, Angelique could almost feel more angelic traces nearby. They'd obviously been covered by more demons coming and going through the gardens. Her expression falters ever so slightly, but she doesn't mention it as she glances over to Stellar. The demon hasn't reacted to the traces, still admiring the shimmering leaves above them.

Should I tell her? She looks so happy and peaceful... I don't want to stress her out or make her corruption worse, so maybe—

She cuts herself off when a familiar voice calls from behind them. "There you two are! Glad you didn't get lost!"

They turn around to see Selene, Ryver, and Haley all standing at the edge of the emoticast willow's grove.

"Oh, hi again!" Angelique responds, suddenly a bit hesitant to interact with them. When the demoness approaches the others, her anxiety falters. *Must be they're not more corruption fragments...*

"Did you all have fun on your little date?" Stellar teases.

"We did, thank you!" Ryver cheers, their tail wagging wildly as Haley pulls them close by the waist once again.

Selene looks between the two of them. "Did something happen while we were away?" she asks.

"Uh... Well..." Angelique glances to Stellar, unsure if they should tell the others about the corruption fragment.

"Nothing you all need to worry about," Stellar says nonchalantly, "Let's say it's a good thing we'll be heading to Sloth after this."

"Sloth?" Haley echoes, "What do you need there?"

Selene glances to Stellar's arms. "Ah... Corruption getting bad again?"

The death demon sighs in defeat and nods. "Yeah. This mission's just a little bit stressful. We haven't found any solid clues the whole time we've been here."

"At least the place is beautiful and the people are nice..." Angelique suggests in an attempt to stave off the tension. She kneels and picks up a tiny, discarded twig of the emoticast willow. The warmth of her palm makes the leaves on the stick turn the same cherry-pink color as the rest of the leaves on the tree, and a bright smile makes its way onto her face. "Do you think anyone would care if I kept this stick as a souvenir?"

"I doubt it," Stellar answers.

Angelique beams and makes the stick disappear into a flurry of pink-and-gold sparks.

Selene laughs brightly as she places her hands on her hips. "Well, it's getting close to opening time for the party district. Shall we head over there?"

"Yeah, that sounds like a plan," Stellar agrees. As the group heads out of the botanical garden, Angelique can't help but look back at the now-pink tree. The vibrant, warm hue makes her heart flutter as her mind drifts to the heat she'd felt when she and Stellar had held each other's hands. She forces her body to fight the heat in her cheeks as she turns and races to catch up.

Fourteen
Neon Lights

The three lust demons lead the way through the city as it bustles with evening-goers and nightlife. Restaurants quickly fill with patrons as the sun begins to set and the nearby street lamps flash to life. Bars and clubs turn on their vibrant business signs which glow in all different neon hues.

They approach a large club with a sign that reads, **[The Eclipse]**. Selene saunters up to the muscular wrath demon standing guard at the door, her lovers on her heels, and greets the other woman. "Good evening, Topaz!"

The woman's attention snaps to the newcomers. "Duchess Selene! What brings you to The Eclipse tonight?"

"We're looking for a bit of fun, obviously! A couple of our friends are also looking for an audience with Azzie. She *is* still here tonight, right?"

At the mention of their presence, Stellar and Angelique step forward. They both wave in greeting, which causes the wrath demon's eyes to widen in surprise. "I see! Here I was worried there would be an unfamiliar face, but I would recognize you anywhere, Princess Stellar." The bouncer bows her head respectfully to the Princess of Death. "Should I trust your companion is not a trouble-maker?" she queries with a half-joking tone.

"Yes, please." She grasps Àngelique's hand. "We're a package deal."

"Well, then I won't keep you out here any longer." The bouncer steps aside and allows the five of them inside the club.

Angelique's senses are immediately accosted as soon as she steps foot into the club. The lights are dim, aside from the bright, colorful spotlights near multiple pole-dancing stages throughout the building and the warm lights near the large bar off to the right. Glitter can be spotted all over the floor, where it had obviously fallen off of multiple people's bodies and become one with the thin carpet despite the cleaners' best attempts. Loud, beat-heavy music fills the air and makes her head pound. She lets out a tiny groan as the scents of alcohol and various perfumes mix together and swirl into a headache between her eyes.

The noise that subconsciously emits from her throat catches Stellar's attention, the demon's ears twitching as she looks back to her companion. "Are you okay?" she asks, concern lacing her voice. "Do you need to wait outside?"

"Um... No, no, I should be fine," she stammers out, unsure but trying not to distress her friend. "If something comes up, I'll let you know."

"Alright, if you're sure..." Stellar squeezes Angelique's hand and leads the way to the large bar. "Take a seat here and see if you can adjust. Do you want a drink or anything?"

As the angel sits on one of the tall bar seats, her tiptoes dangle a few inches from the floor. "Sure. What do they have to offer?"

"Depends on whether you're looking for a hard drink or not."

"... You mean alcohol?"

"Yep! I'm a sucker for one specific drink, but I'm not sure how it will affect you."

"I'm willing to try it."

Stellar pauses and quirks an eyebrow. "Are you sure?"

"I know you'll take care of me."

She hums, a sudden pink tint to her cheeks, and turns to head over to the bartender. Angelique watches Stellar chat with them as they serve a crystal clear drink poured over ice in a whiskey glass. Once the bartender has portioned out a second drink, Stellar brings them back over and passes one of the cups to Angelique. "Hopefully it's not too strong for you."

The angel grasps the cup tightly in her hand. She brings it to her nose, but finds the drink does not smell of alcohol… Or anything, for that matter. In combination of curiosity and caution, she takes a sip. The drink is crisp and refreshing with an odd aftertaste of sugar and aromatic spices. After a moment, she registers the aftertaste of ambrosia—and that the drink is none other than holy water. With the realization, her heart freezes in her chest and her gaze darts to her demonic companion. "Don't drink that!" she yelps, only to watch in horror as Stellar easily downs the substance.

"Ah~!" She pulls the cup from her lips, "Delicious~!" She turns her attention back to Angelique and smiles innocently. "How is it?"

"You… You just drank holy water…"

"Yeah? This type is strong booze."

"Doesn't holy water burn demons?"

"Eh, it mostly depends on the source of the holy water, and even then it mostly gives us a rash or, at worst, a mild burn. It acts like any other alcohol when ingested, and some even get high off the smell and use it to relax." She waves to the bartender and orders a refill.

The bartender agrees and brings over a large bottle of holy water, which they skillfully pour into the glass without spilling a drop. As soon as the glass is full, Stellar grabs it again and sips at the liquid instead of drinking it all at once.

Angelique's shocked stare circles between the glass of holy water in her hand and the one that's pressed to Stellar's lips. "You're so casual about this…"

"Why wouldn't I be? It's only a couple drinks."

"Forgive me for being worried about you," she huffs, "I've always heard this... *Drink,* apparently, is dangerous for demons."

"Well, I have a relatively high alcohol tolerance, so you won't need to worry about me for a while." She leans in close enough that their faces nearly touch, and her breath ghosts over Angelique's lips as she speaks. "Okay, Angel?"

Angelique bites her lip at their closeness and the words whispered across her mouth. "Okay," she whispers back around the sudden knot in her throat. "I trust you."

"Thank you, Angel," Stellar coos. She leans in further, their lips nearly touching, before she pulls back and downs the remainder of her drink. "I'm going to try and find Azzie before her show. Wish me luck." She turns on her heels and wanders off into the livelier parts of the club.

"Good luck," Angelique calls after her, letting out a quiet groan as her words are lost amidst the pounding music. She turns her attention back to the cup in her hands. After contemplating for a moment, she sips at her holy water once again. Its crisp and refreshing nature, combined with the ambrosia-like flavor, reminds her of her life back in Heaven.

I don't know how I'll be able to go back after this, especially if everything they tell us is a lie... she muses to herself, *I'm not good enough at acting to pretend everything's okay.* Her blood runs cold at her next question. *What if Heaven finds out what I know, and they kick me out?*

"What's on your mind, sweetie?"

She startles out of her thoughts and shoots to a proper sitting position on her bar stool. Next to her stands a woman with loose curls that gradually change from a platinum-blonde color to a vibrant magenta at the ends. She stands confidently in a tight-fitting black bodysuit that has a fishnet-pattern mesh covering from her chest up to where it cinches around her neck. High hip cut outs expose even more of her long legs, and belts at the lowest hems of the leg openings accentuate her thick thigh muscles. More fishnet patterns appear on her thigh-high tights, which are also held up by garter belts. Magenta platform pleaser heels add a few extra inches to her height. A long spade-tipped tail wags playfully behind her, and her horns match Selene and her lovers, which further indicates her identity as a lust demon.

"Oh, it's... Nothing," she stammers, "I'm just... Homesick."

The demoness tilts her head, blue eyes with heart-shaped pupils filling with concern. "Are you far from home?"

"Ah... You could say that, I suppose."

"Do you want to talk about it?"

"Not really..."

The woman shrugs, a soft smile on her face. "Alright, I just wanted to check in. You seemed sad."

"Thank you. I'm not used to this kind of atmosphere, and my friend is looking for someone."

"Any idea who they're looking for?"

"Queen Asmodeus. Stellar had a few questions before her performance."

"Oh! You're looking for me?"

The angel pauses and looks the woman over again, a vibrant blush to her cheeks. "Wait, *you're* Queen Asmodeus?"

"I sure am! You mentioned you're here with Princess Stellar?"

"I am. We also came with a few of her other friends... Selene, Ryver, and Haley."

"Oh, my cousin and her lovers!"

Angelique blinks, taken aback. She groans and hangs her head in her hands as she continues. "... I forgot that Selene is your cousin, Your Majesty..."

Asmodeus giggles brightly, covering her mouth so as not to burst out laughing. "You're not from Hell, are you?"

She swallows thickly and shakes her head.

"Ah, then it makes sense as to why your traces are such an odd mix. Life and death... Stellar's been rubbing off on you quite a bit."

"... She has?"

"Mm-hm. Something tells me you're special to her."

"Really? Why?"

"You'll see soon enough."

As soon as Asmodeus is finished speaking, someone presses so close that their chest and stomach are squished against the angel's back. Warm arms loop around her waist and pull her even closer to their body. "Is everything okay, Angel?" Stellar whispers into Angelique's ear. "Nobody's been bothering you?"

Angelique squeaks and turns around as much as she's able to. Her burning cheeks are less than an inch away from Stellar's own flushed face. The demon's eyes are a bit hazy as her glance slowly shifts from Asmodeus' figure to meet the angel's gaze. "What? No, nobody's been bothering me."

"Good..." She nuzzles their faces against one another, and a rough, crackly purr escapes her throat. Her grasp around Angelique's waist tightens slightly as well.

The angel grows tense at the sudden affection from her demonic friend, confusion clear as day on her face. "What...?"

"Aw, it looks like she's tipsy!" Asmodeus giggles, tail wagging even more. "Are you okay, Stellar?"

"Mm... 'M fine..." She cuddles further against Angelique, her own tail wagging in a combination of joy and laziness.

The Queen of Lust giggles, obviously amused by the display in front of her. "Well, you two, I don't have long before my performance begins. I'm guessing you're going to stay until after the show is done to have whatever conversation you were aiming for?"

"Um... Yes. I'll see if I can get Stellar to sober up."

"If you want! And if she needs more time to come to her senses, you can always stay at the Palace of Lust once I head out for the night."

"Um... Okay!"

Asmodeus turns and hurries off, waving as she leaves. Angelique turns her full attention back to her cuddled-up companion.

"You only had two drinks and you're tipsy?" she asks with concern, nuzzling her face against Stellar's in an attempt at comfort.

The bartender comes over and passes them another glass of holy water. "Miss Stellar's alcohol tolerance is much higher than other demons I've met. She's tipsy after two glasses of holy water, whereas others are incredibly *drunk* after one."

"I see..." she murmurs as Stellar releases her grip on her waist. She grabs the cup of holy water and sips at it once again, her tail wagging more lazily as she drinks. She curls up on a nearby barstool and leans onto Angelique's shoulder, smiling a bit dumbly. After a little while, the music shifts and there is an announcer's voice over the speakers.

"Ladies, gentlemen, and others, welcome once again to The Eclipse! Tonight is an extra-special performance, brought to you lovely people by our beloved, Her Majesty Queen Asmodeus of Lust!"

The announcement is superseded by loud applause throughout the facility, as well as cheers and whistles. Asmodeus struts out onto the large central stage, waving to the audience and her tail wagging at all the attention. She approaches the large, sturdy dancing pole in the center of the stage and twirls around it, grinning brightly.

Angelique's face burns brightly as she watches the Queen of Lust's performance. She grasps onto the pole and hoists herself up, pressing her thick thighs together to keep herself upright. She dips herself upside down, showing off her sensual curves to the audience, then allows herself to slide down the pole until she's laying on her back on the stage, heaving her chest dramatically to accentuate her shapely bosom. Her eyes close and a confident smile makes way onto her face as applause roars from the gathered crowd.

The angel squeaks and looks away from the center stage, her face burning red-hot. *I can't believe I watched all of that! What is wrong with me?! Stellar's right here, and—*

She freezes when she notices movement out the corner of her eye. Stellar is rising from her seat and making her way over to an empty stage in a quieter, more secluded section of the club. Without a second thought, Angelique darts after her companion.

Stellar hops onto the stage and wraps her tail around the pole, pressing her back against the cool metal. Angelique watches as she sways her hips and grabs the pole in an iron grip, her gaze never leaving the lone audience member. She unravels her tail from the pole before performing her first trick. She kicks one leg up, followed closely by the other, and wraps her ankles around the pole, allowing herself to dangle almost from the ceiling thanks to her leather boots. Once her legs are secure, she removes her hands and spreads them out to imitate a pair of wings. She then lessens the pressure of her legs around the pole and slowly lowers herself to a more reasonable height, before tightening the grip of her thighs once again. She pulls her right knee closer to her chest and presses the outside of her ankle against the pole, before lowering her left leg and making her body almost completely perpendicular to the pole.

Angelique can't help but watch in awe as Stellar moves through her own personal performance, her confidence unwavering and balance level despite her drunken state. She feels her hidden head-wings flutter as her face burns, and her trembling knees force her to sit on a nearby plush chair as Stellar continues through a few routines.

The drunk demoness ends the performance with a twirl around the pole and a bow to the sole audience member. Once she stands back up, she hops off the stage and cuddles up to Angelique, a loud purr escaping her throat as she clings to her companion. She mumbles something against the angel's neck, but her words are so slurred they're practically unintelligible.

"What was that?" Angelique asks, trying to fight back her shock, awe, and mild embarrassment. She runs a hand along Stellar's back, petting her.

The demon groans, still dazed from the alcohol, and nips at the skin of Angelique's neck.

"Wha—?! Did you just bite me?!"

A sleepy chuckle escapes Stellar. "You make pretty noises~!"

"Oh good grief." She glances over to the stage where Asmodeus is finishing her lengthy, equally skillful performance. "Well, at least now we'll be able to get you somewhere to rest until the alcohol wears off..."

Sure enough, only a few minutes later, Queen Asmodeus finishes her performance with a confident flourish and an elegant bow. "Thank you all so much for coming tonight! May the remainder of your night be filled with joy and passion!"

The audience cheers and disperses as the Queen of Lust exits the stage. Some head to the bar for more drinks, while others head over to the smaller stages to watch other performers or try out their own skills. As soon as the remaining patrons spread out, Angelique nudges Stellar. "Come on, we've got to go now."

A whine escapes her. "But I'm comfy!"

"You'll be comfier in bed."

"I don't want to get up..."

"I know, but you don't want to sleep here, do you?"

"... No..."

"Alright, then we need to get up."

Stellar heaves a heavy, melodramatic sigh and tears herself away from Angelique long enough for them both to stand. As soon as they're both on their feet, Stellar takes Angelique's hand, clinging tightly to her as they begin to walk.

"Where are you two heading?" a familiar voice calls from behind them. Angelique turns her head and finds Selene making her way over to them. As soon as the duchess notices Stellar's dazed state, she falters in her steps. "Ah, heading back to your hotel for the night?"

"We were told we could even stay at the Palace of Lust, but I'm not sure where it is... Or even the way back to our hotel."

"Ah, so you did manage to find Azzie! I can run to the dressing rooms in the back and see if she can help guide you to the palace. After all, it looks like Stellar won't be much help like this..."

"If you really don't mind, could you ask her? I want to get Stellar resting as soon as possible."

Selene scurries off to the dressing rooms. While the two other women wait near the entrance to the club, Stellar leans her head onto Angelique's shoulder.

"Missed you..." she slurs.

"Huh?" Angelique queries.

Stellar slurs again as she speaks, tears filling her hazy purple eyes. "I've missed you..."

"We've been together this whole time, silly." The angel pets her head. "You don't have to worry about missing me."

Stellar purrs more at the affection, tail wagging happily. After a few minutes, Selene and Asmodeus approach them, the latter lugging a small bag on one shoulder.

"Ready to go?" the Queen of Lust asks.

"Yes, please. I want Stellar to lay down and get some rest."

"Then we're off." The queen turns to her cousin. "You know the drill; call me if something comes up."

"Will do, Azzie. See you later!"

Asmodeus leads the way out of the club, turning back every so often to make sure the others are close behind. As they catch up, Angelique notices that the Queen of Lust is wearing a pair of fuschia-colored sneakers instead of her platform heels from their encounter in the club.

"What happened to your other shoes?"

"I took them off for the walk back home. Heels are *never* comfortable for long periods of time." She glances to Angelique's footwear. "Surely you understand, since you're in those wedge sandals."

The angel blushes at the comment. "I mean... Yeah, sometimes they make my feet hurt, but that's normal, right?"

She sighs. "Heaven doesn't treat women any differently than they did thousands of years ago, do they?"

"... Huh?"

"The high-ups are too focused on their reputation to care about the comfort of the other people in their lives, right?"

"I... I guess?"

She pauses in her steps and turns to face Angelique. "You're a guardian angel. How does Archangel Barachiel treat you?"

"Um..." She thinks as far back as she can, but her most recent memory of her boss comes to the forefront of her mind. "... He's dismissive of his staff and doesn't let us get a word in edgewise."

"So he hasn't changed a bit," she snarls, clearly angered by the revelation, but continues. "You should look into getting more comfortable shoes. Maybe even a spare outfit or two."

"May I ask why you're suggesting this?"

"It's not uncommon for people's eyes to wander in Heaven... Especially up a girl's skirt. All I'm suggesting is safety shorts, so any prying eyes don't get what they want." She pauses in her words, as if debating if she wants to continue. "... I'm sorry if I overstepped, I'm just giving you the advice I wish I'd gotten."

Angelique bites her lip, unsure of how to soothe the demoness in front of her. She finally settles on a brief, all-encompassing statement of, "I'm sorry."

"I appreciate the sentiment, but it's all in the past. I want to protect people, if I can." She looks over her shoulder at Angelique. "We're almost to the palace, I promise."

"Thank you..." Angelique turns her attention back to Stellar, who is still leaning against her and cuddling close. "I'm not sure how much longer Stellar's going to be awake."

Thankfully, Asmodeus' word proves true, and they arrive at the Palace of Lust in only about five more minutes. The outer wrought-iron gate is decorated with hearts on each of the rods, and the bricks of the palace itself are a beautiful shade of rosewood. Asmodeus pulls open the gate, revealing a large, blossoming garden filled with dozens of different romantic blooms. Rose bushes, carnations, sunflowers, and tulips all greet the women as they walk down the pristine concrete path. The front doors have large panes of stained glass set into the thick cherry wood. The palace's owner pulls open the door and holds it open for Angelique.

They make their way through the candlelit halls to a large guest suite, and Asmodeus holds the door open as they enter the room. Angelique sits Stellar on the bed and bids the Queen of Lust good-night as the platinum blonde woman leaves.

Angelique turns to Stellar as is about to speak, only to get cut off by the demon.

"Is she gone?" she grumbles.

"Asmodeus? Yes, she is."

"Good." She kicks off her shoes, the force sending them flying into the opposite wall. After Angelique recovers from the whiplash of Stellar's sudden attitude change, she redirects her attention back to her friend... Only to gasp and let out an embarrassed yelp when she realizes that the demoness is stripping off her shirt. She lazily tosses her top over in Angelique's direction, leaving her torso bare except for her snug-fitting bra. Stellar grumbles as she tries to unhook the clasps in the back, pulling it tighter against her body and making a bit of her cleavage spill out over the cups.

"W-Wait! What are you doing?!" Angelique shrieks, heat burning her cheeks as she tries to cover her eyes. She splays her fingers just enough to see her friend without getting too much of an eyeful of her bare chest.

"I'm tired," she murmurs, "So I'm going to bed." She yanks her bra off and once again tosses it over toward Angelique, uncaring as it falls into a heap with her other clothes. As soon as her upper body is fully bare, she crawls under the covers of the bed, leaving her thigh-high socks, shorts, and underwear still on her body. She settles in easily enough, nuzzling her face into the pillow.

Once her companion is covered by the blankets, Angelique heaves a sigh and prepares herself for bed, as well. She slips out of her shoes, contemplating Asmodeus' words about needing more comfortable ones. She uses a surge of magic to change from her uniform into a comfortable nightgown, then climbs into bed beside Stellar. When she looks over to her companion again, she finds Stellar fully asleep.

"Sleep well," she whispers, "Something tells me you're going to have an *awful* hangover."

Fifteen
Medical Mystery

The following morning, Angelique wakes to the sound of pained groans next to her. Her eyelids flutter open and immediately catch sight of Stellar, face buried in her pillow with her nose and eyebrows all scrunched up. The demon is *definitely* suffering from a horrible hangover, which becomes more apparent when she tries to open her eyes and lets out another loud groan.

"Stellar?" Angelique calls softly. She brushes some of Stellar's hair out of her face.

"Ngh... What is it?" she whines as she presses her face into Angelique's warm palm.

"Are you okay?"

"Head hurts... Body aches... Thirsty..."

The angel runs a gentle thumb over Stellar's cheek. "You drank quite a bit last night. How about I get you some water and medicine?"

Stellar whines as she gives a tiny nod in agreement and curls the blankets tighter around herself. "Okay..."

Before she can leave the room in search of refreshments, there's a knock on the door to their room. "Miss Angelique?" a timid voice calls, "Are you and Princess Stellar awake?"

"Oh! Yes, we are! I'll be right there." She scurries to the door and opens it, revealing a young lust demon with a servant's cart. The cart has a bottle of medicine and two plates of breakfast food perched on top. Angelique takes the cart with a quick and quiet

"Thank you," then shuts the door and brings it back to the bedside.

"How are you holding up?" Angelique asks, making sure to keep her voice quiet.

"I feel like shit," Stellar groans from where her head is covered under the blanket. "My headache has turned into a light-sensitive migraine, and I'm worried if I move too much I'll be sick..."

"Well, I'll get you the hangover medicine and see if you can eat something. Does that sound okay?"

The demoness groans out a "Yes" and slowly sits up, propping herself heavily against the pillows near the headboard. She keeps the blankets wrapped tightly around her torso so as not to accidentally flash her angelic companion.

Angelique sets the tray down on the bed and fusses with the medicine bottle's cap for a moment, but successfully opens it and presents her friend with two of the pills. Once Stellar has popped the pills into her mouth, Angelique hands her a cup of water and helps her carefully tip it back. Stellar drinks as if she hadn't had a drop of water in days.

"Feel a bit better?"

Stellar nods, closing her eyes to try and block out more of the morning sun that filters beautifully through the thin curtains.

"Can you eat a few bites of breakfast for me?" Angelique pleads sweetly, motioning in the direction of the plates stacked high with omelet rice and sausage. She brings over a plate and sets it on the demon's lap. Stellar grabs the fork and picks at the offered food, her movements slow and deliberate thanks to the ache in her head. As she watches her friend eat, Angelique decides to take part in the meal, as well.

Even with Stellar taking slow bites of her breakfast, it doesn't take long for the both of them to finish their meals. Once they've finished, Angelique's attention diverts to the pile of Stellar's clothes near the wall.

“Do you want to wear the same clothes as yesterday, or are you going to figure out a new outfit?”

Stellar’s face reddens as she speaks. “I can wash my clothes with a bit of magic and wear them again.”

“If you want to, I won’t fight you.” The angel smiles. “I’m glad you’re better than you were last night. You were so out of it...”

“Don’t remind me...” She flops back against the pillows and hides her face behind her hands. “I got drunk, didn’t I?”

“Well... A bit more than tipsy, so yeah,” she confesses, “But it’s okay! You weren’t an angry drunk or anything, so nobody got hurt!”

“... I wasn’t?”

“Nope! You were quite clingy, actually.”

“Hm... Usually when I get drunk I end up starting a fight.”

“Well, you stuck to my side all night.” Her cheeks heat up as she asks her next question. “Before I forget, do you want me to leave the room so you can get changed?”

“Not necessarily. If you’re uncomfortable with me being topless for a few more minutes, though, I won’t keep you here.”

She shrugs. “I can keep my eyes closed and covered.”

“Alright, then I’ll get dressed.”

Angelique closes and covers her eyes as suggested. Her ears twitch at the sounds of blankets shuffling and the bed creaking slightly, followed by a quiet whoosh of magic and the sound of more shuffling fabric.

“Alright, you can look.”

The angel removes her hands and opens her eyes. Her gaze is immediately drawn to Stellar, who is sitting on the bed and brushing the wrinkles out of her shirt.

“Since we’re in one of the Palace of Lust’s guest rooms, I take it you talked with Azzie last night?” she guesses as she pulls on her shoes.

"Yes, I did. I was talking to her when you came over and started clinging to me." Her cheeks flush at the recollection of her conversation with the Queen of Lust the previous night.

"Hopefully I didn't act too weird," Stellar murmurs, her voice breaking Angelique from her memories. The angel contemplates whether or not to inform Stellar of her pole-dancing endeavor the previous night.

Would she be embarrassed if she knew what she did? Would it make her feel worse if she knew I liked it?

In the end, she shakes her head. "No, nothing too weird at all."

"Good..." She yawns and rubs her eyes. "Mm... I suppose we should both formally meet with Azzie before we head out to Sloth."

"Well, if you let me change out of my pajamas first, we can get going sooner than later this morning." Angelique is met with a nod, and she heads into the en-suite bathroom to change her clothes. With a wave of magic, her pajamas disappear and leave her uniform in their place. She exits the bathroom and motions toward the door. "Shall we?"

Stellar grabs the empty plates, places them on the cart, and follows closely behind Angelique. She occasionally clutches her head to try and fight back the last remnants of her hangover headache. They head down to the dining hall, where they find Asmodeus, Selene, Ryver, and Haley all seated around the large table.

"There you are!" Haley cheers. "We were wondering if you went too hard last night."

"I was beginning to wonder that, myself," Stellar grumbles softly. "How much trouble did I get into?"

"Nothing too terrible, I promise," Asmodeus coos. "The worst you did was give your friend here a private show."

Angelique's face burns, and as Stellar turns to stare at her in shock, she can't help but look away.

"I did what?" the death demon gasps, horror in her voice. "Why didn't you tell me?"

"I... I didn't want you to be embarrassed. It's not like you did anything inappropriate, so there's nothing to worry about."

Stellar heaves a sigh, her tail wrapping around her leg as she digs through her mental library for the situation she doesn't fully remember. "Alright... So long as I didn't make you uncomfortable."

Angelique looks back to her companion and brushes their hands against one another. "I would let you know if you did something upsetting to me," she assures, "I promise."

"Alright, lovebirds," Selene laughs, "Take a seat so we can talk with Azzie like you wanted."

Angelique fights back a flustered, embarrassed retort as she and Stellar sit at the dining table. They settle into their seats and turn their attention to Asmodeus, who smiles with a combination of sweetness and knowing.

"Is this about the angelic traces?" she asks.

Stellar frowns worriedly. "Let me guess, they've already been found leaving the sector?"

Asmodeus nods. "Yes... They were faint, but I believe the traces were headed for the Sloth Sector."

"Then I suppose it's a good thing we're going to Sloth after this," Angelique cuts in. Her gaze lands on the ink-black coloring of her companion's arms, and a concerned frown forms on her lips. "I'm really worried about your arms, Stellar..."

The Death Demon responds with a dismissive wave of her hand. "Like you said, we're already going to be heading to Sloth. King Belphegor should be able to help with this."

"Oh, since you're off to see Belphie, can you tell them I'll send another shipment of herbs next week? I know they were waiting for some dried chamomile for their relaxing tea."

"Sure thing, Azzie. And thank you for breakfast. It really helped the hangover." She stands and exits the dining hall, tail lashing a bit as she walks.

"Have fun and be safe!" Asmodeus calls, turning her gaze from the door to Angelique.

"We will," the angel agrees, also standing from the table and leaving the room. As she walks through the halls, the stained-glass windows display colorful floral patterns on the floors. Once she catches up to her companion, Angelique latches onto her wrist. "Stellar?"

The demon pauses in her steps, barely looking over her shoulder to the angel. "What is it?"

"Are you okay? You seem really upset—"

"My hangover's not completely gone yet and I'm frustrated. It feels like we're running all over Hell on a wild goose chase and making no progress." Her tail lashes again as she speaks.

Angelique frowns deeper, more worries encasing her heart. "I know what you mean," she confesses, "But... It's nice to be spending time with you and learning about your home. If you hadn't invited me to come with you, I'd still be wary of demons and know nothing about Hell." She steps in front of Stellar so their eyes can more easily meet. "So, even if this chase is for nothing right now, I have to thank you for everything."

Stellar looks into Angelique's eyes. "You mean that, Angel?"

"Of course I do. I'm not a good liar, remember?"

She's suddenly wrapped in strong, warm arms and held close to the demon. Thanks to the tight hug, she can clearly feel Stellar's gentle laughing and quiet purrs. As soon as her body relaxes into the embrace, she wraps her own arms around the demon's waist, holding her close in response.

"Alright, let's go to Sloth and see what else we can find," Stellar declares once the hug breaks, "I'll even let you worry about me once we're there."

"Deal!" Angelique cheers, brightening at the offer of caring for her companion.

After another subway ride, Angelique and Stellar step out into the region of Sloth. Similar to Aria of the Lust Sector aside from the lower humidity, trees and other plants can be seen all throughout the Sloth Sector's capital city of Caister. They make their way through the sweet-smelling streets and take note of the various pharmacies and herb shops scattered throughout the streets.

"It smells so fresh here..." Angelique murmurs as they look around the city. "But not the same type of floral freshness from Lust. Does that make sense?"

Stellar nods, tail wagging lazily behind her. "Yes, because there's a more medicinal, herbal smell instead of the sweet scents of flowers. It's less aromatic but more relaxing."

"Yes! Exactly!" They continue through the city, watching as demons enter the pharmacies in search of their medications. "Do you ever take other medicine, Stellar?"

"Well..." She sighs. "I probably should, since there might be some medicines that could help with my corruption and other issues, but I don't exactly... Remember to take anything."

A frown makes its way onto Angelique's face. "Why not?"

"My memory isn't great, especially when my focus hones in on my hobbies... Or at least, the hobbies I used to participate in."

"You don't have any hobbies anymore?"

She hugs herself with an arm. "My art wasn't very good, I never finished any writing, and I don't have the attention span to read books anymore. Sometimes I play music on my guitar, but even that's losing its spark, so I've been throwing myself into my work."

"Is that why you were spending so much time on Earth with King and Spyr and... Well, me?"

She nods.

"Well... If you wouldn't mind, I'd like to see some of your old works. Maybe if you get a fresh pair of eyes, you'll want to take up your old hobbies again." Angelique smiles, a pleading expression to her eyes. "Please?"

Stellar's cheeks turn pink as she glances away, huffing. "Alright, fine. When we get back home, I'll dig around and see what of my old art and writing I may have saved. If I'm lucky, I won't have destroyed too many of my more recent works..."

"You destroy your art?!" Angelique squeaks.

"If I hate it enough, yeah. If it's a digital piece, I delete the file from my computer. The only catch is that I have an external hard drive with automatic backups of everything, even the ones I get rid of."

The angel brightens. "Wait, so you might still have some stuff to show me? I can't wait!"

The two of them cling to each other as they continue down the street, hands intertwined. After a while, they reach a large hospital, which makes Angelique freeze in her steps.

Why am I freaking out? This isn't like the last time I was at a hospital... I haven't been decapitated again—

"You okay?" Stellar asks, breaking her out of her panic. "You look like you just saw a ghost."

"Ah... I... Um..."

It takes a few moments for Stellar to think, at which point her eyes widen. "Wait, you were in a hospital not too long ago, right?"

The angel brings her free hand to her ribbon-covered neck. As her trembling fingertips touch the silky fabric, she flinches from how cold they are. "I... I can't..."

"It's okay. Let's find somewhere away from here to sit; we can talk about what's going through your head and your adrenaline system."

They scurry away from the hospital and take a seat in a nearby cafe. After ordering drinks and snacks, Stellar helps Angelique sit in a chair with her back to the window, hiding the hospital from her view. "So, do you want us to sit here in the quiet for a bit, or are you okay with me asking a few questions?"

Angelique stares at the small iced mocha latte in her hands. "You can ask questions. I'll be okay."

Stellar takes a sip of her fruity smoothie. "Do you know why you froze outside the hospital?"

"I don't know. Maybe?"

"It's perfectly fine if you don't. Has this happened to you before?"

"No. This is the first time."

"What was running through your head when you froze up?"

"... I was wondering why I couldn't move. I kept telling myself that I didn't get hurt this time, so I shouldn't be afraid..."

"So it's a trauma response," the death demon notes.

"What? Why would I have a trauma response at a hospital?" Angelique asks, confused.

The demon gives her an unimpressed look as she takes another sip of her drink, her gaze flitting between Angelique's eyes and the pink ribbon wrapped around her neck. "The last time you were in a hospital, you were waking up from a *very* traumatic incident you couldn't remember."

"... Oh." Her face heats up, and she sips her latte in order to fill her embarrassed silence. "I... I guess that makes sense."

Stellar nods. "You don't remember going into the hospital the last time, and it turns out something horrible happened to you prior. Your body is afraid of something bad happening to you this time, and doesn't want you to lose another 100 years of memories."

"... Yeah," she agrees quietly, "I don't want to have lost another century of my life to an incident I don't remember."

"Anyone would feel the same way, Angel," the demon soothes. "Since Belphegor's most likely working in the hospital at the moment, I'll go in and see if I can schedule a meeting after they get out of work. That way, we can both attend."

"I don't want to abandon you," Angelique counters.

"You're not abandoning me, you're taking care of yourself. I'd much prefer you do *that* instead of acting tough and making your mental health worse."

Angelique sighs, defeated. "Alright, I suppose I'll take it easy..."

"Thank you. It means a lot to me." They spend about another ten minutes in the cafe so Stellar can finish her drink and snack. After she's emptied her cup, she stands. "I'll be back soon," she reassures, before turning on her heels and leaving the cafe.

Angelique takes another sip of her drink as her mind wanders. *At this rate, I'm Stellar's tag-along. I'm not doing anything productive for this mission. Maybe I shouldn't have come here to begin with...*

You're still learning about the cultures, a kind inner voice responds, *After all, Heaven seems to have a lot of facts about Hell all wrong.*

I guess, but how would I go about telling people in Heaven the truth? If I'm not careful, I could get banished and end up here permanently...

Would that truly be so bad?

She nearly chokes on her latte and coughs harshly to keep from inhaling her drink. Once her coughing fit has stopped, she finishes off her raspberry pastry. As she clears her tiny plate and carefully sips the final remnants of her coffee, Stellar enters the cafe and makes a beeline over to her.

"Our after-hours appointment has been made. They'll be expecting us at the Palace of Sloth later this evening. While we're there, they'll take me in for a check-up on my corruption to see how fast it's progressing and if there's anything they can supply to slow it down."

"Thank you for setting everything up. Will we be staying at the palace, or...?"

Stellar pauses, tail lashing a bit as she stares at her companion. "... I completely forgot to ask."

Angelique bursts into giggles, smiling brightly. "Aw, you're so cute when you're forgetful!"

The demon huffs, face reddening as she crosses her darkened arms across her chest. "Yeah, yeah, I'm sure. How about we go wander around until it's time to meet with Belphie?"

"So long as we stay away from the hospital, I won't have a problem with it."

"Deal."

The two women venture around the city, admiring the colorful herbal gardens and taking in the sweet, delicate smells. They take the time to relax at a bathhouse run by a kind, hybrid sloth and envy demon. When the sun begins to lower in the sky, they make their way to the Palace of Sloth.

The fence is made of wrought iron like at most of the other palaces, with large silver stars decorating several of the bars. The silver moons on the front gates are so well-cared for and polished that they shine with an almost mirror-like quality, to the point they nearly reflect their faces. Stellar pulls open the gates with ease and leads the way inside.

The entryway to the Palace of Sloth contains a garden, similar to the Palace of Lust. Medicinal herbs and plants frame the stone walkway up to the dimly-lit manor. The Princess of Death knocks firmly on the front door, tail swaying as she waits patiently for an answer.

They stand outside for only about two minutes before the door slowly opens, revealing a demonic servant with wrath demon horns and sloth demon eyes. "Can I help you?" they ask, voice meek and quiet.

"I am Princess Stellar of Death, and I spoke with King Belphegor earlier today about an appointment. Have they arrived home yet?"

"Ah, Princess Stellar! My apologies, I almost didn't recognize you. King Belphegor arrived home not too long ago, and I believe they are adjusting their attire to be a bit more... Comfortable."

"That's fine. It's not like my friend here and I are exactly... Dressed to the nines to meet them."

"Thank you for your understanding, Your Highness. Please, come in." They push the door open further, allowing the women entry into the palace. The hybrid demon leads the way through the palace, her short, hair-coated tail swaying back and forth rapidly as she walks. "Their Majesty was complaining about a migraine when they arrived, so if you could keep your meeting relatively quick, I believe that would be in everyone's best interest."

"Thank you for the warning; we'll try to keep this quick so they can rest," Stellar assures.

The hybrid demon servant leads them to a large room filled with carpet that tickles Angelique's toes. The room has more soft items throughout, most of which gather into a large mountain of pillows, blankets, and plush toys. The mound almost resembles a couch, based on the person-sized indent in the form. Thick cushioned seats are placed in front of the plush toy pile as opposed to stiff and uncomfortable chairs, which makes the casual atmosphere of the room blend well together. Stellar steps forward and takes a seat on one of the seats, her tail wrapping around the base as she settles in.

Angelique takes a seat on the other cushion as the servant shuts the door. "This is... An interesting throne room," the angel murmurs, admiring the decorations all around.

"Well, everyone tries to be accommodating to Belphegor so their illnesses don't get worse," Stellar explains. "As a chronically ill person myself, I can only imagine the relief they feel to be surrounded by so many who accommodate their plight."

It takes a moment for Angelique to comprehend Stellar's casual explanation. "... Your corruption is classified as a chronic illness, isn't it?"

The death demon sighs. "Yes. I've had it for a long time, and it never fully goes away. Most of the time, I'm able to manage it with treatment, but the stress of this mission has made it flare up a bit..."

"I'm so sorry," Angelique whispers, "If you need a break—"

Stellar laughs. "Man, I wish a break would be the relief I need! But as far as I've tested, rest doesn't help as much as I'd like it to... Besides, this mission could become a time-sensitive matter at any time, so I can't exactly go slow in order to stave off the inevitable flare-up."

"I see..." Angelique hugs herself a bit, rubbing her thumbs along her upper arms to try and calm her nerves.

Taking you on this mission and 'cultural exchange' is making her condition worse, the bitter voice in her head hisses. *You should run away so she doesn't have to deal with you along with everything else!*

She said it's not an issue, a softer voice counters, *A flare-up is going to happen whether we're here or not. If nothing else, we can help take care of her when she needs it.*

Just then, a door off to the left opens and a demon enters the room. They're wearing a cutely oversized lilac sweater over a black turtleneck tank top, with blue-and-purple buffalo-check pajama pants draping to the floor. Their feet are swallowed by large, fluffy, white slippers. A thick pillow in a fluffy pillowcase is tucked under their arm. Their long purple-and-silver hair is pulled into a messy braid that starts about halfway down the length, and their bangs drape around their short horns and into their tired, dark-rimmed purple eyes. Crescent moon shaped pupils also convey their exhaustion, but a small smile makes its way onto their face nonetheless.

"Thank you for your patience, Princess Stellar," they murmur in a deep, sleep-addled voice, "My shift at the hospital took a bit more out of me than I'd anticipated."

"I bet," she responds, her voice low in volume, "We heard you're dealing with a migraine..."

The demon nods, trudging over to the large pile of pillows and plush items. They practically throw their full weight into the mountain, laying on their side once they settle into the softness.

"I apologize for the rush," they continue, "But the sooner we get down to business, the sooner I can examine your arms and send you both on your way, and the sooner I can go fight off this migraine in the darkness of my room."

"Of course, Your Majesty," Stellar responds. She looks over to Angelique. "How about you ask the questions this time, Angel?"

Angelique turns her full attention to the King of Sloth. "Have you heard about the angelic traces that have been sensed around Hell?"

"I have not been made aware that the traces have been all around Hell, but I know the traces of which you speak."

"In the other Sectors, the royals were not aware of the traces until they were already leaving the Sector..."

Belphegor nods. "The traces found here were sensed in the direction of the Greed Sector."

Angelique turns back to Stellar. "Then we're still on track."

The Princess of Death hums. "I suppose you're right, but I still don't like that we're losing the culprit because of my illness."

"If your corruption is acting up, Your Highness, then it's good for you to come get examined and treated," Belphegor interrupts. They turn onto their side and sit up, beckoning the other demon to come closer. "Speaking of, you mentioned it was getting worse. Let me have a look at you, no glamor spells allowed."

Stellar sighs, but stands and approaches the King of Sloth. She holds out her fully ink-black hands, a bit apprehensive as they examine her. They have her flex her fingers, extend her arms, and roll her shoulders, before they let out a thoughtful hum.

"Your corruption is past your elbow already..." they murmur. They turn their tired gaze to Angelique. "How long has this been worsening?"

"Uh..." She thinks back to when she was first informed of her companion's condition at The Gemstone Diner. "... Ever since we started investigating this case, it's gotten worse. I first noticed it back in the Pride Sector, about a week ago."

The final comment makes Belphegor's eyebrows furrow in concern. "Less than ten days, and it's gotten this bad..." They sigh. "You need to take time to care for yourself. *And* take your pain medication, but I know how you are when it comes to remembering your pills."

"I don't *have* time to relax; I'm working on a case right now!"

"If you don't take the time, your body will *make* the time. You don't want this to get to *that* point again, do you?"

Stellar's back grows rigid at the implications, and her tail lashes harshly enough to nearly crack the air like a well-swung whip. Angelique, however, looks between the two of them in confusion.

"Stellar, what are they talking about?" she asks, voice small. When she's not given an answer, her tone changes to reflect her frantic worry.

"It is something Stellar will have to tell you herself. I will not divulge my patient's conditions and trauma," Belphegor says.

Her blood runs cold at the King's words. "Trauma? I thought corruption was like any other illness, what does trauma have to do with—?"

"It's fine, Angel," Stellar says, turning back to face her companion with a well-crafted emotional mask. "I'm fine. It's just... Not something I want to talk about right now."

The angel fights down the urge to argue as worry gnaws at her. "Okay. You'll tell me when you're ready, though, right?"

"I make no promises, but I can tell you that I'll try." She turns on her heels. "Come on. We have our answers, so we'd best make Greed our next stop." Before she leaves, she looks over her shoulder at Belphegor. "Thank you again, Doc. I'll... I'll see what I can do to mitigate this."

"Might I recommend stopping at a pharmacy for some pain medication?"

Stellar groans, but nods in agreement. "Yeah, we'll... We'll make a stop somewhere."

"Good. If you need anything else, Princess Stellar, do not hesitate to stop in."

Stellar leaves the room in a hurry. Angelique bids Belphegor an equally-hurried farewell and gives chase to her companion.

"Stellar!"

Her voice doesn't make her companion slow down, however. In fact, her name being called almost makes her walk away even faster than before. The angel frowns at the realization and dashes forward, grabbing tightly at a darkened wrist.

Stellar wrenches her arm out of Angelique's grasp and latches onto her wrist in exchange, only freezing and loosening her iron grip when the angel lets out a startled yelp. "Angel..."

"Are you okay?" Angelique interrupts.

"... Huh?"

"What Belphegor said freaked you out, so I wanted to make sure you were okay." She gently pulls her arm from the barely-there touch and wraps her arms around the demon's shoulders in a tight hug. She buries her face into Stellar's shoulder as she whispers her next words. "No matter what they were talking about, or if you're *ever* ready to tell me about it, I'll always be here for you. It's all going to be okay."

Hesitant arms snake around the angel's waist and hug her close. "... I know," she murmurs, nuzzling her face into Angelique's long, dark hair. "I just... There were memories, and it scared me. I didn't..."

"Shh, it's okay. If you're not ready to talk about it right now, I'm not going to push you. I want you to remember that I'm here, whenever you are."

They loosen their holds on each other enough to pull back and look into each other's eyes.

"... Promise it didn't freak you out?"

"I was more worried for *you* than myself. Promise me you'll be gentle with yourself?"

"... I promise to *try*."

"You know what? I'll take it." She squeezes her hand reassuringly. "Now, let's go get some food, grab *you* some medicine, and take a rest for the night. We'll be on our way to Greed tomorrow morning."

Stellar leads the way to a nearby restaurant, where they sit for a quick dinner. As they eat, Angelique watches Stellar's stiff movements and finds the ability to fight back her worry wavering. "Are you sure you're okay?" she asks quietly, her voice barely above a whisper.

Stellar nods, swirling the mashed potatoes and gravy around to make a creamy slurry on her plate. "Yeah, I'm fine. Doctor's visits always make my body go out of whack for a bit."

"Alright..."

Stellar shrugs. "At least Belphie doesn't treat me any differently based on my weight."

"... Huh?"

"Yeah. A lot of doctors don't take overweight people seriously when they come in for an issue. They usually suggest weight loss and call it a day... Luckily, with Belphie in charge, that's a rare occurrence."

"That's good, at least..." Angelique sips at her cup of water, unsure of how to continue the quiet conversation. "And... I'm glad you're okay."

"Thank you. Your protectiveness means a lot to me," Stellar murmurs.

"You're my friend; I will always worry about you."

It only takes about another fifteen minutes for them to finish their meals, pay the tab, and make their way out of the restaurant. Stellar once again leads the way down the street toward the nearest pharmacy and through the aisles to the pain relief section. Oddly enough, none of the bottles are marked by a simpler, brand name; instead, they've got the full, generic names of the medications written on the labels instead. The only way to tell them apart is by the color of the caps, and how the bottles are neatly sorted into sections labeled with ailments such as "joint pain," "stomach ache," and "headache/migraine."

Angelique stares at the bottles of medications, completely lost. "How do you know what to get?"

Stellar grabs a red-capped bottle from the "joint pain" section of shelves. "A lot of the system is similar to how it works back on Earth. The over-the-counter medicines are easy to find, and the prescription drugs are locked behind the counter. Once the pharmacist verifies the dosage and stuff with the doctor, they're able to answer questions and dispense the medicine the patient needs."

"So branded medicine just... Doesn't exist?"

"Nope. King Belphegor has a philosophy that companies shouldn't control medicine, so they also created a universal health-care system; that way, nobody can be denied the care they need to either save their life or help improve its quality."

"Interesting..." Angelique murmurs, "I know Heaven has a lot of different companies that help make medicine and other things... It never occurred to me that they might all be the same ingredients."

Stellar laughs. "The same thing happens to humans. They consider 'brand names' more reputable than the nameless medications, but they all work pretty much the same. The only differences would sometimes be the additional ingredients."

"And demons are accustomed to this system?"

"Pretty much. If a new demon were to come in, it could be a bit of a learning curve, but overall it's pretty easy." Stellar grabs a small bottle of water and leads the way to the pharmacy counter, where she places both bottles onto the surface. A sloth demon turns to greet them.

"Hello," they greet, "Is this going to be everything?"

"Yes, please."

The pharmacist scans the bottles and Stellar passes them a small handful of shiny silver coins. They take the money, place it in the register, and pass the bottles back across the counter. "Thank you so much; have a lovely day."

"You, too," Stellar responds, turning around to face Angelique. She opens the bottle of pain medicine, rips off the paper covering the mouth of the bottle, pulls out two pills, and cracks open the water bottle. She slams back the medicine and chases it with the entire miniature bottle of water, letting out a sigh of relief once it's empty. "There; now I've taken my medicine, which should appease both you and Belphie."

Angelique laughs and nudges Stellar with her shoulder. "Good. Now, let's head to a hotel and get some rest."

"Yes, yes," Stellar teases, using a small burst of magic to make the medicine bottle disappear from her hand. "Let's go rest."

They make their way to a nearby hotel and check into a room for the night. Once they find their room, they change into their pajamas and curl up in the large bed, wrapped in the warm covers. As they lay only a few inches from each other, Angelique could swear she heard the rapid thumping of the demon's heartbeat. They remain curled close to one another for a while, relaxing into each other's company. Before long, Stellar presses her face into her pillow, a smile on her face as she falls asleep thanks to the comforting quietness between them. It doesn't take long before Angelique also falls asleep.

As she drifts through a dreamless sleep once again, she feels a familiar presence emanating from behind her. She turns to find the figure of Aurora hovering in the darkness. Her old partner's eyes, however, are still shrouded in the darkness under her bangs.

"Aurora!" she cheers, floating over to her, *"It's so good to see you again! I've missed you!"*

"I've missed you, too, Angie," the other angel responds, taking Angelique's hands in her own. *"You're still not forgetting me, right?"*

"Never! I could never forget you!" As soon as the words leave her mouth, though, she notices Aurora's hair is shorter than it was the last time she saw her in a dream. Her messy brunette hair now falls only to her shoulders, and her bangs are longer than they had been at their previous encounter. *"What..."*

"You're not forgetting me... Right, Angie?"

"No! No, no, I'm not! You, uh... You changed your hair!"

"You're not... Replacing me, right?"

"No! I would never..."

The visage of Aurora pulls her hands from Angelique's grasp. *"If you say so... I'll keep waiting for you, Angie."*

"Thank you, Aurora. I promise, it won't be long before we see each other again!"

"I'll hold you to that."

Angelique slowly wakes, unsure of what time it is. One glance to the clock on the opposite wall shows her that it's currently one o'clock in the morning, which makes her groan. She shuts her eyes, trying desperately to fall back asleep, until she registers a pair of arms wrapped around her waist. She startles a bit, her eyes immediately opening and locking onto a blue-purple gaze.

"Wha— Stellar?"

"Why are you awake?" the demon whispers.

"I don't know!" she huffs, "Why are *you* awake?"

"Bad dream."

"... Oh. Are you okay?"

She shrugs, unable to meet Angelique's eyes. "My mind's traveling a million miles an hour, and it can't settle. I have my share of skeletons I'd prefer to keep hidden in the closet, you know?" She lays one of her corruption-darkened hands between their bodies. "That fact is painfully obvious, thanks to this."

"We'll keep an eye on it," Angelique assures her.

"Mm... Thank you." The demon presses close enough for her face to almost become buried in the junction of Angelique's neck and shoulder.

"Uh... Stellar?"

Before she can get more of her question out, she receives her answer in the form of a gentle purring that resonates from the demon's chest and throat. The soft, soothing vibrations travel through her body. Before she knows it, she's nuzzling her cheek against Stellar's head.

"Mm..." the demoness murmurs against her shoulder.

Angelique lets out quiet giggles. "You're like a clingy cat," she comments.

"You enjoy it, right?"

"I don't mind you being cuddly, if that's what you mean."

"Then is this really an issue?"

"I never said it was," the angel huffs.

"Good," Stellar murmurs. Before the demon pulls away from her, Angelique could swear she felt a pair of soft, warm lips press a kiss to the back of her neck. A shiver spreads down her spine and across her shoulders as a heat forms in her cheeks. The angel's attention diverts to watch as the demon stands and extends her arms high above her head, groaning with the stretch.

"While I'm awake, I may as well use the bathroom. Try to get back to sleep, okay?"

"I'll do my best, but I make no promises."

Stellar chuckles. "That's my line."

"I know. You don't mind if I borrow it, do you?"

"Not at all."

"Good." As her brain settles, she finds herself still awake when Stellar comes back from the en-suite. "I figured out why I woke up at this hour."

"Oh? And why would that be?"

"I guess I'm still mad at myself for yesterday. I wasn't able to enter the hospital to talk to King Belphegor, which caused us a delay and now we may have fallen even further behind the traces we've been tracking."

Stellar climbs under the covers and grabs one of Angelique's hands in a tight, comforting grip. "You don't have to be mad at yourself for having a panic attack. It's a natural response when it comes to fear and trauma. I'd never want to put you through a scary situation like that if I could help it."

"But... Your corruption doesn't keep you from doing your job."

"Not *always,*" Stellar clarifies. "There are plenty of days where my pain level makes it harder to work. I tend to push through, but... Some days I can't force myself."

The angel settles at the demon's words. As her stress levels slowly ebb away, she finds a heaviness overtaking her eyelids. "Ngh... I want to stay up with you..."

"If your body wants to go back to sleep, don't fight it, Angel," Stellar soothes, "I'll make my way back to dreamland, and I'll see you bright and early in the *actual* morning."

"Alright... We'll head to Greed."

"Exactly." She leans in close and nuzzles their noses together. "So good night, my dear."

Sixteen
Family Values

Sure enough, as the morning light streams gently through the curtains, Angelique finds Stellar already getting ready to head out for the day. The demon stretches out like a cat, soft groans escaping her as she arches her back. Angelique blushes, admiring her companion as the demon summons a wave of magic to transform her pajamas into her daily attire.

Stellar turns back around to neaten up her side of the bed, but pauses upon noticing the angel's wakefulness. "Good morning, lovely!" she coos, tail beginning to wag. "Did you sleep well?"

"I did. When did you get back to sleep?"

"I'm pretty sure it was sometime between one-thirty and two o'clock."

"Oh, so it wasn't that bad."

"Not at all. Once you're ready to go, shall we head to Greed?"

"Yes!" Angelique yelps, surging to a sitting position, "We need to get back on track!"

Angelique dresses in her uniform, and they make their way out into the busy streets of the Sloth Sector. They make a quick pit stop for breakfast before heading to the subway station. Once there, they take a seat on a nearby bench and wait patiently for the next available train to the Greed Sector, sipping their drinks all the while. As they sit, Angelique leans her head on Stellar's shoulder.

"So, what do I need to know about the Greed Sector?" she asks, swirling the latte in her hand.

"Greed is full of businesses, similar to Pride," Stellar explains. "Though instead of it being filled with artisans, it's full of shops that sell appliances, home goods, and repair services."

"I see..." Angelique sips her drink until another memory crosses her mind. "Wait, King Mammon endorsed the DHA, right?"

"He did. He heard about King and Spyr's efforts and goals and decided to endorse them so other earth-wandering demons know they're an official safe haven in the human realm."

Angelique frowns worriedly at her almost-empty coffee cup. "It makes me sad that demons need to be protected just for existing. I wish everyone could get along in peace..."

"Well, in order for everyone to coexist, Heaven would need to stop spreading rumors that say we're horrible people."

"I know..." She sighs. "I wish I could help, but I doubt anyone in Heaven will listen to me. Nobody ever does..."

"I do," Stellar counters.

"Well, you're different. Nobody *up there* does."

"I'm sure your partner did."

Angelique pauses at the mention of Aurora, her heart suddenly climbing into her throat. "... I know she did. She would always tell me I had a lovely voice, and she could listen to me for hours."

The demon hums into her hot chocolate. "It sounds like she was in love with you."

"I'm not so sure..."

Stellar's eyes glimmer with amusement. "Well, once you find her, you'll have to ask her about it. She might have cared for you more than you know."

Angelique smiles weakly. "I'll keep that in mind."

It isn't much longer before the subway train pulls into the station and opens its doors, beckoning awaiting passengers to board. Angelique and Stellar throw away their empty drink cups and hop on, easily finding open seats in the car. The ride to the Greed Sector isn't very long—only about an hour and a half—before the train stops again and they're allowed to disembark into the capital city of Langdale.

The city, as expected, is booming with business. Shops filled with home decor, appliances, and repair tools line the streets. Small, family-run businesses can also be found between the larger shops, and each of them have clients leaving satisfied.

"Greed is a very productive sector," Angelique murmurs, amazed by the busy streets.

"You could say that again," Stellar chuckles. "Greed is the business hub of Hell, after all."

They wander through the city until they make their way to the gates of the Palace of Greed. The gates themselves look incredibly high-tech, with luminous screens spanning the distance between each of the silver, tower-like rods. The screens are lit by bright LEDs, which display shadow-like forms in a pastel rainbow of colors as the demoness and angel approach.

"Oh, whoa!" Angelique gasps as the colorful shadows appear on the gate's screen, "This is so cool!" She moves around, watching in awe as the LEDs track her movements and display her rainbow-colored reflection accordingly.

Stellar laughs as she watches her angelic companion dance around in order to make the LEDs shine back at them. "You're like a kid in a candy store," she giggles, tail wagging. The movement reflects in the screens before them, bringing Angelique's attention to it even more.

"Uh-huh, and I'm sure you've never done something like this before?" she counters playfully, attempting a cute pout despite the broad smile on her face.

"Absolutely not. I've always been mature for my age," she jokes back, laughing more. She grabs onto one of the sleek silver handles in the center of the gate and pulls, opening it easily. They slip inside as the gate shuts behind them, leaving them in the small garden. They make their way through, occasionally admiring the bright foliage, until they reach the front door of the Palace of Greed. Stellar knocks heavily on the front doors, announcing her presence to the occupants inside.

Instead of a servant, however, the doors open to a man with a blood red, pirate-style blouse and black business slacks that skim close to his legs. His long, wavy, black hair is pulled into a messy bun, with a few loose strands drooping into his face from around his curled horns. His sunset-colored eyes widen in surprise upon seeing the two women standing before him.

"Stellar? What are you doing here?" he asks, voice tinged with surprise and confusion.

"Oh, hey, Malek," Stellar greets casually, "We're here to speak to your father, if that's alright?"

"Oh, actually—"

"Auntie Stellar!" a small voice cheers. A young girl who can't be older than six races out the door and crashes into Stellar's legs, beaming. Her messy black curls are pulled into a half-up style and tied with a lavender ribbon, and her matching lavender lolita-style dress fluffs out behind her as she stands on her tiptoes to hug as much of the Princess of Death as she can. Her vibrant red-and-pink eyes shine up at the two women as she greets them with a toothy smile.

"Oh, hey, Lilia!" Stellar greets, patting the young girl's head. "How are you doing?"

"Good!" She giggles, her inverted-star-shaped pupils dilating as she looks at the Princess of Death. She turns back to Malek, still clinging to the demoness' legs. "Papa, can I play with Auntie Stellar?"

The man heaves a dramatic sigh, but opens the door wider in an invitation to the sudden guests. "I suppose you can, if it's alright with her."

Lilia's attention immediately snaps back to Stellar with large, pleading eyes. "Pleeease, Auntie Stellar?"

The demoness laughs and nods. "Yes, we can go play," she agrees, grabbing Lilia from under her arms and picking her up. She easily props the young girl on her hip and slips into the Palace of Greed. Angelique stands awkwardly for a moment before also stepping inside.

"I don't believe we've met before, Miss," Malek begins, "I take it you're a friend of Stellar's?"

"Um... Yes, I am; my name is Angelique. Stellar and I are working on a case together, so she's showing me around Hell while we're working."

"I see," he muses, almost humming, "Well, if Stellar deems you safe to be around, then I will not argue with her. She of all people knows her intuition the best."

"People keep mentioning that about her," Angelique notes, "What do they mean?"

"She isn't known as the Executioner for nothing." He turns and leads the way through the Palace of Greed. "She is ruthless when she finds someone untrustworthy. From what I've heard, she's been known to attack first and ask questions later, in some cases."

"That's... A bit dangerous, isn't it?"

He hums in thought. "Honestly, it could be, but sometimes people are brought here and not turned into imps when they probably should be. When they're *barely* spared, she keeps a special watch over them. If it turns out her intuition is right—which it almost always is—she will neutralize the threat before making a report to King Elias."

"Oh, wow... She must keep good tabs on people, if she's able to figure those sorts of things out... Especially if they're spared by the skin of their teeth."

"She is." Malek's arrow-tipped tail sways from side to side as they approach a large sitting area. Despite not knowing all the differences between the subspecies of demons, Angelique's brows furrow in confusion at the presence of so many pride demon features on an inhabitant of the Palace of Greed.

"Please pardon me if I come across as rude, but are you a pride demon?" she asks.

Malek's pointed ears twitch and his tail perks up at the inquiry. "You're quite observant, aren't you? Yes, I'm a pride demon. My daughter is, too."

"I see..."

"I'm sure you're curious as to why the two of us are living here at the Palace of Greed?" he offers with a knowing glint to his eyes; as she takes a better look, Angelique notices that they, also, convey his pride demon ancestry thanks to his inverted-star-shaped pupils.

"Um... Yes, but I don't mean to insinuate anything. I'm just curious," she clarifies quickly, suddenly struggling to swallow around an anxious lump in her throat.

Malek chuckles, tail wagging at the sound. "I don't mind answering your question; it's a simple answer, after all. I'm the Prince of Greed."

"... Wait, what?"

"I'm the Prince of Greed," he repeats, "Mammon adopted me when I was young, and since he has never had any plans to take a spouse or have any biological children, he has raised me as his own."

"And Lilia is..."

"She's my daughter. I adopted her two years ago, when she was four."

"How lovely!" Angelique cheers.

"I do. In fact, I should go find my husband... He should be in his studio."

"Your husband is an artist?" she guesses.

"He is!" Malek beams brightly, "He's very talented; you should see some of their work! I... I will admit, it may sound awfully self-centered of me, since I have been his muse for a while, but I promise you won't be disappointed!"

"It's not self-centered to enjoy being a loved one's source of inspiration," she counters, "I'd love to see his art."

The Prince of Greed brightens even more at the sincerity in the angel's voice. "I'll see if I can snag one of his most recent paintings. Maybe they'll even be willing to take a break once I explain we have guests."

"I'd love to meet them, if they want. In the meantime, I'll sit with Stellar and Lilia."

"Thank you. I shouldn't be long." He turns and scurries down another hallway, tail whipping around joyfully at the prospect of showing off his husband and their artwork.

Angelique smiles to herself at the sight of a husband excited to brag about and show off his spouse. *That hardly ever happens in Heaven...* she muses silently as she steps into the living room. Once her attention turns to the large space before her, which is lit warmly by the massive floor-to-ceiling windows, her gaze catches on Stellar and Lilia. The older demoness is holding the giggling young girl snugly against her stomach, grinning as Lilia laughs.

"Again, again!"

"Alright. A-one, a-two, and... Dip!" She leans forward, still holding the young demon against her. Lilia throws her head back, her messy black curls flying wildly around her face as her body hangs upside-down. She even hangs her arms above her head, like one would while riding on a roller coaster. She bursts into bright laughter and uncontrollable giggles as Stellar sways her from side-to-side.

Angelique freezes in the doorway, a bright blush making its way onto her face as she watches the two demons interact. The way Stellar interacts so easily with Lilia, a child so young... It makes a pleasant heat form in her lower stomach, and her thoughts travel to a universe where Heaven and Hell aren't at each other's throats.

She thinks of herself chatting with Stellar as they hold a young, dark-haired girl and a small baby swaddled in a baby-blue blanket close to their bodies, cuddling close and acting like a family.

She's abruptly ripped from her fantasy, however, when Stellar's surprised voice reaches her ears.

"Oh, crap, did I leave you behind with Malek?" the older demoness guesses, bringing Lilia back to an upright position and cradling her against her body. "Sorry, I always get distracted when there are little kids around... They're so fun, you know?"

"Yeah... Yeah, I get it." Angelique clears her throat, embarrassment burning even hotter at her cheeks. "Malek went to fetch his husband, but I have a question to ask before they return."

Stellar's pointed ears twitch curiously at the mention of the question, but she keeps a smile on her face as she sets Lilia back onto the floor. The little girl scurries off to play with a nearby dollhouse, at which point Stellar turns her attention back to Angelique. "What's your question?"

"I... Well, when Malek was talking about his husband, he'd sometimes use 'he,' but other times he'd use 'they.' Is that... Normal?"

Stellar nods. "Yeah, I'd say so, considering Lyric is nonbinary. I am too, and I like to use gender-neutral pronouns— but most people call me 'she' since I don't correct them."

The heat in her cheeks drains quickly as a lump forms in Angelique's throat. "... Wait, have I been misgendering you this whole time?" she asks quietly, her voice overtaken by horror at the sudden revelation.

Stellar shrugs, obviously unbothered by the issue. "I mean... Yeah, I'm nonbinary, but I don't mind what people call me so long as I'm not called 'he.' I look like a girl, some days I feel like a girl... So it's fine."

"Would you prefer if I use gender-neutral pronouns for you, too?"

"Like I said, so long as people don't call me 'he,' I don't care what people call me."

Angelique puffs out her cheeks in a cute pout. "That's not what I asked."

"Look, before I became a demon, I was only ever referred to as 'she,' so it doesn't exactly matter to me. I know people will keep calling me that even if I choose to correct them, so I've grown accustomed to it." She looks over to where Lilia is playing with her dolls. "It's not exactly easy to explain to someone when I'm having a gender-neutral day."

"Well... What do your more gender-neutral days feel like?"

The Princess of Death snorts at the inquiry. "They're the days that I don't want to be perceived. I want to just... Turn into goo, hide in the shadows, and not be acknowledged."

"Ah..." Angelique frowns. "Well, that's a bit hard to do with your status..." She places her hands on her hips. "I'll use gender-neutral pronouns for you more often, then, so you can be comfortable no matter what!"

"You don't have to," Stellar counters.

"I know I don't *have* to. I want to! You're my friend, and I want you to be as comfortable as possible around me. You don't have to pretend to be a girl all the time 'just because it's easier.'"

The demon stares at her for a moment, surprised at the easy acceptance. "... I suppose you have a point," they muse, "So I'll let it slide this time. Next time, I may not back down so easily."

"You say that, but I'm starting to think you have a soft spot for me," the angel giggles.

"And what would you do if I did?"

Angelique freezes, taken aback by the question. "... Huh?"

"You heard me." Stellar leans in close, with her hands tucked behind her back. "What would you do if I said I *did* have a soft spot for you?"

She blushes, glancing away as she grows more flustered. "Well... Consider it a gift, since you're known for your flawless intuition?"

Stellar pulls back, a bright laugh escaping them. "I like your answer!"

Just then, the doors to the living room open. Lilia looks over from her spot on the floor and beams. She scurries to her feet and races over to where Malek and a blonde human are standing. "Papa! Daddy!"

The latter picks her up easily and cradles her close to his body. They're wearing a loose white blouse similar in style to Malek, but with the sleeves rolled up to expose their elbows. A pair of high-waisted black pants covers their legs, and the bottoms of his bare feet are colored in pale hues of dried paint. Long, wavy, blonde hair is pulled back and fastened into place by a large claw clip.

"Miss Angelique, this is my husband, Lyric. Lyric, this is the young lady I was telling you about," Malek introduces.

"It's a pleasure to meet you," the blonde greets, his voice quiet and smooth. Their gaze shifts over to Stellar, and a wider smile forms on his face. "It's lovely to see you again, Princess Stellar."

The princess laughs softly. "You know you don't need to address me so formally, Lyric."

He huffs. "I want to make a good impression on your friend!"

"Trust me, Angelique and I are *incredibly* casual. I haven't heard her call me 'Princess' since she learned my title," she teases.

"Wha— You never told me you wanted me to—!" Angelique argues, only to cut herself off as her face flares hot in embarrassment. "... You're picking on me, aren't you?"

"Yes I am," Stellar giggles, "You know I *prefer* when people are casual with me."

"Right... And you'd tell me if you wanted me to call you by your title."

"Exactly. Good girl." She wraps an arm around Angelique's waist and tugs her into a lopsided hug. Their attention diverts back to the family standing before them. "So, why don't we take a seat and discuss what we came here for?"

"Yes, that's a good idea," Malek agrees, turning to his husband. "Do you mind playing with Lilia while we talk shop?"

"Not at all, my love." Lyric turns to Lilia and smiles brightly. "Do you want to play together with your dolls, sweetie?"

"Yes!" the little girl cheers, dropping from the blonde's arms. She scurries over to her dollhouse once again, dragging Lyric behind her. They kneel in front of the toys and begin to play.

After taking a moment to admire his family, Malek takes a seat on one of the plush couches. "Have a seat, you two, and we'll get down to business."

Stellar and Angelique both sit on the couch across from Malek. Once everyone is situated, a young greed demon maid wanders in and pauses upon finding the visitors.

"Shall I prepare tea for everyone, Young Master?" she asks.

"If you don't mind! Thank you."

She curtsies and leaves. As soon as she's gone, Malek's attention snaps back to Stellar and Angelique. "If this matter is as important as it seems to be, I believe we should get into the discussion before she gets back."

"Agreed. Is your father here? He should hear this," Stellar murmurs.

"Ah... That's what I was trying to tell you at the front door. My dad is actually visiting with Aunt Bee."

Angelique perks up at the mention. "Oh, right; he and Beelzebub are twins!"

"I see Stellar has filled you in on a bit of the family tree," Malek snickers.

"Ah... Yes, she has."

"Good!" He leans back against the couch. "Then it will come to no surprise that he's visiting his sister."

"It doesn't surprise me at all; after all, he's a doting uncle, right?" Angelique asks.

"At least, that's the role he plays."

Angelique frowns. "You make it sound like he's an actor in a play..."

"Well, in a way, he is. He gets overstimulated easily around young children, but he doesn't want to outright ignore the little ones in my aunt's care, so he puts on a facade. He goes over bearing gifts like snacks and toys, spends time with the kids and does a check-in with Aunt Bee to make sure she has everything she needs. Once he's home, he crashes for a while."

"Ah... I understand. I'm easily overstimulated by crowds and screaming children, myself," Angelique confesses.

"Do you know how long your dad will be visiting Queen Bee?" Stellar asks, "We don't want to pass by him on our way there."

"He should be there for an extended visit this time, since Aunt Bee is looking into building a playground addition for the kids. Dad wants to make sure everything goes according to the schematics he and Aunt Bee have created. He'll be home in about a week, so if you decide to head to Gluttony after your visit here, he should still be there."

"That's good to know. Thank you, Malek."

The door opens and the young maid returns with her arms full. On her right arm, she carries a large tray of tea supplies, and in her left hand, she carries a small tower of sandwiches and sweets. She sets everything on the coffee table and pours three cups of tea. "I hope our guests enjoy hibiscus tea...?" she offers.

"I'm a fan," Stellar comments, taking a cup.

"I've never tried it," Angelique confesses, taking her own cup.

"If you don't like it, please let me know. I'll prepare a different type of tea you should enjoy." She curtsies before leaving the room once again.

Malek grabs a creamy egg salad sandwich and takes a bite before continuing the previous conversation. "So, what exactly is the business that brought you to our neck of the woods?"

"Ah... Well, about that—" Angelique begins.

"You might not want Lilia to hear this," Stellar cuts in, "I don't want her to be scared."

Malek frowns, eyes darting over to his husband and their daughter, who are playing out a domestic situation with two of Lilia's dolls. When he sees how excitedly the young demon plays, he turns back to the other women. "She's distracted enough that she shouldn't be able to fully listen in. Please, I implore you to continue."

"As you wish. There are rumors of an angel that has made its way into Hell, and there are traces throughout each of the sectors to corroborate the claims."

"An angel in Hell, huh..." His tail lashes. "I see. You two are looking for any information on the source of these traces, I take it?"

"Yes," Angelique confirms.

"Well, I'm sorry to say I've heard nothing about any angelic traces. While I can't speak for my dad, I'm sure he'd inform me if that was the case."

"Of course. Thank you anyway, Malek."

"If you two want to spend the night here, go ahead; but if you'd prefer to head over to Aunt Bee's palace and get right to business with the two of them, that's understandable, too."

The two women look to each other, meeting their eyes in an attempt to gauge the other's preferences. When they both see indifference in their gazes, they snort and look away, holding their stomachs as they burst into fitful giggles.

"We'll stay to finish off the tea and treats, and be on our way to Gluttony. Thank you for the offer, though, Malek," Stellar declares.

"I do want to see Lyric's paintings before we go," Angelique adds, "So long as it's no trouble."

"Of course! We'd be happy to show you around his studio." Malek beams and takes another bite of his sandwich. "Speaking of... My love, would you like some tea and sandwiches?"

"Ah, in a moment, darling!" they call over their shoulder. He turns back to Lilia, and they agree to put their respective dolls to bed. They come over and take a seat on the sofa next to Malek. Lyric cuddles into his side and Lilia sits comfortably at the Prince of Greed's other side. Lyric fills a cup of tea for themself and Lilia eyes a strawberry shortcake sandwich.

"Papa, can I have cake now?"

"You can have one piece," Malek coos, petting her head, "I don't want you to spoil your dinner."

"Thank you, Papa!" She takes a piece of cake and puts it on one of the small saucers. She munches happily on the sweet sandwich, getting a small dollop of cream on her nose in the process. Malek easily wipes it off, a bright grin on his face as he dotes on his daughter.

Angelique watches with soft eyes and finds a forlorn smile making its way onto her face. She quickly plasters on a happier expression, but can't help the feeling of Stellar's protective eyes on her.

After they finish their tea and sandwiches, of which Angelique had chosen one with ham, cheese, and a thin layer of dijon mustard, she and the demons all stand up.

"My art studio is right this way, Miss Angelique," Lyric says, heading to the doorway of the living room. They lead Angelique down a hallway and into a large studio, which has prepared canvases of varying size stacked to the left of the door. Several easels are spread throughout the studio, each with a drying painting perched on top of them.

Each of the paintings includes a figure that looks almost exactly like Malek, with tan skin, long dark hair, and glowing orange-and-teal eyes. They're even painted in a style reminiscent of classical romanticism paintings one would find in a museum on Earth. One of the paintings depicts the demon cradling the face of a long-haired blonde figure whose back is facing the viewer. Another shows him covered in draping red fabric and standing under a tree, holding an apple in one hand.

The most recent painting, however, depicts a domestic sight between Malek and an infant wrapped in a purple blanket, who's obviously meant as a stand-in for Lilia. The man is cradling the child in his arms, an incredibly fond expression on his face as the baby holds his index finger in an iron grip.

"These paintings are beautiful, Lyric..." Angelique whispers, mouth agape as she stares at each brush stroke lovingly and meticulously on the canvases.

"Ah, I'm glad you think so, Miss Angelique."

"Do you ever display these? I know Pride has art galleries..."

"I have once before, but it was a while ago. I've been debating whether or not I want to hold another showcase, since my inspiration clearly hasn't run out in the ways I expected it to."

"I think you should," a familiar voice suggests from the doorway to the studio. Stellar stands leaning against the doorframe with their hands tucked behind their back.

"You do?" the human asks.

"Of course. So long as you have the inspiration and aren't burning your candle at both ends, why not show your pieces to the world?"

Angelique hums to herself. *There they go again, giving art advice she probably needed to hear... I wish I could find some of her old artwork so I could see what she could do before they quit drawing.*

She snaps herself out of her thoughts when she's addressed by her companion.

"Now that you've seen Lyric's art, are you ready to go? I don't mean to rush you if you want to stay and chat for a bit."

"No, no, I'm ready to go." She turns to the blonde and smiles kindly. "It's been a pleasure to meet you and see your paintings, Lyric. I hope we can see each other again soon."

"As do I, Miss Angelique. It's been a pleasure."

Angelique hurries over to Stellar and takes their hand. They wave good-bye to Malek and his family as they leave the Palace of Greed, making a beeline for the nearest subway station.

Seventeen
Honey Barbecue

As they sit in the car of the next subway train, Angelique bounces her leg rapidly. She keeps her eyes on the scenery outside the window, but it does little to ease the anxiety coursing through her chest and arms. Thanks to her leg bouncing, she barely feels when a comforting hand is placed on her thigh until a firm squeeze yanks her out of her head.

"Is everything okay?" Stellar asks, frowning worriedly, "You're bouncing your leg so much I think the entire train car's shaking."

The angel leans her head back against the cushions. "I'm nervous."

"I can tell, but *why* are you nervous?"

"We're nearing the end of our journey and we're getting *nowhere,*" she groans, "We've found no clues, and the other Royals haven't had any leads either."

They relax back against their seat. "Well, let's hope Mammon or Beelzebub have found something. Even if they have, we should plan a stop in Blasphemy to check in with Tyrian. He's the one who's most likely to know about it."

Angelique opens her mouth, only to shut it almost immediately. "Right. The only reason we didn't start with him is because he's taking care of his family."

"Exactly. I'll try to remember to send him a message before we leave Gluttony and let him know we're on our way. Hopefully we'll give him enough notice..."

"Alright, if you say so." Angelique leans her head against Stellar's shoulder. The closeness relaxes her, and she finds she's no longer bouncing her knee. *I could get used to this comfort I feel around Stellar...*

But what would Aurora say?

Her mind screeches to a halt as she remembers her former partner. *Right... I've found no clues to her whereabouts either... I hope she's not angry with me.*

What are the chances Aurora would be angry? You know what she was like; she never got mad at anything.

That's true... But 100 years might have changed things.

Well, you'll have to figure that out once you find her.

Right...

As her internal debate grows quiet, the subway car rings with an announcement. **["Now approaching Berxley station,"]** comes the mechanical voice over the intercom.

"This is our stop, right?"

"Yes," Stellar confirms. Once the train slows to a stop and the doors open, the two of them exit and make their way into the streets of the Gluttony Sector's capital city. The main road is filled with various stalls one would normally find in a farmer's market. Each stall advertises a different type of produce, and a few small butcher shops can be seen down the road.

"Whoa... I take it Gluttony is full of farmers?" the angel queries as they pass dozens of vendor stalls. Each of the demons watching over the market stalls is donning some type of typical farmer's clothing, whether it be a pair of overalls, some piece of flannel, or a straw sunhat.

The death demon brightens at the observation. "Yes! The Gluttony Sector is mostly farmland and small towns. The capital, though, is a bustling market! There are also more libraries in Gluttony than the other sectors, and the most prestigious university in Hell is found here, too!"

"Wow... So Gluttony doesn't just apply to food, I take it?"

"Exactly. 'Gluttony' has often been watered down to mean the overconsumption of food, but it also applies to things like knowledge."

"You can over-consume knowledge?"

"Well... Yes and no. A thirst for knowledge is generally a good thing, but if it becomes an obsession, it can cause a whole slew of issues. Anxiety, of course, but it could also lead someone to neglect their health if they're too focused on learning."

"Ah... It's like college students, then. They neglect their health in order to make sure they pass their classes..."

"Well, that's closer to a fear of failure, but it's in a similar vein of thinking." Stellar leads the way through the market until they reach their destination.

The Palace of Gluttony is unlike the centerpoint of any other sector. Instead of the building appearing to be a more deluxe mansion, the Palace of Gluttony is instead shaped a bit like a beehive. It's several stories tall, likely to accommodate the children and staff living inside. The honey-colored bricks make the palace inviting, acting as a pleasant reminder that the children under Queen Beelzebub's care are well-loved despite everything they could have gone through. The fence guarding the outside of the grounds is shaped like rows upon rows of wrought-iron honeycomb, complete with thick glass panels in the center to prevent any small children from getting stuck.

"Whoa..."

"Queen Bee has quite a sense of style, wouldn't you say?" Stellar's tail wags as she opens the gate.

"Yeah... I take it she likes insects?"

"Well... Some of them. She's terrified of spiders."

"Really?"

"Mm-hm. She's fine with things like butterflies, ladybugs, dragonflies... And bees, of course. Wasps, though? She'll knock them back with a steel pan."

Angelique giggles at the mental image of a Queen of Demons beating back invasive wasps with a frying pan. "I can't wait to meet her."

"Good!" They follow the path of hexagonal stone pavers to the Palace of Gluttony. Scattered throughout the front yard are dozens of raised garden beds, each sprouting various types of produce. Based on the labels stuck in the dirt, there are carrots, onions, broccoli, potatoes... Even trellises standing guard around tomato, pea, and cucumber plants. "Queen Bee likes to garden, huh..."

"She does! She likes the taste of fresh produce and uses them in her cooking more often than not. You can definitely tell the difference, too."

Angelique places a hand to her mouth, finding herself thankful she's not drooling at the thought of fresh, crisp vegetables being used in a homemade stew. "I'm guessing they don't keep animals here, so they can protect the gardens?"

Stellar laughs. "Bee has about two-hundred chickens."

"... *Two-hundred* chickens?"

"She says since they're small, they're only good for their eggs. Apparently she uses them to teach the little kids how to treat animals, and the older kids get to learn how to gather eggs and take care of them as pets."

"Huh... How many eggs does she get per day?"

"At one point, she said they average about eight to ten dozen per day?"

"Oh, wow... I bet she needs them for all the kids, though."

"I'm sure she does."

They approach the front door of the Palace of Gluttony and knock loudly on the thick maple wood barrier. It takes a few moments for someone to answer the door. The gluttony demon on the other side is on the taller side of average, with a thick moustache on his face and a small pair of glasses balanced on the bridge of his nose.

"Hello, Rhodes!" Stellar greets, "Long time no see!"

"Ah, Princess Stellar!" he greets after a moment of recognition. "It's been so long! Is there something we can do for you?"

"I need to talk to Queen Beelzebub and King Mammon. Are they both in?"

"Yes, they're both in the backyard. I believe they were about to finish the playground reconstruction for the day."

"So we won't be interrupting anything?" Angelique asks shyly.

"Not at all." Rhodes steps aside and beckons them into the palace. As the elderly demon leads the way through the palace, the girls admire the framed art projects that cover the walls. Each of the artworks is made in any combination of crayon, marker, paint, and construction paper.

"Does Queen Beelzebub save all of the children's art pieces?" Angelique asks curiously.

"She does until they either get adopted or move out," Rhodes explains. "In those cases, she makes them a portfolio that only the children can get into. Then, if the child were to somehow be put in a dangerous situation, their childhood drawings and any other special personal belongings would not be caught in the crossfire."

Angelique blinks in surprise. "... How would they somehow end up in a dangerous situation?"

"If an imp were to somehow come into contact with the child, or their adoptive family became a subject of suspicion by someone like Princess Stellar over here, they could destroy the child's personal items. Our preventative measures ensure that will not happen."

At the mention of their esteemed intuition and protective nature, Stellar puffs out their chest proudly and preens at the compliments. The sight brings a smile to the angel's face, and she sticks close to the demons as they venture through the palace-turned-orphanage.

They enter a large, brightly lit common area whose floor is covered in toys. Bouncy balls, plushies, and art supplies are scattered across the ornate rug to the point it's barely visible underneath the mess. Several board games lay on the coffee table and floor as well, abandoned without a definitive winner.

Rhodes pushes his glasses up the bridge of his nose. "Luckily, Her Majesty Queen Beelzebub is able to make the children clean up after themselves without too much of an argument."

"I'm sure," Stellar chuckles, "She's never been one for harsh discipline."

"You would be right, Your Highness," Rhodes says as he motions to the plush couches that surround the coffee table. "Have a seat while I fetch Queen Beelzebub and King Mammon. It shouldn't be long before they stop in, and you all can discuss what you're here for."

"Thank you, Rhodes." Stellar takes a seat on one of the plush sofas and leans against the soft backing. Angelique does the same, sighing in relief as she rests against the dark green corduroy fabric.

"Queen Beelzebub must enjoy the comforts of home," she whispers to her companion. "Everything feels so... Lived in, for lack of a better term."

"It is," Stellar agrees, "Because she wants the children in her care to grow up to be responsible adults. Not too messy, but not neat-freaks either. Cleaning your own messes and stuff like that... You know?"

Angelique nods. "That's very nice. Everything in Heaven is pristine, and it's a bit disheartening to see the kids there hardly doing anything fun. It's almost like they're miniature adults..."

Stellar opens their mouth to answer, but is cut off by an unfamiliar voice.

"Who's a miniature adult?" comes a woman's voice that sounds straight out of a 1950's movie due to her mix of southern and Transatlantic accents.

Angelique and Stellar look over to see two other demons approaching them. One is a thin gentleman that stands only two inches taller than Stellar, with curved horns poking out of his shoulder-length, emerald-green hair. He's wearing a white button-up shirt, forest green tie, and black vest with gold buttons, and holding a sage green suit jacket over his arms. A pair of business slacks in the same sage green color as his jacket bunches slightly against his black business shoes. His scoop-ended tail sways behind him as he walks.

The other demon is a short, plush woman with thin, segmented horns protruding from her medium-long, dark brown hair that's pulled mostly over her left shoulder. The black undershirt she wears has scalloped hems around the high neckline and sleeves, which end between her elbows and wrists. The goldenrod dress she wears over the black shirt has loose, cold-shoulder sleeves and a small bumblebee charm attached to the neckline. The poodle-style skirt of her dress is made extra poofy thanks to the petticoat she wears underneath, and a white circular apron is wrapped around her waist. Her legs are covered by sheer black tights, and her Mary Jane style shoes match the color of her dress. Her tail protrudes out from underneath her dress, revealing that the tip is shaped like a beehive.

"Surely you're not talking about my niblings," the man laughs, "They're wild and rambunctious; the way Bee likes."

The woman nudges him with an elbow, at which point it becomes clear to Angelique that the demoness actually has *four* arms instead of the typical pair of two. She does her best not to stare at the extra limbs, which sit neatly at the demoness's waistline, but finds it a *bit* difficult.

Stellar, however, laughs at the interaction between the twins. "Not at all. We were talking about the children in Heaven."

The other demons' eyes soften at the mention of the holy city. "I see. Well, I suppose it makes sense; angels are convinced children should be seen and not heard," the woman huffs, crossing the lower set of arms over her chest as she rests her other hands on her hips. Her gaze drifts to Angelique, at which point a slight flush covers her cheeks. "Well... Most angels feel that way, at least."

"Oh, I take no offense," Angelique excuses with a wave of her hand, "I find it disheartening for a mentality like that to exist anywhere."

"Well, I'm glad you agree!" she cheers, clapping both sets of hands together in apparent glee.

"In any case," the male demon interjects, "We should introduce ourselves." He places a hand to his chest as he bows. "I am Mammon, King of Greed."

"And I am Beelzebub, Queen of Gluttony," the four-armed woman says as she curtsies.

"It's a pleasure to meet you both, King Mammon; Queen Beelzebub," Angelique greets, "My name is Angelique. I'm helping Stellar with a case we're looking for your help with."

"Oh boy," Mammon snickers as he takes a seat on the couch across from them. "Why does Princess Stellar need our help?"

"It has to do with some odd traces that have been detected throughout the sectors," the Princess of Death clarifies.

"What kind of traces?" Beelzebub asks, concern lacing her tone as she also sits across from them.

"Angelic traces."

The two other royals cast a quick glance to Angelique, then turn their gazes back to Stellar.

"I'm going to go out on a limb here and presume you don't mean your friend," Mammon states.

"But if that's true, do you have any idea where the source may have come from?" Beelzebub adds.

"Not at this time," Angelique sighs, "But we only have one more sector to investigate."

"Blasphemy?" the twin royals guess.

"Correct."

"Hm..." Beelzebub places a hand to her mouth as she thinks. "I only discovered something odd toward the edge of our border. It was oddly familiar..."

"Could the source be someone you knew when you were in Heaven?" Angelique asks, her demeanor brightening at the prospect of finally getting a clue.

"Yes, but it would be odd for him to be here..." She looks to her twin. "Are you thinking what I'm thinking?"

"That it's an Archangel? Yes," Mammon agrees.

"Wait, an Archangel?" Angelique quietly gasps.

"Which Archangel?" Stellar demands, their voice an aggressive snarl. The change in tone catches Angelique completely off-guard, and she finds herself jumping as she turns to her companion. The other demon's eyes have narrowed, and their skull-shaped pupils have nearly turned into the slits one would find on a venomous snake. She's sitting forward, shoulders curled in like a tiger going in for the kill.

"We believe it was Gabriel," Beelzebub answers, her tone steady in caution as her eyes lock on Stellar's aggressive demeanor.

"Gabriel?" Angelique and Stellar question at the same time.

"What would he be doing here?" the former continues.

"Nothing good," the latter answers, tail lashing, "*None* of the Archangels are to be trusted."

"It's definitely suspicious," Beelzebub agrees, "But we haven't had any interactions with him to know his intentions."

"We should head to Blasphemy as soon as possible," Stellar declares as she darts to a standing position. "Tyrian would have access to any Oaths of Peace the bastard may have signed, so—"

"Stellar, please sit back down," Mammon pleads, motioning to the sofa the princess had practically leapt from.

"No! If the traces are from an Archangel, then we need to get them out of here as soon as possible!"

"Stellar," Angelique cuts in, placing a calming hand to the demon's back, "Didn't you say that since nobody has gotten hurt, there's not a need to rush?"

"Well, *yes*, but that was before I knew it was an *Archangel* down here!"

"What does the source being an Archangel have to do with—?"

"Archangels are *dangerous!"* Stellar snaps, "Especially for demons. Especially for demons *like me."*

Angelique stares at her friend, confusion and concern filling her expression and her heart. "What do you mean, 'demons like you?'" she asks, her voice quiet and level as she tries to stifle every instinct telling her to run away from Stellar's rage as fast as she can.

Tears fill Stellar's eyes as she hugs herself tightly, the corruption slowly inching its way up their upper arms. "I... Was an angel once, too." The confession sits heavy in the air as the Princess of Death begins to cry, quiet hiccups filling the otherwise stifling silence of the room.

Beelzebub stands from her place on one of the nearby sofas and slowly steps closer to the sobbing princess. "Stellar," she calls, her voice donning a mother's soothing tone, "Do you want to be held right now, or do you need space to let yourself cry?"

Their voice trembles as they speak. "I... I don't know," she admits. A few sniffles and rough coughs later, she takes a few deep breaths in a weak attempt to quell their tears. As her shoulders shake from the emotional drop, Angelique stands.

"I know this is probably the typical guardian angel's 'save the world mentality,' but..." She wraps her arms around her companion in a hug and gently squeezes her. "I want you to know it's going to be okay. I'm not upset that you didn't tell me sooner. In fact, now that you've told me at least a little bit of what you've gone through, your words and actions make a lot more sense." A pair of arms wraps around Angelique's midsection, and she finds herself smiling into Stellar's shoulder. "There you go. You've got it. I'm here. I promise."

The demon clings and allows themself to cry for about another few minutes, at which point she squeezes Angelique's midsection. "Thanks for this," she whispers, "It's... Been a long time since I cried over something like this."

"Of course, Stellar. Any time you need to let it out, I'll be here for you."

The two of them pull back from their comforting embrace and look into each other's eyes. For once, Stellar's eyes are red and raw around the edges, and their cheeks are covered in red splotches. Angelique wipes the remaining tears from the demon's face, a small smile on her lips as she finds herself in the caretaking role.

"Ugh, this is *weird,*" Stellar whines.

"What does, hm?"

"Being treated like this... You're so sweet to me and I have no idea *why.*"

"Isn't it obvious? I want to be. This is what friends do, isn't it?"

She sniffles and rests her face into Angelique's hands. "I suppose I'll let you dote on me this time, Angel."

As Angelique stands there, cradling Stellar's face as though she were a prized art piece, she almost misses how happily the demon's tail wags. Once Stellar is sufficiently neatened up, the two of them sit on the sofa again. The demon's tail still wags a bit until Beelzebub speaks once again.

"Well, now that the issue of the angelic traces seems to have been resolved for the time being, why don't you two stay for dinner? If you'd like you can even spend the night in a guest room."

"I... I don't know. What do you think, Angel?" Stellar asks as she turns to their angelic companion.

"Dinner would be nice," Angelique agrees. "We'll see how we feel after we eat, and determine whether we stay here or not."

"Alright. I guess we'll take you up on your offer, Bee."

"Fantastic! I'll go check on the kitchen." She stands and scurries off to another nearby room, leaving Angelique, Stellar, and Mammon in the living room.

Mammon hums curiously and turns his attention back to the two in front of him. "So, how long have you two known each other?"

"It's been a couple months," Angelique answers easily.

"You two act as though you've known each other for years."

"Sometimes it feels like we have," Stellar chuckles, resting their head on Angelique's shoulder. "I doubt she'd *actually* want to have known me so long, though. I'm sure I was a pain in the ass to deal with when I first came here."

"You were morbidly depressed," Mammon corrects, "And you're well aware there is a *huge* difference between that and being a general nuisance, Stellar."

"Mm. I know that *now.* Back in the day, I was convinced my father would give up on me."

"Well, luckily we know Elias well enough to know he would never give up on someone that easily." The King of Greed leans against an arm of the sofa he's sitting on and rests his face in his hand. "Especially not when they still have unfinished business."

Stellar shoots back to a stick-straight sitting position at the mention. "Mammon..."

"Unfinished business?" Angelique echoes, quirking an eyebrow as she turns her attention back to her companion. "What are you talking about, King Mammon?"

"Don't worry about it—"

"Now, now, Stellar... It's awfully *greedy* of you to keep such an important secret from your friend, wouldn't you say?"

"You..."

As the demon growls, obviously agitated, Angelique notices their corruption slowly making its way further up their upper arms. She grabs onto the Princess of Death's wrist, hoping the heat of her palm will help to calm her companion.

"It's okay, Stellar," she whispers, "You don't have to tell me." She leans her head against their shoulder and squeezes their hand. As predicted, the death demon visibly relaxes at the gentle contact and soothing words. The tension in her shoulders slowly ebbs away underneath the slight pressure of Angelique's cheek.

"Thank you," Stellar whispers.

"Any time."

Beelzebub comes back, tail wagging excitedly. "Alright, the cooks know you're going to be staying for dinner! It's a barbecue night, so we've already got a large amount of food to pick from."

Mammon stands, removing his sage-green business jacket. "Are they going to want help with anything, Bee, or are they mostly set up?"

"Oh, I'm sure they're fine, but if you wouldn't mind helping with the barbecue pit setup, we'd all appreciate it."

"As you wish, dear sister."

"Don't you 'dear sister' me, you know I hate it!"

"If I didn't pick on and pester you, you'd think something was wrong!"

"Ugh, you're such an ass!"

"You know it's true," Mammon teases as he makes his way to the kitchen.

"It is..." She sighs as her twin passes by. Once he's gone, she turns her attention back to Stellar and Angelique. "You don't have any dietary restrictions or food allergies, do you Angelique?"

"Not that I'm aware of, no."

"Oh, good! Then you can take part in anything you like."

"We'll make sure to eat our fill, Bee," Stellar reassures her.

"You'd better! We have a few kids who are still adjusting to being here, so seeing more people taking part in whatever they want for food will be fantastic for them."

"Bee, you should know you don't have to worry about the kids as much as you do. How many of them stay in the 'skin and bone' weight range after being here for a month?"

"Only about two percent," Beelzebub answers simply, "But they tend to be on-par with the rest of the kids once they've been here for three months."

"Oh! That's not long at all!" Angelique cheers.

"In the long run, no, but I still worry about them... Making sure everyone gets enough to eat has always been a concern of mine, even before I came here."

"It's nice to hear that you've always worried about the wellbeing of those around you," the angel says.

"She's not the only misunderstood one," Stellar adds.

"I gathered that a long time ago. Everything Heaven has claimed about demons and why they're down here has been twisted into false truths. They preach about how demons are evil, and yet... I've only met wonderful people."

"Well, that and the occasional imp."

"Right— Wait. Speaking of imps..." The angel frowns and turns back to Beelzebub. "How are there so many orphans in your care, if demons aren't as horrible as they're made out to be?"

"It could be a variety of things," Beelzebub explains. "Sometimes, their parents succumb to their self-doubt and leave their children here, where they know they'll be well cared-for and loved;

other times, their parents are killed by demon hunters or put in danger by imps; and yet still, there are those who have died young on Earth and somehow managed to be barred from Heaven despite their age."

Angelique's hands clench into fists at the final revelation. "That's unfair," she states simply, holding back angry tears.

"It is," the Queen of Gluttony agrees, "But, I am here to make sure that all the children under my care are safe, happy, and healthy."

"I don't know what else to say, other than 'thank you.' So... Thank you."

"You don't need to thank me, Angelique. It's what I was made to do," Beelzebub declares. "Now, why don't you both come with me? I'm sure your first backyard barbecue in Hell will be exciting, Angelique."

"I can't wait," Angelique cheers, rising from the sofa once again. Stellar stands as well, remaining close to the angel as they follow Beelzebub to the backyard.

The vast grounds of the Palace of Gluttony include various designated areas, each with their own unwritten purposes. To the left of the yard, near the side of the palace, there is a fenced-in area containing a chicken coop and a large flock. Off to the right are a half-dozen large fire pits, where kitchen staff are setting up grates and grills for the barbecue. A playground set with multiple tiers of plastic-coated metal platforms, bridges, climbing bars, and slides stands tall in a sandy area about twenty-five yards away, giving the children who clamber through the tunnels plenty of room to run around without the space feeling cramped.

"Wow..." the angel gasps. "This is a child's paradise!"

"Thank you," the Queen of Gluttony chortles. "We're looking into adding more expansions to the playground, so younger or more acrophobic kids have an easier time going up and down the slides and climbing equipment."

"Do you have the space for it?" Stellar asks.

"I've talked with the nearby farmers about expanding our perimeter just in case we tread on their land, and the ones who agreed also signed a contract approving of the expansion. Copies have been supplied to each of them, too, so they can keep us in check."

"What does that mean?" Angelique asks curiously.

"If we have them agree to something, like an extensive expansion of the playground, but something turns out wrong, they can hold us accountable. It's like our own little version of checks and balances, here; we promise certain things to the people, and if the people are unsatisfied, they can voice their displeasure until we fix the issues. It's not often that issues arise, but everyone is liable to make mistakes, so we Royals would rather be safe than sorry."

"Oh, wow… Is that why there are so many differences from Heaven and Earth? Like the subways being fully paid for, jobs being plentiful…"

"In a way, yes. Mammon pays for the subways to be properly upkept. He figures it's worth the price tag for Hell's citizens to get around between their homes, jobs, and hobbies."

"What a good way to think about it!" Angelique exclaims excitedly.

Beelzebub laughs quietly. "I'm glad you agree. Are you sure you're not secretly a demon, Miss Angelique?"

"Not at all. Why do you ask?"

"You seem to agree with a lot of the practices we have here. It's… A curious case, we'll say. Reminds me of a certain Queen of Blasphemy."

"Queen of Blasphemy? I thought the King of Blasphemy had a husband?"

"He does, but his husband adopted the title after their first little one was born. He figured it would be a bit hard to decipher between himself as 'Prince' and his son as 'Crown Prince.' He's not exactly particular about being called a feminine title, either; he's comfortable enough in who he is as a person to not be bothered by being called the Queen of Blasphemy."

"It sounds like the titles here in Hell are more of an indicator of rank, as opposed to a signifier of gender..." the angel murmurs.

"I know you said you've already been everywhere but Blasphemy, so I take it you've already met Belphie?" Beelzebub asks.

"We've met with King Belphegor, yes."

"Then you understand. They chose the rank of 'King' because they wanted to feel more connected with all of us, even though we insisted the title 'Sovereign of Sloth' had a nice ring to it. In the end, it's all about comfort in one's rank, even though we rarely show or exert our true power."

"I see..." Angelique murmurs. "It's refreshing to know that everyone is so accommodating of each other." She freezes as another thought springs to the forefront of her mind. "You rarely show your true strength?"

"We try to rule as peacefully as possible, and save our true strength for emergencies."

The angel finds her gaze drifting to Stellar, who's helping to carry and season some of the meats being placed over one of the fiery barbecue pits. "What counts as an emergency?" she whispers.

Beelzebub glances in the same direction as Angelique, humming. "It seems you've already gathered the implications," she muses. "Corruption is incredibly dangerous if it fully manifests."

"How close is it to fully manifesting in Stellar?"

"Close enough for it to be worrisome. See how it's already halfway up her upper arms?"

"Yeah?"

"She's one bad day away from the corruption fully manifesting."

"Oh..." A tightness forms in her chest as she watches Stellar interact cheerfully with Mammon and the staff. "... How can I help them?"

"I'm not sure. You'd have to ask her, and even then I'm not sure if she'd have an answer for you." Beelzebub looks over Stellar's condition from afar again. "From the looks of it, though, her corruption has progressed oddly fast..."

Angelique's ears twitch. "Huh?"

"Her corruption usually takes much longer to flare up. It's only been a couple weeks that you've been in Hell, right?"

"Yeah..." She pauses as a looming dread turns her blood and bones to ice. "... Do you think I've been making her worse?"

The Queen of Gluttony quirks an eyebrow. "Pardon?"

"We had a small argument early on, and... Her corruption started to manifest a lot faster than it sounds like it normally would."

"Do you mind if I ask what the argument was about?"

"Ah..." Angelique hesitates. "It... She had every right to question my motives. I assured them I want to help figure out the situation with the angelic traces as well as look for my old partner. They were afraid I was using her."

"And ever since then, her corruption has gotten worse?"

She nods. "Back when we were in Lust, the corruption created a fragment that looked like one of her friends, but was talking so horribly... I can't help but worry about them."

"If it's already gotten to the point of fragments forming, it's especially far along... Did she mention that when you stopped in to see Belphie?"

"No..."

"Then it's definitely possible for her to be downplaying her symptoms so you don't worry as much. Don't get me wrong, it'd be a sweet gesture if it wasn't so self-destructive..."

Angelique hugs herself, suddenly sick to her stomach. "… I need to talk to them… Tonight."

Beelzebub watches the angel for a moment before speaking. "I see. Well, until you two are alone, you should at least try to enjoy the barbecue. Sometimes good food helps ease one's nerves."

"Alright… Thank you, Queen Beelzebub."

"Oh, you don't have to be so formal! Call me Bee!"

"If you insist… Bee."

The chefs come out of the kitchens to help prepare the meats and veggies for the barbecue. They make their way over to the roaring grills and place the morsels on specific grates, watching as the flames lick at each piece of food and cook it all deliciously. Angelique finds herself staring at the wide variety of food on the grills. "This is a lot of food…"

Stellar looks over from where she's admiring the roaring flames. "There you are, Angel! What are you looking forward to eating? I'd kill for one of those ribeye steaks and some ribs."

"They do look good," the angel agrees. "I'm guessing there are going to be plenty of side dishes?"

"Yes," one of the cooks confirms, "There are going to be caramelized salt potatoes and craft-your-own salads, with options of greens or pasta."

"Delicious," she and Stellar say at the same time, the latter practically drooling.

Once the food is almost fully cooked, the children slowly trickle out of the palace and wander over to the grills. Some opt to play on the playground instead of immediately making a beeline for the food, and others choose to take care of the chickens in the coop. Before long, though, all of the grilled morsels have finished cooking and the rest of the food is brought out from the palace's kitchens.

Everyone gathers around the fire pits to gather their choice of protein and roasted vegetables, then head over to the large tables with giant bowls of pasta, salad greens, and other traditional toppings like tomatoes, cucumbers, pickles, cubed and crumbled cheeses, and salad dressings. The children gather their plates and make themselves comfortable, some sitting on the ground while others choose to sit on chairs.

Angelique watches in awe as she munches on some of the buttery, crispy caramelized potatoes. "After this we only have Blasphemy left to visit... Right, Stellar?"

Stellar looks up from where she's chowing down on a large cheeseburger. "Right! Hopefully Tyrian can give us the answers we've been looking for all this time..." Her tail flicks. "I wish this case didn't feel like we've been all over Hell with nothing to show for it."

"I'm sure everything will be okay," she says. "After all, we're on the case. How bad could it be?"

"You have a point..." She takes another bite of her burger. "Well, at least for right now, we can take a break and eat. I've been hungry for a few hours..."

"Why didn't you say something earlier?"

She shrugs. "I didn't notice how bad it got. Bad habit."

Angelique huffs, puffing out her cheeks. "You need to break these bad habits of yours if we're going to continue working together."

She laughs. "Yeah, yeah, I will. For you, okay?"

"Thank you. I appreciate it."

Eighteen
Lab Rat

The following day, Angelique and Stellar leave the Gluttony Sector after bidding a quick good-bye to Queen Beelzebub, King Mammon, and the children in Beelzebub's care. As they sit in the subway car, the sun setting shining behind them, Angelique's gaze drifts to Stellar's corruption-coated arms. The demon hums as she looks over at her, exhaustion apparent in their eyes.

"Everything okay, Angel?"

"Huh? Oh, um... Yeah. Everything's fine." She looks away and hugs herself loosely as she refocuses her gaze onto her feet.

A darkened hand wraps itself around her wrist. "You can talk to me, you know," Stellar insists.

The angel leans her head back against her chair. "I... I feel like it's my fault your corruption has gotten so bad in such a short amount of time."

They quirk an eyebrow. "What makes you think *you* caused this?"

"I..." She sighs. "I was talking to Bee, and she told me that you're one bad day away from the corruption fully manifesting... I may not know what she means, but I know it's not good." She looks over at the Princess of Death with tears filling her eyes.

"She doesn't know what she's talking about," Stellar interrupts, squeezing her wrist in a weak, comforting gesture. "She doesn't know my condition better than I do."

"She still made me worry," Angelique counters. "She said it's progressed a lot faster than normal, and the only thing I could think of as the 'cause'... Is me being around." She sniffles, fighting back the floodgates of tears. "We had that argument early on in the Envy Sector, and ever since then your arms have gotten so much darker..."

"It's just stress, Angel."

"How can I be sure? How do I know you aren't saying that to make me feel better?"

"You have to trust me until we get back to my dad's place. Remember what I said on the way to Ship's Haven, about what he keeps in the basement?"

Angelique thinks back to the conversation they'd had on the subway back at the beginning of their journey.

Water with a low concentration of souls acts as a highly-effective healing agent. My father has a laboratory in his palace that's got a few different pods full of a healing soul-water mixture, the memory of Stellar echoes in her mind.

"... A laboratory with healing pods?" she guesses.

"See? You were listening." Stellar squeezes her wrist again. "I'll take a long soak in one of the pods."

"Wait, but aren't we heading to the Blasphemy Sector?" Angelique asks.

"We are, but the Death Sector is on the way. I may as well stop at my dad's house while we're in the area and see how long he suggests I soak in the healing pods."

Angelique frowns. "Depending on what he says... If you wait until after we visit Blasphemy, your condition could get even worse than it is now."

"Then I'll see if I can make it fast."

After about another thirty minutes of sitting in a somewhat tense, but otherwise comfortable quiet, the two of them arrive back at the Petraglow subway station. They disembark from the train quickly and make a beeline for the Palace of Death. Their footsteps click against the familiar path, which alerts the dogs lazing just inside the gate.

The angel slows to a stop as she lays eyes on the three Hellhounds once again. A thick lump of anxiety forms in her stomach, making her arms sting as she fights back the urge to run away. *Everything will be fine,* she soothes herself, *Just stay close to Stellar and they won't get to you.*

She takes slow, quiet, calculating steps forward, until she's only about two paces behind Stellar. The demon is unlocking the gate, keeping a close eye on the dogs inside. As soon as the door swings open, the black labrador maneuvers her way out, slips past Stellar's legs, and leaps at Angelique. Before the angel can let out a cry for help, she's been tackled onto the nearby grass and her face is being covered in slobber.

"Helena!" the Princess of Death yelps.

The dog doesn't react to the call of her name, content to stand over Angelique and continue giving her sloppy puppy kisses as she squeals.

"Oh, no! Oh, no!" the angel yelps, laughing, "I'm getting slobbered on! Gross!"

Stellar darts over and pulls Helena back by grabbing under her forelimbs and making her stand up. "That's a naughty dog!" she scolds, but the Hellhound pants happily and doesn't register the contact as discipline. Instead, her long, fluffy tail is wagging happily between Stellar's legs.

"I am *so* sorry, Angel, I had no idea she was going to be cuddly this time around..."

Angelique giggles brightly as she sits up. "Is this what she's normally like?"

"Yes, she's the youngest and friendliest of our Hellhounds. She must have been following Cerberus' lead the first time you came around..."

"I'm glad to see she doesn't actually hate me."

"Not at all. Helena's a good girl." They let go of the Hellhound, who runs a lap around the two of them, barking excitedly. Stellar helps Angelique stand, keeping her eyes on the other two Hellhounds. Rue and Cerberus are watching the interactions carefully, the former hesitating to come close and interact with the angel.

"It's okay, Rue! You can come here, bubby." Stellar pats her thighs, smiling encouragingly at the long-coated Hellhound. The dog wanders out and sniffs at Angelique, then sits obediently at her feet.

"Whoa... This is quite a change in demeanor!" Angelique gasps.

The demon chuckles. "They know you've spent an awful lot of time around me."

"I have..."

"Hey now, no need to get all quiet! Look at this; it's a good thing! He looks like he wants you to pet him!"

The angel swallows around the thick lump in her throat, but reaches out a hand for each of the dogs to sniff. Helena doesn't even bother to do a smell-check, opting to instead headbutt Angelique's palm in a desperate request for attention. Rue, however, sniffs the offered hand and leans his forehead against the warm skin, even closing his eyes in a sign of trust.

Angelique beams at the display and pets the long-haired dog's head, her thumb brushing across the ridge between his eyebrows. As she pets the two smaller dogs, Stellar waits patiently, their tail wagging back and forth much like Helena's.

"Are all of these your dad's dogs?"

"Hm? No, Cerberus is Dad's only dog. Rue is Adrian's, and Helena is mine."

Angelique pauses. "That's right... Your brother..."

Stellar frowns. "What's wrong?"

"He doesn't trust me."

They roll their eyes, tail lashing angrily from side to side. "He'll get over it."

"He has every right not to trust me. I'm an angel, and—"

"Everyone else trusts my intuition," they counter.

"Well... Siblings are different."

"I'm sure Bella would agree with you."

Angelique pauses again, this time with a chill running down her spine as she looks up at her companion. "... How do you know about my sister?"

The demon's eyes widen, pupils narrowing as a strike of panic makes their back straighten and their tail lash. "Oh, I didn't know you had a sister. I was thinking of someone else I knew."

Angelique frowns, suddenly unsure whether or not to believe Stellar in light of the supposed coincidence. "I have an older sister whose nickname is Bella. Nobody but my family and friends would know that she exists, let alone what her nickname is." She stands tall and grabs onto Stellar's wrist, squeezing just a little tighter than their previous reassuring touches. "Stellar... When you were an angel, did you... Know me?"

The demon frowns, but doesn't pull away from the warm, soothing touch. "You'd remember me if I did," she answers.

Angelique frowns, her memories drifting to the dreams she'd been having surrounding Aurora and her disappearance. Unsatisfied with Stellar's response but unsure of how to press the issue without causing a fight, she huffs.

"... I'm not sure I believe you, but... I'll drop it for now." She pulls her hand away. "Let's get you inside and into one of those healing pods; hopefully it will help ease some of your corruption."

"We can only hope."

The demon heads to the Palace of Death, the angel close behind. The latter chances a glance to the extremely large three-headed dog as the two of them pass by, and while the dog is watching her closely, it's not growling and snarling like it had been during her last visit. Once they're on the front porch, Stellar pulls open one of the large front doors and darts inside unceremoniously.

Almost as if sensing their presence, Elias comes out of the living room, wearing much more business-casual attire. A long-sleeved white button-up shirt, mahogany sweater vest, and neat black slacks replace his tailored pinstripe suit.

"Stellar? Is everything alright?" he asks, worry coating his voice.

She presents their arms, revealing how far the corruption has spread up their limbs. It's covering more than three-quarters of their upper arms, almost to the ball of their shoulders. "I need to go in a healing pod for a bit, Dad."

"Stellar..." He sighs and places a hand to her upper back. "Come along, we'll get you in a pod and see what we can do to stave off a full manifestation."

"Can I come with you?" Angelique calls.

"That's Stellar's decision," Adrian answers as he makes his way down the stairs from the living quarters.

"Of course you can come with me. We'll finally get to show you Dad's lab." She holds out an inviting hand, smiling tiredly at the angel.

Angelique swallows around the lump in her throat, still a bit hesitant due to the coincidence from earlier, but takes the demon's hand nonetheless. The four of them head down the hall, until they reach a staircase that descends deeper into the palace. Stellar takes the lead, leading the way down the stairs without much of a care in the world. The angel follows behind, her knees shaking as she steps carefully, with Elias and Adrian trailing behind her. She fights back a shudder as she feels a glare from the latter.

The basement of the Palace of Death is made of shimmering grey bricks, which almost look silver. There appears to be a medical bay off to the right, but Stellar makes a beeline to the left. Angelique steps aside and watches the death demons enter a room that looks like it's pulled from a classic science-fiction horror movie. There is a large cylinder in the center of the room, full of a bubble-filled, light teal liquid. Along the far wall are five round metal cylinders with glass lids, each also filled with the liquid. At the foot of each cylinder is a control panel, with dials and buttons and a display that reads all zeros.

"Are you ready, Stellar?" Elias asks, standing near the control panel of the right-most cylinder.

She nods and leans down to take off her knee-high boots.

"What... Is all of this?" Angelique asks, looking around in awe.

"This is the soul water I was telling you about," Stellar replies.

"You just... Lay in one of these tubes until you're better?"

"It's a bit more complicated," Adrian murmurs, "The soul water is more of a gel, and it puts the body into a stasis so any wounds can be cured with enough time to soak."

Stellar nods in agreement with their brother. "Pretty much. Dad will set the timer for this session, and we'll see how well it works." She turns back to her father. "What are you thinking, Dad? Six hours?"

"We'll start with six; I may need to increase the duration when I come to check on you."

"That works." She turns to Angelique and smiles. "See you later, Angel." Without a second of hesitation, she climbs into the healing pod like one would climb onto a tanning bed. She lays back, closes her eyes, and rests her arms over her stomach. The lid closes, and the soul water slowly fills until it covers the demon's ears. Elias sets the time on the control panel and steps away as a quiet hum fills the laboratory.

Angelique stands quietly in the middle of the laboratory as the two other death demons leave and head back upstairs. She takes a few steps closer to the healing pod and places a careful hand on top of the glass. She pulls her hand back and follows after Elias and Adrian.

As soon as she makes her way back up the stairs and quietly shuts the door to the laboratory, she's shoved backward into the solid oak barrier by the shoulder. A yelp escapes her, only for her voice to die when she feels a firm hand wrap around her neck. Her blood turns to ice as fingers grip hard around her throat, holding her against the door as they squeeze the silk ribbon hiding her decapitation scar. Her gaze darts around frantically as she tries to steady her breathing... Until her eyes land on a familiar face.

"Adrian, what—?"

"Shut your mouth," he snarls, baring his teeth and revealing especially sharp canines. "What have you done to her?"

"To—To Stellar?"

"Yes, you dumb bitch!" His slightly-sharpened nails dig into her neck. "Her corruption is almost at the breaking point. What happened?!"

Tears fill Angelique's eyes as she tries to swallow around the sudden lump in her throat. "Adrian, I swear, I didn't do anything to hurt her."

"You'd damn well better be telling the truth, or I will use my family's political ties to figure out *exactly* what happened to my sister."

She tries to keep her voice steady as she speaks. "We have had three conflicts between us the entire time we've been down here," she confesses, "But nothing serious enough to exacerbate her condition."

"Elaborate."

"I told her I'm looking for my old partner while I'm here, and she questioned my true motives. When we were in Wrath, I tried to calm her down and she snapped at me. And in Lust... Well, I didn't cause this, but a fragment of her corruption manifested. I've been worried about her the whole time." Tears stream down her heated cheeks as panic continues to ride in her chest, making her hands tremble. "I promise, that's all. Nothing else has gone on between us."

"So two *actual* conflicts."

"Yes."

His navy blue eyes bore into her own blue-green ones as a thick silence overtakes them. "... Fine," he finally growls, pulling Angelique away from the door and dropping her to her knees on the floor. "But if I find out you lied to me, you will be forbidden from ever contacting her again."

Angelique coughs and cries, grasping lightly at her neck in mild relief. As soon as she's able to catch her breath, she looks up at him, meeting his eyes as she whispers out, "I promise... I would never hurt her..."

"I'll be keeping an eye on you both. *Don't* make me regret sparing you." He turns and storms off. As he walks away, Angelique is finally able to catch sight of the small battleaxe held tightly in his left hand.

She slumps against the nearest wall as her panic responses slowly dwindle from her chest and arms. It takes a few minutes, but the knot in her throat and the slight pain in her neck eventually fade. She closes her eyes and allows herself to let go of a few more tears, before she wipes her face and stands.

Everyone seems convinced it's my fault Stellar's corruption is acting up, she laments to herself. *Maybe I should take some time away from her side, just in case... We only have one more sector to visit, so it can't be that bad, right?*

With a slight boost to her self-confidence thanks to her mental pep talk, she moves to leave the Palace of Death. She makes a quick pit-stop in the nearest bathroom in order to clean her tear-coated face before leaving and making her way back to the subway station in the city of Petraglow.

Nineteen
Golden Hour

It takes Angelique significantly longer to figure out where she's going without Stellar at her side. Once she enters the subway station, it takes her twenty minutes and three loops to figure out which platform she needs to wait on, and it's only thanks to the kindness of a young sloth-wrath demon that she manages to find the correct location. As she waits patiently for the train to arrive, anxiety fills her heart and she rapidly bounces her knee.

If I can't even figure out which train platform I'm supposed to wait at, how am I ever going to find the Palace of Blasphemy?

After about ten minutes, the train arrives and she takes a seat inside. As she waits for the train to arrive at the station in Rochwall, the capital of the Blasphemy Sector, she feels a buzzing in her pocket. Confused, she pulls her phone out and finds a message from a phone number that looks vaguely familiar, but doesn't have a contact name attached to it.

> **[I heard about Stellar. You don't need to worry, there will be a guide ready to bring you to the Palace of Blasphemy. See you soon.]**

Wait, what? Who could this be? she questions herself. *There are no other angels in Hell aside from the source of the traces, right...?*

And there's no way a demon I haven't met yet would have my phone number...

She ponders the message for the remainder of the train ride, until she arrives at the subway station in Rochwall. She exits and looks around the capital city, only taking a few steps before being stopped in her tracks by someone calling her name.

"Angelique, right?"

She looks around for the source of the voice and finds a young man with dark, wavy hair and flat, curved horns like a bighorn sheep. He's wearing a green shirt with long, translucent sleeves, black athletic pants, and black sneakers. His long tail, which lacks any spikes or other adornments, sways lazily behind him. His eyes are a deep emerald green, with pupils shaped like bottom-heavy diamonds.

"Um... Yes?" she answers, approaching the man. "Who are you?"

"My name is Ryzen. I'm the Duke of Blasphemy." He bows politely, pressing a hand to his chest like a butler might when greeting royalty. "I'll be your guide to the palace."

She pauses, blinking wide-eyed at the unfamiliar man's demeanor. "... Who sent you here?"

"My brother-in-law," he answers simply, standing back up to his full six-foot height.

"The Queen of Blasphemy?"

"Correct. We'll talk more on the way." He holds out an arm for Angelique to take, the action reminiscent of a Victorian-era man trying to keep his partner close as they walk through a crowded party. "Is Stellar with you?"

The angel blushes and takes his arm, trying to keep a bit of a distance between the two of them. "Ah... No, she's not. She's... In a healing pod."

"So it's gotten that bad already..." He plasters on a bright, friendly smile as he looks to her once again. "Worry not Miss Angelique; we'll get you back to her side as soon as possible."

"Well, um... I'm going to need to consult with your brother, and—"

"He knows you're coming," he interrupts quietly. "In all honesty, he and his husband were expecting you much sooner than now, considering how dangerous the situation could get if things were to go even a *little* bit wrong. What took you so long to arrive, if you don't mind my asking?"

Angelique scowls and rips her hand from Ryzen's arm. "I don't appreciate your tone," she snarls. As soon as the words leave her mouth, she straightens, caught off-guard by the change in her own demeanor at the implications. *I nearly snapped like Stellar did when I told her everything would be okay...*

"I'm sorry, I shouldn't have said it that way," she quickly apologizes.

"Oh, you don't need to apologize. You've been hanging around Stellar all this time; it only makes sense for a bit of her protective streak would rub off on you." Ryzen gives another toothy grin, his demeanor oddly cheerful. "In any case, I was just curious as to the cause of your delay."

"Ah, um... We were told your brother needed some time to rest with his family."

"Is that what Adrian told you?"

She nods.

"So he misconstrued my words..." He groans. "I said Tyrian *will* need a break after this is sorted out, not— Ugh, I'm going to strangle him. Actually, I'm not; he'd probably enjoy it."

Angelique's face burns at the Duke's mutterings, unsure if she was supposed to hear the tail end of his miniature tirade. "Huh?"

Ryzen's tail lashes. "Adrian misinterpreted what I told him."

"... You've got to be kidding me."

"I wish I was, but it's either a misunderstanding... Or he misled you both on purpose."

Angelique tries not to let her bubbling frustration rise into her tone of voice as she speaks. "No matter if it's a misunderstanding or a purposeful distraction, we need to get everything sorted out *now*. This mission is exacerbating Stellar's corruption, and... I don't want to lose her."

Ryzen's tail wags behind him once again. "I see. Come along; the faster we get you to the palace, the sooner you can be on your way to save Stellar." He turns and leads the way down the street, this time without an offer for Angelique to hold onto his arm. He only glances over his shoulder once to check if the angel is still keeping pace behind him.

"So... What should I know before we enter the Palace of Blasphemy?"

"Hm? What do you mean?"

"I... I don't know, maybe what the King and Queen are like?"

"My brother is righteous in his duty, and takes the safety of all Hell-dwellers incredibly seriously."

"Will he see me as a threat?"

"Not at all, especially once the Queen steps in."

She frowns. "You're being awfully cryptic..."

He chuckles. "Sorry, I tend to keep things vague for the sake of my boyfriend's daughter. She's only seven, so I don't want to get too deep into certain topics, you know?" His tail wags a bit more. "Tyrian uses his palace as a landing strip, of sorts, for angels sent on recon missions here in Hell. Once they arrive, he makes them sign an Oath of Peace and goes over the restrictions they have here."

"An Oath of Peace... Stellar didn't have me sign anything when she brought me here."

"Oaths of Peace are only found in the domain of my brother and I. Since you're a temporary guest of another Royal, you don't need to sign one."

"That's... Odd."

"Not at all. After all, since you're her guest, Stellar has been keeping tabs on you this whole time."

Angelique freezes in her steps. "... Huh?"

"Well, not exactly 'keeping tabs' on you, but she's been with you this whole time. With her at your side, we don't need to worry."

"Because of her intuition, right?"

"Well, yes and no. Even without her exceptional intuition, as a Royal of Hell, it's her duty to keep the common folk safe. I'm sure if you were to turn on her and pose a danger to those around you, Stellar wouldn't hesitate to neutralize the threat; even if it's you."

She shudders. "The thought of fighting her makes me *really* glad I'm a pacifist..."

"You are, huh? Considering how ready you were to argue with me only a few minutes ago, I'm almost surprised."

"Well... It's like you said, Stellar's been rubbing off on me."

They continue their trek through the city, until they reach a large manor that more closely resembles a cathedral than the other palaces she'd seen throughout Hell. The outer perimeter is guarded by warm, cream-colored brick fencing with lopsided golden diamonds painted every so often. Wrought iron fencing is twisted into elegant curls along the top ridge of the bricks. The gate in front of them is once again made of the dark wrought iron fencing, with eye-shaped designs in the corners and another lopsided diamond design in the center. Ryzen pulls the gate open easily, humming as it creaks ominously. "We'll have to oil this up..."

"Whoa..." Angelique murmurs as she admires the building before her. "If this is the Palace of Blasphemy... Why does it look like a cathedral?"

"Sometimes, demons will find themselves in a state of denial over their fate, so Tyrian and I arranged for this palace to look more like a church. They come here as a safe place to talk about their issues and process everything."

"I see..." She marvels at the intricate stonework on the outside of the Palace of Blasphemy, which lead into inner halls made of marble. "This reminds me of the courthouse in Heaven..."

Ryzen clicks his tongue, tail lashing angrily. "The old fools in the courthouse wouldn't like you comparing them to us," he warns.

"I'm sure they wouldn't, but it's not as though you're going to report me."

"Of course not. The day I step foot back in Heaven is the day of the Rapture."

"Now, now, don't say that," an unfamiliar voice says from further down the halls. Footsteps and a child's excited giggles fill the quietness of the hall. A man with long blonde hair wearing black-and-gold clerical robes appears from around the corner. As he approaches, it's revealed that he has a facial scar from the right side of his neck, up his cheek, and over the bridge of his nose. The scar resembles a long vine covered in thorns and leaves. On his heels is a young girl with loose blonde ringlets and wearing a red and white, lolita-style dress. The young girl's thick red mary-jane shoes tap against the tile floors, her skirt bouncing as she races to the demon. "Papa Ryzen!" she cheers, leaping into his arms.

The demon catches her easily and pulls her deep red hood up over her head as he balances her on his hip. "Hello again, Amber," he greets, "Did you think I was going to go away forever?"

"Not at all, love." The blonde man presses a sweet, chaste kiss to the Duke's lips, smiling as they pull away. His warm chocolate eyes glance over to Angelique. "Is this the angel we've all been waiting for?"

"This is Angelique," Ryzen introduces, "Stellar's special guest."

“It’s a pleasure to meet you,” Angelique greets, holding out a hand for the man to shake.

“No, no, the pleasure is all mine. My name is Gabriel Roberts; this is my daughter, Amber.” He shakes her hand and bows. “It’s an honor to meet a real guardian angel here.”

“A real guardian angel, huh...?” Angelique glances over to Ryzen, obviously confused by the presence of a clergyman in the Palace of Blasphemy.

Ryzen notices the angel’s confused expression and smiles as he explains. “Gabby’s never met a real angel. He was *sure* he’d never get the chance, since he chose to join me down here. His congregation was full of... Less than desirable folks.”

“They were really mean!” Amber cuts in, “They called Papa Gabby a curse!”

Gabriel’s cheeks flush a vibrant pink. “Amber, honey—”

Ryzen runs a hand over the young girl’s back. “It’s okay now, right Amber? You and Papa Gabby don’t have to get bullied by those mean people anymore.”

She huffs and buries her face into Ryzen’s shoulder. “Right...”

Angelique frowns worriedly at the implications. “Was the congregation abusive to you, Father Gabriel?”

“Ah... One could say that. Most of the abuse occurred before I became the man I am today, but... Memories will always stick.”

“I understand,” she murmurs. “In any case... Are the King and Queen of Blasphemy home? I was hoping to talk to them...”

“Yes, they are. If you’d like, I can go gather them—”

“There’s no need to worry, Gabriel,” another unfamiliar baritone voice calls. A man in a tight-fitting black shirt is carrying long, black-and-gold, priestly outer robes, which he hangs on a nearby coat rack. Draped around his neck is a necklace with a golden six-pointed star and large white crystals that dangle from the lower three diffraction spikes. Loose, deep mahogany pants are cinched into a pair of tall black hiking boots. His horns and tail match

Ryzen's, aside from the lengths of small golden chain dangling from them.

"Uncle Tyrian!" Amber cheers from her place in the Duke of Blasphemy's arms.

"I see you've brought our esteemed guest, Ryzen. Thank you."

"Of course, brother." The duke sets Amber back on the floor.

A knot forms in her throat as she stands stiffly in front of the King of Blasphemy. "I appreciate the hospitality I've felt so far, Your Majesty," she declares, giving a small curtsey in greeting.

"Of course, Miss Angelique. Is your companion Princess Stellar not with you?"

"She is not."

"Ah, her corruption must be worsening..."

"It is."

"Then I shall hurry this along so you can return to her side, Miss Angelique. Come with me." He turns and uses his gold-adorned tail to beckon her to follow after him. She casts a glance to the Duke of Blasphemy and tips her head in a quiet good-bye before scurrying off after the aforementioned King. He brings her down the left hall, which appears to still be made of marble. Chancing a peek behind her, she finds that the opposite hallway fades from the elegant marble of the entryway to a more home-like atmosphere.

That must head toward their living space... And this must be the professional wing...

"Is everything alright, Miss Angelique?"

She startles and looks back to the King of Blasphemy. "Yes, Your Majesty! I was just... Admiring the architecture."

"I see. My husband says this professional wing should make angels feel a bit less threatened, since it is reminiscent of the buildings in Heaven. Is he right?"

"Ah... It reminds me of Heaven, yes."

"Then our goal has been achieved," he chuckles. He ducks his head slightly as he enters a white-and-gold office space. There is a large sofa made out of intricately-carved oak wood and with black cotton cushions sitting before an equally large desk made out of the same wood. An electric fireplace is built into the far wall, where it sits framed by two golden filing cabinets.

"This is... Quite an office space," she murmurs, taking a seat on the sofa.

"Thank you. My husband and I have done a bit of cleaning and childproofing ever since our son was born." He sits in the desk chair. "Now, I presume you came to discuss the angelic traces that have been sensed throughout Hell."

"I am."

"Then I would like you to tell me what you know about these traces."

Angelique frowns, suddenly feeling as though she was back on trial in front of the Holy Council. "We know the source of the angelic traces is traveling with a demonic companion, who has been leading them around Hell for an unknown reason."

"I see."

"The traces have not been sensed by the common folk, and the other Kings and Queens have only sensed them as the source was leaving their respective sectors."

"Is that so?"

"Yes, Your Majesty. From what Beelzebub and Mammon were able to gather, they believe it was Archangel Gabriel leaving these traces."

Tyrian moves to open his mouth again, only to be cut off by the door to the office swinging open with the might of an angry boxer. Instead, though, a toddler is seen hurrying into the room, squealing out excited cries of, "Papa, Papa!"

"Mikhail? What are you doing here, buddy?" Tyrian asks, lifting his young son into his lap.

"I brought him here," states a voice that is both familiar and not to the angel sitting on the sofa. She whips herself around to look at the doorway, waiting with bated breath to see if the familiar voice is who she thinks. Sure enough, a short man who stands only about five feet tall enters the room, his black ankle boots clicking elegantly against the floor. Thin legs are covered by white tights with sparkling gold accents on the outside seams. Black shorts are cinched at the man's waist by a golden wrap belt, with a large opal stone clasping the fabric all together on their left hip. A royal blue vest with extended coattails covers the man's white shirt, with a matching waist-length cloak covering his upper body. A golden halo hovers above the man's horns, which closely resemble Tyrian's. Unlike the King of Blasphemy, though, both his horns and his tail are naked of any golden chains. A pair of white-and-orange angel wings sprout from his mid-back, covered at the base by his cloak. "I heard you were in a meeting with an old friend of mine, and couldn't keep myself from missing her oh-so much."

"... Astro?"

"Hello, Angelique. It's been a while."

Twenty
Heathen's Light

Angelique stands from the sofa, her hands trembling as she looks to the friend she'd lost years prior to her coma. It had been so long since she'd seen him that she'd nearly forgotten what he looked like, but his face is still soft and youthful in its roundness. The battle scars on his hands and forearms are almost unnoticeable against his warm olive-toned skin. He tucks his wings close to his sides as he steps further into the room, his tail twitching with each step closer to the other angel. Once they're only a couple feet from each other, he clenches his fists, takes a deep breath, and moves to speak.

"Angelique, I—"

"I've missed you," the woman blurts, darting forward and pulling the shorter man into a hug. Tears well in her eyes as she holds back the urge to burst into sobs. "Do you *know* how long it's been?!"

"Uh... About 150 years?"

"Yes, you idiot! First you disappeared, then I got attacked 100 years ago, now Aurora's missing—"

"You got attacked?" He pulls back from the hug. His eyes have widened and his diamond-shaped pupils have nearly turned into slits as the words leave his mouth. "What happened?"

"I..." She touches the ribbon choker still wrapped securely around her neck. "I don't remember, but it happened when I was on a mission 100 years ago. I woke up a few months ago and found all of this out." She sighs. "… The Holy Council seems convinced it was Aurora that attacked me, but I'm not so sure."

"That does sound incredibly far-fetched, with how close you two were and how smitten she was with you."

"… Huh?"

He quirks an eyebrow at her query, placing his hands on his hips and huffing in a playful manner. "It was pretty obvious Aurora was head-over-heels in love with you."

"She was?"

"Yeah. Did she never tell you—?" He pauses. "… She didn't, did she?"

"No…"

His tail flicks in irritation. "Oh, my God, I *told* her to tell you!"

"Well… Either way, it sounds like she's here now. Last I knew, she was listed as 'missing, presumed dead.'"

"Ah, like they did for me?"

She freezes. "… Yes. I think you're still listed as missing in action, but it's almost exactly like you."

"Hm. I see."

"What?"

Tyrian speaks up from behind them, still cradling his and Astro's toddler in his arms. "Heaven's reports are full of code words. If an angel is 'MIA,' it means they never returned to Heaven after their last completed mission. If they're listed as 'MIA, presumed dead,' it means they were… Disposed of, for lack of a better term."

"Disposed of…?" Angelique asks, dread weighing heavy on her shoulders as the words pass her lips.

"To put it lightly… Aurora was banished from Heaven and thrown down here in the hopes that she'd die on impact."

The dark-haired angel swallows thickly around a knot in her throat. Memories of the first nightmare she'd woken from, with blood dripping from her head and the flesh melting from her arms, flood back to her. The recollection of the scent of blood, the taste of copper, and the sensation of her body simmering with a soul-deep pain make her stomach churn violently in her abdomen.

"Angelique?" Astro asks, "Are you okay?"

"I saw one of Aurora's memories when I first woke up," she whispers, fighting back the urge to vomit. "I felt *everything* she did when she was thrown here. I saw her memories of silver eyes and black grass and—"

"Whoa, that's a lot," Astro murmurs, placing a hand to his friend's back. "Here, how about you sit back down? I'll go get you a cup of water so you don't throw up."

"Please..." Once she's sitting again, she digs her fingers into the plush cushions in a weak attempt to ground herself and soothe her raging stomach.

Before she knows it, a crystal-clear chalice filled with ice water is being handed to her. She takes it and sips carefully from the glass, shuddering as she tries to once again bury the memories that obviously aren't her own. The weight on the sofa shifts as Astro sits next to her, wrapping his tail around his body so it drapes off the cushion.

"Are you feeling better?" Astro questions gently, offering a hand to his old friend.

"A little..." She takes hold of his hand. "Thank you."

"Of course. What are best friends for?"

She smiles weakly at the sentiment. "Some 'best friend' I am. I didn't know you were still alive until today."

"Our lack of contact was my own doing," he counters, "I made sure to erase my tracks, for the sake of my and my family's safety." He uses his free hand to hug his stomach, which she now sees is slightly swollen.

"Right... You're pregnant."

"I am." He casts his husband a glance, and lets out a laugh when he sees the demon's face turn a few shades redder.

"You wanted another baby!" Tyrian huffs, giving a playful pout as he holds their son by the waist. The young half-demon leans heavily against his father's broad chest as he stands on the man's knee.

"I did, and I can't wait for them to be here." He smiles. "I also said Mikhail was going to be lonely growing up all by himself, and that he would be a wonderful big brother."

"Big brother!" the toddler cheers, bouncing on his father's lap.

"That's right, you're going to be a big brother soon!" Tyrian coos.

"Well... 'Soon' is a relative term. I'm only about halfway to term."

"In any case, congratulations," Angelique interrupts the light-hearted banter with a small smile. "On everything. Your marriage, your kids... Your new life."

"Thank you, Angelique. It means a lot to me."

She looks back to the water in her glass. "... I can't imagine Aurora surviving the wounds I saw in my nightmare, so... Maybe I should stop looking for her."

"Why? She landed in Elias's backyard."

"... Huh?"

"Black grass isn't found everywhere in Hell," Tyrian explains, "It's only found in the Death Sector. And if your friend 'fell' here 100 years ago, there's only one case of an angel landing directly in the Death Sector."

"Really? Then with his healing pods... Maybe there's a chance she survived!"

"Oh, it's a greater chance than you'd expect," Tyrian chuckles, a hint of knowing in his voice. "But that's not why you're here, is it? You want to learn about the traces throughout Hell."

The angel's face burns as she's reminded of the actual reasoning behind her presence in the Blasphemy Sector. "Right. Yes, I would like to see any Oaths of Peace from the last month."

Still holding onto his toddler, Tyrian turns in his chair and digs through the filing cabinet to the left of the fireplace. He hums to himself as his fingers drift over file folders, until he stops and pulls out a manilla folder labeled **[CONFIDENTIAL]** in large, bold, red text. He uses a small pulse of magic to unbind the folder and pull out a stack of documents.

"Here you are, Miss Angelique," he declares with a knowing tone, "The culprit's name, written in ink."

She takes the thick stack of documents, which are all initialed in the margins with a five-pointed star, and begins to look through. The forms are a certified declaration that the signer will not harm any non-impish demons during their stay in Hell. Everything is written neatly, initialed where indicated... And signed at the bottom, in black ink that shimmers with a touch of gold, reads a name:

[Archangel Uriel Tolerantia.]

"What?"

"What's wrong?" Astro asks.

"Queen Beelzebub and King Mammon said they were almost certain it was Archangel Gabriel they were sensing... But this is a different Archangel entirely..."

Tyrian frowns. "I doubt those two could get something like this wrong, considering Uriel has been going around and introducing himself to all of us Royals."

"What do you mean, introducing himself...?"

"He has a sponsor, just like you do. The only reason he came to sign this Oath of Peace is because he'll be here for a much longer time than you probably plan to be." He motions to the paperwork again, bringing Angelique's attention to the signature a few lines below Uriel's. The clause above the signature reads:

[I hereby sponsor the above listed angel and will monitor their behavior to ensure that harm does not come to them or those around them. Should something happen, equal responsibility will befall me, the sponsor, and punishment will be given in accordance with the crime(s) committed.]

And the signature is a much more familiar name.

[Prince Sarien Iram of Wrath.]

"Prince Sarien's fiancé is Archangel Uriel..."

"Correct," the King of Blasphemy states, "When Sarien returned home from college with his fiancé, they stopped in to sign an Oath of Peace in order to make Archangel Uriel's presence known about and... Legalized, for lack of a better term."

"And you allowed this?"

"The Oath they signed allows both of them to be punished, should any harm befall another demon thanks to Archangel Uriel."

She frowns, unease swirling in her stomach. "If he's been introducing himself... Does that mean the traces we've been tracking all this time are...?"

"Older than they seem? Yes."

"And it sounds like the other royals have been covering up Uriel's presence here... Likely to keep Stellar from corrupting further," Astro adds.

"But when everything comes to light, won't this revelation be even worse for her?"

"Based on what I know of Stellar? Absolutely." Astro crosses his arms over his chest. "Ryzen told me about his conversation with Adrian when they were last hanging out together. He warned

Adrian that hiding this information from Stellar would be a bad idea, and that if we want her to 'investigate' the traces Uriel's been leaving behind, it would be best for her to come to *us* as soon as she's back in Hell." He turns to Angelique. "If Adrian is the one that sent you on this wild goose chase, he decided to ignore Ryzen's advice... And got the other Royals to agree to this little game they've been playing."

"And considering Stellar's past with Archangel Uriel... If her corruption has gotten as bad as it sounds, this revelation will be *ugly.*"

"... She has a past with him?" Angelique asks, head swirling with all of the new information.

"All fallen angels have a past with him," Tyrian explains, "Us Royals included. Uriel is the Overseer of Sin, and as the Overseer, he is the one that removes any sinners from Heaven."

"... *He's* the one that threw Stellar down here when she was an angel..."

"Bingo," Astro declares, "And the only reason I'm not a full demon is because I never returned to Heaven, so I was never tried and convicted of being a sinner."

Angelique grips the Oath of Peace tightly in her hands. "I need to tell Stellar about this."

"Are you sure it's a good idea?" her old friend asks.

"I'm not going to keep this from her any longer than it already has been. She deserves to know the truth."

Both Royals of Blasphemy nod slowly in understanding and agreement. "I suppose it's a good thing that you were the only one who came here. If Stellar found out... I would *not* want to be in the vicinity when she's angry."

"I'm sure everything will be fine..." Angelique murmurs, reaching into her pocket and pulling out her cell phone. "It looks like Stellar won't be out of her healing pod for another couple hours..."

"Then why don't you stay for lunch? I can imagine you're starving considering the stress you've been under," Astro suggests.

"I'll take you up on that. Thank you."

After a filling meal, Angelique and Astro head to the living room and spend a bit more time catching up. Before they know it, the final two hours have passed, and the angel looks to her phone once again. "It looks like Stellar should be out of the healing pods by now..." She glances at the cell service icon and groans. "Ugh, my phone doesn't work down here."

"You can borrow mine," Astro suggests as he holds his son close. He digs around in the pocket of his vest and passes over his phone. "She should be one of my main contacts."

Angelique unlocks the phone and makes her way to the contact list, where sure enough, Stellar is listed as one of his speed-dial contacts. She presses the button and holds the phone to her ear, anxiety rising in her chest as she waits for the call to be answered.

"Hello?" Stellar's familiar voice answers as soon as she picks up.

"Stellar, it's me," Angelique declares, "I came to Blasphemy while you were in the healing pod, and—"

"What? Why did you go all by yourself?"

"It's a long story. But I found out something important. There's an Oath of Peace on record."

"There is?"

"Yes."

"Who signed it?"

"That's... It's hard to explain. Just... See if you can gather the other Royals."

"Angel, what's going on?"

"I'll explain everything when we're in-person again. Meet me at Wrath," she says into the phone just before she clicks the "End Call" button. She passes the device back to Astro.

As the former angel tucks his phone back into his vest pocket, determination flashes in his eyes. "I'll get you to Wrath."

"Thank you, Astro."

"It's no problem, Angie. It may have been over 150 years since we last saw each other, but you're still my friend after all this time." He sets his son on the floor and wanders over to a nearby wall. With a wave of his hand, a portal opens up, swirling with blue and orange magic. "This should take you to the throne room of Wrath."

She clutches the signed Oath of Peace close to her chest. "Wish me luck."

"Belive me, you're going to need it."

She steps into the portal, her wings re-appearing and flaring out as she is teleported into a familiar room. Three thrones sit off to her left, and a mousy-looking servant lets out a tiny yelp before scurrying off. She's about to chase after the servant, until footsteps are heard approaching her location.

Satan enters the room, blinking in shock at her presence. "Angelique? How did you get here?"

"Astro."

"Ah... Then you know."

"I do."

"You don't have to do this. An Oath of Peace has been signed, nothing has to happen—"

"With all due respect, Your Majesty, I won't be keeping this secret any longer."

Just then, seven swirling portals form around the room. The various Kings and Queens of Hell step out of their respective portals, including Duchess Selene and Prince Malek. The portal closest to Angelique, which is made of black and purple magic, produces Stellar, Adrian, and Elias. The former's arms are still blackened by her corruption, but the ink-black color is now back to her elbows.

Satan frowns, but tries to keep a calm facade. "Hello, everyone. What brings you all to my neck of the woods?" the King of Wrath asks.

"We were called here by Princess Stellar," Asmodeus explains, a small, knowing frown also on her face.

"We were told there were important revelations to be made," Mammon adds, glancing over to his sister. "Naturally, curiosity got the better of us."

"I see. Let me go get my son—"

"I'm here," Sarien calls, entering into the room and making his way to his father's side. The Royals of Wrath stand in the center of the circle of demons, the younger of the two with a straight back and donning an unfamiliar confidence. "May I suggest we move out of the throne room? Should the worst come, I don't want anything in here to be destroyed."

"Yes... Good idea," Elias agrees. Per the suggestion, everyone shuffles out of the throne room and into the equally spacious grand hall. They gather at the bottom of the stairs that lead to the living quarters.

"Angel, you had something to tell us," Stellar declares, a mixture of concern and confusion in her voice as her eyes lock onto the Oath of Peace tucked in the angel's arms.

"Yes... I do. There's an important revelation in this document. The source of the angelic traces, to be exact."

She prepares to read it aloud...

Only to be cut off by Sarien.

"They already know."

"What?" Stellar scowls as she looks to her friend.

"Everyone here already knows," he repeats. "The source of the traces... Is my fiancé."

"So you're engaged to an angel?" Stellar scoffs, "You couldn't have told us that when we first came by?"

"Stellar..." Angelique begins, gathering her courage, "It's not just any angel."

"... What do you mean?"

"We know it's an Archangel, but we were wrong about *which* Archangel it was. The source of the angelic traces—"

"Is me."

Twenty-One
Secret in the Stars

All heads turn to look at the man making his way down the stairs from the bedroom suite. He has short, wavy, blonde hair and metallic silver eyes with star-shaped pupils. He's dressed in long, flowing, orange robes with a golden collar, belt, and cuffs, all of which don the familiar eye-shaped patterns found on the other Archangels. Two sets of white and pink feathered wings extend from his back; a third, smaller pair of wings protrude from just behind his ears; and a two-tiered halo floats above his head.

A lump forms in Angelique's throat as her eyes land on the man. "Master Uriel..." she murmurs, unease filling her even as she greets him with a title and a hesitant curtsey.

"I deeply apologize for the commotion, everyone," he says, his voice quiet enough to not echo far through the halls but loud enough to be heard by all of the royal demons. He makes his way into the circle and over to Sarien's side, but stops just short of his fiancé as a loud "SHING" rattles the walls. A familiar glaive sparking with black and purple magic whizzes between the two men, nearly cutting them both before it becomes lodged in the far wall.

Stellar stands frozen in a pose reminiscent of an ancient Greek hero throwing a discus, her eyes nearly glowing in rage. The nails on the end of her blackened fingers lengthen into claws as she processes the situation before her.

"You... Fucking... Traitor!" she snarls, nearly foaming at the mouth in her rage. "Not only are you *dating an Archangel,* you led him around *Hell!* Do you even *know* who he is, Sarien?!"

"Of course I do," he counters, voice trembling slightly.

"And you know *all* of what he's done?"

"I do."

The dark corruption, which had already begun to make noticeable progress up Stellar's arms, darts to the balls of her shoulders at the revelation. "Then you know why I've got to kill him."

Sarien freezes for a moment as Stellar holds out her right arm, summoning her glaive back to her side and catching it easily in her hand. As she stands at attention, ready to fight, the Prince of Wrath moves to stand in front of his fiancé, outstretching his arms in a protective stance. "I'm sorry, Stellar, but I can't let you do that."

"Move out of the way, Sarien," she demands, her voice deepening and rumbling in anger.

"No!"

"Then you'll be joining your mother in the grave." Stellar dashes forward, the muscles of their arms thickening and turning almost monstrous in nature, more closely resembling a pair of draconic forelimbs instead of anything one would find on a human. The darkness of her corruption almost seems to melt into thick, inky globules as she takes a swing at the couple in front of her.

Before either of them can be sliced into by the magic-coated blade, Uriel grabs Sarien by the waist and hauls him close. With a strong flap of his four wings, Uriel propels the two of them into the air, dodging the demon's next strikes. He soars down the hall and uses a strong wave of magic to throw open the double doors that lead to the training grounds outside.

Stellar snarls and scrambles to chase after them, her tail lashing and leaving hefty indents in the walls. A few picture frames rattle before dropping to the floor, shattering the glass and making a mess.

The other Royals race after the three combatants, panic rising amongst them at the growing severity of the Princess of Death's corruption. Angelique, who had previously been frozen in fear, chases after the group and manages to push her way through the crowd.

Stellar is clutching her glaive in a tight grip, uncaring of her claws digging into her skin. She remains on one side of the training grounds, panting heavily as she locks Uriel in a fierce glare. Her tail lashes again, nearly cracking the air like a whip. She extends her wings, preparing to take off into the sky at a moment's notice. It takes a moment for Angelique to register that a broken, ink-black halo hovers above her companion's head, just above their horns.

Uriel flutters to the ground, keeping a large distance between himself and his opponent as he sets Sarien down onto the dirt arena. "Your Majesty," he calls, voice level despite the tense situation, "Protect him for me."

Satan rushes over to his son's side, pulling him away from the battlefield and holding tightly onto him as Sarien tries to fight his way back to his fiancé's side. As the Prince of Wrath is held in his father's arms, Stellar's attention slowly shifts to the two Royals of Wrath.

"You *knew* about this," she snarls.

"We all did," Lucifer declares, taking a few steps forward and entering Stellar's line of sight. "Sarien has been bringing Uriel around Hell to inform all of us of their relationship."

Stellar's tail lashes again, this time fully making a loud *"CRACK"* in the air. "So I've been sent on a wild goose chase while you all knew who was here and *why?!"*

"We're sorry, Stellar," Beelzebub says, trying to soothe the death demon, "We knew you'd react like this, and so—"

"Of *course* I'm going to react like this!" she screams, voice breaking as she drops her glaive to the ground. "He's the one who *killed me!"*

The exclamation hangs heavily in the air, a thick silence filling the air of the training grounds. As the revelation sinks in, Angelique's heart clenches tightly in her chest.

"Stellar..." Angelique murmurs, tears filling her eyes. "What do you—?"

"I am aware," Uriel says, holding a hand to his chest, "And for that, I am sorry."

The Princess of Death's attention snaps back to the Archangel. "'Sorry?' *'Sorry?!'*" They grit their teeth, inky corruption leaking from her mouth and down her chin. "If you think your *pathetic* apologies are going to make me spare you, you are *sorely mistaken!*" She practically teleports to his side before taking another swing with her sharpened claws. The Archangel manages to take off into the air just in time to narrowly avoid the strike.

Stellar stands in the middle of the training grounds, arms hanging limply as she hunches over. "You all *knew*... You all *lied to me...*"

"We didn't *want* to keep this a secret from you," Leviathan murmurs, pulling her braid over her shoulder and playing with a few of the loose strands.

"And yet you *did.*" More inky corruption drips from her tail, landing in a puddle on the ground.

"It was for your own good," Belphegor chimes in, "We didn't want you to succumb to your corruption."

"I know my corruption better than all of you! Were you seriously convinced that keeping this from me was going to make it better?" The dark color that coats her arms starts to spread even further, covering more skin as it climbs its way up her neck. "I can't trust any of you..."

Her form shifts, and the inky darkness dripping from her lower body morphs together into the shape of a large dragonoid creature. Instead of her human legs, four inky limbs stretch out from the dark mass, with large claws protruding from each toe.

Her forearms remain enlarged as they drip corruption into Stellar's lower body, making her now chimera-like form grow even larger. Before long, the draconic form of her body stands twenty feet tall, towering over all of the other demons in the grand hall. An anguished half-cry, half-roar fills the air, shaking the earth below them and making the nearby trees tremble as the noise tears itself from the demon's throat.

"Stellar, you need to stop!" Asmodeus calls, worry in both her voice and her eyes as she pleads.

"No!" Stellar screams again, "You all *lied to me!* I *refuse* to listen to another word you say!"

"We don't want to hurt you!" Lilith calls.

"You should have *thought about that!"* She summons her glaive to her side once more, and as soon as it touches her corruption-coated palms... She slashes, narrowly missing the attack on the Queen of Pride thanks to a glowing red shield that forms in front of her.

Lucifer's eyes narrow, and he uses a wave of magic to summon his own weapon: an obsidian-black pitchfork. It glows a vibrant red at the four thick prongs as Lucifer aims for Stellar. "Stand down, Stellar, or we will have to fight you!"

"HA! Do you seriously think I *care?"* she snarls, "Go ahead! Fight me! *Kill me, even!"*

Most of the remaining Royals all brandish their various weapons in a flurry of magic, aiming them at the chimera-like creature before them. Stellar lets out another ferocious roar and swipes at her fellow Royals.

Lucifer slashes at the chimera's ankles while Lilith sends fireballs into the air to try and distract Stellar; the strategy works for only a moment, though, as she swipes at them both with her creature half's sharpened claws. The Royals of Pride let out sharp, pained cries as they hit the ground with a bounce and are flung halfway across the training yard.

While they scramble to recover from the hit and stand back up, Mammon copies Lilith's strategy and uses his own magic to send coin-shaped blasts into the air. While the Princess of Death tries to swipe at the magic blasts, Beelzebub uses two longbows to send a flurry of magic-coated arrows into the inky chimera's hide. Stellar roars in a combination of agitation and pain, and uses her wings to knock the Queen of Gluttony out of the sky.

Leviathan uses a wave of magic to transform into her sea monster form, at which point she dashes forward and sinks her teeth into the inky flesh of Stellar's front left leg. The chimera lets out an anguished cry and moves to wrestle with the sea monster, until they're both reared up and snapping at each other. While Stellar is on their hind legs, Asmodeus wraps a magical chain around both of Stellar's back feet, pulling tightly to try and keep the corruption-coated creature in place.

As Stellar and Leviathan trade blows and throw each other around, though, the former is able to pull with enough strength to unhook herself from the trap and send the Queen of Lust tumbling through the dirt. Belphegor and Uriel move to trade places with Satan, holding tightly onto Sarien's arms to keep him out of the fray while the King of Wrath joins in, throwing rapid punches at the chimera's ankles.

While the rest of the Royals of Hell fight Stellar in an attempt to wear her out, Angelique finds herself backing away in a combination of shock and fear. As she moves to hide herself a bit behind Elias, she finds her voice and whispers out a trembling, "What... *Is* that?"

"*That* is a true corruption manifestation," Adrian declares, summoning his battleaxe in a flurry of navy blue sparks. Before he can charge into the fray, he's stopped by his father, who lowers his son's weapon with a gentle push.

"That is still your sister," Elias growls low, "I would like to keep her alive, if at all possible."

Angelique's heart stutters in her chest. "You might have to...?"

"Corruption is a physical manifestation of one's mental state," Elias explains, watching as his fellow Royals battle with his corruption-coated daughter, "And due to the betrayal of those around her... Stellar's mental state is trying to kill her."

Adrian looks to his feet in shame, his white-knuckled grip on his weapon unceasing. "It's my fault, then."

"So long as someone can break her out of her head, there is no need to grieve her." Elias looks over his shoulder at the dark-haired angel and smiles kindly. "This is where you will come in, Miss Angelique."

"What? How am I supposed to—?"

"You are the one person here she does not feel betrayed by. You have stayed with her all this time, believed every word the two of you were told—"

Another anguished scream tears itself from Stellar's throat, shaking the ground beneath them as she manages to overpower Leviathan and send her tumbling to the ground. The Queen of Envy transforms back into her humanoid form in a flurry of sparks, groaning in pain at the impact.

"—So if you could jump in and save her as soon as possible, we would greatly appreciate it."

Angelique swallows the thick lump of fear in her throat, spreading her wings and taking off into the air. She flutters over to the inky chimera form of her friend as the demon rears up on their draconic hind legs once again and slams back down, practically tossing the other demons and the Archangel into the air. They all land in various sprawled-out positions, unable to stabilize themselves on their feet after the weighty impact. Her mind rushes, unsure of what could possibly quell Stellar's unbridled rage, when she remembers the twig she'd picked up from the emoticast willow. She reaches into her pocket dimension with a shimmer of magic and pulls out the leafy twig. Its petals are still the pure, rosy pink from when she and Stellar placed their hands to the trunk.

"Stellar!" Angelique calls, "You have to stop this!"

A deep, resonating cackle echoes sharply from the demoness. "Who are you to stop me?"

"I'm your friend! We've gone through so much together, I know we can—"

"Friend?!" she snarls, "As if! You could never be *'friends'* with something like me!"

"But I am!" She flies closer, trying to look into Stellar's eyes. "No matter how bad your corruption gets, I'll still be here with you!"

Stellar bats at Angelique with her clawed hands, narrowly missing each strike against the angel. "You don't know what I really am!"

"I do! You're an angel they wrongly threw out of Heaven, aren't you?"

The chimera snarls as more inky corruption flows from her mouth. *"He* threw me down here... *He* left me broken!" she snaps, motioning to the Archangel who's trying to get back onto his feet.

"And he was horrible for that," Angelique agrees, "But you still have your friends and family here. You don't have to attack them, too—"

"They were *protecting him!"*

"I know, and it wasn't fair for them to do that to you, but surely you can ask them *why,* right?"

"Why should it matter?!" Thick, inky tears flow from her eyes and leave black stains on her pale cheeks. "They *knew* about what he did!"

"And he's only here because he loves Sarien," she reasons, "You were thrown down here for loving someone you shouldn't have, right?"

She whimpers and nods, reaching up with a clawed hand to try and clean the corruption from her face. Instead, rivulets of dark, inky blood mix with the corruption-coated tears.

"Then it sounds like he might face the same fate as you: Being left here with no one else at his side."

"It's... Not..." She sniffles. "It's not fair! I don't want him here! He hurt me, and I've had to suffer every day of my life for the past 100 years because of him!"

Angelique freezes. "... 100 years?" she whispers, looking over Stellar's monstrous form once more, then back to the twig she holds in her hands.

There had only ever been one person she cared so deeply for. The person she'd lost 100 years ago, but surely...

She puts the twig away in the pocket dimension once again as she hovers within arm's reach of the chimera before her. "There's no way..." She cups Stellar's face in her hands, uncaring of the mess that Stellar's corruption makes of them both.

"Aurora?"

At the utterance of a name long forgotten, Stellar bursts into sobs. "I've missed you, Angie..."

"Oh..." Angelique darts forward and pulls her into a tight, squeezing hug. "I've missed you, too." As soon as they pull back, she goes back to cradling her partner's bloody, ink-covered cheeks. "Which name do you want me to use?"

"Stellar, *please...* It's the name I chose for myself after I was revived..."

The angel leans in close and nuzzles her nose against Stellar's, closing her eyes as she continues to hold them close. "If that's what you wish, then Stellar it is."

"I'm so sorry I kept it from you, Angie..." she murmurs, voice cracking as she cries. "I thought you'd hate me for the monster I've become..."

"We all have sides of ourselves that we're not proud of—ones we'd rather hide from those we care about," she responds, pulling Stellar into another hug. "I'm glad I found you in the end." Angelique shudders a bit as clawed hands and strong arms wrap around her waist and hold her in return. Her wings twitch as she's held close, and a smile forms on her face as she relaxes into her partner's embrace.

"That's it… I'm here."

"Forever?" Stellar whispers, her voice fragile.

"Forever." She gives the chimera another squeeze, this time as strong as her arms will allow. "So please… Come back to me, Stellar."

As she's wrapped in the firm embrace, Stellar lets out a rough, crackling purr. The demon settles into the comfort, her shoulders slumping as she leans heavily against Angelique. As she calms, the corruption encasing the lower half of her body begins to slough off, each large globule plopping wetly to the ground. Once Stellar is back to standing on her own two feet once again, they turn around to face the piles of thick, ink-like corruption. With a wave of her hand and a large stream of purple-and-black magic, the mess is cleaned and the remaining destruction on the training grounds is repaired.

Angelique steps forward, taking Stellar's left hand into her right one. She notices her partner's arms are no longer an inky hue, and her claws have dulled to almond-shaped nails.

Stellar looks over at Angelique, a weak smile on her face and exhaustion in her eyes. She takes hold of her broken, blackened halo, and in a flurry of magical sparks, the symbol of holiness disappears. After taking a moment to breathe and continue to relax into Angelique's grasp, she looks over the angel's shoulders at the other Royals, who are slowly gathering their bearings and shakily standing back up.

"I'm sorry," the Princess of Death blurts, squeezing Angelique's hand again.

"What?" Angelique and the other demons gasp in surprise.

"I overreacted—"

"What are you talking about?" Lucifer scoffs, holding his wife close to himself as Lilith regains her balance. Once she's stable, he makes his way over to them and gently flicks Stellar's forehead. "It was a pretty understandable reaction to me. Wouldn't you say so, Satan?"

The King of Wrath crosses his arms over his chest. "I have to agree. You've been bottling everything up, so it makes even more sense for a revelation like this to cause such a volatile reaction." He steps forward as well and bows to her. "I hope you can accept my deepest apologies for the stress our decision has placed on you."

"I can do that. You... You all were doing what you thought would be best for me. It may have been done in the wrong way, but I can appreciate the effort you all put into keeping everyone safe." She turns her attention to Uriel. "But even with that said... I'll be keeping an *especially* close eye on you."

"I understand, Your Highness. I don't expect you to trust me right off the bat... But please believe me when I say I love Sarien very much."

Before Stellar can open her mouth to respond, Angelique's wings flare out as a strike of fear courses through her body.

"Angie...?"

"I think someone is watching us."

Twenty-Two
Light of Truth

"What do you mean, you think we're being watched?" Stellar asks, her own wings flaring out and her tail raising into a defensive stance despite the exhaustion in her frame.

"I... I don't know. But I need to go check on King and Spyr."

"Then let's go." Stellar waves her hand, a flurry of purple and black magic forming into a large portal. She grabs Angelique's wrist, and before they can jump into the portal, a familiar voice calls out to them.

"Please be careful, you two," Elias pleads, his voice warm despite the slight tremor of anxiety in his voice.

"Yes... Come back to us," Adrian adds.

Stellar casts a glare to her brother, but ultimately sighs in defeat, her shoulders slumping. "I'll be back, but I'm still mad at you, Adrian."

"I can live with that so long as you return safely."

They sigh again and turn back to Angelique, squeezing her hand. "Ready, Angie?"

The angel blushes at the use of her old nickname. "Of course, Stellar."

The two of them step through the portal, until they find themselves falling out onto the familiar rooftop of the apartment building where Angelique had first stayed while guarding the Lockley family. Looking at the surroundings, everything appears to be the same as they'd left it... Until they spot the three elite demons Stellar had left in her place.

Briar and Viper are holding their greatsword and shortsword out to their sides, creating a barrier in front of the Lockley family. On the roof of the DHA's main office, Nast is perched with an arrow nocked against their bow, pulled back and aiming at a figure standing confidently in front of the other demons. A shock of curly red hair is the only identifier they need to recognize exactly who is confronting their wards.

"Shit, it's that demon hunter bitch," Stellar growls.

"You've got to be kidding me. What does she want with them?"

"I don't know, but we're about to find out." She steps forward, tilting off the ledge of the apartment building's roof.

Angelique grabs onto Stellar's wrist before she's able to fall. "Please be careful," she pleads, "I don't want you to get hurt. Especially after your corruption flare—"

Stellar chuckles, tail wagging. "Don't worry, Angie, this will be easy." She maneuvers her wrist out of Angelique's grasp and dives off the roof, spreading her wings in order to catch herself and send her soaring over to their shared wards.

Angelique spreads her wings and leaps forward off the roof in pursuit. She manages to flutter her wings enough to carry her over to King and Spyr's sides. The latter's tail is lashing, and their horns and canine teeth have lengthened in a defensive measure.

"What's going on here?" Angelique and Stellar ask in unison as they approach the group.

Everyone startles at the unexpected voices, turning in surprise to see the guardian angel and Princess of Death behind them.

"You're back!" King gasps in relief.

"Lady Executioner!" the armored demons all cheer, Briar and Viper still holding their weapons high in a blockade.

"Tch, it's you two," Rachel snarls. The demon hunter is donning three throwing knives in each hand, held tightly between her knuckles to emulate claws.

Angelique's eyes widen, and she squeezes her way between King and Spyr. Once she's in front of the couple, she spreads her wings to hide them from the redhead human's view. "Last I recall, Stellar and I told you not to come back unless you were ready to face the consequences."

"Yeah, and you haven't been here, so what's the problem?" She smirks cruelly, brushing the toe of her boot against the sidewalk. "Now... Will you *actually* try to kill me, now that you're back?"

"Tch, are you seriously trying to piss me off?" Stellar snarls, summoning her glaive with a wave of magic. She turns her attention to King and Spyr, motioning for them to escape while they have the chance. Worldlessly, they turn tail and dash back toward their house, the three elite soldiers chasing closely behind.

Rachel smirks as she's left alone with Stellar and Angelique. "My, my. You seriously don't back down, do you?"

"Of course not. The safety of my wards is at stake; and I won't be allowing you near them ever again," Stellar snarls.

"Ha! Do you truly think a *poor, innocent human* like me is such a threat to them?" She readies herself into a battle stance, her knuckles turning white as she grips her throwing knives even tighter in preparation to fight. "I just want King back. If he would leave that *vermin,* then—"

"That 'vermin' is his spouse," Angelique snarls, summoning her own sword with a wave of magic. "If anyone needs to leave him alone, it's *you.*"

"Well said, Angie," Stellar agrees. Their gaze turns back to the demon hunter before her. "I never joke when it comes to the safety of my wards, and I always follow through on my threats." Seeing the redhead's unwavering, self-confident grin, the demon's eyes narrow like those of an angry mountain lion. "So, ignorant human, I'm going to give you until the count of three to leave. If you choose to stay, I will kill you where you so foolishly stand. Are we clear?"

Rachel remains unmoved. "Oh, we're clear alright."

Angelique's eyes blow wide at the scene before her as her anxiety rises. "Wait, Stellar—"

"One."

"Stellar, I think she—"

"Two."

"She might be—!"

"Three." Stellar thrusts her weapon forward, slicing a clean cut into the demon hunter's chest until the tip pokes out of her back. Rachel coughs as she's sliced, thick rivers of blood escaping from her mouth and chest. Instead of the expected rivers of red, the blood pouring from Rachel's body is a shimmering golden hue. Stellar rips her blade from the redhead's chest in a panic as the body collapses to the asphalt below her. A sickening grin is still placed on the demon hunter's face as the life drains from her eyes and golden blood pours from the wound.

Stellar takes a few steps back as panic rises in her chest. She claps her free hand over her mouth, breathing growing much more rapid as she finds herself unable to tear her gaze away from the fresh corpse. Her glaive drops out of her trembling hand with a clatter, and she falls to her knees almost immediately after.

Angelique darts to the demon's side, her own panic caught in her chest. She drops to her knees in front of Stellar and grabs at her partner's shaking shoulders. "Stellar!" she calls, trying to break her out of the shock and panic. "Stellar, look at me!"

Slowly, the Princess of Death's eyes drift to meet the angel's gaze. Once they lock eyes on each other, Stellar's body slumps as her brain catches up to the current predicament.

"Angie...?"

"That's right. I'm here." She pulls Stellar into a firm, grounding hug.

"I... As soon as I saw the angel blood, I thought I..."

"No," she soothes, "You didn't hurt me. I'm right here."

The Executioner swallows thickly and holds Angelique close. "She's an angel..." she murmurs once she finds her voice again.

"I know... I didn't notice until too late that she had angelic traces on her."

"Then we need to figure out who sent her here..."

"Are you able to stand?"

"I... I think so."

The two of them slowly stand, and Angelique sighs in relief when she sees Stellar steady herself on her feet. They approach Rachel's body and begin to investigate.

"... Why am I not finding anything concrete?" Angelique grumbles to herself after a few minutes, "I *know* I felt those traces..."

Stellar frowns, hugging herself in a small semblance of comfort. "It's like when you were hurt all those years ago. I know I wasn't with you that night, but there were no other traces they found..."

"So they did frame you..."

"They did." There's a heavy pause between them. "Do you... Really not remember anything from that night?"

"I don't."

"... Do you want me to fill you in?"

Angelique freezes where she kneels, her hand hovering over Rachel's body. *This is my only chance to know what happened to me...* She swallows around the thick lump in her throat. "Please. Tell me everything you know."

Tears well in Stellar's eyes. "You were on a solo recon mission. Everything seemed to be fine when we told each other good-night on the phone, but... The next thing I knew, our dorm room was being raided in the middle of the night. They grabbed me out of my bed and threw me to the ground… It was then that I learned you were 'killed.'" She wipes her eyes as a few tears escape.

"I was thrown into a prison cell, and two days later, they brought me before the Holy Council. While they had me on trial, I learned why I was brought before them: they thought *I* was the one who 'killed' you. All they could tell was an angel's weapon had sliced your head from your body, and…" She shudders. "… And since I was the last one to talk to you, they figured I must have done it."

"That evidence sounds circumstantial at best," Angelique grumbles.

"It definitely wasn't as air-tight as they made it seem. But, since they somehow knew I had a crush on you, they decided I had been corrupted by demons and must have hurt you so no one else could have you." She grips tightly at her arms to the point her nails dig into the skin. "But I know I didn't do it. I told them over and over, but… They didn't listen to me. So, they convicted me of your murder and hauled me off to the dumping grounds." More tears stream down her face. "… I never got to say good-bye."

"You were told I was dead; I was told you were missing and *presumed* dead." Angelique clutches tightly at her skirt. "Whoever did this wanted to keep us apart, didn't they?"

"Yeah…"

Angelique wipes her eyes of the tears she didn't realize she'd begun to cry. "And it was Uriel who pulled the lever?"

"Mm-hm. I can never get those eyes out of my memories… I had night terrors for years after my dad revived me."

"I'm so sorry, Stellar…"

She brushes a bit of dirt from her shorts. "We can't change the past now; all we can do is move forward."

"Right..." Angelique moves to lay Rachel's body back against the pavement, cradling her head carefully. As she moves her hand away from the former human's corpse, though, she freezes.

"I feel something."

"What?"

"There's a sigil on the back of her neck."

"A sigil?" Stellar kneels down and moves the woman's long red hair from the back of her neck. Sure enough, an eye-shaped sigil that glows with blue and silver magic is found on the skin.

"An All-Seeing Eye," Angelique gasps, covering her mouth with her hands. "Which means—"

"It was Archangel Gabriel who blessed her," Stellar interrupts, eyes wide in surprise. "He's also the one who dealt the final sentencing blow when *I* was under trial..."

"Wait... You don't think it was *Archangel Gabriel* who...?"

"Who framed me? I... I can't be sure." She hugs herself again, once again digging her nails into her skin. "And if I killed his ward, who also happens to have been blessed as an angel..."

"... She got a one-way ticket to Heaven." Angelique takes a moment to process, before letting out a hefty gasp and shooting straight up into the air, her wings flapping strongly. "Oh, *shit!* I need to get home to Heaven as soon as possible!"

Stellar seems to have reached the same conclusion, because the color visibly drains from her face. "You need to go to the Holy Council, *now.* Take as much evidence as you can, and—"

"Are you able to come with me?"

"... What?"

"You're the best evidence I have that demons aren't the monsters the Holy Council says they are."

"I... I don't know."

Angelique takes hold of her hands and squeezes tightly. "No matter what, I'll be coming back to you. Do you trust me?"

"Of course I do, Angie."

"Good. Now, can you make a portal that goes straight to the courthouse?"

"I..." She swallows thickly, obviously anxious, but nods. "I'm not sure, but I can try."

"That's all I ask."

They pull away from each other as Stellar forms a shimmering portal once again. She turns back to Angelique, holding out her hand like a gentleman would when greeting his date.

Angelique takes hold of her hand, then leads the way through the portal Stellar had created. Sure enough, they find themselves standing outside the opulent doors to the courthouse in the center of Cloud Nine. Determination flashing in her eyes, the angel moves to open one of the doors, only for Stellar to grab onto her shoulder.

"There's a press conference at the foot of the stairs," the demoness murmurs, ears twitching, "Don't do anything reckless."

"Standing up for those who are being wronged isn't reckless," she whispers back, turning on her heels.

"If you do this, they might try to capture and banish you," they warn once again.

"Like I said... No matter what, I'll make my way back to you." She squeezes Stellar's hand. "Go hide somewhere safe. This could get ugly."

"Angie..." She sighs. "Alright. I'll keep an eye on you." She turns tail and darts off into one of the nearby alleyways.

With her partner now safely hidden from view, Angelique puffs out her chest to try and regain her confidence. She hides behind one of the columns and waits, listening in on the press conference. From her position nearby, she's able to clearly hear everything.

"Thank you all for coming today," Archangel Gabriel announces, addressing the microphones pointing at him from the crowd, "And especially on such short notice. I have recently been informed by one of my most recent wards of a traitor in our midst; a guardian who has chosen to protect the demons she's encountered rather than the human she's been assigned to." He looks over his shoulder at a familiar redheaded form.

Rachel, who is now dressed in long white angel robes, steps up to the various microphones, plastering on a tearful expression. "I thank you all for taking this so seriously," she begins, "I just... I can't stand idly by and wait for more humans to be put in danger because of this... This *traitor.*" She dabs at her eyes with her long, flowing sleeves.

"Miss Cooper, what can you tell us about the traitor you discovered?"

"Her name is Angelique Taylor," she blurts out, "She's been in cahoots with demons both on Earth and in Hell. I think she's even been flirting with one of them!"

The crowd of reporters and everyday angels lets out a series of horrified gasps.

"She needs to be found and punished as soon as she gets back," Rachel declares, "I was killed by her demonic companion and she did *nothing* to protect me."

The crowd murmurs at the claim.

"Those vile creatures have preyed on innocent people, human and angel alike, all for some semblance of sick, twisted amusement. She's been corrupted by the demons she's chosen to surround herself with, and—"

"That's enough."

A collective gasp escapes the crowd as Angelique steps out from behind the marble pillar.

"Who are you?" one of the reporters asks, obviously intrigued and confused.

"*I* am Angelique Taylor," she declares, "And we have all been lied to."

"What?!" Archangel Gabriel snarls, clenching his hands into fists as he turns his attention to Rachel. "You told me she—"

"What Master Gabriel and Miss Cooper were just telling you is all false," Angelique continues, "While I *was* there when Rachel was killed, it was for the safety of my wards that I did not step in. She has been threatening them for over a year because the gentleman I've been protecting is her ex-boyfriend. Her heart has been corrupted by cruel whispers, telling her she deserves to be his wife even though he's already a happily married father. And speaking of cruel whispers.... The Archangels and Holy Council have been deceiving us."

She allows a moment for the crowd to murmur amongst themselves in shock before continuing. "The reports of angels who have gone missing and are presumed dead are false. Every angel in those reports has been falsely accused, unfairly tried, and wrongly convicted for something as innocent as falling in love. My own partner was reported as missing and presumed dead after I was attacked by an unknown assailant. They were accused of murder and convicted with little to no evidence, all because they happened to have fallen in love with me."

She turns her attention to Archangel Gabriel, suddenly surging with a newfound confidence. "But it was you who attacked me, wasn't it, Master Gabriel?"

"Tch, you dare accuse me—!"

"I may not have my memories, but I have testimony from my former partner that says *you* were the one who made the final determination of her guilt. What was her crime?!"

"If you are speaking of Miss Grey, she was found guilty of attacking you."

"Her *real* crime! It was falling in love with another woman, wasn't it?!"

He narrows his eyes and snarls. "And what if it was? Miss Grey is gone, and you've obviously been turned against Heaven. I should have you tried for Blasphemy—"

"Like you never could for Astro?" she counters. She steps closer, getting up in his face as she continues her rant. "You listed him as missing in action because he never returned to Heaven after finding a loving husband and community in Hell."

"Master Gabriel, is this true?" another reporter asks, shock and disgust on her face.

"Tch, of course not! Miss Taylor is trying to—"

"Then what about Master Uriel, hm? Why has *he* been missing from the Holy Council as of late?"

He snarls. "Do not utter that name when you know not of which you speak!"

"Ha! I should have expected nothing less from you, Gabriel," another voice tuts. A flurry of orange and gold magic swirls in the air, creating a portal above the crowd. Uriel darts out and lowers himself to the steps of the Holy Courthouse, standing a few steps behind Gabriel and Rachel.

"What are you doing here, you traitor?!" the blue-robed Archangel snarls.

"I'm here to reveal the secrets we always kept," he declares, "Including the reasoning behind the disappearances of so many angels."

"You wouldn't dare—"

"Please tell us!" a member of the crowd calls, desperation in their voice, "Tell us why so many have been marked as missing without a trace!"

Gabriel whips back around, panic plain as day on his face. "I— Well— That is none of your business! Each appearance in court is tried on a case-by-case basis, and—"

"Then why are court cases never published?" another crowd member demands.

Uriel steps forward, smacking Gabriel and Rachel out of the way with his wings. "I will answer everyone's questions," he declares confidently, "In the hopes that these revelations will change the way Heaven treats its citizens and those in power." He glances over to Angelique, who's still standing off to one side in shock. He gives her a simple nod.

"Are you sure?" Angelique asks.

"I am. Go be happy; I'm sure I'll catch up soon."

A wide smile forms on her face as the crowd's attention turns to Uriel, even as Gabriel and Rachel try to stop him from speaking. While the reporters and crowd are busy taking in the Archangel's every word, she takes the chance to make her escape. As she passes by buildings and dark alleyways, a hand reaches out and wraps around her wrist. She's hauled into the nearest alley and almost lets out a shriek, until a familiar pair of blue-purple eyes meet hers.

"Wha— Stellar? You stayed nearby?"

"I had to make sure you were safe," the demon whispers in response.

"I was about to make my way back to you," she counters.

A delicate blush forms on Stellar's cheeks, and her eyes widen a bit in surprise. "Don't you mean the Lock—?"

"I said what I meant."

Stellar lets out a half-squeak, half-chirp, and a loud purr resonates from her throat. She pulls Angelique into a firm hug, smiling against her shoulder.

The angel giggles and pets her partner's head. "What's this about, hm? Are you flustered because I was about to come find you?"

"And what if I am?"

"Then you should learn to get used to it." She cups Stellar's face in her hands, just like she had when the latter had succumbed to her corruption. "I will always come back to you. You're my partner, in life and in death."

The demoness's tail whips back and forth in a gleeful wag. "Do you promise?"

"Of course I promise. I love you."

Tears form in the demon's eyes at the quiet affirmation. She sniffles, trying to hold back the waterworks, but leans into Angelique's grasp nonetheless. "I love you, too."

With the confirmation hanging in the air between them, the angel makes the first move. She pulls Stellar's face close and presses their lips together, the touch soft and passionate all at once. She lets out a deep breath through her nose when she feels her surprised partner return the kiss, and can't help the giddy smile on her face once the contact breaks.

"Jeez, Angie..." Stellar murmurs, her cheeks now a tomato-red shade. Her tail continues to wag back and forth wildly, her usual confident facade having disappeared in an instant.

"What's the matter?" the angel teases cutely, "Lost your swagger all because of me?"

"Of course I did," she huffs, "You are my everything. My strength and my weakness, my heart and my soul..."

Angelique's face burns, and she covers Stellar's mouth with her hand. "Okay, that's enough!"

They sit in silence for a few moments, until a disgusted shriek escapes the angel.

"Did you just *lick me?*"

"Mm-hm~," Stellar hums, licking her lips as the hand is removed from her mouth, "You taste as good as I always imagined. Strawberries and sugar..."

Angelique groans. "You're such a sap. Can we go home now?"

"Hm? Yeah, let's get you back to your apartment—"

"Not there," she interrupts to clarify, face turning a few shades darker once again. "I meant... I want to live with *you.*"

Another squeak escapes the demon. "You mean..."

"Us. Together, in Hell."

"... Yes. Let's go home." She pulls Angelique close by the waist as she summons a portal. "Are... Are you sure about this?"

"Of course I am. We're never going to be separated again."

"Then I guess you'll have to marry me."

"... Did you just—?"

"Propose? Maybe." The demon grins playfully. "Time will have to tell. Now... Ready? On three."

"One..."

"Two..."

"Three!" They both yelp, leaping into the portal and leaving the past far behind them.

Pronunciation Guide

Characters

Angelique (Ann-juh-leek)
Dr. Raphael (Rah-fah-yel)
Barachiel (Barr-uh-kell)
Spyr Lockley (Spear Lock-lee)
King Lockley (King Lock-lee)
Stellar (Steh-lar)
Michael (My-kell)
Gabriel (Gay-bree-uhl)
Selaphiel (Sell-uh-feel)
Jegudiel (Jeh-good-eel)
Rachel (Ray-chul)
Elias (Ehl-lie-us)
Adrian (Ay-dree-uhn)
Lana (Lah-nuh)
Fari (Fah-ree)
Henriette (Henn-ree-ett)
Lucifer (Loo-siff-uhr)
Lilith (Lih-lith)
Leviathan (Leh-vai-uh-thun)
Satan (Say-tun)
Lameia (Lah-may-uh)
Sarien (Say-ree-ehn)
Selene (Sell-een)

Ryver (Rih-ver)
Haley (Hay-lee)
Asmodeus (Azz-moh-dee-us)
Belphegor (Bell-feh-gorr)
Malek (Mahl-ehk)
Lilia (Lih-lee-uh)
Lyric (Lee-rick)
Mammon(Mamm-uhn)
Beelzebub (Bee-ehl-zeh-bub)
Ryzen (Rye-zen)
Gabriel Roberts (Gay-bree-uhl Rob-urts)
Amber Roberts (Am-burr Rob-urts)
Tyrian (Teer-ee-en)
Astro (Ah-stroh)
Uriel (Yoo-ree-uhl)

Locations

Cloud Nine (Klaud nine)
Baystar (Bay-star)
Pearl Hill (Purl hill)
Petraglow (Pet-rah-glow)
Stratsford (Strats-furd)
Ship's Haven (Ship's hay-ven)
Kilmarnock (Kill-marr-nock)
Aria (Ah-ree-uh)
Caister (Kai-stur)
Langdale (Lang-dayle)
Berxley (Berks-lee)
Rochwall (Rock-wall)

www.ingramcontent.com/pod-product-compliance
Lightning Source LLC
LaVergne TN
LVHW041012150826
845672LV00001B/67

* 9 7 9 8 9 9 5 0 5 3 0 2 6 *